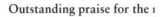
### The Sculptress

"The novel is thoroughly researched, drawing readers fully into the saga with descriptive, often graphic details and strong characterizations. For fans of World War I historical fiction."
—*Library Journal*

### The Irishman's Daughter

"Skillfully blends family ties with the horrors of a starving country and the hopefulness of young love." —*Booklist*

### The Taster

"An absorbing, well-researched story that brings to life an extraordinary period in history, told from within the inner circle of one of the twentieth-century's most notorious characters."
—Gill Paul, *USA Today* bestselling author of *The Secret Wife*

"Alexander's intimate writing style gives readers openings to wonder about what tough decisions they would have made in Magda's situation. The 'taster's' story adds to a body of nuanced World War II fiction such as Elizabeth Wein's *Code Name Verity*, Anthony Doerr's *All the Light We Cannot See*, and Tatiana de Rosnay's *Sarah's Key*. Book clubs and historical fiction fans will love discussing this and will eagerly await more from Alexander." —*Library Journal*

### The Magdalen Girls

"A haunting novel that takes the reader into the cruel world of Ireland's Magdalene laundries, *The Magdalen Girls* shines a light on yet another notorious institution that somehow survived into the late twentieth century. A real page-turner!"
—Ellen Marie Wiseman, author of *The Orphan Collector*

"Alexander has clearly done his homework. Chilling in its realism, his work depicts the improprieties long condoned by the Catholic Church and only recently acknowledged. Fans of the book and film *Philomena* will want to read this." —*Library Journal*

Books by V. S. Alexander

THE MAGDALEN GIRLS

THE TASTER

THE IRISHMAN'S DAUGHTER

THE TRAITOR

THE SCULPTRESS

THE WAR GIRLS

THE NOVELIST FROM BERLIN

Published by Kensington Publishing Corp.

# The
# NOVELIST
# *from* BERLIN

# V. S. ALEXANDER

KENSINGTON
PUBLISHING CORP.

www.kensingtonbooks.com

KENSINGTON BOOKS are published by

Kensington Publishing Corp.
119 West 40th Street
New York, NY 10018

Special book excerpts or customized printings can also be created to fit specific needs. For details, write or phone the office of the Kensington Sales Manager: Kensington Publishing Corp., 119 West 40th Street, New York, NY 10018. Attn. Sales Department. Phone: 1-800-221-2647.

The K with book logo Reg US Pat. & TM Off.

ISBN: 978-1-4967-3482-2 (ebook)

ISBN: 978-1-4967-3481-5

First Kensington Trade Paperback Printing: October 2023

10 9 8 7 6 5 4 3 2 1

Printed in the United States of America

*The roofs that you see are not built for you.*
*The bread that you smell is not baked for you.*
*And the language that you hear is not spoken for you.*
—Irmgard Keun, *After Midnight*

# PROLOGUE

———◆———

This is a story of survival—a story about never giving up despite what comes your way.

Looking back upon my days, I'm ashamed of many. I was neither a saint nor as evil as the regimes I lived under. My deeds, even after the wall fractured Berlin, were matters of life and death. I did the best I could, as one had to do in order to live in fascist Germany and then in East Berlin. For many of my actions, I must apologize—but not for all.

I married a man named Rickard Länger. He was a husband and father, and became a National Socialist after we were wed.

Our lives are part of a story others begged me to tell, but I wrote years later, for myself, with no expectation of being published.

People have told me that I can be as slippery as jelly on toast. By that, they mean I work myself out of bad situations with my skin relatively intact—but my emotions are often bruised. People don't always know the truth behind the story, and that's what I'm going to tell you. I became a celebrity in my own right when my books were published before the Nazis ruled Germany. Because of my novels, I've had more than enough danger in my lifetime.

The world is a better place, at the moment, than during the

seventy-one years I've lived, but history warns us we're often doomed to repeat our mistakes. I've lived through the Great Depression, Hitler, World War II, the Berlin Airlift, and the Berlin Wall. Many mornings I wonder how I survived these catastrophic events. There's no easy answer to that question.

Money flows like a river, sometimes full and flush and other times dry and barren. Wealth was so much more important to me when I was young. Journalists want to tell my story, women want me to come forward because some admire what I did, editors want to reissue my novels and they clamor for an autobiography. The attention and fame I sought when I was young has transformed into a desire for peace and security. Money is good, but I want to write for myself—only because I want to validate my own worth. Happiness is being able to live one's life as one chooses.

I'm content in my little village away from Berlin, with my two dogs and two cats to keep me company. They provide companionship and bring warmth to my home.

Read what I have to say—pay attention to my words before the next Hitler arises, before the next world war blooms. All any of us want is to love, be loved, and to live our lives in peace.

When I was young, I wrote about the "New German Woman." That woman is long dead, and a modern one has taken her place. If someone finds my story, I hope the men and women of today will understand what history has taught us.

*Editor's Note: This fragment was found in December 1983 in a trunk in a deserted farmhouse west of Berlin, Germany, along with the manuscript that follows, both written at least ten years before.*

# BOOK ONE

# CHAPTER 1

―――◆◆◆―――

*Remembering the Weimar Republic*
*October 1929*

The Nazis were scum, *der Abschaum* as my friends and I used to call them. Those outside the National Socialist political sphere knew that, but few stood up to them, and by 1929 Germany was in deep trouble with much worse yet to come. The National Socialist movement didn't burst forth like a spring tulip. The Nazis took their time: bending the truth, propagating their lies, using their strong-arm tactics. The warnings were in front of us, but we didn't pay attention. Who, after all, was this power-hungry, former *kriminell* named Adolf Hitler? In the beginning, many laughed at him and dismissed his threats as the ravings of a madman.

At eighteen years of age, I was a "New German Woman." I stayed away from the Sturmabteilung, the SA Brownshirts, as much as possible because the concepts of freedom and liberty had deserted their boggled minds, even though they espoused such ideals in their fascist propaganda. The world was very *1984* in those days. A few years later, you couldn't walk down the street without passing a parade of them, haughty and smug in their invincibility. They were the living evidence that our freedoms and our lives would never be the same and, in many cases, would be taken away.

During the Weimar years, I smoked Manoli cigarettes and drank cherry brandy, especially when a good-looking man was buying at the Leopard Club. It was a grand establishment, close to the Alexanderplatz, housed in the first floor and basement of a large stone apartment building. God knows what the tenants thought of the ruckus below them until all hours of the morning, but my fellow club devotees and I didn't care. We were having a good time living, loving, and, most of all, surviving.

Sometimes a piece of *schweinefleisch* appeared on a white china plate in front of me as I chatted up a man at the bar, or vice versa. The plate would turn blue, red, green, or yellow in the club's lights depending on the mood of the delicious bartender, Rudi.

He was a man who liked tight pants and even tighter shirts, who had the kind of muscled body that drove women mad—visible but not excessive. He spent many hours in the gymnasium. Rudi, with his wavy black hair, sparkling eyes, and smoky voice, flattered me, but that was the way he operated. I thought he was sexy. We never acted upon our tenuous mutual attraction except for a few arresting kisses in a corner booth of the basement cabaret. I found out later that he had a thing not only for girls but boys as well. Gender didn't matter to Rudi as long as the sex was good.

My girlfriend Lotti often accompanied me in the evening after she escaped her office job as a typist. She was lucky to have it, always aware that work like hers, although common, had little turnover and much competition. A million other girls were always there to take your place if you stepped out of line, or asked for too much time off, or worst of all, demanded a raise. Typing interested me only when I was writing. I decided that I had no use for menial labor. I wanted to be a star like the glamorous women whose photos graced movie magazines. I knew that before I even thought about writing. My mother, despite her Lutheran background, read the publications that I would peruse in secret after she went to bed. There was a deeply buried side to my mother that longed to break free from the drudgery of everyday life. Many women in Berlin had the same fantasy that was unfulfilled in the Weimar years.

One late night at the club, after many brandies, Lotti dubbed me Niki. "It has to have one 'k,' even if it looks Russian," she said. "It's frightfully exotic and suits someone with a face like yours." I had no idea what she was talking about, but I took it as a compliment. I lit a Manoli cigarette.

"Who's that man over there?" she asked, tilting her head to the left. "He keeps looking this way."

I was charmed that Lotti had created a new name for me rather than use the dull one I'd grown up with—Marie Rittenhaus—so I'd barely noticed the slick-looking man at the end of the bar who smiled at us and then slipped away. He wore an expensive black suit and shiny leather shoes, and carried a pack of gold-filtered cigarettes.

Rudi picked up the man's glass from the bar.

"What was he drinking?" I asked, as Rudi drifted over.

He leaned toward me and popped open a button on his shirt, exposing a swath of dark chest hair. "You like him? I'll introduce you."

Lotti sighed. "Why is it always you? I spot them and you get them."

"Courvoisier," Rudi said, answering my question.

"Oh, nice. He's handsome and seems cultured, not the usual type who hangs out here. What's his name?"

"Ah, enough of the insults . . . Rickard Länger." Rudi wiped the onyx bar with a damp cloth. "He's a leading movie producer in Berlin."

"Hmm . . . Länger," Lotti said, wriggling her nose. "I wonder if the name holds true?"

"From what I've heard," Rudi said with a touch of boredom, and went on about his bartending.

"Movies . . . movies."

"The Great Niki," Lotti gushed. "That'll be your screen name . . . or The Sexy Niki."

"The Silly Niki," I said, looking at my watch. "I have to go. Coming or staying?"

"The gentleman left . . . nothing for me here," Lotti said. "Two girls on our own."

"I have an audition tomorrow," I said, referring to a small part in a cabaret show that I'd found listed in a newspaper.

We grabbed our coats, intent on braving a brisk mid-October night. I whistled for Rudi and he came bounding over.

"You're leaving? *C'est dommage.*"

"The next time Rickard Länger settles in for the evening, call my building. I'd like to meet him—in a professional capacity. Is he married?"

"I don't think so . . . I'll give you a call . . . Niki."

Word of my new name had traveled fast. I gave him a respectful kiss on his lips, not as slow as he liked them, but sufficient enough.

Lotti and I walked through the square and then toward my apartment near the Berliner Dom. It was almost midnight, but Konigstrasse was packed with people out for a late-night stroll. The air was filled with mist, the droplets catching on our coats and covering our faces like sweat on a humid summer day. The night lights shimmered on the wet street. Our breaths rolled out in steamy puffs in front of our faces. The cool air felt good on my skin after the stale atmosphere of the Leopard Club. As we walked, Lotti talked about her miserable existence as a typist and encouraged me to pursue my creative careers.

"What if this audition doesn't work out?" I asked. "It's only a small part and doesn't pay much. My stage experience is in school plays—not exactly the kind of work that directors are looking for. This 'profession' got into my head from looking at my mother's movie magazines. I'm running out of money. The temporary typing jobs seem to be drying up. Soon, I'll find myself living with her again. No woman my age wants to live with her mother."

"Then do something else. Write a book. You've told me a hundred times you'd like to write a novel . . . how the pictures go through your head. I wish I could write a book . . . or star in a movie."

"It's hard to earn money these days—a woman has to rely on her wits as well."

"Or whatever she can," Lotti added.

We arrived at my apartment. With no space to entertain, I rarely asked anyone to come inside my two-room flat. For the privilege of living here I paid eight marks a week, furnished. Lotti had been inside many times, but she was one of the few. If I was with a gentleman, I went to his place—to make sure he wasn't married. I didn't have sex with married men, even those who, as a ruse, took off the ring. Some girls would sleep with a married man for a coat, or jewelry, but I couldn't. It was a rule I wouldn't break. Perhaps the Lutheran upbringing that my mother had jammed into my head had warped me, despite her minor obsession with glamour. After all, photoplay girls weren't necessarily harlots. I hadn't been to church since I left home. My refusal to go to bed with a man claimed by matrimony was rooted in the horrible knowledge that I'd betrayed his wife—a living, breathing woman who had feelings like mine. I didn't want that done to me.

I kissed Lotti on the cheek and walked up the stairs, passing the communal telephone that served the building. I hoped that Rudi would give me a call about Rickard. When the phone rang it never went unanswered. Two or three tenants on the lower floors fought over it.

I opened the door, and a scene appeared from a novel I'd been thinking about, *The Last Man*. I was the heroine.

*Buttery light filtered through a window that looked into the courtyard below. A single linden stood there, its branches flexing gray fingers toward the sky.*

*She always looked forward to fall, when the tree would shed its leaves, brown and gold upon the ground, for that meant the low winter sun, nested in the southern sky, would strike her room a few hours a day. In the summer, she felt wrapped in a green cocoon, soothing her when the rain struck the leaves in silver bursts, but ultimately leaving her depressed, claustrophobic, and anxious in the humidity and the photosynthetic world that surrounded her.*

*Nothing could hide her shame. He was coming for a visit and he'd see the bed she'd tried to make as comfortable as possible: the old feather pillows, the green goose-down comforter folded neatly at the bottom of the mattress, the sheets a bit yellow with age. He would notice the old hot plate she'd polished to a metallic glint; the vertical mirror, its gilt frame cracked to white in several places, its bluish tint circling the glass. She kept the small bathroom as clean as possible with an ocean of bleach and soaps. All of this preparation would signal that she had little money, and nothing much to offer except her body. How long would her attractiveness last? How much could she get from him—without falling in love—before he tossed her away?*

There it was—in my mind. How I, and many other women, survived the world we were born into. I closed the door, threw my coat on the comforter, and shut the window I'd left open. My eyes fluttered as I crawled into bed, and I wondered how long it would be before I got a message from Rudi about Rickard Länger.

\*   \*   \*

I didn't get the part, but a call came about 8:00 p.m. a week later from the smoky-voiced bartender. "He's here for another hour. Maybe longer, if you can convince him to stay."

I grabbed my coat, rushed out the door, and even sprang for a taxi, which was a luxury considering my financial state. I'd worked a few typing jobs, but was stretched thin. When I arrived at the Leopard Club, the doorman, who knew me, ushered me in. The chill bite from the wind disappeared as I stepped into the stuffy hallway. Once again, smoke and mirrors filled my senses. A warm blue light spread over the bar and across the tables. It was like stepping into a shimmering pool of water in summer. The cigarette smoke softened the light even more, rendering it fuzzy and semitransparent. The voice of a female singer in the cabaret below flowed up the stairs.

Rickard sat to the right of the bar, tucked into one of the small booths that lined the wall apart from the dining tables. He was a vision in blue and black, the color settling in muted veils on his dark suit, the straight line of a shadow cutting across his face.

The usual denizens of the club sat nearby—girls who dressed like boys, boys who dressed like girls, a few stiff businessmen waiting for the liquor to loosen them up, a sour-faced war veteran from 1918 who looked out of place among the younger crowd, as if he had wandered in from the street.

I waved to Rudi, who pointed in the direction of Rickard's booth. He needn't have, for the man had already spotted me and risen from his seat like a gentleman. My nerves tightened and I smoothed my coat in an effort to calm myself. What had stoked my anxiety? I wasn't sure. I'd been with a few men, nothing serious, most of them allowing me to live on-and-off with them for a month or so until one of us grew tired of the other, providing a few laughs and, most important, some good food and wine. Perhaps my skin tingled because I found this man filled with possibilities, unlike most of the others. He was handsome enough to make my heart flutter; however, I didn't know if he was married. Even Lotti was unclear on that account.

Rickard took my hand and guided me into the booth opposite him. His fingers were somewhat cold despite the heat in the room. I assumed his luminous eyes were blue, but it was hard to tell in the light of the same color. His hair was parted on the left and slicked back in a current style that swept past the crown of his head. The black suit may have been the same as the one he wore when I first saw him, but the shirt was different. It was black as well, the only spot of color being the muted burst of a diamond stickpin through his tie. I judged he was in his early to midthirties. The age difference wasn't a problem for me. I liked a man who was settled.

A large bottle of cognac and two glasses sat on the table, his half-full. He poured me a drink and leaned back in the booth, studying my face and figure as I took off my coat.

"I'm happy you could come," he said, in High German, and, after a pause, "Niki."

I was so unused to the formality and the nickname that I stuttered a greeting in return.

"Sorry, I'm used to dealing with business partners," he said, slipping into a less formal mode of speech.

I sipped the cognac and it slid down my throat in a smooth, pleasant way. I put the glass down and looked at the crowd filling the tables. "Herr Länger, it's a pleasure to meet you. I assume Rudi told you the nickname my girlfriend gave me."

"Yes, I like it. I was interested in meeting you." He tore open the foil pack of the gold-filtered cigarettes and struck its corner against his fist. A smoke popped out and he lit it. "Call me Rickard. We might do business together." He offered me one—I declined—they weren't my brand.

"Are you married?" I asked.

His brows lifted for a moment and then settled as he smiled. "You don't waste time—a debatable personality trait." The raucous laughs from a table of drunken business-men diverted his attention.

"I like to know what I'm getting into—no matter the proposition," I said, when he returned his gaze to me.

"For the moment, business," he said, answering my question. "I like your look. Rudi may have told you that I produce movies."

I nodded.

"I'm making one now—about vampires."

I laughed. "Hasn't that been done? *Nosferatu?*"

He inhaled luxuriously and let the smoke drift out of his nose. "That kind of filmmaking is dead. Angles and shortened perspectives are out. Realism is what I strive for. Murnau's film doesn't go far enough. So many stories have been based on Stoker's *Dracula*, but I want to tell the tale of his brides, his many loves. It's a speaking role—only a few lines—you look the part."

"Should I be flattered or insulted?" I took another drink.

"Definitely a compliment. Turn your head to the side."

I did.

"Yes, a splendid profile—a true beauty."

I wondered if this was his way of making an advance. I'd looked in the mirror on my way out the door and hadn't been fond of the view. My hair was too long for the current fashion. I had purple blotches under my eyes from worries about money. I thought my nose was too big, my bust too small. "You overestimate, I'm sure."

"No, when I see it, I know it." He leaned forward, studying me in the blue light. "You have a classic profile. Don't cut your hair because the style at the turn of the last century was longer—we have wigs to add to the length—and whatever you do, don't erase that birthmark on your left cheek. It adds to your personality . . . and beauty."

I thought of it as an unsightly spot, and many times I'd considered having it removed, but decided the cost wasn't worth it.

"You're tall for a woman." He stubbed out his cigarette in the glass ashtray. "But you're not gangly—you exude a certain style and grace. We start shooting the wives' scenes tomorrow morning. Can you be there?"

"How much does it pay?"

"How much is your rent?"

"Eight marks a week."

"I'll give you ten a week as long as you're shooting . . . but don't tell the other girls."

I extended my hand, like the businesswoman I'd become. "Agreed."

"Your call is at eight . . . don't be late, or I'll have to get another girl." He reached into his suit pocket. "Here's my card, in case you need to get in touch."

"I'll be there."

He rose from the booth, cupped my head in his hands, and turned it gently to each side. "Wonderful." He tilted his head toward the cognac. "Keep the bottle."

After Rickard left, Rudi floated over to my booth, pretending he wasn't interested in what had transpired. He wore a pair of tight slacks that turned the heads of every sex when he walked through the room. Tonight, he'd topped off his outfit with a white shirt and vest that turned blue or gray depending on where he stood in the light.

"Would you like something to eat?" he asked, eyeing the two-thirds full bottle of cognac. "Sauerbraten? Cheese?"

"No, not really. I have a call tomorrow morning." I looked up and smiled at his pleasing face.

"I knew it," he said, smiling back. "I'm thrilled—Lotti will be, too."

"I'm playing one of Dracula's wives."

"A vampire. Perfect casting."

"Oh, be still. Care to join me in a toast?"

Rudi was about to reply when a commotion broke out near the club door. Everyone looked toward the entrance.

Rickard, breath pulsing from his lungs, rushed through the maze of tables and slumped into the booth. He pulled Rudi toward him. "The thugs slugged me in the stomach, and your doorman took a punch to the eye. I don't think the bastards will come inside."

"Walter's been hurt?" Rudi asked.

"He's okay—he yelled for the police. They're out there now."

Rudi strode toward the door.

I leaned across the table, trying to get a better picture of what Rickard had been through. His hair was ruffled, and it appeared that one of his lapels had been torn; his eyes were wide, his lips pressed firmly together.

I slid next to him and poured a drink. He drained it in one gulp.

"What happened?"

"They know who I am." The glass slipped a bit in his hand. "I'm important to them because I have money—they think I have much more than I do." His mouth turned down derisively. "They want payments for protection, for me and the studio, and they'll stop at nothing to get them. For years, I've been able to avoid them like the annoying insects they are, but now they're following me. They jumped me just as I was about to get into a taxi."

I found it hard to believe what Rickard was saying, but the proof was in front of my eyes. The SA had been around for years. I'd heard a few stories about what they'd done, sometimes roughing up a person, calling them names, but I'd never witnessed anything like this. It was hard to tell sometimes whether the tale you heard was true or an exaggeration. Germany was changing and I, like many people, had ignored what was happening because it hadn't affected me.

"Are you all right? Do you need to see a doctor?"

"I'm fine—I fought back—surprised myself. But I do need another drink."

The cognac was down to about half now.

Rudi, his face as immobile as a Greek statue, returned to the booth. "Walter has a small cut under his eye, but he's fine otherwise. Now, I've got to warn the owner to be on the lookout for the Brownshirts. Brownshits is more like it."

"Give Volker my best," Rickard said.

Rudi stormed off to find the man.

"Well, I'll make my exit again," Rickard said. "Certainly, they're gone now."

"We'll take a taxi together," I said, gathering up my coat and the cognac. If nothing else, I could use the bottle as a weapon to stave off another attack.

We reached the door, having walked past the inquisitive eyes that gazed at us from the tables, and stepped outside. The weather had turned colder, and I braced myself against the wind while looking for the SA. None were to be seen. Walter, sporting a bandage under his left eye, asked Rickard if he was injured. My new employer once again declared his good health and tipped the doorman ten marks for joining in the fracas.

We got into the car and I gave the driver my address.

"You live near the Dom," Rickard said.

"Yes, in a very small two-room apartment, with little space for company."

"That's too bad," Rickard said.

A few minutes later, the taxi stopped at my street. "Tomorrow, be prepared to suck blood," Rickard said as a joke. The driver shot us a disgusted look in the rearview mirror.

Rickard held on to my arm as I tried to exit. He pulled me close and kissed me on the cheek.

My face flushed as I said good night. The cab sputtered away. As I walked up the stairs to my apartment, I looked over my shoulder, the first time I'd ever done so. I couldn't shake the feeling that the SA might come rushing after me. I quickly put the key into the lock and hurried into my room.

# CHAPTER 2

I arrived at the studio about 7:30 after a quick breakfast and a smoke. I had no idea what to do with my hair or makeup before I left the apartment, so I left them alone. The studio was about a half hour away, but the crush of workers on the trolley threw me behind schedule. I was jostled about like a juggler's pin. When I stepped onto the lot, I brushed my hair and pinched my cheeks for a little color.

Passport Pictures sat in a field by the airport. Several major roads ran nearby and a railroad spur snaked onto the back of the property. The rusty tracks, harboring a healthy growth of weeds between them, looked as if they hadn't been used for years. Behind the arched entrance, trees bedecked with yellow and brown leaves formed a semicircle around a low brick building. That structure was joined on each side by two massive vertical rectangles of steel and stone that rose like cathedrals from the ground. Those, I assumed, because of their blacked-out windows, were the studios.

A guard met me at the entrance and asked my business. I told him I was here to see Herr Länger about my role in a vampire picture. He instantly knew what I was talking about and directed me to Studio One, which was to the left of the low building.

Because the clock was ticking, I hurried to the location:

impressed, excited, and somewhat overwhelmed by the size of the business in front of me. I hadn't had time to call Lotti to tell her about the role, but I was certain she would share my enthusiasm and anxiety. My mind raced as I reached a small entrance next to a larger opening covered by a hangar door.

I pictured my face on the cover of movie magazines, stylish, made up to look much older than I really was, outfitted in a dress dripping in silver spangles that accented my cleavage and the white softness of my skin. As I pulled on the handle, I also considered that it had been more than a year since I'd done any work onstage, and that in a school play. The image of me, as a star, burst like a bubble in the wind.

I entered another world. The air inside smelled like a crisp winter day. The lights were dim. I felt my way along a wall of black-cotton muslin. High, and in front of me, a yellow beam pierced the dark. I followed its direction through the twists and turns of the hall.

When I turned the final corner, a panorama opened before me, as if I had been transported to the wilds of Romania at the end of the last century. A castle of gray stone sat high upon a thorny crag. On the painted backdrop, a blood-red moon rose above the vampire's lair, a mood trick for the actors because the black-and-white cameras would show only a dark tone and not the color.

A man clad in a dusky sheath, his face powdered to a soft white, bent over the form of a woman whose filmy dress clung to her like snakeskin. As the two actors worked, a large camera moved into position toward them, advancing as stealthily as a prowling panther.

"Cut," a man yelled from a canvas director's chair. "That's what I want in the frame." The actors rose languidly from their positions, still absorbed in their roles. "Thirty minutes before the next shot," the man yelled through a megaphone. The male vampire broke his pose and ran down a series of wooden steps painted to look like stone, stopping briefly at his chair to grab a cigarette. He lit it, taking care to keep the flame and its burning end from his powdered face.

A hand on my shoulder caught me off guard. "Niki," the soft voice said. A man kissed my cheek, his fingers twining in my hair a moment before they brushed against my neck. I liked the feel of his fingers. I turned to see Rickard, looking recovered from the previous night's altercation, dressed in dark pants and a checked sweater that covered an open-collared shirt.

"Sorry I'm so late," I said. "The trolley was a catastrophe."

"Next time take a car. I'll pay for it." He took my hand. "Let me introduce you to Anders Pechstein, one of our best directors."

The name sounded familiar, and Rickard took the time to explain. "He's directed more than twenty films for us and he just turned thirty. His father is German, his mother a Swedish Jew. He's worried. The family has connections and money. We're all walking on eggshells with these Nazis about. And, the irony is we're only trying to make entertainment—nothing else."

Anders was bent over a script as we approached. Rickard tapped him on the shoulder and the director looked up. His body was long and lean, his hair dusty blond, his face as pale as his vampires except for a ruddy spot on each cheek. The knee-length pants and the vertically striped sweater that matched his socks accentuated his thin torso.

"This is Niki," Rickard said, as if he hated to disturb the director, "the woman I was telling you about . . . a perfect wife for our vampire king."

Anders turned, looked up, studied me for a few seconds, and grunted. "She'll do. Take her to makeup."

We didn't dally. Rickard guided me around the set, behind the false front of the castle, to a dingy dressing room tucked into a makeshift corner. "He's in a bad humor," I said.

"No, that's Anders. Always business and nothing more. That's what makes him great. We're all used to it."

A vinegary woman, whose smudged hands displayed a rainbow of color, sat in front of a mirror ablaze with lights.

"This is Inga," Rickard said. "She does it all—dresser, makeup, runs lines . . . by the way, you need the script."

"Yes."

"I'll get you a copy."

"Don't bother," Inga said flatly. "I've got one here. Who is *she*?"

"Vampire Queen Three," Rickard said.

"I've read this miserable trash at least twelve times," Inga said, tossing me the script. "You've got three lines in a silent movie. Shouldn't take long to memorize." She got up from her post in front of the mirror. "Sit. We've got fifteen minutes to make you ugly—if it takes that long."

Inga sniggered and I rolled my eyes at her insult. Rickard disappeared. As I opened the dog-eared pages and glanced at the script, the only thing that kept me in the chair was the ten marks I was earning.

In fifteen minutes, Inga had pasted a greasy, ashen pancake on my face, produced false teeth, and dressed me in a slinky gown much like the vampire dress I'd already seen. I was shocked at my transformation, from my everyday appearance to the dark-eyed, pasty-faced, fanged vamp who looked back at me from the mirror.

If I'd read the lines for Vampire Queen Three correctly, Inga was right: *I won't be discarded, How beautiful is the moon tonight*, and *Feed me your blood*. Where and when those lines would be said still wasn't clear to me.

A young man stuck his head around the curtain that separated the dressing room from the set. "Niki?"

I nodded, ready to leave Inga to herself.

"You're wanted on set."

The Vampire King was waiting when I climbed the terrace steps, the castle towering over our heads. The camera had been positioned at a forty-five-degree angle, its lens looking upward, capturing not only our bodies but the rough texture of the fake stone and the painted moon. The other two Vampire Queens, fangs and claws extended, were positioned across from me, ready to attack as I pleaded to be saved by the King, who reeked of schnapps and cigarettes.

Anders called for quiet and action. The camera whirred.

The King, as if wearing skates underneath his costume, glided toward me. "Why should I make you my queen?" he hissed.

I faced him, transferring all my acting ability into my eyes, along with the words to come forth. "I won't be discarded!"

Somewhere a door slammed and Anders yelled, "Cut."

The lights flickered for a moment and then returned to their intensity for the shot.

"Enough," a man called out. The King and I dropped our poses and, putting a hand over our eyes, looked beyond the director. In the murk, I saw Rickard stride toward Anders.

A Brownshirt in his kepi hat walked briskly toward the two men. A thin, weasel of a man, he reminded me of Joseph Goebbels. "Who's directing this picture?" Two similarly attired men, missing the oak leaves on their insignia, followed. They presented a formidable group in their uniforms, complete with pants flared at the hip, leather straps, cinched waists, Nazi armbands, and, most disturbing of all, pistols strapped to their sides.

Anders got up from his chair and turned to face them. "I am. What do you want?"

"Is this a respectable German picture?" the leader asked.

"Who are you?" Rickard asked in return.

"I am Oberführer Spiegel," the man replied, "and you will address me as 'Oberführer.'"

"Yes, Oberführer," Anders said. "This is a good German picture filmed on good German soil." He started to turn away as if Spiegel didn't matter.

"What is it about?" Spiegel prodded.

Anders hesitated; instead, Rickard spoke up. "The wives of the Vampire King."

"Vampires?" The man sneered, his mustache curling on his lip. "You call that good? We've already seen the decadent filth of *Nosferatu* and want no more of it. You should be extolling the virtues of the Fatherland, the good German men and women who will someday rule the world. The joys of hard work—productivity and motherhood—that's what you should be filming—not this degenerate smut."

Anders rose from his chair and stepped toward Spiegel. The two men were nearly the same height as they faced each other, both with fire in their eyes. "My film is neither decadent nor degenerate. We film what people want to see."

The Oberführer raised his hand, and his two accomplices moved on either side of the director. "You want to see blood? We'll show you."

The two Brownshirts pulled Anders down the hall. We heard the door slam and looked at each other in horror. Rickard moved toward the door, but Spiegel blocked his way, drawing the pistol from his side. "I know you," the Oberführer said. "You're Länger—the producer who refuses to support our cause—who owes us tribute."

"Tribute, my ass. Blackmail. You and your stinking Nazis. Get out of my way!"

"I have many reasons to shoot you, and no one, not even the useless police, would question my motive." He raised the pistol to Rickard's forehead.

One of the other queens gasped and I started to say something, but Rickard held up his hand for quiet.

"If I were you, I wouldn't ignore our Party or our leaders," Spiegel continued. "It would be in your best interest to find the money we require." He lowered the weapon. "I'll check on my men now . . . you should have plenty of blood for your picture." He holstered his pistol and disappeared into the dark.

I rushed to Rickard's side—he was shaking, more with anger than fear I imagined. He took my hand for a moment, then ran to the door and threw it open. I, and the rest of the cast, followed.

Anders lay in a heap halfway across the lot. The two Brownshirts stood over him, but the truly terrible sight was the nightmarish vision of the Oberführer kneeling near Anders's neck and licking the director's wound. Spiegel withdrew his tongue, dipped his hand into the blood, rose like a creature of the night, and sucked the crimson fluid from a finger. "Vampires are real," he said, laughing. "Don't forget, or more of this will be spilled." The three men turned and walked away.

"My God," Rickard said, running to Anders's body. Blood had pooled around the director's head and turned the dirt slick and black.

"Is he alive?" I asked.

The Vampire King, resting on his knees, pressed his ear near the director's face. "He's breathing. I think he's just been knocked out."

"I'm calling the police," Rickard said. "Wait with him. See if you can get him to come around."

And we did wait until the ambulance came and took Anders away. The Vampire King and I managed to get a cloth over the cut on the side of his head that had caused blood to flow down his neck. The director was groggy, but managed to mutter a few words before they took him away. Spiegel was right, the police were ineffectual, asking only a few questions and categorizing the attack as "minor." I got the idea that they didn't want to get involved with anything regarding the SA.

"I'll take over for today," Rickard said as we walked back to the studio. The mood was more than gloomy as we continued shooting.

A few years later, I wrote *Confessions of a Vampire's Wife*, hoping that the Nazis would read it. They did—and hated it. The book was filled with allusions to the SA and their tactics.

*They came for me like they came for everyone else. Clad in robes of scarlet, traveling on wisps of wind, never seeing the sun because their presence alone blocked it out. They were more than vampires; they were parasites. I became part of them because they absorbed me. I could do nothing to stop them. The only way out of my horror was through my own death. But I was already dead from their presence.*

*My husband was the worst. We didn't have sex; we had no children. We propagated our race through violence and insanity. It made no difference to my husband whether he was kind or benevolent. There were no rules, only buried days that slid into nights clouded with death, red and billowing with smoke.*

*The golden allure of drink, the breaking softness of flesh against our teeth didn't satisfy us. Blood drove us, and the more we drank the thirstier we became. I never forgot the night I saw him bent over the body of a beautiful young man he'd killed. He had done so not for sex, nor for greed, not for anything but the warmth and vigor of fresh, running blood. He kneeled over him, his incisors piercing the jugular, the life of the youth gushing out in bursts until he was as white as alabaster. Then, with a roar of lust, my husband dipped his fingers into the blood and drank like he was possessed, until he was cupping his hands around his victim's neck, like taking water from a mountain stream. His teeth, everything about my husband, glowed red. From that time on, no one could stop him.*

As we filmed that day, the crimson moon above us, I felt that no one could stop the Nazis. The feeling ran through my blood as icy and sure as an Alpine river.

We were heading toward chaos.

But so many Germans didn't care and worshiped the Vampire King who was rising among them.

# CHAPTER 3

Anders was in the hospital for several weeks with headaches and dizziness from his head injury. Doctors called it a severe concussion and called for complete bed rest until the end of the year. Rickard picked me up in his Mercedes-Benz a few times and we drove to the hospital to give our good wishes to the director.

Rickard gamely tried to carry on with filming, but soon found himself overwhelmed by the technical details that his colleague had already mastered. Rickard was the money; Anders was the filmmaker.

So, after two more painful weeks, production shut down, and I and the rest of the vampires said our good-byes, not knowing if we would see each other again. I got my thirty marks and was pleased to have the money. The Vampire King told me that he was going on to other studios, other projects, and not to tell Rickard about his decision. I understood— even a vampire needs cash.

Lotti and I met a few times at the club after work and crabbed about our respective lives to poor Rudi, who had nothing but solace and liquor to offer. Lotti was most excited, however, to hear about my relationship with Rickard that, oddly enough, had taken a positive turn after the awful beating of Anders. Her fleshy cheeks glowed pink when I told her about our time together, having dinner upon occasion or visiting Anders.

One day as we drove to the hospital, I asked Rickard what he was going to do about the Nazis.

He was curt. "You shouldn't worry about that. It's not your concern."

"But I do worry," I said, and put my hand on his leg, the only limb that was free since both of his hands were on the steering wheel.

He turned briefly from his driving and smiled at me in a way that no man ever had. I fell for him at that moment—at least a little bit. When we got to the hospital, he gave me a kiss before we got out of the car. I felt warm and alive, not like a gold digger, or a woman just out for the comfort of a man's money and home.

I had been with men before, of course, much to my mother's displeasure. I kept her in the dark—only that I was going out—except for a few names scattered here and there. She was a churchgoing Lutheran, like my father had been, and had devoted herself to rearing me in a Christian home. My mother prayed regularly during the day, before meals, before bedtime, and in church. I went along with her but could never see the benefit. Our prayers didn't bring money or prosperity to the household—neither did the glamour magazines that appealed to my mother's fantasies beyond our small home. Life crawled along like a tortoise. Any change in our circumstances was slow and incremental, mostly downward. My father had been killed in World War I, so I never really knew him. I believed that God had taken my father and deserted us, even though my mother rhapsodized about his death, calling him "an angel who had flown to the Heavenly Kingdom much too early." Life became even harder for my mother after his death. A small pension and what money she could make from taking in laundry barely supported us.

I always liked lists, but there was one—the men in my

life—that I kept secret from my mother. It started at sixteen with a kiss, progressed to fondling, and then a year later to fumbles in the alley, or, if the man could afford it, the back seat of a car. I lost my virginity just before I turned seventeen, several weeks before my mother told me I had to leave—she couldn't stand to see me ruin my life with "soiled men." The man's name wasn't important, but I recall my first sexual encounter as painful and unpleasant. Mothers seem to know when their daughters are having sex. Perhaps she knew because I felt so guilty—at first. Later, the sex became a matter of survival.

Thereafter, I made my way from man to man, enforcing the requirement that they be single. I looked for dinner, cherry brandy, a warm bed, and a job if it was part of the arrangement. My looks got me into apartments but didn't keep me there. The sex faded and the men got bored with my company, sometimes threatening to kick me out if I didn't pack up. Rickard, at least on the surface, seemed different, but I wasn't certain that he wouldn't throw me to the gutter as well. I hoped he wouldn't because I liked him—sometimes loved him.

In my young years, I couldn't define the difference between survival and love. I wanted to believe that any relationship was more than hormones and sexual urges. Rickard seemed to walk in brightness and I felt good when I was around him, but my mistrust of the world tarnished his halo as it had for all men. When we visited Anders in the hospital, I would study Rickard, his form resplendent in the sun as it poured through the window, his face relaxed and smiling, cheering Anders on to health, regaling him with stale jokes that sometimes brought a smile to the director's face. But I read concern for others in Rickard as well, more than I'd seen from any other man, and that quality simultaneously buoyed me and scared me to death.

We'd kissed and hugged during the few weeks we'd been

together, but never made love. Even my vocabulary had shifted from "sex" to "made love." Rickard was too much of a gentleman to push, and I was afraid of what I was falling into. I was losing control of my singularity—my sense of self.

Then the day came that changed everything.

It began like any other. I had taken a bath in the washroom at the end of the hall, returned to my apartment, and was combing my hair in front of the blue mirror when a man knocked on my door—I knew that from the vigorous pounding and the smoker's hack. A surly neighbor from the first floor, a veteran of the Great War who always wore ill-fitting pants and scuffed shoes, stood in front of me twirling the end of his gray mustache and staring at my robed body with his suspicious, dreary eyes.

"A call for you," he said. "A man. Who else?"

"Thank you, I'll be there in a moment." I shut the door in the rude, old bastard's face. I didn't want to see him after his stinging assessment of my character, so I waited a moment before padding down the stairs. The phone was dangling against the wall by its cord.

"Hello?"

"Have you heard the news?" Rickard seemed out of breath and filled with dread. I'd never heard him so distraught.

"No?"

"God, Niki, do you even know what day it is?"

"No. Why should I?" I was irritated by his tone. A growl came through in my voice.

"Wednesday, October 30th, 1929. We've been in this shit for a while now, but it really hit bottom yesterday in America. The New York Stock Exchange lost billions. Thousands are now penniless, and the damn panic is leapfrogging all over the world." He took a breath. "There's a bit of a recovery today, but I don't think it will last. Too much has already been lost."

I didn't know what to say. The stock market never interested me. I didn't have money in it, let alone any to invest. Frankly, I was more concerned with getting through each day, trying to figure out who I was, and wondering where the future would take me. However, Rickard's news and his obvious fear weighed on me.

"That's terrible," I said, softening my tone. "Is there something I can do?"

"Unless you can save world markets, I doubt it." He paused for a time—so long I thought the line had gone dead. "The studio is finished. Without our investors' capital, we're sunk." His voice broke. "Everything I've worked for is gone. Everyone will be looking for a job, including me."

Again, I struggled for words. "I'm sorry."

"Oh, it'll be tough for you, too. It won't be easy finding work now. Thousands of Germans are unemployed already—now it'll be a flood."

"I have enough from my typing jobs to buy us coffee," I said, hoping to cheer him up, but his only response was a sigh. My mother would take me in if I couldn't find work, but that was the least desirable option.

"What would you say to living together?" he asked. "We could combine our incomes, help each other out."

I was taken aback by his question. There was little financial advantage for Rickard unless he wanted me to help with the rent, and I probably couldn't afford half the amount he was paying. I knew he had a swanky apartment on Unter den Linden, named so because of the trees that lined the walkways. Or was it his way of saying he was interested in me, maybe even cared for me? Curiously, he sounded younger when he asked the question, almost like a teenager. Was he nervous . . . or did the thought of me moving in excite him?

"Are you serious? I couldn't afford my half of your rent."

"We could share food expenses . . . we'll worry about the

money later. Of course, I'm serious. The first night I saw you at the club, I was entranced—"

I didn't respond immediately after the sudden drop in his voice. I gauged how I was feeling while holding on to the telephone and looking down the grubby hall toward my small room. My luxuries were nonexistent. My days consisted of temporary jobs with stingy employers who left me wondering how I would pay for my next meal, fighting the sour growls in my stomach when I didn't have enough to eat. Rudi was kind enough to slide some food my way when Lotti and I showed up at the Leopard Club, and more often than not, Lotti paid for the drinks because she was working full time. My past had been filled with "just getting by," and Rickard offered me something more. Comfort. Security. "I was entranced," he said. No man had ever said those words to me.

My mother wouldn't have approved, but it didn't take me long to make up my mind. "Tomorrow is the thirty-first. My rent is due November first. I'll be there in two days."

He inhaled, as if a weight had been lifted from his shoulders. "Come at eleven in the morning."

I hung up and scampered back to my little hole of an apartment. I didn't have much to pack. I felt like celebrating and couldn't wait to tell Lotti.

The banking district in Berlin Center wasn't awash in blood, but I didn't doubt that a few ambitious investors took their own lives. As I walked down Unter den Linden, I imagined that some had leaped from the tops of the massive stone buildings lining the streets, and that the hundreds of banks and their branches in the area had suffered great setbacks. Certainly, sadness ruled at the Berlin Stock Exchange on Hackescher Markt. There were stories of men throwing themselves from skyscrapers in New York City, of withdrawing pistols from their desks and blowing their brains out—

because they'd lost money. How would those men have dealt with the Brownshirts we walked by every day? Life is a process of choices, a question of priorities.

Carrying my suitcase up the steps, I arrived at the gated door of Rickard's building. I set the leather case down on the cold stone and considered what I was doing . . . moving in with yet another man; one who had money when I met him, but now might be in the same dire financial straits as most of my previous romantic interests. Yet, I hoped for his sake, and selfishly for mine, that he had saved some money from his business earnings.

The ornate filigreed gate covering the massive glass door caused me to pause. Since I'd left home, I'd lived with several men, none offering much more than the apartment I'd just left. I'd lived an eggs-and-toast life, with a pleasant sticky jam sometimes thrown on top. One push of Rickard's buzzer and the deed would be done. I could always leave if things got rough, but I didn't want to think about that. Something inside my head told me that I wanted this to work. Outside of my mother's home, only Lotti had offered me the use of her apartment if I got in a bad way—and by that she meant pregnant.

I looked up at the stone façade and held my breath.

I half expected a well-manicured, stiffly dressed butler to answer the buzzer. Instead, Rickard, dressed casually in a white sweater and dark pants, bounded down the stairs with a broad smile on his handsome face. His enthusiastic reception lifted my spirits. What could possibly go wrong in a place like this?

The door opened to reveal a large hallway glistening with black and white tiles, and a creamy marble stairway lit by the warm light of an electric chandelier. Rickard gathered me in his arms and kissed me in a lovely way—not forced or overly passionate, but calm and steady—as if he meant it.

"Come in," he said, grabbing my suitcase from the outside

landing. "I'm happy to see you. It's been a trying few days, but things are looking up."

"I can tell," I said, certain that I'd added to his emotional lift.

We walked up three flights, past doors with rectangular white panels outlined in gold leaf. The hall was as hushed and tranquil as any place I'd ever been. Usually, my ears were assaulted by the roar of motorcars or horse-drawn wagons rolling outside my open window, even the screams and laughter of children echoing from within an enclosed courtyard. The silence here was eerie.

"Here it is—3D." The door was unlocked and Rickard swung it open. The room before me took my breath away. Broad windows of shiny glass overlooking Unter den Linden were cut into the walls. My eyes took in the irregular skyline of buildings that stretched to the horizon under the clouds. I stepped upon reddish-beige parquet inlaid with strips of black marble. A bank of rounded, rust-colored sofas sat under the windows, while two tables of glass and chrome anchored the room. Matching comfortable chairs of creamy leather, sculpted into a relaxed V, rested next to them. Carpets of geometric design cushioned the floor in spots.

"It's magnificent," I said. "I've never seen anything like it."

I spotted the bedroom to the left, a symphony of white and silver, fashioned into one corner of the building.

At the height of my awe, a voice called out from a room concealed by French doors on the right side of the apartment. "Länger? We need to conclude our business."

"A moment," Rickard shouted back. "Niki. Unpack. I've cleared space in the wardrobe for you. I'll explain in a few minutes."

I did as he asked, unable to look back or hear what was going on behind the doors. The large piece of walnut furniture that Rickard had referred to rested against an inside wall. Two rounded corners thrust out from a recessed center panel, which held a full-length mirror. The space to the right was filled with Rickard's suits and jackets, the middle probably hid his shirts and pants. I opened the left—there were more than enough hanging space and shelves for my meager collection of clothes.

After unpacking, I sat on the comfortable bed, running my hands over the silky comforter. Rickard was absent for more than a few minutes. A half hour drifted by, then forty-five minutes, leading up to an hour. I kicked off my shoes and lay back, nearly falling asleep by the time I heard voices outside the bedroom.

I crept to the door and peered around it. Rickard was talking quietly to the Oberführer whose thugs, weeks earlier, had assaulted Anders and pressured Rickard for "tribute." Spiegel raised his right arm in salute. My companion half-heartedly returned the gesture. In a few seconds, the Nazi was gone.

My heart crumpled and an angry heat rose from my chest to my throat. Rickard's expression soured the moment he entered the bedroom.

My fingers bunched the comforter. "Why was that bastard here?"

He sighed and sat on the bed next to me. "I thought he would be gone by the time you arrived . . . but the Nazis, if nothing else, talk endlessly about the Führer and their proposed rules and regulations for the new Reich. They act as if they've already taken over the government."

"They're not even in power. Why is everyone bowing to them like they're God?"

"That's what they want to be—and more. I need a cigarette. Have you read *Mein Kampf?*"

"No, and I don't care to."

He rose from the bed and walked to a dressing table snuggled in a corner between two windows. A match flared and he sat in the dresser's white leather chair. He bent over and the light struck his back and body in such a way that he seemed old and sad and tired of living. After a puff, he rested the cigarette between his fingers and spoke. "They're ruthless . . . and they're not going away. They have more than one hundred thousand members . . . as the good Herr Spiegel gleefully informed me today. That's not a large figure compared to the number of people in Germany, but they've infiltrated high places . . . courts and bureaucratic offices. When you combine that with the growing number of shock troops they have, they're a potent force. And they intend to use them—ultimately ending German democracy any way they can."

He lifted his head and stared at me, his eyes watery yet phlegmatic.

"Their leader, this Adolf Hitler, blames the Jews for Germany's failures, but who knows who he really is?" he continued. "Some people listen to him; others think he's a joke. I don't think he's going away. People are blinded by his nationalism and truth twisting. Goebbels spouts the Party's lies, and Germans eat it up like apple cake. I fear what's coming, and I want to protect . . . *us* . . . if I can say there's an 'us.' I like you Niki—a lot." He twirled the gold filter of his cigarette between his fingers and then stubbed it out in the crystal ashtray on the dresser.

"You can say there's an *us*, but I don't know if that's true."

He walked to the bed and sat. "I want us to get through the mess that's coming. Knowing that I've lost quite a bit of money, they still want me to pay them." He spread his arms in a broad gesture. "I could lose my apartment. I have to deal with these people—they've threatened me."

I wondered for a moment, if I should take my bag and head down the stairs, but I was so sick of scraping by and Rickard seemed sincere. I looked at the bedroom and the magnificent room outside. Instead of leaving, I turned to him. "Tell me how this is going to work."

"Us . . . or the money?"

"Both."

"The Nazis have Party members in the banks. Spiegel knew how much money I had before Wall Street failed, and he knows how much money I have now. He offered me a way out if I cooperate—that's the only way to reason with these people. Maybe I have to sell my car . . . or some of the expensive furnishings." He got up. "Come into the other room. I need a drink. You?"

I followed, after grabbing my cigarettes from my coat. "Do you have any cherry brandy?"

He wrinkled his nose. "Nothing that sweet. Will cognac do?"

I nodded and sat in one of the V-shaped chairs that faced the wide windows. Rickard walked to the ebony bar, poured the liquor into two heavy crystal glasses, and handed one to me. I took a sip and asked, "What about us?"

"There's something you need to know."

I didn't like the sound of his voice.

"The Nazis have threatened my wife and son if I don't pay up."

I clutched my drink, my fingers turning pink from the pressure. "You're married?" I sunk in the seat, thinking I'd violated my cardinal rule before I even got started.

"Ex-wife," he said, slumping onto one of the rust-colored sofas. "She left me and took my son with her. He's six now, but I haven't seen him in five years. It was an ugly divorce. I don't even know where she lives, but the Nazis do—as I said, they have officials in high places."

I put the half-finished drink on the nearby table. "Why was it ugly?"

His body tensed for a moment and his eyes slowly met mine. "Do you want the truth?"

"Always."

"I had an affair with an actress. It got out of hand—the woman talked and word got back to my wife . . . she was not forgiving." He leaned back and stretched his arm across the back of the sofa. "I assume you've had some affairs?"

I felt I could answer truthfully. "Yes. I'm not a virgin."

He smiled. "Good. Then we've both been spoiled."

"Rickard . . . are you sure this living arrangement is going to work . . . life is difficult enough these days."

He got off the couch. "Please, don't leave—give it some time. Maybe we can help each other, help each other find a way through this bad time." He stood in front of me and took my hand in his. "I'd like you to stay." The smile turned melancholy and melted my heart a little. "I'll be honest with you—I don't like living alone—and you're the first woman I've met in many years that I felt might make this place a home." He released my hand and turned away. "Well, it's too early to lay everything on the table."

I didn't have anyplace to go. I had little money. I'd been with men who'd had less to offer than Rickard. Maybe we could make a go of it, but what were the odds? Still, what was a month or two or three? By then, I'd know if it was going to work out.

"Have you unpacked?"

"Not yet."

"Go ahead. This is your home now." He sipped his drink.

I retrieved mine from the table and headed to the bedroom. *What's a month or two? Don't I deserve to live like a queen for a while?*

I put my suitcase on the bed, opened the wardrobe, and unpacked. The room seemed cold and darker now, as if the sun had been blocked by thick clouds. Maybe it was going to rain. I didn't even have an umbrella.

# CHAPTER 4

Our first night alone, we slept together. We got to know each other, exploring with our hands and mouths, settling into the warmth and curves of our bodies. Sex was like building a nest, I thought, starting a home together. The play of Berlin's light that washed over us during the night, and the trappings of the opulent room, lifted the experience to the exotic. I wanted to please Rickard, even though my motives were selfish. Like most single women who lived during the Weimar Republic, the constant specter of poverty and hunger lurked over my shoulder.

Rickard was kind and patient during that early time, never pushing me for sex or forcing me into an uncomfortable situation. We danced around each other, sometimes slow and loving, other times nervous and wild, still gauging our interest and the depth of our affection.

I enjoyed getting to know my new home: falling asleep on my new comfortable bed, sitting on the couch with Berlin's skyline outside the windows; the dawn slipping past the curtains like silver mist; the ease of a sausage and eggs breakfast with Rickard; the laughter over a bottle of wine at dinner. For the first time in my life, I knew what it was like to have some comfort and not feel as if a creditor's hands were crushing my throat.

The apartment was divided by the great room. A full bath, with a porcelain tub, adjoined Rickard's bedroom. The room where he'd met Spiegel had been turned into an office, including floor-to-ceiling oak bookcases filled with volumes on movies and art. The builders probably had intended for it to be a dining room. A small but serviceable kitchen was connected to the right of the office, along with a compact bathroom containing a toilet and sink.

Most days, we stayed inside getting to know each other. The weather was becoming colder; Berlin duskier as fall turned to winter. During our talks, Rickard was a mass of conflicting emotions, ranging from optimism about the future to predictions of a coming apocalypse. Sometimes we listened to the radio and paid attention to the news. A couple of times a week he would travel to Passport Pictures to make sure "the place was still standing." Before those trips, Rickard would pass twenty-five marks or so my way and tell me to buy what I wanted. "Get a pretty dress— something for a party," he said, and I did after saving some of his money.

But I also prepared for the worst, and asked myself how I might earn a real living if the relationship didn't work. The studio was dead as far as I knew, and my paltry acting credits wouldn't carry me far with another film company. I kept thinking about Lotti and what she used to say when we met at the Leopard Club. "Write a novel. You have it in you."

I met her there one late afternoon when Rickard was out. The place was oddly quiet with only a few patrons at the bar, the lighting a pale white. Rudi was off for the day, and a woman I didn't know with short black hair was serving the few customers. I ordered a brandy, lit a Manoli, and waited for Lotti in the same booth where I'd met Rickard.

She showed up about fifteen minutes later than expected, her chest heaving from her frantic effort to make up time, her normally pink cheeks flaming red from the bitter wind.

"I'm sorry," she said. "My boss is a bastard—kept me over without pay. If I didn't need the job so desperately—if everyone didn't need a job so desperately—I'd walk out and be on my way." Eyes twinkling, she took off her hat and coat and tossed them into the booth. "But I can't wait to hear about you. Rudi and I have been talking about your prolonged absence at the club. Is everything going well?" She made an obscene gesture, pulsing her right index finger into a circle made with the thumb and index finger of her left hand.

"Stop it," I said. "I'm not a whore."

"You enjoy men and I'm wildly jealous because you can have your pick."

"It's been nice, even the sex."

Lotti's eyes widened. "What? Tell me!"

The barmaid came with a schnapps for my friend. Apparently, all Lotti had to do was make an appearance and liquor was served.

"He has a gorgeous apartment, a beautiful office . . . and a lovely bedroom."

"Hmm." Lotti burst into a smile.

"It's true . . . but I never think all's right in heaven. I haven't allowed myself to do that with Rickard—all my previous relationships have been so tenuous."

"You should relax," my friend said, sipping her drink. Lotti leaned forward, anticipating a good piece of gossip. I knew Rudi would be the next to hear.

"I don't know how much I should tell you," I said. "Can you keep this to yourself?"

She put her hand over her heart. "Promise."

"Rickard's being blackmailed by National Socialist thugs," I whispered.

Lotti relaxed a bit, apparently unimpressed by what I'd said. "I'm sorry to hear that . . . but it's as common as wind these days. They're looking for money. Making threats or beating someone up are their ways to get it."

"Did you know about Rickard?" I asked, somewhat perplexed.

Her fleshy arms jiggled against the table. "Rudi, gorgeous man that he is, has an even bigger mouth than I do. Rickard has a tendency to talk when he drinks too much and the next day he forgets what he's said. Besides, I would have expected it after what happened here."

I sipped my brandy. Surely everyone in the club knew about Rickard's predicament. "He's a mystery to me sometimes. He's been nothing but kind, but beneath all the movie glamour and the supposed fortune, I think he's scared."

"Everyone who's paying attention is scared," Lotti said. "My God, the doorman here, what you told me about the studio director—they've been beaten because they challenged the thugs. They stood up for what was right."

"Did you know Rickard was married and had a son?" I asked.

"You asked me if he was married, remember? I didn't know. That's one secret he kept to himself."

"That little secret came as a surprise. If Rickard and I don't work out for some reason . . . I've got to figure out what to do."

"How are the typing jobs coming?"

"A few now and then."

"I have one word for you—"

"I know . . . if you can't act—write."

Lotti nodded.

"What will I write about?" I asked.

"That's easy. Me."

"Be serious."

Lotti called for another shot of schnapps. "I don't mean *me*, but women like you and me. What we're going through, how we're surviving going from man to man, pay period to pay period, living under the thumb of bosses and politicians who seem to work for their own benefit and not the people."

Her eyes sparkled in the light, and I thought perhaps she might have hit upon a good idea. "Who would read it?"

"I would," she said, "and all my friends, and probably every girl in Berlin who's ever had to sleep with a man to get by, and every wife who's been jilted by her husband for another woman."

We drank a few more glasses together and talked about writing, life, and the future. Time passed quickly and I had to get home to Rickard. I was excited to tell him the news about my big career decision, but wondered if he would react favorably.

After I left the club, I thought about the long nights of my childhood, alone with my mother and without the benefit of a father. Those lonely days, with few friends my own age and my own awkwardness, left me in the company of books. Novels became my friends, and with the help of a kind teacher who provided them for me, I entered other worlds inhabited by strange creatures, magical fairies, evil gnomes, knights, and lords and ladies. These characters became my friends— friends who were so much more interesting than the life inside my house or outside my window.

Before I reached the apartment on Unter den Linden, I spotted a man who looked familiar. He was in full Sturm-abteilung uniform, like the hoodlums who'd beaten Anders at the studio. The sun had set but identifying him was easy because of his walk and the curve of his back and stooped shoulders. I'd known him as the Vampire King in the scenes we'd done together, but Rickard had called him Wolf when exercising his unsatisfactory directorial skills before the picture was shelved.

Wolf sauntered down the street, swaying a bit as if he'd had too much to drink. His gait was loose and careless, unlike the hundreds of stiff-backed SA members whom I'd seen on the Berlin streets. His face retained the same pasty color that he'd donned for his role as a blood-sucking fiend. I began to wonder if he might be a true creature of the night. He ducked into a shop entrance to escape the wind and light a cigarette.

"Hello, Wolf," I said, appearing in front of his startled eyes. His expression remained blank, however, clearly indicating that he had no idea who I was. "It's me, Niki—Vampire Queen Three."

A dim light flickered in his eyes as a sparse recognition dawned. "Oh, Niki." He put his cigarette case in the pocket of his brown shirt. "How are you?" His words slopped over his tongue.

"I'm fine," I replied cautiously, trying to refrain from my intended cynical question—but I relented. "You've joined the National Socialist Party?"

He took a drag off his cigarette, threw his head back, and howled with laughter. Liquor had loosened him up. He motioned with his index finger for me to step out of the wind into the shop entrance.

"Are you insane?" he asked when I was within breathing distance. His breath smelled like sugar laced with stomach acid. "That's the last thing I'd do. I'm an actor, an *AR-tist*." He hit the first syllable hard, spitting it out. "Those cretins have no idea what art is, and I doubt they ever will." He steadied himself against a glass pane separating us from a display of red and blue crockery.

"Then, why the costume?"

"I'm making a film."

Under my coat, the hairs on my arms rose. "Really? You said you wanted to do other projects, but I never imagined . . ."

"Some mucky-muck with the Party is directing a film about a rally in Nuremberg. He's obsessed with young people and Hitler. If I didn't know better . . ." He swayed a bit, looking at me, and I could tell that, even inebriated, he had enough sense to drop the sentence, in case it got back to the Nazis. "I'm getting paid—it's been hard finding work since so many studios have closed."

"Where are you filming? Would there be any parts for me?" I asked these questions because I was fishing, not because I wanted a part in a Nazi film.

"Do you remember Rickard Länger?"

I nodded, growing uncomfortable.

"You ought to go to Passport and ask him. He got in touch with me."

I tried to hide my shame, my building anger, for a man who'd failed to mention that his studio was making a film for the Party.

Wolf smiled and I realized that I had no desire to continue the conversation. "It's wonderful seeing you again. Maybe I'll go to the studio . . . as you suggested."

As I left him, he looked somewhat bemused, probably wondering if our meeting had happened at all. In the morning, Wolf's memory would be foggy at best.

Rickard wasn't at home when I arrived, so I fortified myself with a large glass of cognac. My nerves tightened, my skin itched with each passing minute.

When he arrived sometime after eight, I'd downed two drinks and was wondering how I'd reconcile Rickard's work with my disgust for the Nazis and all they stood for.

Taking off his hat and coat, he offered a cheery hello. "Care for dinner out this evening?"

I sulked in one of the V-shaped leather chairs, looking out the window, drink in hand, saying nothing.

Analyzing my icy silence, he asked, "All right, what's wrong?"

I swiveled toward him, a little more hatefully than I should have. "I ran into someone this evening—someone we both know. Wolf."

His lips pinched and he settled on one of the couches, his body backlit by the gray, fuzzy light of Berlin. After a moment, he said, "Before you—"

I wasn't going to let him silence me. "No! Tell me why you're making a National Socialist film, and why you've said nothing about it."

He sighed and his face drooped, sad and worn. "Because I have no choice. The day you arrived, Spiegel came to see me about the film. Produce this picture, he said, and the threats against you and your former wife and son will disappear."

"They beat the club doorman and nearly killed poor Anders! Isn't that enough? My mother would say we have to love one another, but I can't love them. The sight of the SA makes me sick. They don't like women like me." My anger bubbled near the surface.

He talked over his pained expression. "Do you think the SA would have any regrets about killing or maiming anyone who doesn't give them what they want? If so, you're naïve. Hitler and his thugs aren't a joke." His voice peaked and he rose from the couch, then stalked toward me. "I'm protecting *us* . . . I'm offering you a home . . . and safety . . ." Then, his voice faded, a signal of defeat, and he turned away. "I'm sorry. I'm tired of keeping secrets and dealing with these murderers. Don't fool yourself—they are murderers. Fucking swine."

I put my drink down as he trudged back to the sofa. He seemed broken, defeated not only by the Nazis but by life itself. I walked to him. "Don't keep secrets."

He faced me, his eyes steely blue, his lips pressed together in grim determination. The tall clock near the door struck eight thirty. Rickard inhaled and said, "I thought you might leave me if I told you the truth. I couldn't take that. I've been deserted by a woman before—a woman who took my son with her—and the pain was like a lance piercing my body. I never want to go through that again. I thought the pain from my betrayal and her desertion would lessen, but it hasn't."

I took his hands in mine. "Just tell me the truth."

He withdrew from my grasp and looked out over Unter den Linden. Berlin was below: lines of people, cars revving by, and the clop of horses pulling carriages—all defined, all lit by the city. Between us, the air grew cold.

"What's next for us?" Rickard asked.

Feeling my own sense of defeat, I stood beside him. "I'm not sure. I want to believe what you tell me, but I've been deserted by men as well. In that way, we're alike. You have some money—I have only a little. For now, perhaps we should trust each other and see how it works out."

Rickard lowered his gaze. "If you want to leave, I won't stop you. I'm not a monster." He faced me, his eyes glistening. "You think I have it all . . . I've been successful, but so much has been taken from me. I don't want that to happen again."

He kissed me on the cheek, letting his lips linger on my skin.

I leaned back, pulling away from his affection.

"I'll never force you to do anything," he said. "Please understand why I have to work with them."

"All right," I replied, somewhat mollified. "How about another drink before we have supper out? Cognac?"

He nodded.

I got the drinks, pouring a little more in his glass than mine. I'd had enough. "I'm going to write a novel," I said as I handed him the glass.

He looked up, eyes a little wider. "That's good. Maybe we can make a film of it."

"Wait a moment," I said. "I've got to write it first and it's got to be good—a book I'm proud of. I want to create something, make something of myself, by writing a book people will remember."

"What's it about?"

"Lotti wants me to write about her."

Rickard groaned. "Oh, that'll be interesting."

"Not her, but us, the young women of Berlin who are struggling against . . . well, everything."

"There has to be some drama, some action," Rickard said. "Take my word as a producer. A film needs something to hold viewers' interest; otherwise, the paying customers will be bored. They'll walk out in droves."

"Vampires? Nazi rallies? I sense a theme." Rickard may have blushed, although it was hard to tell in the dim light. "The women of Berlin have much to offer. Each one has a story."

I grabbed his arms and pulled him close. He sank against me and kissed me on the neck. "Vampires," he said.

"Come on . . . let's make the best of the evening."

"Yes, let's."

As we were putting on our coats, I added, "Can I use your office typewriter? I can't afford one."

He looked at me and cocked his head. "Of course. You can use it whenever you like."

That night, I dreamed I'd begun to write, and I made a list in my head about how to treat my character—Niki.

Niki could have all the men and sex she wanted as long as it was behind closed doors or "off camera," out of sight. No writer, and certainly no woman novelist, could write about sex in 1929. My heroine would smoke and drink and hop from man to man because she needed men to survive. She'd take and give favors in order to put food in her mouth. She'd talk and joke with her friends and sometimes they'd get into trouble without her, and she'd come to their aid. They could be eccentric, or even normal like Lotti. They'd appear and disappear from Niki's life, like people often do. But what would happen to these characters? Would they live or die? How would the story end? In my dream, I wrote a new novel called:

### The Berlin Woman

*Martin leads her to the bedroom, which smells of lemon cologne and leather. A shaving strap is hooked over a towel rack in the bathroom.*

*Niki doesn't resist for it's been a long time since she's been with a man. She enjoys the pleasure that sex brings. He takes off his shirt and lets it fall to the bed. She unbuckles the straps of her black shoes, dropping them and her orange sheath dress to the floor. The next step with Martin, the final step, will culminate upon the bed.*

*She steps toward it, using each movement as a cue to erotic excitement. A tension, a pulse in the bloodstream rockets through every fiber in her body. Martin, always the unwavering gentleman, pulls back the sheet and fluffs the pillow. He drops onto the bed and, with a pat of his hand, invites her to join him.*

*Longingly, she savors his skin, whitened by the long winter months; the muscles of his chest and arms tightened by hours at his job on the rail yards; the dance of his brown eyes; the dark thatches of hair that adorn his body. Even though she's known him for months, she can still smell the masculine heat rising from his body that reeks of sex, a musky scent, not unpleasant, not rank.*

*Naked, she curls up beside him on the cool sheets, but turns her head away.*

*"Is something wrong?" he asks. "We don't have to do this."*

*"No," Niki responds. "Everything is right . . . so much that it scares me. I'm not sure what to do with the feelings I have for you."*

*"I love you," he says, as if replying to a compliment, and strokes her arm.*

*Relenting, she turns toward him. Vulnerability— that's what she feels—as if giving herself to him will somehow wound her, keeping her from living her life, throwing her in a direction she never expected, reducing her from a woman to a motherly slave. But those thoughts are insane.*

I will be the same as I ever was—won't I? He's protecting me. I have nowhere else to go. My God, what is happening? Damn it all.

*She turns, finds herself kissing his lips and chest. The sheet covers their bliss. Something animal in Niki takes over, and when the act is done, they look at each other, tired and spent, she having traversed a line of intimate passion that she'd vowed never to cross.*

What is love?

The dream was so much like her life.

# CHAPTER 5

Rickard cleaned his typewriter the next morning and then excused himself while I gathered the courage to write the first few pages of the novel. I had no real idea where I was going, although I knew Niki needed to tell her story.

The machine gleamed, gray metal with a black platen and a ribbon that smelled like fresh ink. The odor permeated the study, and its presence filled me with awe. Rickard also had a book on shorthand and typing delivered to the apartment, thinking I might be able to hone my office skills even more than I had.

I worked most of the day, plunking out a few words here and there, making time for lunch and coffee and then returning to the study to enjoy my new-found profession. Perhaps writing was where my talents were best used. I hoped it would bring me success and lead me to my purpose in life.

By five, it was growing dark. I turned on the study lamp and looked at my output—one page. But I could see Niki before my eyes and hear her voice in my head as I listened to her story. She even told me what to write the following day, which seemed insane, but I made notes on a piece of paper. Those steps counted as a victory.

Rickard and I had supper at home: sausage, potatoes, and a bottle of white wine. During the hours that we ate and talked, a feeling of pride surged through me, along with a case of nerves that set me tingling. Writing was real. I believed I could write *The Berlin Woman* by setting a reasonable goal each day.

"I'm proud of you, Niki," Rickard said, and raised his glass. No man had ever given me such hope and validation before.

"Thanks for the use of your typewriter. . . ." I said. "And for protecting me."

He didn't have to say "You're welcome," because it came through his kind and loving eyes.

That night, as the gauzy lights of Berlin filtered through the bedroom curtains, I struggled to find sleep.

Rickard lay next to me, a haze of blue and green falling across his form like a scene from a dream. I saw the curve of his chin, the left profile of his face turned softly on the pillow, his black hair contrasting with the white linen.

I settled next to him. He stirred, moaning gently in his sleep, as my hand worked the buttons on his pajama top. The silk was cool to the touch, but his chest was hot and slightly damp, as if he suffered from a fever.

His eyes fluttered open and he gasped to find me bending over him.

He kissed me, turned me on my back, and we made love until the sun scattered the night's diffused light and sent its beams shining upon us. I realized after the act, as I was falling asleep in his arms, that I'd made love to him this time because I knew he cared about me. I wanted to be loved. I knew he did as well.

At breakfast, Rickard asked me something I hadn't expected. "Would you like to wear that new dress you bought several weeks ago?"

"Of course," I said, as I dug into my eggs, my body ravenous after a night of passion.

"Herr Spiegel is having a party tonight at his estate. He's invited both of us. . . . It would be best if I went. You can come if you'd like."

I'd seen the man twice and had no fondness for him, after what his henchmen had done to Anders and how he'd blackmailed Rickard. He was oily, with a look similar to Joseph Goebbels, a high forehead sloping to slicked-back hair, thin lips pressed into permanent ambiguity, eyes at once beady and disturbing. Perhaps the only distinguishing feature between the two Nazis was the nose. Spiegel's was sharper, more linear than the bulbous tip of Goebbels's.

I took a few minutes to think about this unexpected invitation while I finished my eggs and sipped my coffee. "Normally, I wouldn't have anything to do with him or his cronies . . . but, isn't there something about knowing your enemies?"

"'Know thyself, know thy enemy.'" Rickard said, gripping his cup. "Words by Sun Tzu, an ancient Chinese general who wrote a book about battles and war."

I gave him a look, one of raised eyebrows and openmouthed awe. "How do you know that?"

He smiled. "The studio almost did a film on him—a war drama, of course—but it turned out to be too costly to produce. The costumes and extras alone shattered the budget."

"I'm impressed."

"'You need not fear the result of a hundred battles—if you know yourself and your enemy,'" Rickard said with a magisterial voice, and then lowered his gaze, as darkness covered his eyes.

"Is that what you think? A hundred battles are before us."

"Possibly, if the Nazis have their way. I'm more interested in knowing my enemy."

"Then I suppose it's time."

He leaned back in his chair. "How would you like to be introduced? As a charming young actress or my fiancée?"

"Is this a proposal?"

"Not yet."

I smiled. "A charming young actress with great star potential." I paused. "No, that's wrong—as a talented young writer with great potential."

"You shall be a writer then." He grasped my hand and kissed it. Everything at that moment seemed perfect, but the evening hadn't arrived.

I tried on the dress in front of the wardrobe mirror. It shimmered in the light—a one-piece, sheer at the top leading to a bust of black silk, a cinched waist set off by a belt accented with a diamond pin, and a flowing black skirt glistening with silver pleats. A modesty shawl encrusted with spangled accents came with the dress.

Rickard whistled when I finally emerged from the bathroom, fully dressed and made up.

"I have another gift for you," he said, casually.

Smiling, I twirled in the dress, liking the way I felt and looked. "Really? What's that? You've been more than generous."

He rose from the bed and patted the breast pocket of his black tuxedo. "It's in here."

I spotted the outline of a small box pressing against the cloth, hardly noticeable unless you were looking for it. "And?"

"At the party."

I nodded, thinking that a ring was soon headed for my finger. I wasn't sure how I felt at that particular moment about marrying Rickard. I glanced at myself in the mirror again, taking in the quick vision of the beautiful dress, taking in the serene feeling of security, of having something as opposed to the lack of money that had been so prevalent in my life, and wondering why on earth I would give up any of this. How could I be comfortable with Rickard if I wasn't comfortable with myself?

"Are you ready to face them?" Rickard asked, taking my hand.

"Yes, I'll be on my best behavior." I grabbed my handbag.

"That's boring," he said, and laughed.

We walked to the door, down the stairway, and out into the cold, clear night. I pulled the shawl around my shoulders as we walked to the garage. The Mercedes gleamed under a light bulb surrounded by wire mesh, the roadster's long green nose topped with its recognizable hood ornament. The cold stopped us from putting the tan top down, so I snuggled next to Rickard as he drove.

We sped through Berlin and were soon in the country north of the city. The cluster of buildings gave way to sleepy villages lit by yellow lamps, and then the lush stillness of a forest harboring black pines that rose along the sides of the road. The Mercedes purred along, taking the straightaways and the curves with ease. Rickard fumbled with the steering wheel while searching for the address on a piece of paper. I guided the car as he downshifted.

We spotted the turnoff on a remote road far from the city. The car veered into a long, tree-lined drive that seemed to curve endlessly, but eventually led us to a magnificent, stone mansion bathed in the light of white lamps that shone like beacons in the darkness. Rickard stopped the car, and two footmen attired in outfits from the Germanic Middle Ages approached the Mercedes. They wore quilted, high-collar gambesons and leather gloves extending to their elbows. I expected a lance or a sword at their sides.

One opened the door for me. Rickard handed the keys to the other, who drove the car away in the night. My footman pointed to the mansion's entrance, and Rickard and I proceeded up the long flight of steps.

My heart fluttered. I didn't know what lay behind the mighty oak door carved with stags and other creatures of the forest. Perhaps this was a home used for hunting in the spring and fall but left vacant during the height of winter snows. I shuddered—Rickard thought it was from the cold—because if I had been another kind of woman, a National Socialist, I would have savored each step toward the house and those inside. I imagined Lotti would be jealous when I told her about the house and the glittering gathering—if only it hadn't been hosted by Nazis. The party left me uneasy and wary of the people behind the doors.

After Rickard announced us, a third servant at the top of the stairs told us to proceed down the hall to the ballroom at the back of the house.

The rather dim corridor was lit only by candelabra, possibly for effect. The pronged heads of stags and other kinds of horned animals lined the walls. Their sad and vacant eyes looked down upon us as we walked toward the bright lights burning ahead. A nave of death surrounded us. Our heels clicked on the marble floors; the thick walls hid rooms secreted behind the stone.

Two French doors opened to the ballroom. In one corner, a string quartet played Viennese waltzes. Tables filled with steaming chafing dishes of food, and hearty drinks, lined the walls. In the center of the room, an undulating crowd of about thirty people milled about in a slow-motion shuffle as they greeted each other for mere moments and then lumbered on at a snail's pace. Most of the men wore dinner clothes, but a few Brownshirts stood out, as well as the crisp, smart, and terrifying black uniforms of the SS. The bejeweled women wore glittering formal gowns, sparkly and white, as if they were expecting Adolf Hitler himself. In my fashionable black dress, I stood apart. The men, stern and stiff, looked uneasy and preoccupied, some with jowls, sturdy necks, and pushed-in noses like bulldogs—but I had no desire to disparage another species.

Wearing his SA attire, Herr Spiegel spotted us and sauntered toward us in his slick manner, leaving his wife behind.

This time the SA master, although I'd only had the unfortunate pleasure of being in his company twice, was all smiles.

"Welcome to my home," he said with a hand extended toward Rickard. It quickly shifted to a Nazi salute. My companion shot our host a brief smile and gave a milquetoast return of the gesture.

"I'm so glad you came to our party . . . and who is this lovely young lady?" Spiegel asked, his lecherous eyes taking in the curves displayed beneath my dress. From that moment, I knew that the Nazis not only loved power but also relished their sexual dominion over others.

"This is a rising young star in the German literary firmament," Rickard countered, laying it on thick. I discreetly nudged him with my elbow. "In all her work she goes by the name 'Niki.'"

"Niki. Charming." Spiegel bowed, took my hand, and then kissed it. My stomach turned as his clammy lips touched my skin. "As you can see, we have a hospitable group here. Please help yourselves to food and drink and mingle with the other guests. The Gruppenführer should be along soon."

Rickard gave a curt bow in response and moved us toward a food table adorned with china, silver candlesticks, and carving stations.

"Who's coming?" I asked Rickard as our obliging servers piled our plates high with roast beef, potatoes, and sauces.

"The Gruppenführer—Hermann Göring, a confidant of Hitler, high up in party circles. I've never met him, but I've heard he's full of swagger, bluster, and a morphine addict to boot. He was an early SA member, so I wouldn't be surprised to see him here."

"What joy." We stepped away from the table.

"Look, Niki, play along. This is uncomfortable for us, but remember who we're dealing with. We don't have to like them, but we can use them to our advantage. Right now, they're keeping Passport Pictures afloat."

I took a bite of the beef and then whispered in his ear. "I don't like them, and I'd rather be anyplace else than here. Look at them. They're positively inhuman. They're not Germans. They're automatons, something out of *Metropolis*, standing around like demigods." The glamour and pomp in the room were suffocating, and I wondered what lay beneath those cold hearts and minds. Did these women really have lives outside of their devotion to their husbands or, more likely, their allegiance to the Nazi Party? Could they possibly think of women like Lotti and me, the German women I was writing about, as equals, or were we dust beneath their feet? I suspected the latter.

"Do you mind if I act like we're having a good time?" Rickard asked. "It might benefit me to chat with some of them."

"No, chat all you like. You won't mind if I'm a bit more selective?"

Rickard shook his head and put his unfinished meal on a serving tray. I picked at my food—having lost most of my appetite—listened to the string quartet, and watched the interactions playing out before my eyes. The music soothed my nerves a bit, but I soon found it necessary to use the washroom. A server took my plate and I asked him where the ladies' powder room was.

He directed me to a location outside the French doors. An elegantly attired young woman in a white dress laced with salmon-colored sequins emerged just as I arrived. She stopped briefly and adjusted her bejeweled belt and the diamond pendant dripping from her necklace.

I took care of business after tussling with my dress, which, despite its beauty, required the physical machinations of a gymnast to get in and out of. Blessedly, the powder room was empty, a rather stark and dull place compared with the rest of the house—one might call it utilitarian—except for a white rococo desk resting against a wall. It held a bureau mirror, an obvious station for checking or reapplying makeup.

I breezed by the desk and something glinted in my left eye. I stopped, turned, and walked to the glittering object. A diamond bracelet bearing seven good-sized emeralds in its center lay in front of the mirror. My thoughts ran to the woman I'd seen leave the room seconds before I arrived, but the bracelet didn't fit her style. She was young and fashionable, as modern as a young National Socialist could be without courting ridicule from the Party elite. This bangle was much more than a trifle and shouted "old money." I imagined that an older woman had taken it off for some reason and had forgotten to put it back on. But who could "forget" such a beautiful work of art? Perhaps she'd had too much to drink? Was she tired of it? Hardly. What if it was some nefarious plot to trap a potential thief? Would someone jump out of a corner and accuse me of stealing it?

I picked it up, feeling the luxurious weight of it in my hand, the hard smoothness of the diamonds, and relishing the cat-eye green of the luscious emeralds. I fully expected a Nazi matron to clamber into the room, claiming the bracelet as her own, excoriating me for having the audacity to touch it—but the room remained quiet.

An audacious thought entered my mind. Through the years, many men had given me baubles, tokens of their love—as long as it lasted—in exchange for sex; in blunt terms, the use of my body, which, often, I had given willingly. Rarely was I proud or ecstatically happy about my situation. Living in Weimar Germany was a struggle, and for women that task was doubly hard. Sometimes I had fun with my companion. Sometimes I was happily wrapped in his arms, but more often than not I was content just to live, to eat, and to see another day. Survival was the point.

I draped the beautiful bracelet across my cupped palms and the promise of money flashed before my eyes. These diamonds, these emeralds, could be my insurance policy, a source of cash, a ticket out of Germany, if needed. And Rickard didn't need to know anything about it. This would be a secret I must keep, mostly for me, but possibly for both of us. I looked in the mirror and was satisfied that I didn't need any touch-up. I walked out with the bracelet clutched loosely in my right hand, fully prepared to give it up should any woman come rushing toward me. But none did.

I'd never stolen anything before, certainly nothing on this scale, and guilt did creep into my head for a moment. Then, I considered who I was stealing from. Carelessness aside, the woman who lost this bracelet probably didn't need it. From the Nazi tactics I'd witnessed since I'd met Rickard, I felt that this theft was like a declaration of war, a further assertion of my independence against a hideous political party.

I dropped the bracelet into my purse, securing it from National Socialist eyes. I found Rickard, who had left Spiegel and other Brownshirts a few moments earlier, and we toasted each other with a brandy.

Within minutes, Göring strutted into the room surrounded by three men whom I assumed were bodyguards. The Gruppenführer was in full SA attire, complete with Nazi armband and an audacious display of Iron Crosses and war medals pinned to his portly chest. Rickard whispered that in 1918 Göring had cut a dashing figure as a revered World War I ace. He was no such figure now. He was soft and flabby, his skin white, and his face gripped by a silly smile that made him appear rather like a spoiled child than a leader of thugs.

The adoring crowd gathered around him as if worshiping an idol, while Rickard and I stayed to the rear. This portion of the entertainment went on for nearly a half hour as Göring made his way through the crowd, shaking hands, saluting the men, and kissing the hands of the fawning ladies. Eventually, he made his way to us. Spiegel introduced Rickard as the owner of a film studio dedicated to "Party ideals," and me as a "woman who idolizes German culture and literature." The ranking Nazi dropped his goofy smile for an instant and looked at me with his jelly-like eyes, scrutinizing the black dress that so stood out from the other women in the room. Few words were spoken in this awkward time.

As if by magic, a platform appeared in the center of the room. Spiegel led Göring to it, and the flamboyant leader stepped up to make his much-anticipated speech.

He cleared his throat and began. "Ladies and gentlemen, fellow National Socialists . . . Herr Spiegel, my compliments on your home filled with art and beauty. I'm sorry that my wife couldn't be here this evening; she sends her regrets." He spread his arms and the smile deepened on his face, his teeth glowing in the light. Distracted for only seconds, he then proceeded. "You could use more paintings, however. Some Old Masters, perhaps? I'll see what I can do." Chuckling, Göring bowed to Spiegel, who looked as pleased as a youngster receiving a birthday present.

"What a marvelous gathering we have here this evening to honor the National Socialist Party that continues to grow each day." He raised his fist in a defiant manner. "Soon, the world will know our power, but more than that, the leaders of all the countries on earth will *believe* in our might and the will of a German people that will not be vanquished. We only have to look to our Führer to see where the future of Germany lies. He will guide us. He will save us from poverty, the moral corruption, the lies that our enemies spread. Germany will be great again! Germany will only live through our Führer!"

A chorus of cheers broke out from the crowd, all the attendees raising their arms in the Nazi salute.

Göring quieted them and plowed on. "I will be brief because I want to speak to each of you personally, but first I must issue a stern warning to those outside this room. Believe in us, swear your loyalty, or be destroyed. There will be no room for the corrupters, the prostitutes, the pimps, the money lenders, the spoilers, the men of the press, or those who hoodwink Germany and call it 'patriotism' or 'a normal way of life.' They will be the first to go, the first to feel the sword of National Socialism upon their necks. There will be no mercy for those who stand against us. That day will come soon, dawning as clear and bright as the spring sun. That day is almost upon us—do not doubt it."

He shouted his devotion to Hitler amid the cheers resounding through the room, and stepped down from the platform.

Spiegel took Göring's place and called out for the crowd to hush. "We have another exciting announcement this evening. Herr Länger and Niki, please come forward."

I hid my astonishment as Rickard grabbed my hand and led me to the platform. We stepped up and stood beside the oily man.

"Many of you know of Rickard's efforts to promote the Party through films, but I had the pleasure tonight to be introduced to his soon-to-be bride, Niki." Spiegel clapped and the men and women followed. "Another pure German family will join our ranks. Please, Herr Länger . . ."

I could only turn and look at Rickard with uneasy eyes, a blush rising in my cheeks, hoping the others in the room wouldn't spot my discomfort.

He took the box from his breast pocket, said a few words of love, and asked me to be his wife. I smiled and looked across the crowd, the men smug and confident in the fulfillment of their manly duties, the women misty eyed and bursting with romantic Aryan notions. He opened the velvet cover and handed me a gold band carved with interlaced runes.

Under all those eyes, crushed by the pressure of the audience, I said yes. But I couldn't wait to get him into the car and berate him for such an engineered performance.

I put on my own performance, smiling, accepting congratulations, but I wanted to kill Rickard.

That would come later in the evening.

# CHAPTER 6

"Why?" I asked as the temperature between us in the roadster dropped like the frigid night air. We sped away from Spiegel's house with barely a word spoken until I finally parted the frosty curtain. Everything seemed black, even the brilliant stars had lost their luster, and my nerves and muscles were strung as tightly as piano wire.

"Why did you do this?" I asked again after receiving no answer.

I could tell Rickard wanted a smoke, but I didn't offer one of my cigarettes. He stomped on the brake, swerved the Mercedes to the side of the road, the car coming to rest in the dirt near a swath of tall pines.

He turned to me, face taut, jaw set. "Use your head, Niki. Sometimes you amaze me—and not in a good way." He reached into his breast pocket for the ring, which I had returned to him. "If you don't want it, throw it into the woods. It's only fourteen carat gold."

I thought of the emerald and diamond bracelet stashed in my purse and wondered if they might be costume jewels. I took the box and opened the lid. The ring looked dull and unimpressive in the dim light . . . but it was a ring.

"I didn't say I didn't want it—or you." I turned to him.

"Why the big show, the big production, as if we were filming a movie?"

He snickered. "That's the point. Of course, it was a production. Another level of protection against these beasts . . . so they won't come after you. If they think we're getting married, they'll infer that you're on their side. Do you understand?"

I closed the box and handed it back to Rickard. "You should have told me," I said in a softer tone.

"Would you have gone along with it?"

"Maybe . . . maybe not."

"Yes, and that's the problem." He turned his gaze away from me and toward the road. "The scene worked perfectly as it played out—you were the surprised fiancée, bowled over by the ring and all the attention."

"I could have turned you down."

"But you didn't. That would have been a very hard thing to do under all that Nazi scrutiny." He put his hand on mine. "Let's go home."

I realized then that Rickard seriously underestimated my ability to make my way in the world. I'd done everything possible to survive as a New German Woman, including moving in with Rickard, but I had no intention of bowing to a Nazi. I pushed my back hard into the seat, folded my arms, and waited for the roadster to carry me home.

We sat in tomb-like silence on the drive back to Berlin, collapsing into bed with a curt kiss. In the morning, Rickard was off to the studio and I was left by myself to continue my writing. Instead, I dawdled over breakfast and examined the bracelet that I'd pulled from my purse.

When the sun broke through the clouds, I went to the window and held the emeralds and diamonds to the light. If they were inferior pieces, they certainly didn't look it. The diamonds sparkled with the clarity and fiery color of the real thing. Gazing at the facets was like looking into the colors of a rainbow. The emeralds were as cool and green as a mossy forest glade. Their color hardly varied from one stone to another.

I took a bath and then decided to visit a jeweler not far from the apartment on Unter den Linden. I had no idea whether the man was Jewish or not. Many such jewelers suffered from Nazi harassment. Herr Schlager, of Schlager and Co., happened to be the closest. He was a small man with gray hair and close-set blue eyes. One of them was covered by a jeweler's loupe attached to his head by a wire band. He wore a white shirt and buttoned gray vest and looked like he'd been in the business since watchmaking began. I think he was taken somewhat aback by my unassuming presence. I neither looked nor felt like a moneyed German woman or a society matron procuring an estimate on an expensive bracelet.

After exchanging greetings, he removed the loupe and turned his attention from the gold watch he'd been working on. "What can I do for you, fräulein?"

His eyes widened as I pulled out the bracelet. I'd observed enough human behavior to know surprise, bordering on astonishment, when I saw it. I'd prepared an answer to a predicted question, cutting him off before he could get out the words. "My aunt died recently and my mother and I think this is costume jewelry. I was wondering if you could give me an estimate of its worth?"

He took it in his almost trembling hands. The look on his face turned from astonishment to envy, as if he were holding an object of great historic and artistic interest.

"Your aunt must have been a very wealthy woman, or had a husband who doted on her."

"Oh, my uncle died a few years ago," I lied. "Of course, it came to my mother."

Herr Schlager sniffed. "It isn't particularly old, probably not more than ten years, but I can assure you that it is real. An excellent piece of work." He positioned the loupe over his eye again and turned the bracelet, taking his time, examining the gold band that held it together. As if coming up for air after a dive into a pool, he took a breath and said, "It's Cartier, made in Paris. The diamonds are exquisite; the emeralds, Colombian, of the finest quality."

I didn't want to appear overeager, so I waited a few moments, tempering my voice. "Thank you, we'll keep it in the family." I held out my hand.

He drew back a little. "Don't you want to know what it's worth?"

"It makes no difference to me," I said, taking it back from his sweating palms.

"I'd have to keep it for a day for a closer examination, grading the color, carat weight, and other factors," he said, removing the loupe.

"No, thank you. Not today." I placed the precious cargo in my purse.

"I can offer you ten thousand marks for it, right now." He leaned forward, his blue eyes flickering with excitement.

That figure meant the jeweler would sell it for at least double, twenty thousand marks. "I'd never make a decision about my aunt's bracelet without conferring with my mother." I clutched my purse in my hands and turned to go.

"Please keep me in mind," he yelled.

"Thank you," I said over my shoulder. "I will." I left, crushing my bag against my chest, convinced that the bracelet I'd lifted from Spiegel's house would be the leverage I needed to get me, or us, out of a bad situation.

The frost between Rickard and me melted over the next week as we settled into Christmas and the welcoming of the New Year—1930. We purchased a small tree together and put it on a table in front of the great room windows. The effect was quite magical as the reflective glass balls and decorative candles melded with the lights of Berlin. The cold, the time of year, pushed us together in bed and we found ourselves making love more often.

The holidays reminded me, in a melancholy way, as days of that nature often do, of incidents in my childhood: snow, sledding, vague memories of my father, before he was sent to war, bundled against the cold as we picked out our tree, the woody odor of my mother's tea that she drank only on special occasions, flashes of light and color, overcast Christmas mornings turned whitish-gray by snow. And, as always, the books at my bedside that kept me company when the holidays extended the feeling of time.

One evening, after Rickard went to bed, I sat for hours and watched the candles burn on the tree until they were stubs in their metal holders, extinguishing themselves, sending their powdery smoke into the room. In that time, I took stock, asking myself if what I'd constructed on Unter den Linden was real or simply a pleasant bubble that would burst under sustained pressure. I came to no answer, but I knew the stasis wouldn't last.

Despite a relatively quiet boil, the kettle was heating up. The Nazis continued their march under Hitler's direction despite minor political setbacks. No one, except those closest to the Führer, knew of his determination to lead the new Reich. The Brownshirts were never out of view. Hitler courted the army while stirring up treason against the government. The breadlines, the terrible unemployment, did nothing to enamor the German people to the Weimar Republic. Hitler promised a new way of life, a new prosperity, based on promises that would become war. Who cares about fighting, the destruction of countries, the slaughter of millions, when one's stomach is empty? Starvation and poverty are persuasive motivators for political gain.

Early in the year, Rickard told me of a rumor that worried me but came as no surprise. A person high up in the Reichsbank was colluding with the Nazis, and the cash that would flow from that union would provide a powerful income source for the National Socialists. I hoped with that kind of funding Spiegel would exert fewer demands on Rickard.

The puffed-up man paid us a visit one late afternoon in January, entirely for my benefit. Rickard had spent the day at the studio when the two men walked into the apartment together. Spiegel looked more like a businessman, clad in a dark suit and shiny shoes, than an obnoxious SA thug. Still, he made my skin crawl.

I stopped my work on *The Berlin Woman* and met them at the office door. Spiegel sat in one of the V-chairs in the great room while Rickard fixed him a drink.

"Working?" Spiegel asked as I stepped toward the couches.

"Yes," I replied, as politely as I could.

"A novel?" he asked with a slight air of condescension.

"Yes." I didn't want to carry on the conversation.

"Tell me about it."

How could I tell a National Socialist about a novel portraying a rudderless woman who struggles to make a living, surviving any way she can, and then grows stronger and finds it within herself to make a new life on her own with or without men? Not the stuff of Nazi dreams.

"Oh, I think you'd find it dull," I said.

"No, go ahead."

"Yes, tell the Oberführer about your book," Rickard said from the back of the room near the bar. He shot me a sly look and tilted his head as if to say, *Make up something to satisfy him.*

"Well, it's a complicated plot, but I'll compress it to a few sentences." I sat on the red couch and looked into his slippery face. "It's about a woman from Berlin who takes her son from her weak, ineffectual, religious husband and, struggling against a society that shuns her, raises him to be a soldier who fights for the new German Reich. Her son becomes a battle-tested hero and a leader of the people."

I wondered if Spiegel believed the preposterous story I'd spewed out, but one could never underestimate a Nazi's capacity for flattery. His eyes, narrow in their sockets at first, expanded as I told the lie, until his happy smile practically lifted him from the chair. "What a wonderful story! I must tell Göring, even relay this news to the Führer!"

Rickard's eyes widened as well, but in an entirely different way, a look of shock and concern crossing his face.

"Please, Herr Spiegel, you flatter me, but the novel is far from done," I said, attempting to put a damper on both their reactions. "And, who knows, books always change, the plot evolves along the way. By the time I'm finished, the story may be completely different."

Spiegel frowned, leaning toward me, almost rising from the chair. "Don't change a thought. You've created a great work of art. Don't destroy it." He clasped his hands. "In fact, when the first draft is done—before it is published—let me read it. I can even pass it on to Hitler—not that he has the time to read with his busy schedule, but he may make an exception in your case for such a faithful National Socialist." He turned to look at Rickard.

"Please . . . your praise is making me blush," I said.

Rickard forced a smile, like an actor playing a part, but I didn't know if the Oberführer even caught the nuance. However, like their capacity for vanity and flattery, one could never underestimate a fascist's intelligence.

"Rickard, bring me a drink, too," I said, hoping to deflect the subject.

An odd silence ensued as Spiegel and I smiled at each other and Rickard finished making the drinks. He brought them on a silver tray.

"To the Führer and the Reich," Spiegel said, as he lifted his glass.

We toasted, but my heart wasn't in it. My thoughts were consumed with the awful possibility that my manuscript might be plopped on Hitler's desk. I couldn't let that happen.

Spiegel sipped his drink and settled back in the seat. "I've come today because I have a serious matter to discuss."

I looked at Rickard—he seemed to be as much in the dark as I was about this "matter."

"An unfortunate incident occurred at my recent party," the Oberführer continued. "A very valuable piece of jewelry, once owned by the Baroness Hofstetter, disappeared from the powder room that night—an emerald and diamond bracelet of some worth. Unfortunately, the woman wearing the piece is inconsolable about the loss. It was on loan to her. She and her husband, though they are good Party members, haven't the means to replace the bracelet. Such restitution would cause them considerable financial harm."

I leaned toward him. "On loan? Who would loan such a valuable bracelet and trust it to someone so careless?"

Spiegel's eyebrows rose. "You do ask probing questions . . . Niki."

"I'm a writer. It's my job to ask questions and speculate about human nature."

He put his drink on the glass table near him. "The circumstances of the loan must remain confidential, but I can tell you that the owner was glad to give it after the bracelet was *requested* by the SA. The wearer only took it off to wash her hands and, being tipsy from the influence of champagne, didn't notice the loss until the next day. A search of all the rooms used that night yielded nothing."

I leaned back and lit a Manoli. "You suspect that I had something to do with it?"

Spiegel blanched, his face turning as white as the chair.

"Oh, no. I'm only alerting you to its loss. My intention is to ask every woman—or her husband—who attended the party."

"I'm sure if Niki had seen it, she would have told you," Rickard interjected.

"I did use the powder room, but I saw nothing," I said. "A woman did come out before me, wearing a diamond pendant on a necklace, but there was no bracelet on her arms."

"The thief could have been one of the servants, or one of the cleaners, but I've interrogated each one to no satisfaction," Spiegel said. "You understand that I bear some responsibility because this happened at my home."

Rickard and I nodded.

"How much is it worth?" I asked.

Spiegel sighed. "Depending on the expert—between forty and fifty thousand marks."

I gasped, remembering the jeweler who, in his eagerness, offered me ten thousand. It took a few moments for me to respond. "I certainly hope you find the perpetrator. I don't have information for you, but if either Rickard or I find out something we'll come to you."

"Of course," Rickard said. "May we offer you dinner?"

"No, no. I must be going. I'm meeting a few fellow officers tonight." He gulped his drink and rose from the chair. "Thank you for the cognac."

Rickard escorted Spiegel to the door. After the Oberführer left, my companion sighed and leaned against the frame. "Niki? Niki?" He asked my name, the inflection on the first syllable, in such a way that I knew he suspected me.

"What?" I asked, taking a draw from my cigarette and spreading my arms across the top of the couch.

"Did you see that bracelet? Tell me the truth."

I feigned shock and disappointment. "Rickard . . . I can't believe that you would believe that I would stoop to thievery—to stealing a piece of jewelry from a Nazi."

"I think it might be something you'd do—to teach them a lesson—a bit of revenge. Let me see your purse."

I was surprised by the force of his demand and the determination in his voice. "Certainly not," I replied. But, in a way, I was happy because his demand allowed me to prove my innocence.

"Please . . . for my own peace of mind."

"All right, but I'm very disappointed in you," I called back as I gathered my purse from the bedroom. I made sure that Rickard could see my every move as I brought it to him. "Go ahead, give it a good searching."

His shoulders sagged. "I can't. I was wrong to doubt you."

"No, you must be satisfied." I took it from him and dumped its contents on the couch: a waterfall of lipstick, Reichsmarks, cosmetics, pens, and notepaper scattered across the cushion. "See . . . nothing."

He ran his fingers through the items and then looked up at me with eyes as sad as an abandoned dog. "I'm sorry. I shouldn't have doubted you."

"No, you shouldn't have." I tossed the items back in my purse and returned it to the bedroom. I made sure not to glance at the wardrobe, for I'd stashed the bracelet behind a panel on its back. Even if Rickard searched my clothing drawers he wouldn't find it.

# CHAPTER 7

It's been said that money can't buy happiness. The same could be said for pleasure. Before I moved in with Rickard, I felt the modern woman should be unmoved by life's ups and downs, like a ship bouncing over ocean swells. Survival, overcoming doubts and adversity, was all that mattered—at least that was the way I thought of it.

Somehow, even with Rickard by my side, I felt unsettled. The cause of this melancholy was difficult to ascertain: the continued rise of the Nazis, my insecurities about writing, the lonely wanderlust that had guided my actions before I met Rickard—one or all could be the cause.

Aside from modernity, perhaps the most humble woman in Germany hoped for an endless round of parties, beautiful dresses, shopping, and trips to the salon, where she would try on the most fashionable shades of lipstick, indulge in the latest beauty creams to keep her face firm and youthful. Breakfast would be delivered in bed, luncheon served on the patio, in the garden, or by the pool. The ladies' maid would pick out evening wear for cocktails and dinner, and then one would be off to the theater, the opera, or a grand party hosted by someone famous. If she wasn't on the cover of a glamour magazine, she would at least be pictured in a glittering gown, next to the hostess, both of them brandishing extraordinarily long cigarette holders. What a farce!

Reality was quite a different matter.

The world's economies were wrecked, the unemployment rates staggering. Hunger, homelessness, and poverty ruled Germany and we called it home. Rickard and I, by all rights, were lucky. Thanks to him, I was never hungry, and despite the tough times the studio was going through, we always had enough money to get by. I tried hard not to think of what was going on at Passport Pictures, but I feared the time would come when I would have to confront Rickard and take a stand against the SA. Would he, or I, be strong enough to do so. If we did, the money would be gone. I, of course, was getting occasional typing jobs and still working on my novel, *The Berlin Woman*.

*I'm ashamed that I live in ease while everywhere around me people are in trouble, even my friends. Martin tries hard to cheer me up, as does my friend Angela, who recently moved back to Berlin from Cologne. She lost her job and returned hoping to find work. So far, she hasn't found anything and is living with three other girls in a tenement apartment. Hers is a sad life compared to mine.*

*I, however, despite my easy relationship with Martin, feel incomplete. I creep through the small rooms, sit in the one chair, read the three books that he has on hand. His job is secure, but I'm having trouble finding work. The hours drift by with the sun or rain beating down, and, at the end of the day, I've accomplished nothing of worth. I simply exist—like so many women in Berlin.*

*I'm clouded with doubt, shrouded in melancholy. Martin tempers my moods, but the days drag by, one after the other, from the first light of dawn to the dark-est midnight, with little to distinguish them. Our rou-tines have become commonplace.*

*I drag him to art galleries, or to the theater—the inexpensive seats, of course. I wear my best dress, and dab on perfume, and turn my head to look at Martin's dark features. How handsome, how wonderful a man he is, with a strong chest and arms, brown eyes that flash when he looks at me. A good man. I appreciate him as I sit beside him. He's been so kind, yet the fire grows no stronger. God knows not because of Mar-tin, but because of me. What have I done with my life? What do I want to make of it? I can't answer those questions through Martin, and no friend, no woman, no man, no politician can offer the solution. I wonder what it will take to make me comfortable in my own skin.*

*Martin, the poor dear, is unaware of how I feel be-cause our intimacy, strangely, has created a gulf as wide and deep as a canyon. Funny how, as time goes by, secrets become enshrouded, never to be revealed. Desires, wishes, erotic dreams, I keep to myself rather than share them with my lover. The truth hurts too much to tell. It saddens me, but perhaps all men and women do the same.*

I worked hard on the book, never quite satisfied with it, always questioning my ability as the plot drifted here and there, while Niki, Martin, and the other characters did things on the page I never expected. Thoughts came out I'd never dreamed of writing. Rickard was always there to give me encouragement, never interrupting my time, even on days when there was no work for him at Passport Pictures.

As the months drifted by, I became so absorbed in my writ-ing that I'd failed to notice that what was happening to Rickard and me was happening to Niki in *The Berlin Woman*. Time was pushing us in the same direction, but my insecurities were pulling us apart, like a river split by a mound of stones.

When my fears struck me, I came to him one day in the late summer. "When are we getting married?" I asked. Buried deep within me, I failed to understand that the question was a defense against losing everything we'd built together. How many men and women have experienced the same while unaware of their subconscious thoughts: like couples who have a baby, or buy a house, or give each other something expensive in the hope of keeping their relationship from falling apart? One may not recognize it at the time, but the subconscious does.

He looked somewhat surprised, but nonetheless pleased. "Anytime you want." He took my hands in his. "We've been together for almost a year. How about next Saturday? I still have the ring."

"Fine," I said. "I don't want a big wedding. I don't want Spiegel or the SA crawling about, just a civil ceremony and a small dinner after. I was thinking of inviting Lotti and Rudi. Only them. You know how I am about lists. Just the four of us."

"Spiegel will want to make a big show of it, but I'll handle him."

"Like you always have," I said, with too much sarcasm, while putting my arms around his neck.

He stepped back. "Don't be cruel, Niki. It doesn't suit a woman who's about to be married."

I relinquished my embrace and walked toward the office. "Look . . . I have something to show you."

The day was hot and the windows were open. The heat rose from the street and filled the apartment with the smell of motor-car exhaust. Occasionally, the befouled breeze would sweep in and ruffle the papers on the desk. I'd secured my work with a weighty tome on Roman art from the bookcase. I pointed to the stack of papers. "Here it is . . . the first draft of *The Berlin Woman*."

A broad smile broke out on Rickard's face. He lifted the novel and gazed at the title page. "That's wonderful, Niki. I'm so proud of you. I can't wait to read it."

I sat in the office chair. "I'm not sure I want you to. What if you don't like it?"

His face tightened. "I'm sure I'll love it."

I took the book from him and placed it back on the desk. "Perhaps, but that's the point. You can't be impartial."

"No, you're wrong. How do you think I've worked with Anders and all the other directors and actors at Passport? Many of them are my friends, but I was able to tell them when something's rotten."

I frowned and ruffled the manuscript pages. "I certainly hope it's not rotten . . . Spiegel and his cronies aren't going to like *The Berlin Woman*. The book is not at all like the plot I made up for him. It's as far from that as from here to the moon. This can't end up on Hitler's desk, or any Nazi for that matter—not with my name on it."

"You told me what it was about—the new modern woman." He perched on the edge of the desk and looked at me expectantly.

"Yes, and that's exactly what it turned out to be. Niki is her own woman—she's not subservient; a bowing, pale imitation of a female. She doesn't want to be 'loyal' to a good Nazi husband, provide him with sons to send off to war, or any other National Socialist nonsense."

Rickard picked up a pencil from the desk and twirled it in his fingers. "I never expected it to be like that. I would have been disappointed if it was—although what you told Spiegel would make a great propaganda picture. He would pay good money for the rights."

I sighed. "Not this. The Nazis would burn it if they could."

"So, what do you want to do with it?"

My lungs itched for a cigarette. "If this manuscript goes to Spiegel or Göring or Hitler, I'm done. If I can find a publisher, I'll publish it under my real name—Marie Rittenhaus—and hope that the SA isn't bright enough to figure it out. Their only clue would be my heroine's name—Niki—unless I change it." I stopped and gazed at him. "Frankly, I'm a bit scared."

"And, at the same time, exhilarated?" Rickard asked. "Remember my warning. They have ways of finding people—friends in high places."

I nodded. "I'll change the character names and publish it under a pseudonym if I have to." At that moment, I felt the dream of publication within my reach. "Exhilarated. It's a very odd feeling. I suppose it's like an explorer charting new territory, visiting a part of the earth where no one has ever been."

He leaned across the desk and kissed me. "I'm proud of you. I mean it, but don't think that the SA couldn't figure out who you are. They are ingenious and crafty beyond belief. It might be better to use a pseudonym and change the heroine's name, if it isn't too much trouble."

I sighed. "Work and more work. Writing a novel isn't easy. I haven't even begun to edit it."

For the first time in months, I felt like Rickard and I had really talked and come to an understanding. Neither one of us had said much about our work lives recently. I kept to my writing, and he maintained his detached view of the studio and his work. Although I didn't want us to keep secrets from each other, the excitement about my book took my mind off the films being made at Passport Pictures.

The Nazis gained some success in the September 1930 elections. Shortly thereafter, three young Reichswehr officers were tried in Leipzig for high treason for promoting Nazi doctrine to army members. The true star of the trial was

Adolf Hitler, who was called as a witness for the defense. Hitler made his position clear to the court, stating that the Nazis had no interest in replacing the army, calling such rumors "madness." He said that when the National Socialists came to power they would create a great army of the German people, adding that "we will form the State in the manner which we consider to be the right one." He also called for a Nazi Court of Justice, so revenge could be taken on all those who opposed him. Most of us were unaware of the trial, the words spoken there, and their implication for the future.

Our wedding in late October, nearly a full year after moving in together, was a modest affair. As I'd hoped, the guest list was small. Only Lotti and Rudi attended the afternoon ceremony at the courthouse. I didn't invite my mother. I debated whether to invite her, but decided against it, opting instead for a pleasant day for all, my mother included. She didn't know Rickard, and I had no idea what she would think of him or my friends. Perhaps I underestimated her capacity for restraint. I would fill her in later and she could come to her own conclusion about his worth as a husband.

There were no objections to our union, so we were married.

After the wedding, the four of us dined in a restaurant near the Alexanderplatz. Rudi was the only one with a commitment for the evening, a late shift at the Leopard Club. The weather was warm for the time of year. We sat, loosely bundled in our coats and sweaters, at an outside table under a red umbrella promoting a popular beer.

Rudi and Rickard got along well, the two of them smoking and drinking, reminiscing about good times at the club. Apparently, their history was longer than I knew.

"Did you know I wanted to be an actor?" Rudi casually asked me after he and my husband had shared a laugh.

"No," I replied.

"As Rickard can testify, my talent was no match for my ambition. I'm a terrible actor." They both laughed again. Rickard winked at me.

"I'm a much better lay," Rudi added with a spit of bravado.

Rickard's cheeks flushed crimson and he lowered his gaze, letting his hand drop from his beer glass. I tried to remember what Rudi had said at the club the first time I mentioned wanting to be introduced to my husband. He had commented on Rickard's last name, Länger, and said something like "from what I've heard." I certainly could attest to that, but apparently so could Rudi. He had confessed without directly implicating himself.

*So many secrets.*

Lotti noticed my strained look and tapped me on the shoulder. "So, you've finished your novel?"

Her question jolted me and brought me back to the table. I looked at her as if coming out of a dream. "Yes . . . yes . . . the draft."

"Tell me about it," she said, pressing me, drawing my attention away from the two men. Their conversation halted abruptly, even Rudi now looking like a stricken dog.

I turned toward my friend, a glass of champagne in my hand. She had coiffed her blond hair for the wedding, even braiding curls into a half circle that ran from one ear to the other across the top of her head. Her cheeks were fleshy and pink with a flaming spot of rouge on each.

"I'm editing it," I said. "The manuscript needs to be retyped. Then, I'll look for a publisher." I glanced across the table. Rickard was smiling faintly and whispering into Rudi's ear.

"I know an editor who might look at your book," Lotti said, her cheeks puffing up with a smile. "At Verlangen Press. My company does business with them."

"Do they publish fiction?"

She nodded. "Of course. I'll get you his card."

"Thank you," I said, picturing my husband in bed with Rudi.

The remainder of our meal was quiet and restrained. When we returned to the apartment, I took off my dress and lay on the bed in my slip, a headache coming on. This one was real, not an excuse to forestall sex, but a product of too much champagne and the suddenly expanded nature of our relationship.

Rickard turned on the bureau lamp and settled on the bed near me, stroking my bare arms. The sun had gone down and Berlin shimmered in the October haze. My husband's fingers felt cold against my skin and I wondered why. Was I imagining the way he really felt about me, or was I anticipating the future? I shivered and turned away, but regretted doing so. Was I really such a traditionalist that I couldn't see beyond the strict definition of a man and a woman? In an afternoon and evening filled with images, another popped into my head—my mother's stark wooden crucifix nailed to her bedroom wall.

"Niki," Rickard said softly, a deep sense of loneliness pervading his voice. "Look at me. I don't want our wedding night to end like this. I love you."

I was frozen to the bed, unable to move. I felt the mattress sink as his body snuggled against me. The wardrobe was to my side; the emerald and diamond bracelet almost within reach—in case I needed to leave. *Stop acting like a child!*

My silk slip rustled against the spread as I turned to him. I was surprised to see tears in his eyes, one running down his cheek. He swiped it away before it hit the bed.

"Let me ask you something. . . ." His voice caught, as if he was about to ask the hardest question in the world. "Have you ever slept with a woman?"

I sighed, knowing where he was headed. How often had I been offended at the Leopard Club by men who dressed like women, or women who dressed like men? Never. I had enjoyed my time there, actually reveled in the freedom, the ability of some to live their lives as they wanted, unencumbered by strict tradition. The true German freaks were the Brownshirts who prowled the streets, not the patrons of a club who only wanted to be themselves and live in peace. The modern German woman wouldn't object, finding no moral outrage in the Leopard Club. She would applaud the men and women who had the courage to define themselves as they wished.

"I kissed a school chum once and we helped each other try on bras," I said. "I never . . . but I didn't . . ." Articulating my sexual feelings was difficult. I'd slept with men and admired the figures and faces of beautiful women, but other than a jealous crush on a popular schoolgirl, I'd never wanted to go to bed with a woman.

"Two times with Rudi," Rickard said. "The first was an experiment. The second a confirmation that I preferred and loved women—meaning that the first time had been an aberration, a curiosity, an expression of feelings that needed to come out. He's a very sexy man."

"I don't know why I was so shocked." I put my hand across his shoulder, feeling the soft wool of his suit. "Because I never suspected you? Sometimes it's hard to see inside others . . . just as hard as seeing inside yourself."

"Rudi was safe," Rickard said. "I'd had opportunities with other men in the industry, but never acted upon them. I wasn't interested. And I knew Rudi slept with women as well. I didn't have to worry about a commitment or falling in love."

I took a deep breath. "Life is strange, often wonderful, sometimes terrible, but I feel I've learned two things on my wedding day. You're more than I ever imagined . . . and I'm not as modern as I thought. I live through my characters. Niki in *The Berlin Woman* is much more of a free spirit than I am. I must work on that."

"You're perfect as you are," Rickard said, managing a smile. "Do you want to make love? I'm all yours."

I pulled him close. "No, I want to fall asleep in your arms."

"We can do that, too," he said, kicking off his shoes.

And we did fall asleep wrapped around each other. Sometime in the depth of the night, Rickard took off his suit and we did make love and I felt he totally belonged to me. And like Niki, I wondered if our relationship was some grand dream, along with the unsettling feeling that we might not last.

# CHAPTER 8

Herr Artur Berger was the publisher and an editor at Verlangen Press in Berlin-Tempelhof, not far from Passport Pictures. Lotti had given me his business card. After I sent an introductory letter, Berger expressed an interest in the manuscript. Rickard dropped it off on his way to the studio in early November. I met with the publisher the first week of December 1930.

Berger was buttoned-down, strict-looking, and reminiscent of old German aristocracy with his monocle and pressed gray suit, but underneath the armored exterior I detected his love of books and a concealed concern for humanity. Verlangen had published numerous German writers, current and past, and I was excited to be an invited part of the venerable institution.

The details of our meeting were as boring as any business transaction: dates for final edits and publication, my paltry advance, publicity, and other mundane details, which Berger handled adroitly. However, it was all new to me, and I was thrilled to get my first novel published by such a respected house. I made few demands of the publisher, particularly after Berger pointed out he was taking a chance with the book and had decided to publish it because he'd "never read anything like it." A book about the struggles of real women, he'd said.

After much consideration, we agreed that the novel would be published under a pseudonym rather than Niki or my real name, Marie Rittenhaus, and there would be little biographical information given on the dust jacket other than a few lines describing a debut novel by a Berlin writer. Author pictures were uncommon, so I didn't have to worry about that. The Nazis would have to dig to find the writer—if they even cared. I'd also come to the conclusion that Niki shouldn't be the heroine's name. After all, the Berlin SA knew me by the nickname. So, after great effort, correcting the manuscript by hand as Berger allowed, I changed the heroine's name to "Charlotte." My only concern was that the Nazis might use their ham-handed SA tactics on the publisher. I was determined to go to Spiegel myself if it came to that, and also warn my mother that there might be a negative reaction from National Socialists after the book was published.

The book was scheduled for publication in August of 1931, before the fall and winter reading season.

Politically, Germany was in flux, but few cared about politics beyond the headlines. A succession of chancellors filled the office before Hitler assumed power. Paul von Hindenburg, the country's president, was losing his physical and mental faculties and his control over the office. Most people were concerned with jobs and promises, not the behind-the-scenes machinations of politicians. That didn't stop the Nazis from consolidating their power, always chipping away at the republic in their bid to form their fascist state.

I began working on a second book, the morality tale called *Confessions of a Vampire's Wife*. I'd written a few scenes for it long ago, including the one inspired by Anders's beating. Berger gave me begrudging approval to proceed with the work, but urged me to take a lighter tone with a novel that might be categorized as horrific. I assured him that it would be "romance with a little blood," and I would be as "ironic as possible." Of course, the National Socialists would be my ironic target.

The months slipped by with Rickard and me devoting most of our time to work, which put an unintended strain on our relationship. We enjoyed each other's company when we could, along with our forays into sex. On balance, I felt that we were both defined by the separate worlds of our professions. His job was taking more of a toll than mine. He would come home defeated after a day at the studio, his spirit and body sagging. I tried to get him to open up about his troubles, but he would brush them off saying only that Spiegel and the others wanted him to go deeper, farther, into the reaches of National Socialist doctrine.

"Can't you say no?" I asked, not knowing what the far reaches of Nazi doctrine really meant.

He shook his head. "You need to ask that question? You already know the answer."

"If *The Berlin Woman* sells, we can do without them," I said.

He scowled at me, as if his masculinity, his power to provide, had been challenged. The idea that we could live on a woman's earnings was nothing he'd ever considered. I wondered how his ex-wife was faring, and if she was getting a portion of his income. I'd never asked because he'd only talked about her and his son once and I didn't want to bring up a painful subject he avoided.

"I wish it were that simple," he replied, his gaze downcast, as he wandered to the bar.

"Do you want to talk about it? Remember, no secrets."

He swiveled, his eyes flaring. "It's no secret. They control the money and the films. There's nothing to talk about."

The conversation about his work ended there.

One spring day in April 1931, during an early afternoon of warm sun and cool, fresh air, someone knocked at 3D. I wasn't expecting any guests, and Rickard, as usual, was gone for the day. I got up from the desk and looked at the door, acting as if I could see through it. The knocks subsided for a moment, but then returned stronger, more persistent.

I looked at my typewriter and wondered whether I should abandon my work for the day.

"Who is it?" I called out.

"Anders . . . Anders Pechstein," came the rather meek reply.

It took me a moment to shake off my surprise and recall the face of Anders Pechstein. The last time I'd seen the film director was in a Berlin hospital, where he was recovering from the beating he'd taken from Spiegel and his henchmen. I remembered our first meeting at the shoot—how focused he'd been, and also his long and lean body. All business, Rickard had said.

When I opened the door, a different man walked in. He was Anders Pechstein, but the dusty blond hair was streaked with gray; his face had shifted in color, from a healthy flesh tone to a rather sickly yellow. His eyes were as hollow and dark as caves. An ill-fitting dark suit fell about him like folded newspaper. I didn't know what to say. He walked in as if he'd been inside the apartment before and sat on one of the red couches lining the wall.

"It's a beautiful day," he said. "I'm glad you're here." The words sounded almost cheerful, as if he was visiting a friend, but they made no sense to me as I viewed the wreck of a man sitting in front of me.

"Can I get you something? Water? A drink?"

"A drink would be nice. I'll take whatever you have." He interlaced his fingers and folded them into his lap.

I walked to the bar and poured a half glass of our best cognac. My guest looked as if he needed it. I handed him the drink and sat looking past the couches into the sunny Berlin skyline. What a shock! How could one fall from good graces to the man sitting in front of me? Easily, in 1930s Berlin.

We said nothing for a moment and I studied him as he

looked into his glass. After a time, he leaned back and exhaled in a relaxed manner, as if the cares of the world had escaped him.

"Is Rickard here?"

"No."

"Do you expect him soon?"

"What's wrong, Anders?"

"It's no matter where Rickard is . . . I can tell you my troubles." He patted his suit jacket as if looking for a cigarette but came up empty. I offered him a Manoli, which he accepted with a smile. I lit it for him and he resumed his pose. "I really shouldn't bother you with my problems, but I didn't know where else to go. No one has any money these days." His eyes reddened, and he grasped the drink, fighting back a veil of tears. All the self-confidence I'd witnessed when I first met the man had disappeared.

"Do you need money? We're pretty rough ourselves."

He flinched and gulped the cognac. "My mother has money, but it's tied up. She's Jewish and afraid that, even in Sweden, she'll need everything she has to get by . . . maybe to get out of the country if the Nazis come to power. My father is here because of his business, but the Nazis are threatening him because he has a Jewish wife. He's thinking of going back to Sweden where it's safer."

"What about you?"

He looked at me with a vacant stare. "I haven't worked in more than a year. My wife and I are fine because my father's been channeling funds our way, but that can't go on forever. The Nazis are more than willing to put the screws to me. They know my work, know my communist politics, and they keep a record of whom they beat up. Spiegel is a monster." He looked out the window for a moment and then turned his attention back to me. "You realize, Niki, that when they come to power—and they will—Hitler is too smart and the masses are too blind to see what's in front of their eyes—everything will change. In six months, Germany will be crushed under the thumb of a dictator."

"It's very depressing, but I don't know what we can do—other than vote."

"When Hitler comes to power, voting won't matter . . . but that's not the real reason I came here."

I stared at his sallow face and wondered if this was what the German people would look like in two or three years. I dared not think beyond that time.

"I came to plead with Rickard to stop making films," he said with a renewed determination in his voice.

I lit a cigarette and offered Anders another. How could I tell him that the unholy arrangement with the SA was the only way that food appeared on our table? "I know it's awful, but Rickard—Passport Pictures—has no other way of surviving." I didn't want to tell Anders about our personal business, how we were using our pact with the Nazis as personal security, fearing for our lives; how Rickard had been threatened by Spiegel; how we would be in Anders's position, equally broken, if the money wasn't coming in.

As these thoughts went through my head, a creeping sickness, like a bout of nausea, filled my stomach. Anders was right—Rickard and I both knew what was happening at Passport was wrong, but the choice was to go along with these monsters or fade into oblivion and die.

Anders's eyes flared and his face stiffened. "Survive? His films are going to cost thousands of lives."

"What are you talking about? They're making pictures about rallies—I think he's made some about camping and the health of German youth also."

"May I have another drink before I go?" he asked.

I got the bottle, returned to the couch, and poured another stiff round into his glass.

"Spiegel and Rickard are making films about Jews."

"Jews?" Anders's words shocked me, but I didn't know what he was getting at.

"Yes, stirring up hate . . . belittling Jews . . . calling them war mongers and ugly, deceitful creatures, coming to take your jobs and money, and even eat your children. The Jews are the cause of all the world's problems, according to the National Socialists. It's only one step from this hate to destruction."

I almost laughed out loud. "You must be mistaken. Rickard wouldn't be a party to that." I said the words, but doubt covered me like a shadow. I hadn't been to the studio since the vampire picture was shelved, so I had no real idea what was going on. The sickness rose into my chest.

"I ran into Wolf," Anders continued. "He was quite happy to work again. He told me he was playing a monstrous old Jew, a lecher who beats German children with sticks, then kidnaps them and holds them for ransom. The poor parents give the fiend everything they own to get their children back before he can eat them. The Jew leers and kisses the sacks of gold before he's found by the good National Socialists, who take matters into their own hands and stone the old man to death. Another dead Jew. *Fini*."

I didn't know what to say. I felt like throwing up. Rickard had never mentioned that the studio was now churning out propaganda films against Jews.

"It's called *The Wicked Jew*. It's the first of many planned for production. Wolf will be employed for as long as he wants. I came to implore Rickard to stop—to save the lives of Jews . . . and possibly his own. The hate will become a terrible trap that will kill him."

I didn't want to believe him, and I held my breath for a moment as I considered what to do.

Anders finished the drink, handed me the glass, and rose from the sofa. "Maybe you can save him . . . convince him to stop these horrible pictures. It's a warning for his sake as well." He started for the door, but stopped beside my chair and looked down upon me. "It's hard to have dignity in Germany during this time, and I fear it will only get worse. Ending these films would be a step against the fascists. Believe me, I know their power."

I grasped his hand as he stepped away. "I'm sorry, Anders, and I hope that we'll all live through this. . . . I'll talk to Rickard."

"Good luck." His cold hand slipped from mine and he was gone.

As soon as the door closed I knew what I had to do.

An hour later, I was on the tram headed to Passport Pictures. I wanted to see if Anders was telling the truth. I didn't doubt the man, but I thought perhaps he'd gotten confused about the intent of the film; maybe *The Wicked Jew* was a fairy tale, like something from the Brothers Grimm. As I rode, the crowd jostling against me, the more I believed that Rickard had fallen under the Nazis' spell. I looked at the drab suits, the faded dresses, the worn faces of a people crushed by economic uncertainty who sought any sign of hope to lift them from a wearisome world. The joys of spring could do nothing to raise the spirits of the German people. But there was one man—Hitler—waiting patiently for his time onstage, who promised much to those who would follow him.

The guards at the studio had been replaced by the SA. After telling a pair of brown-shirted, booted men, whose faces shone almost crimson in the light, that I was Rickard's wife, they let me pass. I walked to the studio where the vampire picture had been filmed, supposing that production was going on there rather than the building to the right, which looked vacant and unused.

I wound through the dark hallway and soon found myself staring at a set. Dracula's castle had been converted to a mansion, although the creepiness surrounding it had been preserved. The blood-red moon still hung on the backdrop, bare trees dotted the crag. The gray monochromatic scenery supported the film's bleak atmosphere.

A man stood on center stage, taking direction from a uniformed SA officer. The actor was made up with a large, hook nose, scraggly hair, a long black beard, and hands that resembled claws. The man could have been Wolf, but it was impossible to tell under all the makeup. Several uninterested blond children dressed in traditional German lederhosen and pinafores, possibly the sons and daughters of the rabid SA men, sat nearby awaiting direction. The "Jew" was surrounded by bags filled with his bounty, wooden bars painted gold protruding from their tops. In the wings, Nazis, in full regalia, stood ready to save the children from their captor.

I surmised that the next scene would be just that—a brutal attack on the Jew to rescue the children.

"Niki, what are you doing here?" I hadn't noticed that Rickard had crept up behind me.

I wheeled to face my husband as the director called out for action. The actors took their places and the mayhem began.

Through the shouting and the beating of the Jew, I shifted my gaze between Rickard and the action on the set. "You're supporting this violence?" I asked, my voice rising above the commotion. A few of the SA men standing by looked in my direction.

"Hush," Rickard said. "Come outside. We can't talk here."

He encircled my waist with his arm and guided me through the dark hall to the door. As we stepped into the bright light, I was blinded temporarily by the sun.

"What's going on?" I screamed at him. "I knew you were making party rally films, but not these horrors.

"I'm sorry," he said. "I knew you'd be upset. . . ."

I looked past Rickard and gasped. The SA men from the gate were sprinting toward us, guns drawn. "Herr Länger . . . Is everything all right, Herr Länger?" they shouted.

Rickard nodded and sent them back to their posts with a wave of his hand.

"I don't understand you," I said. "Anders Pechstein came to the apartment this afternoon. He told me everything. I had to see for myself."

"Ah, Pechstein, the former director who's become a beggar because he refuses to acknowledge the truth about what is going on in Germany. It's on his head, you realize. Now you know . . . now you know the dirty secret I've been hiding."

"No secrets, remember?"

"One thing I've learned is that secrets are a way of life. Standard behavior between a man and woman, and all but the ones hidden by the National Socialists are coming to light."

"I see that clearly." The emerald and diamond bracelet stashed behind the wardrobe flashed into my mind and I felt ashamed—but only for a moment.

Rickard sank against the studio door. In the spring sun, I saw a man unrecognizable despite our evenings in the apartment. The skin around his eyes had turned dark, the rest of his face pasty after months of work and submersion in the cavernous studio. He looked as sad and defeated as the passengers on the tram.

"We've been through this before. Eat or be eaten. I'm not going to let us be devoured by the Nazis. If that means playing along with their fantasies about how they're going to solve Germany's troubles, I've no problem with that. As long as we live . . . as long as we're safe . . . we're making money . . . and my ex-wife and son are safe. In my case, the National Socialists are living up to their promises."

I responded with a stony silence.

"You wouldn't believe how much money they have," he continued. "Everything is falling into place for them. Hitler knows he can't do it alone, and he's promising the manufacturers and producers that they will have contracts and workers to fulfill those obligations. The bankers are lining up, too."

"What happened to 'fucking Nazis,'" I said. "What happened to 'I fear what's coming'?"

He touched his cheek as if he was wiping away a tear. "I used to fear them, but I don't—can't—as long as I'm on the winning side. They'll not be turned away." He paused before continuing with a voice as firm as an iron rod. "I will never allow what happened to me and my son to happen again. Nothing will be taken away from me again. If there's a God in heaven, I swear it."

"What if we left Germany? We could go someplace else—make a new life."

Rickard shook his head. "No, I can't. I've lost too much already. I won't give up my business, the life we've made together. This is where we belong."

"I've seen enough. I've no stomach for what's going on inside the studio. You should be ashamed."

I started to leave, but he grasped my arm and in a low voice said, "Understand what the consequences would be if I back out now. A grave situation would develop . . . for both of us. What do you want me to do? Burn down the studio?"

"If that's what it takes." I wrenched my arm free and stormed through the gate under the watchful eyes of the SA. The heat rose on the back of my neck as I made my way to Unter den Linden. A hot flush of tears threatened my eyes. Only by choking back sobs was I able to retain control over my emotions.

I thought of packing, grabbing the bracelet, buying a train ticket, and heading somewhere—anywhere away from Rickard and his Nazi friends. I thought of calling Lotti, begging her to put me up until I could sort out what had happened. Maybe I could move in with Rudi, a move that would anger Rickard. Not only was I furious, but my thoughts were shifting to revenge as well. I patted my cheeks with a handkerchief and settled my mind.

As I was climbing the stairs to the apartment, calm overcame me as if coming from the depths of my soul. I couldn't be too hasty or revengeful. I had no source of money, other than the bracelet. The SA probably had issued a warning to local jewelers to be on the lookout for it. I would be arrested. And I couldn't wait for the profits from book sales—if the book sold at all.

But there was something else that caused my measured step, and I hadn't even told Rickard about it—let alone Lotti or Rudi.

I was pregnant.

# CHAPTER 9

By August 1931, when *The Berlin Woman* was scheduled for release, my belly was large and I was well on my way to delivery. In the spring and summer, after my trip to the studio, I'd come to the conclusion that it was safer to stay with Rickard and have the baby—due sometime in mid-November—than strike out on my own. At least with my husband, I still had a home and the means to pay for medical care, even though Rickard's association with Spiegel and the SA weighed upon my mind. And I couldn't rid myself of the feeling that pursuing my own career would get us into trouble.

I'd talked to Lotti several times on the telephone and, in one of our early conversations, told her I was pregnant, but I didn't tell her about the rough time that Rickard and I were having. When I told her about the baby, there was a subtle shift in her attitude toward me. I didn't blame her. She was a single woman looking for a husband, a working girl who was used to living alone, doing as she pleased, like late nights at the club followed by the occasional male visitor to her apartment. She had offered her place to me before, but this time the subject was never broached. I think she was a bit jealous because I was having a child. Motherhood wasn't in sight for her. Also, she was losing me as a carefree companion. I had cut down on my smoking and drinking as well.

Was I happy about having a baby? My joy or sorrow depended on my mood. I would have been much happier had the world been a better place, not descending into madness thanks to the Nazis. I'd never considered myself an overtly political person; however, my politics came out in my books and my characters' lives. The past had formed me despite any objection I might raise in the present. Perhaps, I'd never recovered from my father's early death. Perhaps the undercurrents of my Christian upbringing bubbled beneath my skin—another factor that had led me to my place in the world. I would have been happier if Rickard had been his own man and not become a Nazi pawn. After my visit to the studio, we rarely talked about his work. I knew that any conversation about National Socialism would lead to an argument and bad feeling. The New German Woman lived on the hope of survival, and each day it became clear that her future would be as challenging. Everyone in Berlin asked, "What would you do? What can be done?"

On the day *The Berlin Woman* was released, Artur Berger, the publisher, invited me to lunch in his office at Verlangen Press. I found myself in the hushed atmosphere of his sanctuary: a refuge of oak furniture, leather chairs, oriental carpets, glass, and chrome, with wide-paned windows that looked out on industrial buildings muted by leafy tree tops.

After congratulating me on my obvious pregnancy, he offered his own good news.

"The initial orders for the book are going well," he said, offering me a glass of water with my meal of salad and cold, poached fish. A white-coated waiter attended the table, setting up the luncheon and pouring my drink. "The retailers are excited, as well as the critics who've received the book. I expect good reviews within a week."

I leaned back in the comfortable leather chair after each

bite. My protruding stomach barely allowed me to touch the white tablecloth. "That's excellent news."

"Those who have read it say it's a different voice . . . one that hasn't been heard. I knew that from the first time I read it. Berlin women are going to react favorably. That's why I wanted to publish it." He adjusted his monocle and balanced his fork delicately over his plate.

"I have an unusual request, Herr Berger," I said. "I hope you won't take offense."

He raised his head and looked at my slyly. "As long as it's not illegal. . . ."

"No, I don't think so. I'd like my sales to be paid in cash after earning out the advance. You can take the taxes out of the royalties, if that makes your bookkeeping easier." I smiled. "Assuming the book sells."

"That is a bit unusual," he said. "We don't usually pay our authors that way." His brows lifted as if an explanation was owed for my stipulation.

"It's my wish . . . for personal reasons."

"Of course," he said, nodding. "I understand how to conduct business. Publishing is a business."

"I'd like to pick up the money personally when payments are due." I'd discreetly impressed upon him my need to get cash—the thought of leaving Unter den Linden never far from my mind. I was relieved that Berger agreed. The rest of lunch went well, with the publisher telling me which booksellers had ordered the most copies, and how the company existed on such a "slim profit margin." He finished by regaling me with the past successes and escapades of Verlangen authors.

In September, I walked past bookstores and marveled at the sight of my novel displayed in the shop windows. Berger called me and explained that the initial printing of 2500 copies had sold out and a second printing of the same amount was on order. I was thrilled at the news, but my success had become a threat as well. Rickard reported that Spiegel had seen the book and asked his wife to read it. She, being the good Nazi, was outraged at Charlotte's, my heroine's, behavior. Verlangen was deluged with requests from newspapers in Berlin, Nuremberg, Cologne, and Munich for interviews with the author. I agreed to give the interviews under my pseudonym, by phone, from the publisher's office.

Celebrity had accompanied my dream come true. Fame was throwing me and Rickard into danger. I hoped that the Nazis' authority, still not solidified by the government, would be kept at bay until after our child was delivered.

Laura Länger was born in a Berlin hospital early Monday morning on November 16, 1931. As I delivered, without complications, in a private room, Rickard paced in the waiting area—that was what the nurses told me. He saw our daughter a few hours later and then went back to the apartment, but I could tell from his demeanor and the way he held Laura in his arms that he was truly in love with the child. Perhaps he was feeling the loss of his son, or was swept up in the miracle of birth. I could have sworn that a tear crossed his eye.

Lotti came by for a visit. Later, my mother, Frieda, showed up. It was the first time I'd seen her in more than two years. Laura was her first grandchild, and I wanted her to see the newborn. I had gotten the message to her—where I would be, the expected time of delivery. Frieda came into the room wearing a brown coat over a blue housedress, looking somewhat bemused, as if the process of giving birth was something to be avoided by any woman with a brain. She still retained her ample figure, red cheeks, and brown hair dusted with auburn highlights, as well as the subtle smirk of condescension that often lived upon her face. I tried to be nice, but remembered how much I'd struggled to leave my birthplace.

"Well, it finally happened," she said, flatly. She sat in a folding chair across from the bed, keeping her coat on and her fingers interlaced on her lap.

"It?"

"You know what I mean." She growled a bit at my question. "The baby . . . at least you got married."

I fluffed the pillow behind my head. I was in good health, but Rickard insisted I stay a couple of days at the hospital to make sure Laura and I were both fine. "I don't need a lecture, Mother. I'm not fifteen anymore.

"Are you hurt that I didn't invite you to the wedding?" I asked. "Only two friends attended. We wanted a small affair."

"I suppose it was for the best. We've had our differences. The day was like any other in my life." A thin smile appeared on her lips. "I'm glad you finally settled down."

It was the second time she'd used "finally" in a sentence, as if my wanton life had come to a halt with marriage. That was good news as far as she was concerned.

"I'd like to meet your husband . . . someday," she added.

I nodded, thinking that it might be good for her to see the life I'd made—how I'd survived. Frieda might blanch at the "luxury" of apartment 3D on Unter den Linden, the furnishings, the trappings of Rickard's profession as a producer, the ostentatious display of a life she never could or would have. She might even be jealous. Perhaps it would remind her of the home of those glamorous movie stars she read about in her magazines. But when to do it? When would the time be right?

As we sat there, rather at a loss for words, a nurse in a starched white uniform came in. Laura had been taken away for a bath and a brief visit with a doctor, who pronounced her in good health. The nurse, young and pretty with shiny black hair bursting forth from underneath her cap, held Laura against the bosom of the apron that covered her dress.

I asked the young woman to hand Laura to my mother so she could hold the baby. My mother's eyes sparkled and then dimmed, but she took the baby anyway despite what looked like a forthcoming objection. I supposed it had been many years since she had held a child in her hands.

The nurse left and I watched my mother's uncomfortable dance with Laura, the baby shifting this way and that, then kicking her legs in a revolt against the wrap covering her. Finally, Laura settled and my mother ran a finger through the baby's fine, dark hair.

"She's beautiful, isn't she?" I asked, not really caring whether my mother agreed.

She nodded, not saying a word.

"How's home?" I asked. "Are you comfortable?"

Again, she nodded. "I must come for a visit—with Laura, of course. Would you like that?"

Frieda rose from her chair and carried the baby to me, placing her carefully in my arms. "Of course. I'm always home. If I'm not, I'm at the market. It's the same place it always was." She returned to her seat and assumed the identical position—coat on, hands locked—looking at me in a quizzical manner as if I'd said something odd. "Why would you visit me now . . . after all these years?"

I didn't want to tell her the truth—that I feared that I'd have to leave Rickard; that my growing disgust wouldn't allow me to live with a man who'd become embroiled with the Nazis; that I might have to live with her. I'd seen the National Socialists' handiwork and had had enough. I was also scared that my identity as the author of *The Berlin Woman* would be compromised, possibly by Rickard himself. All of us, including my daughter, could be harmed. I was growing paranoid under the Nazi threat.

"Now that I'm older and have a child . . . and husband . . . I'd like to see you more often. Maybe you'd like to visit us in the city?"

"Perhaps," she replied, but the answer was half-hearted. She stood, having had enough for one day.

As she was preparing to leave, I said, "There's one more thing . . . I've written a novel and it's doing quite well. It's called *The Berlin Woman*."

The title meant nothing to her. My mother was never a reader except for her magazines. I was the one who'd written poems and short stories, taken books out of the library, filling the dark days of autumn and winter—a child who considered the glamour publications a superficial exercise in reading entertainment, passable only for a new word now and then or an interesting picture. "I wanted you to know because Hitler and the National Socialists don't like it." That caught her attention. She returned to my bed and looked down on me.

"Why would you write a book like that? Are you mad?" Her eyes narrowed to tight, gray balls. "You've seen what they can do. You must know what they can do? They could come after me."

"No one knows who I am—no one except Rickard. I wanted you to know in case someone questions you. You don't have to admit anything."

"Why write at all?"

"Because the urge is in me—more so than acting. I write about life—what's it like for the modern German woman."

"Bahh," she said, almost spitting out the interjection. "Modern German woman be damned. That's the kind of thinking that'll get you into trouble."

"I'm sorry if you don't approve, but I'm making real money for the first time in my life. I could live on my own if I wished to."

She scowled, then turned to the door, but stopped before opening it. "You are my daughter, and as much as I don't understand you, God says I must love you." She stared at me. "You've made mistakes because you believe the world is for you. You can't have everything like you want it. That's the thinking of a lunatic." She trundled out and left me alone with Laura.

I sighed and wondered if my mother might be right. I had made some terrible choices. Why write about the New German Woman? Because I lived that life. Why resist the National Socialists? Because it was the right thing to do.

I cradled Laura to my breast and, for a time, forgot about the world's troubles. I looked into that innocent face and basked in her love.

When Rickard picked me up after my hospital stay, I was surprised to find how much he had changed. He was dressed in black pants and a white sweater. The puffy darkness under his eyes had disappeared. The stiff, stress-induced attitude he'd displayed in previous months had been replaced by a breezy, pleasant demeanor that almost obliterated the tension bubbling in our relationship.

At home, he took Laura from my arms and led me to a corner of the great room next to our bedroom. There, in sight of the bed, but far enough away to give us nighttime privacy, sat a new bassinet and a bentwood rocking chair. "It's for our daughter . . . and you." He placed the baby on her back in the bassinet and pulled a beautiful red silk comforter up to her chest. He cooed over her, took off her cap, and stroked her hair. "My God, she's glorious."

My heart was once again shifting in Rickard's direction. His contradictions continued to confound me—how he could be such a loving father and at the same time support the hideous regime that threatened to wreak destruction? Was I the only one in Germany who sensed a coming disaster?

"Where did you get all this, and how did you know what to buy?" I asked.

"I went shopping with a little help from Mrs. Spiegel," he said. My stomach dropped, but I kept the smile on my face. "I telephoned and she told me what we absolutely had to have. Cloth diapers, a rattle, some kind of swinging contraption with toy birds positioned over the bassinet, to occupy her time." He dug the rattle out from under the comforter and placed it near Laura's tiny clenched fist. "The kitchen is loaded with baby formula if you need it." He looked at my breasts.

"I'll be fine for a while," I said. "She's already partaken."

"Would you like a drink?" he asked. "You deserve it."

I shook my head.

He walked to the bar. "No? Still not drinking?"

"No stomach for it now. The thought of cherry brandy makes me gag."

"Lotti won't believe her ears," Rickard said.

"I suppose Rudi won't either."

He stopped mixing his drink and turned to me. "Let's forget about the past."

I pulled the rocker next to the bassinet, trying it out, and looked at Laura, who squirmed happily one moment and then scrunched up her face the next as if she was suffering from cramps.

He walked toward me with a cocktail I didn't recognize. "Something new?"

"Scotch with soda water." He sipped the drink. "If you know the right people . . ." He sat on the floor, his legs crossed in front of me. His demeanor darkened a bit before he began. "Seriously, Niki . . . I know things have been strained lately, but Laura gives us a chance to start over. I'll be a good husband and father."

I felt sorry for him as he sat there looking doe-eyed. He was a victim of the modern world rushing toward Hitler. As that thought crossed my mind, I remembered what I saw at the studio. Wolf dressed as the hideous Jew about to be beaten. I recalled all the hate and anger that had been directed at

Anders, even the doorman at the Leopard Club. The continual parade of the SA thugs hadn't ended in Berlin, if anything it had swollen like a blood-filled leech.

"My mother came to see me," I said, deflecting his comment about fatherhood.

"Really? I didn't think you got along."

"We usually don't, but I wanted her to meet her granddaughter. I'll be visiting her more now . . . working to mend our relationship . . . she might even come here." I wanted to introduce the idea that Laura and I might be out of the house more often. "When I'm not writing."

Rickard nodded, and said almost casually, "I read your book." He pointed to the office. "There's a copy on the desk."

"You didn't need to buy it. I can get copies from Verlangen."

He put the glass on the floor and leaned back on his elbows. "I didn't buy it. Artur Berger was here."

I cocked my head, somewhat astonished that my editor and publisher would come to the apartment.

Rickard took note of my look. "Yes, he was here. He dropped off copies himself . . . told me how well the book was doing. Sales have surprised even him."

"I'm glad." I wasn't sure what to say.

"You never let me read it, Niki. It's a dangerous book. Spiegel's wife was fuming . . . he was too."

"They don't—"

"No, they don't. You were wise to change the character's name to Charlotte and publish it under a pseudonym. They'll have to dig to find out who wrote it—unless they go after Verlangen, but Berger doesn't seem the kind of man who breaks easily."

I exhaled and looked at my daughter, who had blissfully fallen asleep in the bassinet.

"I told Berger he should never come here again," Rickard said. "He could give everything away." He rose from the floor, bent over Laura, and kissed her forehead. "Are you tired?"

"I need to feed her; then I'm going to bed."

He watched as I breastfed Laura in the rocking chair before placing her in the bassinet. I knew a long night was coming. Rickard must have sensed it, too, because he lay next to me on the bed, the warmth of our bodies making me feel comfortable and drowsy—to a point.

Nazis infiltrated my dreams. Laura and I might be safe with Rickard for a time, but what would that safety cost us. I couldn't condone what was happening in my country. Politics was tearing Germany apart, a feeling so deep that I couldn't be rid of it. The specter stood in the shadows as Rickard kissed our daughter. I fell into an anxious sleep dreaming of Brownshirts . . . the SA were stalking me like I was a hunted deer.

As if to echo my nightmares, Laura cried every couple of hours and I raced to comfort her.

# CHAPTER 10

The good wife of Herr Spiegel, and who knows who else in the Nazi Party, read these words near the end of *The Berlin Woman*:

*I pack my two leather suitcases for I must leave Martin. Everything is clouded, empty, and confused. A woman can look out for herself, and, when in need, even cry out for help, but the world looks down on her. Sympathy extends only to men. Men save sympathy for themselves. They are empathetic, a band of brothers, a controlling lot who see the world only through their eyes.*

*I'll miss the apartment with the touches I added: the ivory drapes, the black shades that blocked the light, the red chairs where we watched the sun go down. Now that he has successfully come to an understanding with those he doubted, he feels fulfilled.*

*I don't. The long voyage of discovery is just beginning.*

*The last valuable that I dare give him, I'm taking with me—our unborn child.*

*I lift the bags from the silk sheets of our bed, take*

*a last look at the rooms that were my home for longer*
*than I ever imagined, and walk to the door.*
    *As I close it, a soft hiss echoes in the hall.*
*Good-bye, Martin.*

I wondered what Rickard thought of those words, or if they registered at all. People often see themselves in novels, despite the author's objections; perhaps Rickard was too close to the material to grasp it, or perhaps he was so immersed in the world of movies and fiction that he felt those words couldn't be real. The novel was about our life together, and it seemed that every word, every scene, predicted the outcome of our relationship, ending in a break that I didn't look forward to, but had been ordained by the writer.

I didn't move out immediately, and for the rest of 1931 and into 1932, Rickard and I suffered no consequences from the book's publication. Berger and I met several times in his office to discuss the plot of my second novel, *Confessions of a Vampire's Wife*. He'd convinced me, for the sake of Verlangen's readership, to make the book a romance with minimal bloodshed and somehow steer the book in the direction of a modern, German vampire. So, I revised it, making my blood-sucking fiend less bloodthirsty and more of a hero. My early draft was thrown out, and *Confessions* became a contemporary vampire novel set in Berlin with lots of lovemaking and limited ferocity. I wasn't happy about the editorial direction the book had taken, but I opted for money rather than art as the Nazis continued to make progress toward their political goals.

My wish to leave Rickard fluctuated even as we "got along." I had to admit that part of me loved him, while another part of me couldn't stomach his relationship with the Nazis. The main reason I hadn't moved out lay in the bassinet outside our bedroom. Laura was getting stronger every day, but I wanted to make sure that my baby could travel, be shuffled from house to house if required, and suffer no ill effects.

*Confessions of a Vampire's Wife* was published in the fall of 1932. To my surprise and the great glee of my publisher, the book was an even bigger success than *The Berlin Woman*. Herr Berger told me that the book didn't sell well the first week because of the implied horror, but after my readers learned that my vampire was a hero, in love with his wife, and dedicated to saving her and their love every sunset, the novel sold out in stacks. The book was the fastest seller in Verlangen history. I believed that the figures had more to do with the times we lived in than my command of my art. Women were looking for a romantic escape.

I marveled at the sales and collected my royalties on our prearranged basis when they were due. I hid the money, in larger bills, in an envelope taped to the back of the wardrobe. Rickard asked me if I was getting paid, but I told him that the novels were breaking even and not much was to be made. I don't know if he believed me, but he never asked if I was secreting funds. One day, I saw a group of women standing outside the front of a bookstore chattering about my novel. It was handsomely displayed in the window, surrounding a rather Germanic-looking mannequin dressed in evening clothes and showing fangs. I was the proud author that day, although I never revealed myself.

But then at noon on January 30, 1933, the unimaginable happened and the world paid dearly for it for more than twelve long years and for many decades after the war ended.

Hitler became Chancellor of Germany.

Were we prepared for what was to come? Many of my fellow Germans saw Hitler as a savior, a man prepared to restore our country to its past greatness. Most only wanted to be prosperous and happy in the face of economic uncertainty. However, a powerful flood flowed over the people, a movement that began as a ripple and led to waves of hysteria, culminating in war. I could only speak for myself, but I saw the smiling faces of the boisterous Germans who stood along Hitler's parade routes. War may have been on their minds, but something far more sinister warped their emotions—the notion of invincibility—the feeling that the state was without fault and would fulfill its grandiose obligations, crushing any people, institution, or country that stood in its way. The German people accepted this "invincibility" as fact.

But there were those, myself included, who believed Germany was headed for destruction. Those who rejected Hitler might as well have lived in the sewer. Our thoughts and feelings were buried, relegated to the underground, and the feeling of paranoia grew proportionally as the Nazis consolidated their power. For us, dread, loathing, and fear were fast becoming a way of life.

It didn't take long for the Nazis to reveal their true selves.

Rudi, his ears ever open at the Leopard Club, heard the rumors first. He called Lotti, who then called me.

"Tonight, at the Opernplatz," she said somewhat breathlessly after I picked up the office phone. Whatever she had to say was weighing upon her.

"What? Calm yourself."

"I'm fine," she protested. "It's you I'm worried about." She paused to take a few breaths. "Rudi overheard a few university students at the club. They're planning a book burning tonight. Goebbels is to speak, and many books are to be torched in the square. They've already raided the library of Dr. Hirschfeld's Institute for Sex Research." She paused again, and the connection between us tingled with danger before Lotti resumed, a chill in her voice. "I think your books will be among them."

The idea was so preposterous that I almost laughed out loud. "My books? The German woman I write about is a threat to the Nazis?" Of course, I wanted to reassure myself that I wasn't in trouble, that I wasn't a threat to the National

Socialists, but I'd suspected the worst for years. The icy cold that permeated my body on that late Wednesday afternoon of May 10, 1933, confirmed my suspicions.

I looked at Laura, now a strong little girl nearing two years of age who lay napping in her bed, and knew that the purge had begun. But despite whatever fear, trepidation, or intimidation I felt, I needed to be strong for her.

"Rickard should be home soon," I said. "He'll look after Laura. Come at eight and we'll walk to the Opernplatz. I'll tell him we're going for coffee. I want to be there when history is made."

Lotti agreed, but as soon as I hung up the phone I wondered if I'd made the right decision. I wouldn't be able to tell Rickard . . . another secret between us. And I asked myself if my eyes and stomach were strong enough to withstand the sight of any book, let alone mine, being burned in the square.

Rickard raised no fuss when he got home from the studio; in fact, I think he liked the idea of spending the evening alone with Laura. I told him that Lotti and I were going for coffee and I might be later than usual because we hadn't seen each other in several months.

The spring night was deceptively calm as we left the apartment and headed to the Opernplatz. As we neared it, I felt the sparks filling the air before any fire had been lit.

"I'm nervous," I said to Lotti. "What are we getting into?"

"I told Rudi that we might go," she replied. "He said to be careful because these are members of the National Socialist German Students' Association. They're just as rabid as the SA."

She looked at me as we walked, her florid face shining like the sun under the streetlamps. Lotti was anxious, too, but I was driven forward by some force greater than myself. I wanted to see this travesty with my own eyes. I wanted to see the power over people generated by this new regime—people who might be considered normal in other circumstances.

We stopped for coffee before heading to the Opernplatz, and after sitting for a brief time, we continued our trek. As we approached the square my mood grew as dark as the night. I don't remember whether the weather was clear or cloudy. All I know is that the air and my thoughts turned as cold and desolate as the black sky.

A large crowd had gathered by the time we arrived. The square, dominated by the dome of St. Hedwig's Cathedral and the massive buildings surrounding it, thrummed with activity. As far as I could see, thousands awaited the arrival of the Propaganda Minister Joseph Goebbels. Mostly the participants were young with that optimistic, no-care-in-the-world look on their faces, many wearing Nazi armbands and strutting about the Opernplatz as if they owned it. On this night, they did.

A few, like Lotti and me, wandered about, taking in what was to be one of the first spectacles of Hitler's new power. Apart from the Nazi regalia, this gathering might have been a congregation of university students having a good time, but a closer look revealed the true purpose. Among the young men and women dressed in their school clothes and over-coats were the SA in their kepi hats, leather straps, ties, and black boots. Clearly, they were in charge while the rest of us remained interested or awed bystanders.

Singing broke out: the Horst Wessel Song, other *lieder* that sounded as if they had risen from the grave of Wagner, oaths declaring the perfection of the German race and promising death to traitors of the state. All of this was done and orchestrated by the student association to entertain the crowd. This planned event was more than a book burning—it was among the first of a long line of Nazi performances.

At one point, as the night passed by, I clutched Lotti's arm. "I'm not sure I can go through with this," I whispered to her as we brushed through the crowd.

"You can't back out now," she said. "I recognize a few

faces from the Leopard Club. It wouldn't be good to disappoint . . . if you know what I mean?"

I gazed at the fervent National Socialists around me and reluctantly agreed.

In time, we stood in the rim of people encircling a pile of books that had been thrown upon the stones. My throat tightened as I looked at the volumes strewn about. I didn't know at the time what books had been tossed upon the square. I found out later that Ernest Hemingway, Helen Keller, Jack London, Freud, and Einstein were among the authors burned that night, along with tomes by the great Germans Heinrich and Thomas Mann. Other notable, and lesser-known novelists, myself included, were destined for the flames.

After a florid introduction, Goebbels, bottled up in his double-breasted tan coat, arrived and assumed his place behind a lectern decorated with a large swastika. The Propaganda Minister, invited by the students, gave a perfunctory speech, punctuated by accented words and the theatrical thrusting and lowering of his arm. However, his style didn't interest me. I paid attention to his words.

"The era of extreme Jewish intellectualism is now at an end," he said. "The future German man will not just be a man of books, but a man of character. It is to this end that we want to educate you. As a young person, to already have the courage to face the pitiless glare, to overcome the fear of death, and to regain respect for death—this is the task of the young generation. And thus you do well in this midnight hour to commit to the flames the evil spirit of the past . . . from this wreckage the phoenix of a new spirit will triumphantly rise."

As he ended his barrage, I looked at his rat-like face and saw instead death's head—a living being, skeletal, grinning, calling those young students to their demise, intellectually and physically. Those who followed would have their minds warped by the power of his words and, most likely, die.

I clutched Lotti's hand as Goebbels left the lectern, signaling the burning to begin. I looked at my watch—it was midnight. We stepped back a few rows from the rim to conceal ourselves from the ritual that was about to play out.

A group of male students dressed in knee-length pants and white shirts began their circular march around the pyre. They carried Nazi flags, and their chants rose into the air as the first torch was thrown; other torches followed in flaming spirals. The books ignited in a conflagration, lifting yellow flames into the sky and scattering heat through the crowd. Brownshirts, guarded by fully uniformed Nazis, gathered armloads of confiscated books and threw them gleefully on top of those already burning. The students continued their chants and circles around the fire.

"What are they saying?" Lotti asked me as the books were thrown.

I shook my head, trying to listen. "They're oaths of some kind." I listened hard before replying. "They're saying why the author's books are being burned, and declaring their loyalty to Hitler and the state."

A young man brushed by me. Out of the corner of my eye, I saw the covers of *The Berlin Woman* and *Confessions of a Vampire's Wife* clutched in his hands. He was headed toward the fire. I grabbed his shoulder, pulling him back. I wasn't much older than he.

"Why are you burning those books?" I asked, despite the surprised looks of the students crushed around us. The question caught him and the others off guard. He turned, his face obscured by the shadows, but I caught the sneer curling on his lips, the white teeth reflecting the flickering light.

"You dare ask me that question? Just look at these covers. They're immoral!"

I tried to calm him down. "The writer is so popular, though."

He raised the books level with my eyes, almost pushing

them against my face. "For two good reasons—*against* decadence and moral decay, and *against* the soul-shredding overvaluation of sexual activity. That's what I will declare as I toss them into the fire."

"There's no overt sex in those books," I said.

"You've read them? Perhaps *you* should be tossed into the fire."

Lotti tugged at my arm. "Let's go."

"Yes," I said to the man. "Go ahead and do your duty. Everyone will be watching."

His eyes burned like the flames and he trotted off. From the edge of the circle, he shouted oaths and tossed my books onto the swirling pyre, now rising at least six meters into the air.

I stomped away from the students, Lotti behind me, and didn't speak until we were well away from the crowd.

"I don't know whether to be scared and sad, or happy to be in the company of such subversive authors," I said as we walked back to the apartment. The lights of Berlin that I so enjoyed seemed strangled and mute. The anxiety that had plagued me as we walked to the square had transformed to a deep sadness.

Lotti put her arm around my shoulder. "Everything will be fine."

I stopped and gazed at the cars parked along the boulevard. "No, everything's gone to hell, including my writing career. That came to an end tonight. They'll be looking for me. I have to be one step ahead of them."

"What do you mean?" Lotti asked.

We walked a bit before I replied. "I'll sue them."

"Sue the National Socialists?" Lotti's face turned even more florid than before. "That's ridiculous. You don't stand a chance of winning."

"Maybe not . . . but at least I will have stood up to them. But it means more than just time in court. It means revealing my identity and leaving much of my life behind."

Lotti sighed, but said nothing.

Soon, we arrived at the Unter den Linden apartment, the stone steps leading up to the massive glass door covered by the ornate ironwork—the most glorious place I'd ever lived. I looked at its windows. Everything was dark and quiet, far removed from the chanting crowds of the Opernplatz. The future under Hitler sickened me as I remembered the optimism I'd felt when I first climbed those stairs. I'd worried about my relationship with Rickard, as I did with any man, but I had the hope that it would work out. If it didn't, I knew the way to the door. Now, our lives together had become much more complicated. There was no easy way out.

"Try not to worry too much," Lotti said, after giving me a kiss on the cheek. "I'll call you in a couple of days. Must be off—work tomorrow."

I said good night, climbed the staircase, and traversed the hallways to 3D—still as quiet as the day I'd arrived.

I opened the door, trying not to make any noise that would wake Laura. I walked to the bassinet near the bedroom door and studied her sleeping form bathed in the soft light of the city. She was on her back, the covers pulled up to her neck, her right thumb nestled against her mouth—as angelic a vision as I could imagine.

Not far beyond, Rickard slept in our bed, relaxed, unaware of what I'd just seen and experienced. In slumber, his soft breaths gave me some comfort, but the feeling was short-lived.

Germany had changed since Hitler had assumed power a few months before. In the past hours, I'd witnessed firsthand the consequences of a frightening new birth in our country.

The book burning had confirmed what I'd long dreaded. The time had come to take Laura and leave Rickard for both of our sakes. From this night forward we were all in danger, and more than anything, I wanted to protect our daughter. Rickard couldn't do that as long as he bowed to the Nazis.

# CHAPTER 11

My parents lived in a small house on Rosen Strasse in Rixdorf, part of the Neukölln borough of Berlin. According to my mother, my father had tired of paying rent and convinced the owner to sell him the modest dwelling in 1910. I was born a year later. I can't help but think that for the first time in their lives my parents had felt some degree of comfort and confidence. Fortune might have swung in their favor. That was probably the reason I was born.

But then the Great War broke out and everything changed for my family, including my father's death in the trenches of France.

The Knights Templar had settled Rixdorf almost eight hundred years earlier. Tempelhof Airport and Passport Pictures found homes nearby centuries later. Rixdorf always had been a haven for workers and the home of a large Bohemian community, which was not part of our ancestry. During its history, Neukölln moved in and out of the ever-expanding city of Berlin but finally became incorporated into it for good. The Nazi foothold in Rixdorf was tenuous. The Communist Party had a large following, culminating in the Bloody May riots of 1929 between the Berlin police and communist demonstrators. I'd moved out of my childhood home by then. My mother remained safe during the disturbances despite the actions of the police, who sometimes fired into residences.

I never loved the neighborhood, especially after my father died and my mother became a strict woman who felt it necessary to take on the role of two parents. I always dreamed of leaving when I looked at the old-fashioned cobblestones of Rosen Strasse from my bedroom window. I wanted to see more, to live in the city. Rixdorf had its share of nice, grand buildings and pleasant churches, but our home was like many others, cramped and small, a white-washed stone building with pale-blue trim around the windows, topped by a red-gabled roof.

The house had two "eyes," as I saw them, which looked out on Rosen Strasse. There were trees, verdant green in spring, yellow in the fall, and patches of grass that also changed colors with the season. Most of all, after my father died, I remembered the magazines my mother would read about Hollywood stars, glamorous women and handsome leading men. One might find it incongruous that a devout Lutheran would indulge in such fancies, but I think it said more about my mother than the magazines. Frieda was an expert at hiding her feelings beneath the plain clothes, the scrubbed face devoid of makeup. She was a prisoner in her own skin and having no way to escape her circumstances, she wished for more and lashed out when her own dreams and desires were foiled at every turn.

As a young woman, I had the choice to absorb her pessimism and fall into the same hole she'd dug, or strike out like any modern girl and make my own way. There were consequences to be borne, however, with any action regarding the latter. The price of freedom wasn't cheap.

I'd come to think of apartment 3D as something separate from me. As I stood in Rickard's office, on Monday morning, May 15, 1933, looking at the typewriter on his desk, watching Laura squeal and play with her doll near my feet,

I remembered what I loved and hated most about my childhood in Rixdorf.

All the memories that made me happy: the smell of baking bread; reading by firelight; the switch from a wood-burning stove to one of coal, which warmed the house so much I could feel the heat soaking into my skin; the golden, slanted rays of light that poured through my window during the summer as the sun moved north; shivering under my bedcovers during the winter when snow hushed the world, the bells of a horse-drawn sleigh being the only sound breaking the frozen silence. Reading and more reading; writing my poems and stories. My books kept me company.

All the memories that made me sad: my mother's loneliness and fear, the moments when I would catch her crying in front of the stove for no reason; the silence that greeted me when I touched her shoulder or kissed her cheek, trying as best I could to comfort her; my own struggle with isolation, and the feeling that I was alone in the world except for my books.

Laura grabbed my shoe and I flinched, having lost track of her for a moment. I didn't want my daughter to grow up like I did. I wanted to give her all the love I could, all the opportunities that Berlin could offer. But the world had descended into madness. The thought of taking her from her father, a man who loved her, caused my throat to tighten, my heart to crash in my chest.

But I'd made the decision. Laura and I had to leave—not only for our sakes, but for Rickard's as well. He was safer with me out of the apartment, as I would be. And I was taking my daughter with me. If the Nazis discovered who'd written *The Berlin Woman*, Rickard could claim that he had no idea and that "his wife" had deserted him—a woman on the run from her own decadent ways.

But before I could pack our things, the doorbell buzzed with the kind of insistency that marks bad news. I looked out the office window and, from above, spotted the figure of someone I knew—at least I thought I did. I picked up Laura and headed downstairs to find Artur Berger standing beyond the glass door, his form dissected by the filigreed ironwork. Rickard had warned him not to visit, but he had returned at some risk to himself and to me, I suspected.

When I opened the door, I clearly saw the damage that had been done. Beneath Berger's shiny monocle, a bruised face and black eye blossomed.

"Niki, may I come in?" the man asked in his usual refined tone. He wore a lightweight black coat over his gray suit and stood with his polished shoes firmly planted upon the stone steps. The walking stick that always accompanied him rested at his side. "I won't be a moment." His driver stood by the passenger door of a black sedan that idled behind the parked cars on Unter den Linden.

"Of course," I said. "This is my daughter, Laura." The two had never met. "Whatever happened? Were you in an accident?"

"One might call it an accident if politics can be considered as such," he replied as we walked up the stairs. "We should talk in private rather than in the hall."

Once inside, I gave Laura her toys and put her next to her bed to play. She stuffed her dolly into her mouth and swiped at the bird contraption that Rickard had attached to its side. I sat on one of the couches overlooking the street, while Berger stood, staring through the windows at the roofs and buildings of Berlin.

"Your husband told me not to come back," he began, "but, under the circumstances, I feel it worth the risk to bring you this unpleasant news."

I nodded, waiting for him to continue.

"The short version of the story is that on Friday the SA raided Verlangen and roughed me up." He turned and studied me with his sophisticated face. Even under the glare of lights and the purplish bruises that scarred his face, the man exuded confidence and determination. "They are animals, but they haven't seen the last of me—a man who loves Germany for all her faults. These beasts admire nothing but an insatiable disrespect for life and freedom." He tapped his walking stick on the parquet floor.

"I'm sorry," I said. "We've always known they were thugs and miscreants."

"Yes, a man named Spiegel called upon me. You may know him?"

I nodded uncomfortably.

"There's more to the story—there always is." He pivoted toward the window, staring out once again. I let him rest for a moment.

"God, how I love this city," he finally said. "I'm afraid it will be in ruins . . . all too soon." His voice caught and he reached into his pocket, brought out his handkerchief, and dabbed it demurely on his cheek. "They wanted you—they want to find the woman who wrote the two books that made you a literary success. They tore through the files, hoping to find your name, your address, anything about you. Apparently, Herr Spiegel's wife was offended by your books, calling them anti-German, heretical, and practically pornographic. Of course, I asked Herr Spiegel if he had read the books. He shook his head. I knew he hadn't."

"Please, sit for a moment. Can I get you anything?"

"I'm afraid not. I'd rather stand and face this atrocity."

"Did they find anything out about me?" I asked.

He eyed me again, adjusting his monocle with a wince. "No, they didn't get that far. Spiegel came with two men, but four of my rather burly pressmen escorted them out of the building after they went at me for trying to stop their uninvited investigation. 'Escorted'—that's the polite word for it. I was afraid we'd all get shot, but apparently murder wasn't on their minds." He lifted the walking stick, wrapping his hands around its gold-tipped handle, planting it like a pillar in front of him. "Fortunately, after they left, I had the sense to remove all the author files and place them in the company safe, where only I can get to them at the moment."

"Oh, thank God. What a nightmare."

"Verlangen is not unscathed," he said. "Later in the day, a couple of Nazi toughs presented themselves to my secretary. They said nothing, but dropped an envelope addressed to me on her desk and then left . . . now I'm forbidden to publish your book, among many others . . . on orders from the Propaganda Minister . . . approved by the Führer, of course. Included in the envelope was a list of suggested and approved books I could publish, all with a National Socialist bent." He took a deep breath. "According to Goebbels, if I continue to break the government's orders, there will be consequences. The order didn't specify what those consequences would be, but I imagine they would be dire. If they can burn the Reichstag, as I imagine they did, they can burn my publishing house. If I want to keep my company, I have to follow their directions."

I was at a loss for words. I knew what Goebbels's order meant for me and for the press. I looked at Laura, almost on the verge of falling asleep on the floor, and thought about our future together. "I was at the book burning last Wednesday night—purely as an observer. My books were thrown on the fire."

"Germany has come to this. No one believed that Hitler would exert such authority, or that his followers would be so rabid."

"Rickard and I have known for years not to underestimate them. We've survived by bowing like slaves to them . . . but I will no longer."

"What about your husband?"

"I don't know. . . . He's survived by giving in to their demands. I'm going to sue them for loss of income." Needing a cigarette, I rose from the couch.

"Sue the National Socialists? Don't be mad. You could never show your face in court—it would be suicide."

"I'll get a lawyer."

Berger watched as I lit a Manoli. "It might bankrupt you. Hitler's courts would drag out your case until you have no more funds, time, or energy. They will never lose."

"Then, what am I to do?" I asked as I returned to the couch.

"Let my lawyers fight them. You won't have to be in court. My action will be on behalf of all my authors who've been banned. This is not just your struggle. We still have rights at the moment, but I'm afraid those won't last long. That's why we need to go to court now."

I knew that Verlangen was likely to lose as well, but what Berger said made sense. Perhaps, I could observe the trial from afar. I also had no idea what Rickard would do after I left with Laura. He might turn me in immediately to Spiegel, severely limiting my options. Everything was closing in on me and my daughter because I'd written two successful novels and defied the ideal National Socialist woman.

"I have something to tell you, but you must keep it in confidence," I said, extinguishing my cigarette. "It's too early for a drink, but I feel I need one." I walked to the bar and lifted one of the crystal glasses. Soon, even the feel of such glassware would be a memory.

"I'm leaving Rickard."

Berger looked at me, his lips tight, and his expression grimmer than when he arrived. "Do you think that's wise?"

"It's the only choice I have." I put down the glass. "I always wondered if our relationship might end up this way, but I didn't want to believe it. Rickard has fallen under the Nazi spell . . . and my career is ruined. When they find out that I'm the author—that I created my art, made my way in the world—they will go after him as well. The only positive in this whole affair is that he is useful to them. He provides a service they need. He'll probably walk out of the muck with his shoes clean."

"Well, good luck, my dear. I sympathize with and understand your reasoning entirely. My run-in with them was enough, but I'm prepared for more. Where will you go?"

"This you must keep secret . . . probably my mother's home on Rosen Strasse in Rixdorf. Everyone knows her, so you won't have any trouble finding me. That's a cause for worry, but I have little choice, unless a friend takes me in."

He started toward the door, but then stopped as if he'd remembered something important. "Naturally, your sales ended when the books were banned. I'm sure a little money will find its way to Verlangen—some final royalties—but don't count on them. If we have any additional payments, I'll get in touch with your mother. I hope you saved some of your earnings."

I nodded, thinking of the money and the bracelet still stashed behind the wardrobe. They were my security.

"Watch the papers for news of a lawsuit. I'm sure a publishing house suing the Propaganda Minister will make headlines. If nothing else, the Nazi Party papers will devour it . . . prepare for the worst."

He closed the door. I ran to the window and watched him get into his car. I admired the old man, thinking how brave he must be to take on the Nazis. I wished I had the same level of courage, but thoughts of bravery were extinguished by my child who had fallen asleep with her doll cradled in her arms. As Berger's car pulled away, I was reminded that I had one very important item to take care of—a note to my husband.

*Dear Rickard:*

*I can't say that the past year and a half has been fun or easy. Neither can I say that it's been a dreary disaster. In my way, I've loved you and I know that you've loved me, but the time has come for us to pull away from each other for our own sakes.*

My books have been banned, blacklisted by the National Socialists, and I suppose before too long they will find out who wrote them. When that happens, you will be in as much danger as I am, but I believe you will be able to charm them more than I will. It's better for me to be gone than for my stain upon their politics to smear you.

I'm taking Laura. This will cause you great distress, I'm certain, but I believe she needs a mother who now has much more time than a father who has little room in his life for her. Please don't look for us—I don't know where we're going. I implore you to act cautiously. Don't let revenge dominate your life.

Please know that I have loved you, but I love Laura more than anything on earth. I will do anything to keep her safe from harm.

I'm taking only our clothes and a few toys for Laura. When you walk into the apartment this evening, everything that remains will be as it always has been. I'm leaving the typewriter because I have no desire for writing now that my life has been turned upside down. Perhaps later, I may ask you to use it again. When I do, I hope I find you well. I've gotten rid of my books from your office, along with papers and notes. The Nazis will be thorough.

My best,
Niki

I signed the note and rested it on the typewriter keys, where I knew he would find it. It was better to let him know with words than with a brutal fight in front of Laura. Picturing the shock, fury, and tears to come this evening, I hoped that Rickard would find it in his heart to leave us alone for at least a little while. I was certain that after he read the letter, his mind would be racing with thoughts of how to get his daughter back. He'd sworn never to endure such a loss again.

The rest of the morning I packed, gathering everything essential that would fit into my suitcase and purse. I hid the bracelet and cash in a secret pocket I'd created in the lining of my coat. I'd wear it while carrying Laura and my luggage to Rixdorf.

I didn't even know if my mother would let me and Laura in the door.

# CHAPTER 12

I locked the apartment and put the key on the frame above.

I slung my purse over my shoulder, cradled Laura in my right arm, and carried the suitcase in my left hand. The trip to Rixdorf wouldn't be easy. Rickard, Spiegel, and the SA could find Lotti and Rudi easily. They'd have a harder time finding my mother because I rarely talked about her with Rickard, and he'd never met her. I could spend only a few days with her before they would come after me. I hoped that my husband, for the sake of his daughter, would honor my request not to look for us.

By the time we arrived at Rosen Strasse, Laura was spitting up and crying. I was exhausted. The walk and a series of tram rides had set my nerves on edge. The door to my mother's house was closed, but unlocked, as it always was, except at night. I stepped across the threshold, dropped my purse and suitcase near the couch, got some milk for Laura from the icebox, and calmed her in my old bedroom.

The house was almost the same as when I'd left it four years ago. My starched pillowcase, not used by another person since I'd gone, smelled of soap and bleach. Despite having no guests, I was certain my mother washed the bedding every week just as she did when I was living with her. The sheets were folded crisply underneath the spread. I lowered the shades and sang to Laura as she drifted into a restless sleep.

I closed the door and walked to the large room at the center of the house, plopping down on the couch my mother had used for years. The tan fabric was stained in spots, which I'm sure infuriated her. Scrubbing marks had scratched the fabric. Two needlepoint pillows resting on top of it were the only additions to the room. The pillows depicted rabbits, foxes, and other creatures cavorting in the woods. The artist had been influenced by the romantic notions of the Black Forest.

A pile of movie magazines sat on a utilitarian end table. The center table was equally ordinary, showing watermarks and nicks from usage. I marveled at how luxurious Rickard's apartment was in comparison to my mother's home. The odors of cooked cabbage and sausage lingered in the room. My nose was no stranger to those smells. No liquor, fancy barware, expensive furnishings, or expansive views could be found here. My mother's house was plain and claustrophobic, just as it had been years ago.

But I hadn't come to my mother's for babysitting services. When the home was built, a closet had been cut into the wall opposite the kitchen, very near the front door. As a child, I'd often retreated to that space, concealing myself behind the ironing board, the mops, and brooms that resided there. After I'd stumped my mother several times, she discovered my secret hiding place. Before my father left for the war, he created a false back for the closet so my mother could conceal what few valuables we had. Unintentionally, he'd made it large enough to hold a child. The space was too cramped for an adult. Laura could hide inside that closet—even if I couldn't. The problem would be keeping her quiet.

I fell asleep on the couch and my mother woke me up late in the afternoon. I bolted upright, staring at her with wide eyes, wondering whether she would admonish me for setting foot in her house. She held me in her gaze with an inquisitive look. I looked at my watch. It was still early enough in the evening that I doubted that Rickard had made his "discovery."

"I see you've come for a visit," she said, putting her shopping bags in the kitchen. She took off her sweater and draped it over a chair.

I suddenly felt contrite and humbled in her presence. She wore a pale-blue housedress and black shoes. Her reddish-brown hair was tied back in a bun from a face unadorned by cosmetics, the natural ruddiness of her cheeks being the only color. Her legs seemed a bit swollen at the ankles; a wreath of blue veins snaked under the skin. I became a child again, transported back to the days when I could do no right and she lorded over me with her vise-like grip. She busied herself with the groceries for a minute, placing a cut of meat in the icebox and pulling up a handful of carrots by their green tops. She was unaware that Laura slept in my former bedroom.

"I've come to ask you a favor," I said, feeling shaky, my hands trembling a bit.

"Yes?" Her eyes were blank.

"I've no place to stay. . . . I was hoping to impose on your kindness until I work things out."

She left the kitchen and sat in a chair across from me. "You've left your husband?"

"Yes . . . it's a complicated story, which I will tell you—but first I need to know that it's all right to stay here. Laura is in the front bedroom."

"Your old room." Her left eye twitched.

I caught the motion, a sign that she was nervous, too.

"Tell me now," she said.

I was in no mood to recount the tale of my marriage to Rickard, but my mother had me at a disadvantage. So, I told her everything, including my final days at the apartment, the book burning, and the visit from Herr Berger, my publisher. At times she seemed fascinated, at other times revolted by what I'd revealed. I warned her that Rickard, and possibly

the SA and National Socialists, were looking for me. Rosen
Strasse might figure in that search. She said nothing while
I talked. I was dying for a cigarette, but I knew she would
never let me smoke in the house.

The time dragged on. I looked at my watch and urged her
to say something—anything, because I wanted her anger and
dismissive attitude to blossom now rather than later.

Finally, she pointed to the stack of movie magazines on the
end table. "You wanted to be one of those women, living the
glamorous life, your face known around the world, making
pictures, drinking champagne, never having to worry about
money. Do you have any money?"

My coat with the cash and bracelet lay on the couch beside
me. I nodded. "You've dreamed that as well; otherwise, you
wouldn't read those magazines."

"You should have never crossed the National Socialists . . .
you should have never married a man who associated with
them."

The recrimination was building. "I told you . . . it was a
gradual process. Rickard said it was a matter of survival, and
I believed him because it was the same for me. My life has
been a game of 'getting along.'"

"You were a fool to listen to him. Now you're scared.
You've learned a lesson."

I wanted to lash out at her. She'd been the one who'd forced
me out of the house with her suffocating and controlling iron
fist. My mother had no idea how hard it was for a woman
with little money and no support to get along in Berlin. However, as I was living high with Rickard, she had retained her
small home, doing without, taking in laundry, cooking for
others, earning money here and there. We had both made
our own ways, and for that reason I had to respect her, if not
admire her fortitude.

"Mother, I don't want to get into an argument," I said.
"I've learned a lesson. Perhaps I made a mistake with Rickard,

living a modern life; but like thousands of women in Berlin, I survived, even though the choice may have not been the best."

She leaned back in her chair, her gray eyes piercing me. "You are my daughter who has carried my granddaughter into this world. God commands me to forgive and love you despite your faults. You've returned like the Prodigal Son . . . and I won't turn you away. But now you are under my roof and you must obey my rules. You won't smoke or drink here, you will say prayers, and you will honor me as God commands."

"Of course," I said, feeling my stomach tightening—a natural response to her demands.

"I don't care about politics," she continued. "If I had my way there'd be no politics, no man grasping for power, but you can't fight powerful men. I've learned that over the years. All the great Prussian and German men who wanted conquest got nothing but spilled blood in return. Your father paid with his life for their folly in the Great War. Communists still live in Neukölln, even after what happened in May 1929. I ignore them—I don't want any part of their politics any more than I want to be part of the Nazis. Still, you can't ignore what's happened in Germany." She paused. "You can move into your old room—I've left it the same—then you can help me with supper. With two more mouths to feed, there's much to do."

"I'm grateful," I said, hiding my disappointment at how much I'd fallen in one day. For a brief time, I'd been the toast of Berlin, albeit an anonymous one. I'd embarked on the longest relationship of my life, navigating my way through its often murky waters, as people do when they're young and uncertain.

How long could I stay here? I was certain that Rickard wouldn't be smashing the door down at midnight. He was more sophisticated and calculating than that. Even so, he might show up a day or two later, after he decided that Laura meant more to him than anything in his life. Maybe he'd take my note to heart and leave us alone, but I doubted it. In the meantime, Laura and I would try to get a good night's sleep.

The next morning, I told my mother that we needed a plan in case Rickard showed up. I knew she would never see her granddaughter again unless we protected Laura. My mother's heart had melted within hours of their meeting. In a short time, Frieda had grown to love Laura in the way that she loved me as a child—strict and disciplined in her fashion. Frieda showed Laura the proper way to eat her mashed carrots, the way to hold a spoon without spilling its contents, the way to say a prayer before breaking bread. I didn't stop her because I had no right to do so in her own home. Before long, I realized that it was more important for Laura to survive Nazi Germany than either my mother or me.

As a rehearsal, Laura and I got into the closet near the kitchen, but we couldn't fit into it. My daughter broke into tears when I playfully attempted to hide her alone in the tight space. The exercise was too cruel, so I gave up. The only other way of escape was through the back door, crossing through the neighbor's garden, making our way to a safe place.

For two days there was no sign of Rickard or anyone else who didn't belong on Rosen Strasse. But late in the afternoon of the third day, my mother flung open the back door, holding Laura in her hands like a sack of flour. I was sneaking a cigarette in the backyard because I couldn't smoke in the house. Fortunately, I'd stored all of our belongings in the closet's secret compartment in order to avoid discovery.

I could tell from my mother's eyes that danger lurked nearby. I grabbed Laura, who must have thought we were playing a game, for she began to laugh and throw her hands in the air. The day was splendid, the sun splashing gold upon the flowering bushes and plants of spring. My mother slammed the door as I cut through the garden. The tulip stems, without their colorful blossoms, shuddered in the breeze; the purple lilacs spread their potent perfume in the air. A rose's thorn scratched my right leg, and I looked down to see a trickle of blood just below my knee.

I turned west and was soon far enough away from the house that I was able to look down Rosen Strasse without fear. I recognized Rickard's green Mercedes parked at the curb. I wasn't sure that he was alone. A brief panic jolted me as I thought of Laura's doll in the front bedroom. I hoped that my mother had remembered to hide the toy.

Laura could walk in little steps as long as I held on to her, so I grabbed her warm, chubby hand and guided her to a small park near the town center. I found a bench surrounded by bushes. If I craned my neck I could look over the hedge and see who was approaching. We sat for an hour, watching sparrows hop across the stones and peck at the ground. Finally, Laura got cranky and began to squirm and holler, so I picked her up and retraced our route.

The Mercedes had disappeared. I walked behind the house, avoiding the thorns, and was soon at the back door, which I found open. Laura was eager to go inside, but I was anxious. My mother was nowhere in sight, so I softly called her name. She rose from behind the kitchen counter like a ghost with Laura's doll in hand.

"Oh, thank God you're here," I said. "I thought they had taken you."

Frieda scowled. "They? They'd never get away with that. All Rixdorf would have heard me scream. Come in . . . he's gone."

"So, it was Rickard—no one else?"

She handed Laura the doll and we sat together on the couch. "Yes. I can see why you married him. Nice looking, a gentleman if he wants to be, beautiful car. He must have had a wonderful apartment."

I sighed, irritated at her. "Mother, what did he say? I'm not interested in your opinion of Rickard or his possessions. He's in bed with the Nazis."

She pressed her palms against the ivy-patterned green housedress covering her legs. "He can be persuasive . . . very much so. He offered me a great deal of money if I would return you and Laura to him—if I saw you. He even brushed a tear from his eye."

Her words shocked me, but her stiff back and steely determination revealed that it would take more than money to betray her granddaughter.

"I told him that I hadn't seen you," she said almost blithely. "I asked how he'd found me. He said finding anyone is easy when you have friends in the Party. But he said he was concerned with your health and that of Laura's—that was how he put it. He begged me for help. He wants you to come back, saying all will be forgiven if you return."

I hugged Laura. "I can never return . . . and I don't believe him."

She turned toward me, her slate-colored eyes placid and resolute. "I wondered what you would say . . . if you had the stomach to turn him down . . . I don't believe him either. I don't believe any man who has too much money and power. Such men took my husband from me. As long as such men exist there will be wars, but I won't allow them to take my granddaughter. I saw him coming up the walk . . . I had just enough time to hand Laura to you and put her doll in the icebox."

I laughed as I thought of my mother rushing to rescue a doll. "Did he look around?"

"No. I told him to search to his heart's content. The offer seemed to satisfy him."

"He'll be back," I said.

"He or the SA." My mother closed her eyes and leaned back, resting her head on one of the needlepoint pillows sitting on top of the couch.

A sudden panic swept over me and I jumped up with Laura. "What am I to do? I can't stay here—I'm putting you in danger as well. I'm a pariah."

"I'm not even sure what that means. Calm down. We'll pray and the answer will come."

I shushed Laura, whom I'd alarmed with my sudden movement. "Prayers won't help. I'll move to an apartment," I said as I paced the room. "One nearby so you can see Laura. I can't live with Lotti or Rudi."

"Who are they?"

"My friends."

"Don't trust anyone." She picked up a Berlin newspaper a neighbor had given her. "I thought you should see this." She pointed to a small story on the bottom right of the front page. The headline read: *Verlangen Press Sues National Socialists.*

I grabbed it with one hand and read the story. The trial was to start the following Monday in a Berlin court. That would give me only a few days to find an apartment. As I stroked Laura's hair, I wondered how I could be a spectator in that courtroom without giving myself away. Perhaps it would be wiser not to go at all.

# CHAPTER 13

Let me define the word "paranoid."

You can't sleep because you're scared that SA thugs will knock down the door; you wake up in a sweat next to your daughter, crushing her to your chest so hard she almost loses her breath; you can't eat because your stomach is churning from anxiety; every unannounced movement is a threat, even those you catch from the corner of your eye—the branch bending in the wind, the shadow across the street that hides an assassin. The fear is so great you wish you had eyes in the back of your head. Life becomes a series of vivid flashes as you struggle to keep your sanity. Every sound becomes a shot that sends your heart racing.

Take those and magnify the paranoia by one hundred times and you'll know how I felt. I couldn't think clearly. My arms and legs acted as if they were immersed in concrete. My mother helped me through the terrible days after Rickard's visit. Would my fear grow worse? I saw no end to it.

Before the trial, Frieda and I plotted like spies. We decided that getting an apartment would be too much of a risk. I could adopt another identity, falsify my name, but papers would have to be forged. I didn't have the time or the expertise to do so. I couldn't use my name or my mother's without exposing myself. Documents could be easily traced. Rickard had had no trouble finding my mother after a couple of days. The Nazis would have an easy time as well now that they knew to keep their focus on Rixdorf and Neukölln.

We talked about the trial. The court would be stacked with Nazis and I dared not show myself. It was rare for a woman to be on trial, let alone an observer in court. Even if I disguised myself, or sent a friend like Rudi or Lotti, the SA would be watching for me or anyone associated with the banned books of Verlangen—anything out of the ordinary, anyone acting out of suspicion or fear, would be marked. It made no sense to put myself or my friends in danger just to witness a trial.

Late Saturday afternoon, two days before the trial started, I called Lotti in a panic from a booth. Although my mother had a phone, I didn't dare use it. By this time my paranoia was so deep, I even imagined that my friend's phone might be tapped. I hadn't told Lotti that I was leaving Rickard, only that there was trouble between us. Herr Berger had been the sole recipient of my secret.

I sobbed into the phone while my mother remained at home looking after Laura.

"I don't know what to do," I blubbered, thinking that my life was finished with the Nazis looking for me. "Nothing seems to work. Every possible solution leads to a dead end."

"It's simple," Lotti said. "Move in with me. We can sleep in my bed, and Laura can sleep on the couch. I have friends in the building who'll hide you if the SA comes calling." She chuckled. "A few in my building despise the Nazis."

I wiped my tears with a handkerchief and blew my nose. "But they will question you . . . about me. And I don't want to inconvenience you . . . what about your boyfriends?"

"Rickard has already been here. I told him I hadn't heard from you. I didn't even know that you had left him."

"Oh, God."

Lotti sighed. "He told me that Spiegel and the SA didn't know you were missing. He said he was most concerned about you . . . and Laura. I told him that I would give you that message if you contacted me and then I would call him. A bit of a ruse, but I don't think he'll show up again unless he gets desperate. He's not there yet. And don't worry about my boyfriends. I'll go to their place. You can stay here while I'm at work. When I come home, you can go out, concealed by darkness, and I'll take care of Laura. It'll be good training for my eventual motherhood . . . because that's what the Reich wants—happy mothers." She snickered. "Or we can find a babysitter and go out together."

"Are you sure? I don't want to put you in danger. I'll split the rent and food. It would help me so much."

"I pointed out Rickard to you at the Leopard Club, if you remember. Therefore, I've known him longer than you have. He doesn't want us dead, and he certainly doesn't want to hurt Laura."

"Would tomorrow be too soon?" I asked.

"Of course not. Come for lunch."

The weight dragging me down lifted somewhat. "You're such a good friend . . . I couldn't ask for better."

With the plan in place, I went back to my mother's and told her the arrangement I'd made. She avoided my eyes when I talked, gazing lovingly at her granddaughter. It pained her to see Laura go. I made no mention of her visiting me at Lotti's apartment because I didn't trust Rickard or the SA.

Sunday morning, I gave my mother fifty marks and left home, but not before it was prudent to do so. Satisfied that Rosen Strasse was safe, I left her, once again, to her solitary life. She kissed Laura many times and brushed away a tear.

"It won't be the last time you see your granddaughter," I assured her.

Lotti's apartment was about an hour away, a little east of my former room between the Berliner Dom and the Alexanderplatz. The building was of similar construction, about the same height, but without a central courtyard. Lotti's second-story rooms looked out on the street and were as noisy as Rickard's when the windows were open.

We had a good time that afternoon, talking and playing with Laura. Lotti prepared a nice lunch. Exhausted, we went to bed early because my friend had to work the next morning. It felt strange getting into bed next to her—that had never happened before—but it also was comforting. I fell into a deeper sleep than I'd experienced in weeks.

Monday morning after Lotti left, I called Verlangen and left word with Herr Berger's secretary that he or his attorney could reach me on the building phone if necessary. I gave her this information in confidence and told her that any caller should ask for the apartment number rather than my name.

The day dragged by, for I had nothing to do except entertain Laura, who at times was as cranky and bored as I was. Lotti had a few magazines scattered about and I read them all within a couple of hours. I listened to music on the radio and prepared lunch. Laura and I were napping in the midafternoon when a knock awakened me.

A young man stood in the hall, asking for Lotti, saying he had a call for the apartment number. He looked similar to the male students who'd attended the book burning. However, his smile was softer, his expression kinder, than those men. I explained that Lotti was at work—I was just visiting—but that I would take the call. He brushed his black hair away from his forehead several times as I talked.

"The phone is near the stairs," he said, and trotted off.

I looked back at Laura. She was asleep on the bed and I thought it safe to leave her for a few minutes to take the call. I closed the door but didn't lock it. I recognized Herr Berger's voice when I picked up the line.

"We lost," he said with a melancholy growl. "The trial was short . . . a travesty." He sounded tired, the usual enthusiasm in his voice giving way to defeat.

"I'd like to hear about it," I said.

"You were right not to come. It would have been dangerous." The line crackled and for a moment I thought he'd hung
up, but he came back on. "Meet me at Die kleine Rose at
seven. I'll be at a table inside."

The line went dead. I suspected that Berger was unnerved
by someone he'd seen.

I told Lotti what had happened and she agreed to look
after Laura while I met with Berger at Die kleine Rose near
the Alexanderplatz. The establishment was a typical *biergarten* with tables inside and out, a roof of colorful umbrellas
sheltering the terrace, and an accordionist playing German
songs approved by the Reich. A few young couples sat among
the older men and women who made up most of the clientele.
Die kleine Rose had been in business on its corner for many
years, although I'd never been inside. It had a reputation of
catering to a higher social class, charging a few extra marks
for "fine" beer and liquor. The triangular terrace, wider near
the street than by the door, held about twenty tables and
was surrounded on its three sides by high shrubs and flowering plants. Expansive windows that swiveled open in fine
weather separated the interior from the exterior.

I found Herr Berger seated at a small table at the back
of the restaurant, a glass of sherry sitting in front of him.
His hands were folded over the head of his walking stick.
He stood as I approached, and offered a pinched smile. The
bruises on his face from his run-in with the SA had faded to
a soft purple.

"The day has not been pleasant," he said, as I sat.

I took a cigarette from my purse and lit it. A waitress came
and I ordered a brandy.

"Before we go further with this conversation," he said,
"you should know that the owner of Die kleine Rose bends
with the political winds. He reminds me of your husband,

Rickard—he wishes his business to survive—and will do most anything, short of shooting people, to ensure that it does. I've known him for years—a good man at heart—he doesn't like the Nazis, but he's bowing to them."

The accordion music, a militaristic tune, seeped in from the front garden. I looked over my shoulder just in time to see two Brownshirts find seats at one of the last unoccupied terrace tables. The two men looked around, surveying their surroundings, making me very nervous.

Berger noted what I'd seen. "It's as safe for us to meet here as any place in Berlin. I've come here for years . . . I know the building much better than those young men."

"I feel like I can't make a move without someone watching me," I said. "Every day grows worse—because I wrote two books they hated."

He sipped his sherry and then frowned. "It's not just you, Niki. They're out to destroy anything they don't approve of—literature, art, music . . . people."

Our conversation halted before I asked, "What was the verdict?"

"In three hours, Verlangen was found guilty of publishing unhealthy, incendiary, and seditious material. Of course, those charges are crimes against the Reich. A man that Hitler apparently prefers to adjudicate such cases, Roland Freisler, the Ministerial Director of the Prussian Ministry of Justice, was handpicked for the trial." He shook his head. "He's a disagreeable man with a balding head and heavy-lidded eyes. He could have easily been a train conductor, but he's a fervent Nazi who spouts the same sort of bombast as our leader. He loves to yell in his red robes."

"I'll remember not to cross him," I said, looking once again at the SA men behind me. They seemed to be enjoying their beer.

Berger smiled. "You already have . . . and so has Verlangen. The company was fined five thousand marks for each offense—and the books have been banned for life. I must pay somewhere in the range of fifty thousand marks plus the expense of the trial. Freisler was adamant that the defendant pay all the court costs."

My jaw dropped at the sum. "Do you have that much to spare?"

He put his hand on mine and patted it, as if he were my elderly father. "Don't worry. The sum isn't a dinner bill, but the company has enough to cover the fines. It will hurt. The broader issue is the question of making a living in the future." He adjusted his monocle. "It may be time for me to retire."

"I'd hate that."

"So would I, but I have no confidence in Germany's future. The courtroom was filled with SA members and Nazi officers of ranks I didn't even know existed. They hung on Freisler's every word. Hitler has created a monster with his National Socialist Party."

He stopped, his eyes darting briefly around the room, at the oak bar across from us, and then outside.

"Get out," he whispered, "and don't come back to the table." He clutched his walking stick with his right hand and held it as if he were brandishing a sword. "The door at the end of the hall behind me leads to an alley and a side gate. Go through the gate to the neighboring restaurant and then out to the street."

I grasped his hand and said a quick good-bye. I looked back as I neared the door. Two more Brownshirts had taken places by the two already seated. All four were gazing into Die kleine Rose, as if they had spotted something of interest.

Once outside, I ran down the alley. After opening the gate, I found myself on the crowded terrace of another restaurant a couple of buildings east of Die kleine Rose. Sidestepping my way around the tables, I passed through the restaurant, finally finding myself outside. I crossed the street.

From my vantage point, I looked into Die kleine Rose.

Berger was surrounded by the SA men. They harangued him, their fists raised, arms swinging wildly. The customers stared at the scene inside but did nothing to help. A few robust men on the terrace, attired in their business suits, seemed to be enjoying the assault on my publisher. My face grew hot and my body shook, but I could do nothing to help poor Herr Berger. I thought of Laura, who I hoped was safe in Lotti's apartment.

A crowd had gathered opposite the *biergarten*. I withdrew inside its circle, watching as the men lifted Berger from his seat, pushing him down the narrow aisle, onto the terrace, and then shoving him into a black sedan that had pulled up to the curb. All of them climbed into the car, and, after a few seconds, the engine roared and the vehicle disappeared in the evening traffic.

Scared that I might be followed, I took a taxi to Lotti's. Nothing seemed out of place when I arrived. I trudged up the stairs to the apartment. The windows were open, and the gritty noise of cars and trams filled the room. Lotti sat on the couch, next to Laura, reading a story from *Grimms' Fairy Tales*, a book that nearly every German owned. Regardless of their content, I had read them when I was a child. The often brutal tales fueled my young imagination—fables that were supposed to instruct, to teach right from wrong. After a particularly gruesome tale, I found it hard to sleep, the story forming a nightmare in my head. I was unhappy when I saw the book in Lotti's hands, for Laura might suffer from the same nightmares, but now wasn't the time for a lecture about fairy stories. I preoccupied myself with the ordinary environment until my friend came to the end of the tale; then, I told her what had happened at Die kleine Rose.

Shivering, my arms covered in gooseflesh, I dropped to the couch ready to burst into tears. A rather savage knock interrupted us. Instinctively, I grabbed my daughter, rushed to the bathroom, and closed the door.

"Lotti . . . phone for you," a gruff male voice complained. "Tell your gentlemen that they mustn't call at this hour. It's almost nine, nearly my bedtime."

"Thank you," I heard Lotti say. "I'll tell him." The apartment door closed.

A few minutes later, Lotti returned, while I sat on the toilet with Laura in my arms. "You can come out," she said, after knocking.

I walked out with Laura in my arms.

"My God, Niki, you're pale as death."

Her complexion was equally wan. "You don't look much better. What I saw this evening was nothing compared to the book burning." Laura squirmed, eager to be placed on the couch with her toys.

"I don't know how to say this," Lotti said.

"Herr Berger . . . they've killed Berger!"

"Don't think it! No! Berger instructed a man from Verlangen to call the apartment number. The SA demanded immediate payment of the fine. Berger complied, otherwise things would have been much worse. But in the car, they made threats. . . ." Lotti seemed unable to go on.

"Please, tell me."

"They threatened to kill the authors of the banned books."

I slumped on the couch with Laura in my arms, wanting to cry, but the tears wouldn't come and my voice seemed locked in my throat. I didn't want to believe what I was hearing, but I knew Lotti was telling the truth. A sickness flowed through me, weakening my limbs, and I sank to the floor unable to move.

"They want me dead," I managed to whisper. Laura, my mother, Lotti, and even Rudi were in great danger because of my books. "Oh, God, Lotti, what am I going to do?"

She cried out like a wounded animal and shook her head. "I don't know."

# CHAPTER 14

The next few days, I confined myself to Lotti's apartment. Each day I expected bad news, which, fortunately, didn't come. Laura was the only bright spot in my miserable life. She kept me occupied; otherwise, I would have gone mad from boredom. I couldn't write, couldn't take walks during the day, and couldn't socialize with anyone. I even dreaded making a phone call from the building. I might as well have been in a nunnery, taking vows of chastity and silence. Those were the physical aspects.

Emotionally, nightmares of violence and abduction haunted me—Lotti shook me awake at night—the isolation had me teetering on the edge of depression. Only the weather cheered me. Summer had turned the grass green, the trees to full leaf. The breeze, silky and warm, brushed against my skin; the sky radiated a serene blue on most days. The lovely air pouring in the window kept my spirits up.

Lotti held up well, but I knew the longer I stayed the harder it would be for her. Our arrangement had to end.

One evening, Lotti came home in a shambles from work. Her eyes were red and puffy and her hair, usually braided with never a strand out of place, fell down to her neck in unruly curls. I studied her with concern.

"Rudi was attacked this afternoon," she said, wiping her eyes. "He called my office. He's at home and needs help."

"What happened?"

"I don't know. He wouldn't talk about it on the phone."

The sun was still out, for the evenings were long. Of course, Lotti and I answered Rudi's call. It was too short notice to find someone to stay with Laura, so I grabbed my daughter and her doll and we were soon on our way.

I hailed a taxi to Rudi's apartment in Friedrichshain. The ride would be faster and safer than walking. The car carried us east, the sun warming our backs through the rear window. Rudi's apartment building was constructed of white stone, rising five floors above the street in a neighborhood filled with similar structures. The façade was dotted with small balconies, while a pointed turret stretched to the sky from its center.

I paid the fare and we got out of the taxi. "Have you been here before?" I asked Lotti.

"A few times," she answered rather meekly.

The door was open and we walked in. The hall smelled of boiling water and noodles, not unpleasant, but a bit suffocating in the heat.

"He's on the top floor," Lotti said. "That may be why he needs help."

We trudged up the stairs, both of us sweating and out of breath by the time we reached the landing.

Lotti knocked on a red metal door and a weak voice, almost a whisper, answered. "Come in, it's unlocked."

My friend opened the door to the small one-room apartment, much like the one I'd had before moving in with Rickard. I cringed when I saw Rudi and tried to shield Laura's eyes from the sight, but she knocked my hand away, apparently more interested in the man lying on his back on the bed than being frightened or sickened by the view.

Crutches lay across the foot of the crumpled bed. Rudi's right leg was wrapped in bandages as was his right cheek. His eyes were blackened, and his nose appeared lopsided and flushed with blood. As we entered the room, his grim expression turned sour when he saw Laura and me.

"What's she doing here?" he asked Lotti, while pointing in my direction. "I asked you not to bring her."

Lotti moved toward the bed. "Rudi . . . Niki's come to help . . . besides I don't remember you saying that. I was so confused—upset when you called."

"Well, it's too late now, isn't it?" He moved his head toward the window and groaned.

I didn't know what I'd done to deserve such treatment, but I felt terrible for Rudi.

"Can someone close the curtain?" he asked.

I walked past his bed to a glass door that opened to a small balcony overlooking the street. A heavy, red velvet curtain had been hung over it. I pulled it shut, plunging the room into darkness.

"Now the light," Rudi said.

Lotti flipped a switch and a bedside lamp burst on. "Who did this?" she asked, standing near him.

"Who do you think?"

Neither Lotti nor I answered.

"Volker brought me home."

I remembered the name—the owner of the Leopard Club.

"I was just about to start my shift when they tried to pull me into a car. I think it was Spiegel, whom you've talked about, and two of his men. I think they were the same ones who attacked Rickard and Walter, our doorman, that night long ago."

My skin crawled at the mention of Spiegel's name. I moved to the foot of the bed, where I could see Rudi's face clearly.

"What did they want? Why did they beat you up?"

"I . . . I . . . don't know."

I knew he was lying. The only reason they would have jumped him was to get to me. The question that rang in my head was, *"Did he talk?"*

"I need food—enough for a couple of days." He grimaced as he shifted his head toward Lotti.

"I'll go," she said. "What would you like?"

"Something I can fix with little effort . . . some milk . . . some noodles. I smelled them in the hall. The grocer's at the end of the block. Money's in the drawer." He pointed to the nightstand next to the bed. His arm flopped on the mattress. Raising it had caused him pain.

Lotti gathered the money and left, leaving Laura and me alone with Rudi.

"This is your daughter," he said. "We haven't met."

I looked at his red and raw face and saw the fear that still glittered in his eyes. "Why would the SA do this? Spiegel has Rickard under his control—they didn't rough up Volker or Walter today. You were singled out."

He nodded in a slow, methodical manner, the small movement hurting him.

"Oh, God, it's like fire shooting through my neck," he said, exhaling. "They threatened to break my legs . . . one of them slashed a blade across my face, just deep enough for it to bleed, but they wanted more blood. I could tell from their voices, from the fire in their eyes."

"They want me, don't they?"

He closed his eyes as tears threatened to burst forth. "Yes . . . I had to tell them. They threatened to cut my throat and I knew they would do it. I'm strong, Niki, but I'm not strong enough to take on three of them. I tried to fight, but they were brutal."

"Lotti told you I was living with her." It wasn't a question, but a statement of fact. I should have known that the two friends could never keep that deep a secret from each other. I wasn't angry at Lotti because I knew how close they were, how they relied on each other for fun and company. I was upset with myself for not anticipating it. The SA could have beaten Lotti, but it would have looked bad to beat up a woman, although I'm sure they would've shown no regret. Now, I knew I had to leave her apartment. I had little doubt that Rickard had cracked and told Spiegel about Laura. The SA officer and his thugs had decided to find Laura as a favor for my husband, I suspected. After all, he still was aiding their cause as far as I knew.

He nodded again as Laura squirmed in my arms and wiggled her stubby fingers toward Rudi's bandaged head. "Forgive me," he said.

"You saved your life . . . we know what these people can do."

We stared at each other for a time, waiting for Lotti to return. I wanted a cigarette.

Rudi must have judged my need for tobacco from the look on my face. "Put her beside me . . . as long as she doesn't kick, I'll be all right. Have a smoke on the balcony." Laura was unafraid of the man and more than willing to sit on the bed next to him.

The sun was setting as I stood outside and pondered my fate. The sky had turned purple on the horizon as pink clouds sailed overhead. The breeze was beautiful and at any other time would have felt glorious against my skin. Now, the silky air mocked me, inviting me to enjoy a life scattered in pieces. I sighed and peered over the balcony. I spotted Lotti heading back from the grocer with two bundles in her arms.

Obviously, I couldn't stay at her apartment any longer. Perhaps we'd spend one last night together—then, in the morning, I'd gather my things and move on. But where would I go? That was the question to be answered. Perhaps, Lotti had a friend. . . . Since I'd left Rickard, I had used about one hundred of the five hundred marks I'd saved.

I stubbed out the cigarette on the balcony railing and went inside. Laura's head was snuggled against Rudi's left arm. Both were ready for sleep.

Lotti walked in with the groceries and Rudi perked up.

"Put the perishables in the icebox," he said.

I looked at the white porcelain appliance tucked away in a corner. It was even smaller than my mother's.

"I brought you fresh ice," Lotti said, pulling out a mound of butcher's paper that held the precious frozen liquid within its wrapping. A flashing trail of water dripped from the edges.

Rudi said nothing as Lotti unpacked the groceries. I picked up Laura, knowing it was time to go. Lotti shifted on her feet, aware of the silence in the room.

"I'll check on you tomorrow after work," she said, breaking the stillness.

"Thank you. I'll feel better." He extended his left arm, wanting me to take his hand.

I did.

Lotti glanced at me and then looked away.

We said good-bye and headed for the stairs. As we descended, I said, "Rudi told me. They want me . . . they're looking for me. The SA beat the answer out of him."

Lotti studied me, searching for my anger, her eyes wide and sad. "I'm sorry. I never thought this could happen. We're all friends."

"I'll have to move. Maybe one night longer, and then Laura and I will go."

She stopped at the bottom of the stairs and we stood in the warm hall as the mundane details of life surrounded us: the odor of noodles and beef mixing in the air, the murmur of voices down the hall, the sound of a waltz playing on the radio.

"This is my fault," Lotti said, and she began to cry.

Laura reached out to touch her, not liking the sound of misery. I put my free arm around Lotti. "There's nothing to be done now. If they hadn't gotten what they wanted from Rudi, they would have gone after you."

Sobbing, Lotti took a handkerchief from her purse and blew her nose.

"Let's go home," I said.

We got into a taxi. Lotti managed to compose herself by the time we arrived at her apartment. The sun had set and daylight died in the west. The breeze had dropped, and the thick and humid air clung to us.

I looked around as the car left. The green bushes surrounding the building had turned dull in the light. Nothing moved.

I stepped toward the door with Laura in my arms.

That's when I saw him.

Spiegel stood in the hall in his brown uniform, glaring at me, his hand gripping his pistol. Seconds later, the two companions who had beaten Rudi jumped from behind the vegetation that had concealed them. They grabbed me by the arms. I clutched Laura as she screamed in fright. Her cry cut through my body.

Lotti stood immobilized behind me. I screamed and kicked at the men holding me. Suddenly, my friend bolted toward them, pummeling them on the back with her fists. One of them turned sideways and, with his strong arm, planted his hand on her face, shoving her to the stone walk. Across the street, a few passersby looked on but did nothing but gawk in the presence of the Brownshirts.

I screamed for help, but no one came.

Spiegel stepped slowly out of the hall, the pistol raised in his hand. "Don't struggle, Niki, or you're likely to get shot. You're an enemy of the Reich."

"Don't hurt my child," I said, as a mixture of rage and terror coursed through my body. Had it not been for Laura, I would have fought with greater intensity.

"That's far from my mind," he replied, sauntering up to me, a conqueror assessing his conquest. "I want your daughter, nothing else." He stopped, putting his face so close to mine I could smell the lemon cologne on his skin. His narrow eyes bored into mine and he spoke as if the devil had possessed him. "I could take her, put a bullet in your head, and the Führer would give me a medal. We know who you are . . . we know what you've written . . . and we know how you kidnapped a child from her rightful father—a loyal supporter of the Reich. For those transgressions alone, you should give her up willingly."

"This is all Rickard's doing," I said, seeking confirmation of what I'd suspected all along.

He ran the pistol's barrel along the side of my face. Laura cowered in my arms.

"Your husband is a friend of the Party. The return of his daughter is a reward for his service. I'm sorry that you've strayed so far from him." He tucked his pistol in his holster.

"Leave her alone," Lotti said, rising from the ground. "She's done nothing wrong."

"Shut her up," Spiegel ordered.

One of the men let go of me, turned to Lotti, and slugged her in the face. The other held me tight around the waist as I watched. I could do nothing with Laura in my arms. Lotti dropped to the ground like a stone.

"Now we can talk freely," Spiegel continued as if nothing had happened, "let me tell you what Rickard has offered for the return of his daughter, with our blessing, of course."

I gasped for breath as Laura started to cry.

"He will give her a home and the comforts you cannot, but you will never see her again. Don't try to get her back, or come looking for her. He has his reasons for wanting his daughter." He paused. "Your books are dead. You will never write again, for the Reich will live far longer than you. And if you do write any of your obscene, traitorous words, we will kill you and your friends. If you comply all will be well. It's as simple as that." He smiled. "Now, hand her over, or we will take her by force."

Two headlights flashed over my body. I turned my head to see a black car pull up to the curb. Another SA man was driving.

"Please, don't take her." My body trembled as I spoke the words.

"That's not possible." He reached for Laura.

I held on as tightly as I could but finally had to relinquish her as they pried at my fingers. I didn't want to risk hurting my daughter.

Laura's screams sliced through me, penetrating my heart. She was gone in seconds, whisked away in the dark. I could do nothing but stand and watch.

I managed to stumble to Lotti, who was still stretched out across the stones. I touched her cheek, lifted her head, and tried to rouse her, and after some prodding, her eyes flickered open and she looked up at me. "What the hell?" she asked. "Where am I?"

"In front of your apartment," I said, "but I'm afraid you have a terrible bump on the back of your head."

She rose from the ground slowly, pushing herself up on her elbows. "I remember this man coming toward me . . . where's Laura?"

I managed to get out the words. "They've taken her to Rickard. They took her from my arms."

"Oh, God," she said, managing to hug me while we both huddled on the ground.

I got up and wiped the dirt from my dress. "I will get her back."

"There's no end to this madness," Lotti said, stroking the back of her head. "We'll sort this out."

"There's nothing to sort out," I said, but thought, *I hate them and I will get my daughter back. I will get Laura back.*

We brushed the dirt from our clothes and then trudged up the stairs.

# CHAPTER 15

I stayed with Lotti a few more days, until I couldn't stand it anymore. With Laura gone, nothing seemed to matter. My anger at Rickard, Spiegel, and his thugs simmered until I thought I'd gone mad. There was little to do except cry and beat the pillows on Lotti's bed.

If nothing else, I was convinced that Spiegel would keep his promise regarding me and my friends, if I kept my word. Most of my anger was directed at Rickard. I tried to find him, as discreetly as possible, despite the warning.

In the time we'd been apart, Rickard had moved to a new apartment, but I didn't know that. Of course, he hadn't told me, and I had little hope of finding out where he lived. The Nazis had hidden or blocked his personal records from being seen by ordinary citizens like me. I even enlisted Lotti's help, but she had no luck.

The morning after Laura was taken, I'd walked to Rickard's apartment on Unter den Linden. The building that had once been my home, and that seemed so grand, looked sinister now. The filigreed ironwork protecting the door might as well have been a spider's web, a trap seducing me with its invitation to "come inside," snaring me in its deadly mesh.

I sat for many hours across the street studying the building, analyzing the sunlight bouncing off the windows, expecting the shades to be drawn, the sashes to be thrown open. I imagined burning the building down to get to the truth. But nothing like that happened. Instead, I perched on a bench, moved in and out of the sun and rain showers, hovered in doorways, always hoping to catch a glance of Rickard. I hid my face behind sunglasses and wore a silk scarf. My only concern was that Rickard's former neighbors might alert the police about a suspicious woman prowling the boulevard.

I should have suspected that Rickard would be smart enough to conceal his intentions, on the advice of his SA friends, while plotting to get Laura back. After a few days of watching and seeing nothing, I finally spotted a mover's truck and new tenants. They were a lovely young German couple— a pretty blonde with a faultless face, wearing a beautiful red dress, hanging on the arm of her strong, athletic husband, who was attired in a brown suit with a swastika positioned crisply on the left sleeve.

I was courting danger, but I crossed the street and approached the woman—a bold but risky move.

"I used to live here," I said, hoping to draw her into my confidence. "The neighbors are such nice people." In reality, I'd met very few, and my interactions had been limited to a passing "good day" or "hello."

The woman pursed her lips and looked at me as if it was none of my business to even speak to her. Perhaps she was right. Her husband seemed more interested.

"Which apartment?" he asked.

"3D," I replied.

He offered no answer, but I could tell from his curious expression that I'd been correct in my assumption—the nonresponse along with boxes marked with the apartment number in black ink confirmed my suspicion.

They hurried away, eager to supervise the movers, and I scurried down the street, putting the apartment and my former life behind me, hiding my anger with my scarf.

That night I told Lotti that I was getting my own apartment because it didn't matter now where I lived, or who my friends were, if Spiegel kept his word. A few days later, I moved to a modest building near the Alexanderplatz and the Leopard Club. With no publisher and no creative motivation, I had no interest in writing a new novel. I applied for some typing jobs, but found nothing. I talked to Rudi, who talked to Volker, the Leopard Club's owner. The next day, I accepted a job as a waitress. The pay was low, as were the tips I expected to get from a noon to seven shift, but I was glad to get the offer.

I wondered if Rickard would walk in the door one late afternoon. Truthfully, I hoped he might—I could harangue him about Laura and still be within the bounds of Spiegel's threat. That slim hope was one of the reasons I took the job. We hadn't divorced because I feared it might anger him or the Nazis.

He never came in—until June of 1934, the following year.

The summer of 1933, I'd tried to recover from the shock of losing Laura. The fall and winter were a blur of long, dreary months huddled in bed against the cold, wishing that spring would return. My anger at Rickard and the Party had turned to dismay and depression in my small apartment. Some days, I found it impossible to get out of bed. The world swam by and I would sink to the floor in pain.

Lotti, Rudi, and I resumed our friendship. They were the only ones who kept me from sliding into the abyss. Rudi and I shared hours of working together on some days. We never talked about politics, or the events leading up to Laura's kidnapping. Rudi walked with a slight limp for months. The cut on his face faded to a thin scar. I asked him once if he'd ever seen Rickard. He closed his eyes, shook his head, and said, "Thank God, no. I'd be so angry."

Rickard returned to the club on Saturday, June 23, 1934.

Rudi hadn't arrived for his night shift yet, so I was alone with another bartender when he walked in.

My husband was heavier now, as if the good food and drink reserved for Nazis had triggered his appetite. He was still handsome despite a somewhat jowly appearance. As usual, he wore a black suit. This one was new and cut in the double-breasted fashion. He took a seat in the booth where we'd first met.

I stared at him for a few minutes, silently daring him to speak first. He stared back for a time, then lowered his head while lighting a cigarette. The smoke encircled his head and by the time it had cleared I'd made my way to the table. I kept my words in check while trembling inside with anger. Only my concern for my daughter kept me from exploding in Rickard's face.

"Yes?" was all I could ask.

He sighed and flicked his hand toward the other side of the booth. "Sit down . . . please." His tone was shy, almost contrite.

The club wasn't busy, so I slid into the booth, my brain scrambled with things to say. "You knew I worked here, didn't you?" I finally asked.

"Of course. I've known for months . . . the difficult part was showing up."

"How is Laura? If I find she's been mistreated . . ."

"Our daughter is fine," he said, taking a puff from the cigarette. "She's in good health and growing fast. She has two good nannies who care for her while I'm at work."

"Nannies?" The word came out sour and bitter. "You must be doing well."

He nodded and then added, "You know why."

"Yes, I do." I turned away—for a moment I didn't want to look at him.

Rudi had slipped in. Bathed in pink light, he stood behind

the bar, conversing with the other employee, while keeping an eye on me.

Rickard cleared his throat. "Look . . . I've come with a proposal . . . an offering of peace, and a chance to see your daughter." He lowered his gaze to the cigarettes and the glass ashtray on the table. "Laura misses her mother."

I burst into tears at the mention of her name. I swiped a bar cloth across my cheeks and then held it up to my face, trying to mask my sorrow.

Rickard extended his hand across the table, but then thought better of the gesture and withdrew it.

"We've both been wronged," he said, after I'd had a chance to compose myself. "You were wrong to take Laura from me and I was wrong to take her from you." He stubbed out the cigarette and clenched his fists. "But I warned you, Niki . . . I'd suffered too many losses and I wasn't going to allow that to happen again."

"The SA beat up Rudi and Lotti and ripped Laura from my arms . . . and I'm supposed to forgive and forget?" I spoke louder than I should have and then threw the cloth on the table.

"No, I don't suppose you ever can, or will ever have to, for that matter. All I can say is I'm sorry for what happened and it won't happen again. I promise."

"How can you make a promise like that?" I asked, leaning toward him. "Germany isn't any better now than it was a year ago—it's worse! The SA is stronger than ever. Hitler controls us like dogs on a leash."

My words alarmed him, and he held a finger to his lips. "Don't speak so loudly. You never know who might be listening."

He was right. I placed my palms on the table and breathed in the smoke and liquor-sodden air. The odors of the Leopard Club, which I was so used to, were somehow comforting.

"We're through," I told him. "I haven't filed for divorce because I'm too afraid of what the Nazis will do to me. I'm living alone. My writing career is ruined. They've destroyed me, and you bear a responsibility because you support them."

"I don't support them—I gave in to them. Maybe I'm not the man I should be, but I'm trying to make things right. We have to live with them whether we want to or not." He leaned back, straightening his back against the cushion. "Hear me out. Spiegel is having a party next Saturday night at his place in the country. He knows I've been miserable . . . that you've been miserable—"

"Stop. He's a monster. They're all monsters. The leopard doesn't change its spots. Yes, we have to live with them, but I don't have to like it. What is happening?"

He lit another cigarette. The other bartender dropped off two glasses of water as Rickard leaned toward me. "Spiegel is under pressure from factions within the Party. He's planning this gathering to show solidarity with the SS and the Gestapo, for the benefit of Himmler and Heydrich. I thought it would be a good opportunity for you to see Laura in a safe setting."

I had no idea who Himmler and Heydrich were and I didn't care—all I cared about was seeing my daughter. "It's safe for you—what about me? How do I know this isn't a trap?"

"I'll guarantee it isn't."

"I don't trust you." I stepped out of the booth. "I have to get back to work."

"Then you won't see your daughter." He sighed and lowered his gaze toward the table. "I'm drowning, Niki. I need a lifeline. They're strangling me in their grip—and before you criticize me—I know it's my fault—I couldn't stand the thought of losing everything, including my daughter, as I had before. I'm torn up with guilt."

A low moan escaped from his mouth, and he rested his head on his clenched fist.

I faced him, considering what I wanted to say. I didn't trust Rickard or any of them, but Spiegel had kept his word in the year that I'd been separated from Laura. The SA hadn't come after me. I thought of my daughter again and held back tears.

"Rudi will drive me to the Spiegels'. I'll meet you outside with Laura before I go in, if I go in at all. I will hold her and talk to her and see her for as long as the party lasts."

Rickard rose from his seat. "Agreed—maybe we can even work something out with Spiegel regarding your writing."

"I'm not concerned about my writing. I couldn't write their propaganda. I only want to see my daughter."

He withdrew a piece of paper from his suit jacket and handed it to me. "The directions to Spiegel's country estate . . . in case you've forgotten. Everything you need to know is noted there. It's nice to see you, Niki."

Rickard grabbed his cigarettes and strode toward the door without a nod to Rudi. I stumbled toward the bar, not quite sure what had happened in the minutes we'd been together.

"You're pale, even in this pink light," Rudi said. "Would you like a drink?"

I shook my head, my nerves tight. I had to get through another hour before I could go home.

"What was that about?" he asked.

I answered with another question. "Do you know how to shoot a pistol?"

His dark eyebrows rose. "No . . . but I know someone who does."

# CHAPTER 16

———◆———

The young man's name was Hermann. He looked barely old enough to drive, let alone shoot a pistol. I'd never met him because, according to Rudi, Hermann was an "outdoor" German, the kind who liked to canoe, climb mountains, ski, and trek through dense forests, often camping alone at night. They had known each other since their school days, and kept in touch despite their differing interests. Rudi said his friend didn't smoke, and drank wine only on special occasions—a dramatic difference from the denizens of the Leopard Club.

He was the kind of young man the SA would have drafted into their ranks had Hermann been so inclined. He was shorter than most men, but blond, good looking, with smooth, freckled skin and a vibrant smile. Because of his skiing and other physical activities, he had developed a sleek, muscled body. When I met him, he seemed to be in a continual state of bliss, ignoring anything that didn't concern him directly. Rudi had told me that Hermann had no use for the Nazis, and that he had managed to avoid any run-ins with them.

I made it clear to Rudi that I wanted someone to protect me, not someone to get into a gunfight with the SA or carry out an assassination. Hermann had the car and the weapon, so for twenty-five marks, I hired him to take me to Spiegel's and back the night of June 30, 1934. Rudi had a shift at the club.

No fantasies of kidnapping, or somehow getting Laura back, entered my mind. I knew that this orchestrated meeting was a test, although I was still concerned that Spiegel and his henchman might try to abduct me in retaliation for my literary crimes against the Reich.

I dressed modestly for the night's party. The gorgeous black dress that I'd worn to Spiegel's first gathering, I'd left in the wardrobe at Rickard's knowing that I wouldn't be spending much time at gala parties, especially those hosted by National Socialists.

Hermann picked me up at my apartment at six for the forty-five-minute drive to the country. So few young Berliners had cars, I wondered if the boxy, black Wanderer sedan was his or his family's. His blond hair flashed in the evening sun as he opened the passenger door for me. Looking crisp and neat, he wore a jacket and black pants. Another boxy-looking item lay in the back seat—a black pistol with a long barrel and a massive, rectangular magazine.

I settled into the seat next to him and gave him the directions.

"You were lucky to get me," he said as we pulled away from the curb. "This time of year, I'm usually hiking in the Bavarian Alps on weekends. I'm in the city because I'm helping my brother move to a new apartment."

"Is this your car?" I asked.

"My father's," he said. "I can't afford a car. I don't really want one."

"What about the pistol in the back?"

"Oh, that." He smiled at me as we weaved past trolleys, other automobiles, and a few horse carts. "My father's as well. A Mauser C96, issued to him in the Great War. Holds ten rounds. I'm not a bad shot, but I'm even better with a bow and arrow."

"You're a hunter?" I asked, feeling somewhat assured that Hermann might be able to shoot his way out of a difficult situation if necessary, not that I sought violence during the evening. My stomach was already in knots thinking about my daughter. What if she didn't recognize me? What if she wanted nothing to do with me? What would she look like? The questions rolled through my head as Hermann drove north.

"So the Nazis are out to get you?" he asked in a devilish tone. "Rudi told me about it. It was rough the way they pummeled him. I don't like it when my friends get beaten up."

I nodded and told him the pertinent parts of my history and about what I believed might happen this evening, reminding him that I wanted a bodyguard, not an assassin. "I'm supposed to meet Rickard and my daughter in front of the house at seven," I explained. "I feel safer with you here. If I decide to accompany Rickard inside, stay with the car. Don't let the attendants park it elsewhere."

He nodded. "Are you nervous?" I asked.

"Should I be? They're a tough gang."

"We'll be all right. I just have to remain calm."

As we drew closer to Spiegel's country home, the terrain, the winding road, the thick forest, looked vaguely familiar. Hermann drove past the road leading to the house, which I happened to spot. He maneuvered the Wanderer into a three-point turn and returned to the drive.

"Hold on," he said, stopping the car. He turned and grabbed the Mauser from its resting place and placed it under the front seat. "Are you ready?"

I nodded.

We traversed the long, tree-lined drive that seemed to curve endlessly, but led us to the magnificent, stone mansion that lay in the shadows of dusk. The white lamps that had illuminated the house during my previous visit were dark. The footmen that had parked Rickard's car also were missing. My throat and chest tightened, feeling as if I had been drawn into a trap.

I asked Hermann to stop the car a safe distance from the residence. In the gathering gloom, closer to the house, I spotted a black Mercedes sedan. It had been requisitioned for the Nazi Party, a swastika emblazoned on its passenger door.

"Wait here," I told Hermann. "I'll go alone."

"Be careful," he said, reaching under the seat to get the Mauser.

"Keep the car running," I said.

I opened the door and walked up the drive—slowly, taking in everything around me. The house was quiet, no lights shone in its dark windows. The large oak door carved with forest creatures was closed.

A driver, attired in a black uniform and cap, got out of the Mercedes and opened a rear door. A little girl, clutching Rickard's hand, appeared. She wore a black skirt, a white blouse with a triangular patch on the left sleeve, and a cinched black tie—the girl's outfit of Hitler Youth. She was nearly three years old now, walking, her ruddy cheeks glowing in the semidarkness.

My first instinct was to run to her, but I still suspected a trap.

Rickard, also cautious, guided our daughter down the drive. Laura's eyes brightened a bit as we neared each other. Was it from recognition or just her interest in someone who stimulated her curiosity?

They stopped and I walked to my daughter.

"Laura, this is your mother," Rickard said. "Do you remember her?"

"Hello, Ma-ma," she said in a small, prim voice. The nannies had taught her well.

I reached for her and Rickard allowed me to hold her. Laura was on her way to becoming a girl, more than a child. She was heavier, her limbs stouter than I remembered. She clung to me, but not in a way that indicated that she missed me. Her affection was more polite, as if she had been told that a great aunt was her visitor. When I realized what had happened in the time since Spiegel had taken her—my tears flowed.

"I'm sorry," I said to Rickard. "I can't help it."

"I understand," he said.

"Did you bring me a present?" Laura asked, resting her soft cheek against mine.

"Laura, don't be rude," Rickard said. "Can't you see that your mother is upset? She's made a special trip to see you."

"Father always brings me presents when he comes home," she insisted.

"That's because I work a lot . . . and you deserve them for being such a good child," Rickard said.

I hugged her, pressing her against my body. "I promise the next time I see you, I'll bring you a present—perhaps a piece of chocolate."

"I still have my doll," she said. The remembrance of that toy brought more silent tears to my eyes.

Rickard looked past me to the Wanderer. "Who's in the car?"

"A friend of Rudi's. I asked him to come . . . for protection."

"Is he armed?"

Rickard saw through me and my improvised plan to protect myself. The cloak of invincibility in which I'd wrapped myself dropped like a fall leaf. "Yes."

"So is my driver—a dedicated Nazi with deadly aim. Let's hope it doesn't come to that." He paused, as if considering what to do next. "Please, come inside and talk to Spiegel. There's no party. That's where I led you astray. I was afraid you wouldn't come if you knew it was only Spiegel and me."

"I came to see my daughter. Why go inside to see a butcher?"

"Because I've asked for a favor . . . he's willing to offer you a chance to write again—to make money."

"Laura comes with us?"

He nodded.

"One minute." I handed Laura to Rickard and raced back to the car. Hermann was sitting behind the wheel watching me with interest as I approached. He rolled down the window, the evening shadows falling across his face. "I'm going inside. Spiegel wants to talk to me. Leave if things get bad." I knew he'd understand my meaning. "Save yourself. . . . The driver is armed. Rickard says he's an excellent shot."

Hermann frowned and notched his head toward me. "I see." He turned off the engine. "How long will you be?"

"No more than an hour, I suppose."

"I'll be here."

I caught up with Rickard, who was on his way to the steps with Laura. We climbed them, Rickard holding Laura's left hand and I her right, pulling her up with a bounce on each step. She giggled with each flight into the air.

A servant opened the door and escorted us to an office off the long hall. Spiegel sat behind a desk that dominated the room, his wife in a chair to his side. Mrs. Spiegel, in a word, was a *matron* of the most Germanic type. I remembered seeing her at the party, but our interaction had been brief because she was playing the hostess, flitting around the room, greeting each guest with gusto. Her face was severe, angular, her hair pulled back in a tight braid behind her head. She wore a black dress and expensive leather heels, and seemed as much in control of the room as the Oberführer. He was dressed in his SA uniform and held a brandy snifter in his right hand. The room was heavy with oak furniture, sturdy paneling, and two panels of bookcases filled with expensive volumes. A blue marble fireplace was cut into one wall. A large ledger book lay open on his desk.

The servant retreated and Spiegel asked us to sit in the two wingchairs in front of his desk. I took Laura. She settled into my lap, as Mrs. Spiegel managed a weak smile.

Her husband smiled as well, his demeanor becoming more affable, a trait that I'd seen him display more than once. However, like a poisonous snake, he could strike at any moment.

"Can I offer you a drink?" he asked.

I declined. Rickard accepted a brandy, which the SA leader poured.

"I'm glad you decided to visit us, Niki," Spiegel said, an acidic bite in his voice. "Rickard has been at a loss lately . . . work occupying too much of his time. Of course, he's an asset to the Reich and our plans for the SA, some of which even he hasn't heard." He leaned back in his chair and chuckled.

"As I told Rickard, I came to see my daughter."

"Yes, that evening at your friend's—Lotti, is it?—that was unfortunate." His wife shifted in her chair. "But, since that night, you've upheld your end of the bargain and so have we."

"Most of my interactions with you have been unfortunate."

Rickard shot me a look, as did Mrs. Spiegel. The Oberführer took the comment in stride.

"We need help, Niki," he said. "That's why I asked you here tonight. I thought your beautiful daughter would act as an enticement."

So, I was correct in my assessment—it was a trap. "What do you want?"

"Something that someone of your talent can provide," he said. "Words."

My thoughts jumped ahead to Spiegel's thoughts, but I waited until he explained himself.

"You wrote so eloquently—as some would put it—about the New German Woman," he continued. "Unfortunately, that woman is not the ideal espoused by the Reich." He rose from his desk and stood behind his wife, placing his hands on her shoulders, lording over her. "You can write scripts that Rickard will produce, that we can film at Passport Pictures, about the women who will carry the Reich forward. Even the new director Leni Riefenstahl has been urged to put her talents to work for us. Think how exciting it would be to work with such a talented woman!" He clasped his wife's shoulders a little too hard and she flinched.

I had a sudden urge for a drink and a cigarette. I knew little of Riefenstahl and, of course, didn't know her personally. What Spiegel wanted me to consider was the same business that Rickard had been in for several years—propaganda. I wondered if I should consent—only to be close to my daughter and perhaps win her back. The same sickness of the past creeping into my stomach told me otherwise. I could only stall for the moment.

"I'll have to think about it." As my words came out, I caught a glimpse of Rickard, who seemed to suspect that I had other motives on my mind. Did he really believe that I would write movie scripts for the Nazi Party? Did he really want me back in his life, so we could raise our daughter together?

Spiegel kissed his wife on the cheek and walked to his desk. "Don't take too long to make up your mind. Time is short."

"May I speak to my husband privately?" I asked.

The Oberführer nodded and then pushed a buzzer under his desk. The servant who had answered the door arrived a few moments later. "Take the Längers to the library so they can have a private discussion," he ordered.

The man directed us to a room across the hall, between the pronged heads of Spiegel's hunting trophies, let us in, and then closed the door. The opulent library was lined with half-sized bookcases on three walls, again filled with costly volumes bound in gold, red, and black leather. Bronze sculptures of stags and hunting dogs sat on their walnut tops. Mountain landscapes in swirling gold frames hung above them. Still holding Laura, I settled into a couch positioned in front of another grand, marble fireplace that took up one wall. Laura jumped off my lap wanting to explore, enthralled by the surroundings. I let her, as Rickard watched like a doting father.

"What is this really about?" I asked him. "Do you have a cigarette?"

He took out a pack, not my brand, but I gratefully accepted one. "I don't know what to say, Niki. Maybe I was naïve enough to think that you might change your mind and that we could give it another try." He walked the room looking for an ashtray, finally finding one on top of the fireplace mantel.

"After what you did to me and our friends?"

"I could say the same thing . . . after what you did to me? Taking my daughter away when you knew that losing you both would wreck me?" He handed me the ashtray and sat on the couch.

"I was scared, Rickard. Scared of what the Nazis would do to me . . . and us . . . when they found out that I wrote *The Berlin Woman*. I was protecting my daughter because I knew you would never give up the business. Do you think it was easy? The only easy part was spitting in the face of these disgusting people."

He leaned toward me. "I wanted you both so much, but I knew you wouldn't come back to me as long as you had Laura. I worked it out with Spiegel—the arrangement—you leave me alone, I leave you alone. But I was hoping we could work something out."

I took a puff on the cigarette, got off the couch, and walked to the fireplace. The humid, woody scent of smoke flowed down the chimney, forced into the room by the summer breeze.

"You know I will never write for them, so why even ask? I will never promote their vile views—"

I was interrupted by a tremendous pounding on the front door that echoed down the hall. I threw the cigarette into the fireplace. Rickard grabbed Laura, who was running her hands across a row of books.

"What the hell is that?" he asked.

We walked to the door and opened it to find the servant lighting the lamps in the dark hall. He stopped his task and strode to the door.

He opened it a bit and was pushed back by a force behind it. Three men, high-ranking SS officials clad in black, strode in.

"Where are Herr Spiegel and his wife?" the leader commanded. The men accompanying him were stern, dressed as threateningly as the first in black boots, flared pants, and caps displaying the Nazi eagle and the Death's Head.

Taken by surprise, the elderly servant fell back against the wall. The men rushed toward us.

"Who are you?" the leader asked, coming face-to-face with us.

"I am Rickard Länger and this is my wife, Marie, and our daughter, Laura. I work for the Reich making movies for the Führer at Passport Pictures. We're only visiting."

Rickard had learned his lessons well—divorcing himself from anything to do with Spiegel. I stood by him as the commander, or whatever rank he was, tilted his head toward one of his men who checked a typewritten list.

"No," the man said bluntly after a few moments.

"Where are they?" the SS man asked again.

The servant, who had recovered his balance, pointed to the office. Just as he did, Spiegel opened the door with his wife behind him. He carried a gun, but as soon as he saw the officers, he lowered it to his side.

The SS men jumped into action, disarming him, pulling the Oberführer from the room, along with his wife. Spiegel shouted his objections: "Keep your hands off me. . . . Release my wife. . . . What the hell are you doing?" They dragged them down the hall. Mrs. Spiegel lost one of her shoes on the stone walkway. The servant dutifully picked it up.

When they reached the door, one of the men turned and shouted at us, "Get out."

We rushed toward the door, Rickard clutching Laura, and I feared that all of us would be shot at any moment. The men turned to their right with their prisoners in tow. The servant followed, voicing his objections as well.

Night had fallen, but a third car shone its headlights against the white stone mansion. The men lined up Spiegel, his wife, and the servant in a clearing between the sculpted bushes. The leader pulled out a pistol and shot them in quick succession in the head—the wife and servant first and then Spiegel. They collapsed like rag dolls in the light, crumpling in a pile in the shadows. The SS man holstered his pistol and led the men casually back to their waiting car. Rickard's and Hermann's vehicles sat in the darkness.

We hid behind an oak tree and watched as the car rolled down the drive, both of us panting in fear. Rickard had covered Laura's eyes with his hand as the shots were fired.

"You weren't on the list," I said, gasping for breath. My body shook against the tree bark. "You saved us because you weren't marked for death, and you knew what to say."

"Hold her," he said, giving Laura to me. I watched as he ran to the car that had brought him. He soon returned, out of breath. "He's . . . dead. Shot between the eyes . . . he was SA."

"The SS is killing the SA? Why?"

He leaned with both hands against the tree. "I don't understand." His voice verged on a sob.

Footsteps squished in the grass behind us and we turned to see Hermann's stern face as he approached, pistol in his hand. As he got closer, he dropped the Mauser to his side. "I didn't want to see that. I ducked down as they drove past me. Your driver put up some kind of fight and they shot him. I ran into the woods when they went into the house." He gazed toward the shadowy pile of bodies.

"We need to leave," Rickard said. "Now!"

"I can't believe that Nazis are killing each other," Hermann said.

"Take me to Unter den Linden," Rickard said. "I'll get a taxi home."

We drove back to Berlin, not bothering to set foot in Spiegel's country home, leaving the door open for people and animals alike, saying little in the car. My body and mind were numb as I tried to understand what we had witnessed.

The Wanderer bounced along, Hermann pushing it to its limits. My thoughts were as jumbled as the drive. It would have been easy to take Laura from Rickard at gunpoint, but what would that have accomplished—another vendetta against me, another reason for bloodshed? I couldn't kill him in front of his daughter, nor did I want to. Everything in me cried out for her, but the silent voice inside me said, "Let her go. She'll be safer with him than you!" He had saved us both by merely being himself in this Nazi regime. What kind of luxuries could I offer as opposed to those Rickard could give? I was defeated.

When we arrived at Unter den Linden in the shadow of the Brandenburg Gate, I watched as Rickard and Laura got out of the car and into a taxi. I didn't know where he was going or if I would ever see my daughter again. Before the door closed, he kissed me on the cheek and I held on to Laura and cried until they could wait no longer. He promised me that he would get in touch and let me see my daughter. I didn't believe him.

I got back into the Wanderer with Hermann. He wiped his brow with a handkerchief and whistled. "What happened tonight? This reeks of Hitler."

"Why do you think that?" I asked, still wondering why Spiegel was shot.

"He's afraid."

Hermann was right.

Hitler was afraid of losing power.

# BOOK TWO

# CHAPTER 17

*Remembering the war and its aftermath*

For days, I tried to block the executions of Spiegel, his wife, and servant from haunting me. As hard as I tried, my mind kept flipping back to that night and the image of them falling in the dark; their blood, warm and red, spattering against the white stone, the deathly silence after the shots. The memory that chilled me the most, however, was the SS man firing his pistol rapidly, with precise aim, coolly embracing the slaughter in front of him. He then lit a cigarette and led his men back to the waiting car. I would never forget their walk down the sloping lawn to the pavement.

Because I'd witnessed the murders, my life became a game of deception. I dressed plainly, even at the club, so as not to arouse interest in me as a person, or as a woman. I became acutely aware of my surroundings, always looking behind me or ahead into doorways and alleys, or other places Nazis could hide. Only under the protection of Walter, Volker, and Rudi at the Club, or hidden away in my apartment behind a locked door, did I feel somewhat safe. The SA wasn't dead, some still ventured into the club, but one could sense their diminished power. The SA hierarchy had been assassinated during the Night of the Long Knives. Even Ernst Röhm,

Hitler's longtime friend, confidant, and head of the SA, was dragged from his hotel room, thrown into prison, and later shot. He'd refused to commit suicide. Other SA leaders were taken from their rooms, some with male companions in their beds, and executed outside the hotel.

Hitler had vented his rage, decrying the traitors, the treachery, and the moral turpitude of the SA. The assassinations affirmed his power and leadership. Those close to the Führer, including Himmler and Göring, had warned him the SA had grown too large, had amassed too much power.

After the murders, the thought came to me that wresting Laura from Rickard's grasp was an impossible task. The power of the Reich was too great.

I could only exist, only survive, much like I had when I left my mother's house to move to Berlin—to be the New German Woman.

I met Emil Belmon in late spring of 1935 at the Leopard Club. He wandered in alone one evening looking somewhat lost, having never been in before. In his black pants, dark jacket, and cotton neckerchief, he looked more like the habituate of a bohemian coffee shop than someone who'd be comfortable in the club.

He took a seat in one of the booths, immediately pulled out a book, and started to read. When I approached, he looked up briefly and asked for a glass of Russian vodka and matches.

He spent the whole evening by himself, reading in the dim light, adjusting his wire-rimmed spectacles now and then, and occasionally looking over the rather sparse crowd. Why had he come to the Leopard Club? As long as he bought drinks, neither I nor that manager could complain.

I found it hard to explain to Rudi and Lotti why I felt attracted to him. There was a sense of something greater about him, a creative intellect that I couldn't match or dare question. The somber mood he projected also appealed to my state of mind. He was a quiet intellectual who seethed inside, I imagined. My fantasy about Emil extended to a wildly romantic personality, a trait subjugated by the realities of Nazi Germany. I took him for a communist from the start, but I wasn't certain.

His face, pale but pleasant, expressed a propensity for study. His hair was black and tousled, awash with curls. Sometimes he shook it like a lion's ruff and it contrasted sharply with his white face. He was the exact opposite of Rudi's friend Hermann.

For several months we saw more of each other, inside and outside the club. We talked about art, philosophy, drama, and politics. He confessed that he had gone from odd job to odd job, didn't have a lot of money, but had found work recently as a typesetter in a printing shop. Later, when I trusted him, I told him what I'd written. A smile broke out on his face, in amazement really, of who I was—something one might witness from an adoring fan. He said a few of his friends had read my books. On their recommendation he'd done so as well. I pictured him, stretched out on his bed, reading my books while copies of Kant, Schopenhauer, Freud, and Marx lay nearby.

"I'd never read anything like *The Berlin Woman*," he told me one evening as we sat under the trees in the Tiergarten. "You opened my eyes."

No one, Rickard included, had ever expressed such a feeling to me, except for Herr Berger, my publisher. In the languid evening I closed my eyes for a moment and Emil kissed my cheek. The fleshy softness of his lips sent a thrill through me and I responded by pressing mine against his.

That evening we slept together for the first time, and my soul swam in a sea of unbridled ecstasy from our lovemaking. Perhaps my romantic fantasies had overtaken me, but all the other men before Emil, including Rickard, paled in comparison.

I found myself falling in love. His fingers caressed me; they didn't grab or burn with heat. His lips stoked every part of my body with passion. I melted into him and his body responded in kind.

On the evening of the seventeenth day of September 1935, he showed up at my apartment. We'd made tentative plans to see each other, but had not confirmed. I could tell when I opened the door that something was wrong. He was wearing his usual attire, but behind the rimmed glasses, his brown eyes had lost their usual sparkle. I invited him in and asked what was wrong.

"I have something important to tell you," he said, in a tone darker than I'd ever heard him use before. He took a seat on the bed next to me, taking off his glasses, wiping the lenses with a handkerchief, as if the act would delay the bad news.

I clasped my hands, shivering a bit on the bedcover, fearing the breakup of our budding relationship, myriad questions coursing through my mind. Perhaps, I wasn't pretty enough, or smart enough, although I liked to think I held my own in our philosophical discussions. He had mentioned girlfriends, but had never indicated that he was in love with someone else. Was that what he'd come to tell me?

He turned to me. I had the courage to face him.

"I'm a Jew," he said.

No happiness, no pride in his confession entered his voice. My breath halted for a second as I looked into his sad eyes. His words shamed me, for in them I found a two-fold response: that it didn't matter that he was a Jew, that I was in love with him, that I knew the truth when he stood naked before me; and, on the other hand, that our relationship was doomed in Germany. The Nazis had struck again, this time with a dagger through my heart.

"I knew. Why have you confessed?" I hoped he'd clarify his thoughts.

"Yesterday, in Nuremberg—decrees were passed by the

Reichstag at the Party rally," he said. "I read the laws at the shop." He kneaded his hands together, as if crushing a piece of paper. "Since Hitler came to power, our rights have eroded to such an extent that we hardly have anything left. And, now this! We've already been told that we can't hold public office or be in civil service positions; we can't work in the radio or newspaper business. The Nazis have cut us off from making money through exchanges or brokerages. . . ." He shook his head before continuing. "Now, in addition to the blood that they've extracted from us, they've made it illegal for me to marry you or to have sex with a German woman. I'm no longer a citizen." He took my hands in his. "It's illegal for me to fly the German flag—the swastika. I would never fly the abominable thing anyway. Screw them! Let me fly the gold star and the hammer and sickle over their damn Reich!"

Rubbing his temples, he rose and paced the tiny corridor between the kitchen and the window.

"You're a communist, aren't you?"

He turned to me. "Of course. I should have told you."

"Why didn't you?"

"After what you've been through? I would have thought you'd had enough of politics. Have you got a cigarette?"

I took a pack from the nightstand drawer and handed one to him. He lit it, opened the sash to let in the cool, evening breeze, and stood flicking the ash out the window.

"It appears that this is an evening for truth," he said, after taking several puffs. He moved toward me again, settling on the edge of the bed.

"I hate the Nazis, and they hate me," he said. "I loathe them every waking hour. Some evenings, I stay after work and print pamphlets calling out their lies. I tell the boss I want to clean up the shop, which I do—he doesn't pay me for those hours. I print the tracts, and make sure I leave no typeset or stray pamphlets for anyone to find. Then I clean and lock up."

"I admire you. You've taken a stand against them. Rickard never could. I tried . . . and failed."

He extinguished the cigarette in the nightstand ashtray. "But you did—you wrote your books, you wanted to save your daughter, you tried to convince your husband. How can you win against a juggernaut?" He pulled me close, his warm breath brushing against my neck. "The answer lies with us. One person at a time against the Nazis until we build a collective that can destroy them."

I shook my head. "I wish it were that easy—one person at a time." My voice caught, and a few moments passed before I could continue. "I don't know if I will ever see my daughter again. That's the worst tragedy." I blinked away tears. "And, I know my daughter is safer with her father than she is with me. That's the crime of Hitler! I'm paralyzed, but I'm not divorcing Rickard after what he's done. I won't give him that satisfaction. Laura will remain part of me whether or not the Nazis will ever let me see her again."

I collapsed against his shoulder and Emil comforted me while I wept. I'd never expressed to anyone, not even Lotti, that I might never see my daughter again. The cathartic release left me drained, but somewhat calmer.

"How can I help?" Emil asked, his brown eyes raking over me.

"Can you stay tonight? Can we fight together?"

He turned my head and kissed me. That night we had sex, and I felt like we were alone in Germany, alone on an island sheltered by love.

During the next month, we explored the path we wished to take. I stayed at Emil's when I could, and my creativity returned in pieces. He let me use his typewriter during the day when he was at work, and I started a novel called *Einsamkeit, Loneliness*. The words came slowly and the daily business of our lives often got in the way. We shuttled back and forth between each other's apartments, noting the incremental tightening of restrictions against the Jews by the Nazis—as well as the increasing brutality toward those who disregarded the Reich's rules.

One night Emil asked to take a picture of me. He hung a sheet across the window and positioned the lights so that my face would be framed in a particular way. He then asked me to do the same for him. I thought the lighting was garish and ugly and I asked him what the pictures were for, but he wouldn't say. A week later, he presented me with a false passport and forged identification papers that had come from his efforts at the printing shop. Fall had come to Berlin and I shivered a bit from the cool breeze coursing through my window along with the realization that I was a "new" person based on this assumed identity.

"Insurance," Emil said, with a hint of a smile.

"In case we need to leave Germany," I responded.

"We'll have to leave. I'm sure of it."

I was somewhat shocked by his words. Not because I couldn't see what was coming—I had known it for years— but of Emil's certainty that there was no other way out. At some point, we would have to leave Germany.

Of course, Laura and my mother figured into my discomfort as well. I knew my mother would never leave her home, let alone travel to a foreign country with Emil, a man she didn't know and probably wouldn't trust. I'd heard nothing from Rickard. It was as if he'd died. I'd thought of going to Passport Pictures, begging him to see Laura, but then thought better of it. The SA had been gutted only to be replaced by the Gestapo and the SS, two vicious and cunning orders. I was sure that one or both of those groups had their investigative and protective services surrounding the studio.

That same evening that Emil presented the passports, I

revealed one last secret to him. If Rickard and I had danced around each other, Emil and I had melded into one flesh—a unit working against the Nazis.

I took my coat from the closet and placed it on the bed. The plain gray wool had weathered over the years, and it was out of fashion, but it was the warmest coat I had and still held the treasure that I'd taken from the ladies' powder room at Spiegel's country home.

The coat felt warm and fuzzy in my hands, the silk lining cool against my fingers. Without damaging the fabric, I delicately unraveled the thread concealing the hidden pocket. Emil watched, fascinated, as I performed the task. When the enclosure revealed itself, I reached inside and removed the bracelet, the sparkling diamonds and lush emeralds glinting in the light.

Emil whistled and shook his head. "Where the hell did you get that?"

I told him the story, knowing that we had about one hundred marks between us.

"Fifty thousand marks?" he asked and sank to the bed. "I've never seen anything so beautiful before—except in a museum."

"I can't sell it here. The SA knew it was missing—Spiegel inquired about it one afternoon when he came with Rickard to the apartment. I denied that I'd seen it. I'm sure they alerted every jewelry store in Berlin." I paused and congratulated myself on perhaps the one thing I'd done right regarding the Nazis. "I think Rickard suspected, but I never told him."

"Then, you'll have to sell it—pawn it—elsewhere."

"Where?"

"I have an uncle who lives in Amsterdam in a Jewish community. You can sell it there. It'll keep you—us—in funds for a long while."

"Amsterdam . . ." I'd never been. In fact, I'd never been

out of Germany. It sounded so far away, so foreign, with a people I didn't know, with a language similar to German, but so different.

"We should go before we're chased out of Berlin, before we can't leave," Emil said, holding the bracelet in his hands. "It won't be long before the Nazis make it difficult for Jews to leave Germany. We must make plans. You'll have to learn some Dutch."

I purchased some language instruction books. We did plan for our future, thinking that such a move might be years away, but something happened that forced us to make the decision earlier than later.

That event saved our lives.

I happened to be there—at Ludwig Printers in central Berlin. I had come to have lunch with Emil before starting my shift at the Leopard Club.

Ludwig Printers was a small shop, pressed between larger buildings, on a street crowded with stores and a few similar printing establishments. One only had to look through the large windows to see the typesetting machines and the presses lined against the wall. A sign in black medieval lettering, showing an old press on four legs with a screw turn, hung above the door. I had been in the shop a few times, just to say hello to Emil. I loved the smell of the place: the sharp tang of ink, the papery odor that mixed with the printing process. The shop always seemed to be warm even on cool fall days.

The owner, Ludwig, was a gruff German who, if one could judge from his stomach, had a fondness for beer and sausages. Like Emil, he wore wire-rimmed spectacles, but, unlike Emil, Ludwig was nearly bald except for some wisps of brown hair streaming from both sides of his head. When I'd visited the shop before, the owner would stop what he was doing, wipe his hands on his dark blue apron, and nod—a begrudging acknowledgment that I had entered his territory. He never said a word, only watched our interactions with some interest.

I expected the same treatment this day; instead, sharp words bulleted out the door and into the street. For a moment, I wondered whether I should even go in, but I heard Emil's voice above the commotion. My interest was more than curiosity. I feared for his safety.

"You'd run me out like a common thief?" Emil shouted as the fracas ignited.

"You are a thief! And a Jew!" Ludwig smashed his hammy fists on the counter.

"I've stolen nothing," Emil protested, but I knew he was lying.

Ludwig leaned forward, his eyes narrow and fiery. "I know what you've been doing. I've seen the remains of your work. One piece of paper you neglected to remove from the trash told the whole story. 'Jews revolt! Overthrow the Oppressors!' What do you call that? What do you think would happen to me if the SS traced that back to my shop? You're lucky I haven't called the Gestapo."

Emil took off his apron and threw it on the counter. "You're like the rest of the Nazis. Thinking you're too good—that everyone is beneath you."

"That's true," Ludwig said, leaning back a bit from the counter. "And you Jews are finding out who the real rulers of the world are." Growling like a bulldog, he slapped his palms on the counter in one final act of defiance. "Get out and take your whore with you."

Emil drew his fist back, but I rushed to his side and grabbed his arm.

"No," I said. "Let's leave, like the owner says."

Emil huffed as I turned him toward the door. "You're

on the wrong side, Ludwig. This building will go down in flames."

"Get out, Jew, and don't come back. You won't get your final earnings from me—they'll pay for what you've stolen."

As I pulled Emil out, Ludwig raced from behind the counter, coming toward us like an enraged boxer. He slammed the door behind us.

"Nazi scum," Emil said.

"Be quiet." I put a finger to his lips. "We'll be arrested."

He shook as we walked down the street, the sun warm on our heads. Despite the fight, it was a beautiful day, as if God had favored Hitler and Germany over all others.

"Walk with me to work," I said, as we trudged toward the Alexanderplatz, attempting to blend in with the crowd. Ludwig's threat worried me, but I felt it was more bluster than action. How would it look if the Gestapo discovered that a Jew had been printing pamphlets in his shop for months? I could hear their questions, see their inquiring eyes, their probing hands dissecting every nook in the shop as they searched for evidence . . . evidence that would lead to Ludwig's arrest. We were safe from his threats.

When we arrived at the club, we stood in the shade of the awning beneath the marquee that rose upward like an arrow to the blue sky. Walter, the doorman, wasn't on duty yet because it was early in the day. In fact, there was little activity on the street other than a few passersby.

"Now, I'm unemployed again with no one to recommend me. I can't even pay the rent." Emil slouched against the stone surrounding the door. Defeat, desperation, defined his voice.

"Live with me," I said, and then kissed him on the cheek. "We can make it work until we move."

"I don't have much . . . a few bags of clothes, my typewriter. I'll have a few pamphlets to dispose of."

I lit a cigarette and offered him one. He took it, but he

stared at the walk beneath us, his mind elsewhere. "Niki, I have a bad feeling, a very bad feeling. I don't know how else to say it. We need to leave Berlin sooner than later."

It was the fall of 1935. Winter was closing in. I thought about it for a moment and then suggested that we leave in the spring of the following year, which would allow me time with my mother, and perhaps even Laura, before saying our good-byes.

Emil agreed, but I could tell he wanted to leave Germany now. He didn't trust the SS or the Gestapo. As a matter of fact, we had begun to trust no one. Ludwig was the perfect example of the German who could turn us in for treason and violations of the Nuremberg Laws. If so, prison awaited us.

Our next hurdle would be moving to Amsterdam, crossing the German border to freedom.

It wouldn't be easy.

# CHAPTER 18

Through the winter, Emil and I planned our escape from Germany.

More than anything, I wanted to see Laura and say goodbye to my mother before leaving the small apartment that had become our home.

In the spring of 1936, I took the tram to Passport Pictures and walked the shabby and deserted street that led to the studio. The trees, still naked from the winter, stretched their gray branches into the sky. Here and there a sprig of green grass sprouted between the cracks in the brick walk. The studio's building suffered from neglect, almost to the point of dereliction. It had become a deserted monument in a flat field outside Berlin's center. Despite that, the structure held striking additions. Two long, vertical Nazi banners—brilliant red with a black swastika in a white circle—draped the façade, the fabric flapping in the breeze. Clearly, Rickard was still drinking the fatal brew the Party offered.

Even more disturbing were the rows of black sedans and military trucks that lined the road leading to the studio. A high fence had been constructed around the property, along with a reinforced gate. Two armed soldiers stood as sentries by the stone columns.

My heart sank. My chances of talking to Rickard were

slim—my hope of seeing Laura scattered like mist in the wind.

My disappointment soon turned to anger bubbling in my chest. The soldiers had spotted me, their arms creeping up to the rifles strapped over their shoulders. I walked away from them, realizing that I would never see Laura as long as Hitler was in power. How suicidal it would be to face these men, to walk up to them and ask to see Rickard. They would want my name and identification papers. I wasn't prepared to use the forged credentials that Emil had given me. Certainly, Marie Rittenhaus, Niki, and my pseudonym would be listed on their clipboard of enemies of the Reich. They would arrest me. I couldn't take that risk.

I wanted to kill them all. After my father's death, my mother had prayed for me and tried to teach me lessons from the Bible. I understood that thinking about killing was wrong, but the murders that Hitler and his power-hungry Party perpetrated every day were sins. I felt guilty—ashamed—that I harbored such thoughts against the men who stood at the gate, the Nazis who'd made my life hell. My hatred, at that moment, even extended to Rickard, who had taken up with them to save his skin. These feelings made my stomach churn.

I took a final glance at Passport Pictures and retraced my steps to the tram stop, hoping that the soldiers would think I lost my way. The anger didn't leave me as I rode back to my apartment. I never wanted to see the studio again unless it was in ashes.

The next day, I visited my mother in Rixdorf. Nothing much had changed since I was there with Laura, except for the red and yellow tulips now blooming in her backyard. She wore the housedress I'd seen hundreds of times and the same plain black shoes that she favored.

I told her about Spiegel's murder and that terrible evening I'd let Laura go. She needed to hear the truth, so I described that night while we sat on the couch. Her eyes glistened and she dabbed them with her handkerchief.

"I told you the Nazis were no good," she said. "Men ruin the world."

I nodded to appease her, knowing that some men were good.

"I want to see my granddaughter before I die," she said.

"Of course you will." I grasped her hand. The two needle-point pillows of forest scenes rested on the couch in the same places where I'd last seen them. "When Hitler loses power, we'll both be able to see Laura."

"Hitler will lose power when he's dead." She dropped my hand and craned her neck toward the open back door, gazing upon the flowers in her yard. "I wish he had the life span of a tulip," she said, referring to the short duration of the bloom.

Dreading what I had to say, I took a breath and settled against the back of the couch. In her house, I was still my mother's daughter. We sat for a time before I spoke.

"I met a man, Mama . . . and we're going away. We're leaving Berlin."

Her face remained stone-like, her gray eyes unyielding. "Another Nazi?"

"Not at all . . . I'm in love with him."

She studied me, like a teacher analyzing a student. "Weren't you in love with Rickard?"

The question pricked me, the hurt palpable. "There's no reason to drag this out. It's exhausting."

"Answer me."

My hands crept toward my purse, searching for a cigarette that I couldn't smoke. "I thought I was. Love was different with Rickard. I was younger then. . . . I was sorting myself out. But I haven't forgotten Laura. I love my daughter. I will get her back. I promise."

"What does this man do?"

"He was a printer. Now, he's managing our move."

She cocked her head. "Why must you leave?" She already knew the answer.

"Because Emil is a Jew."

Her nose wriggled, a clear indication of her distaste. She kept her gaze on the spring tulips as she spoke. "A Jew . . . better than a Nazi . . . I suppose the same as a Catholic . . . but not as good as a Lutheran."

I chuckled. "No, Mama, I suppose not." I took her hand again. "Please, listen to me. I have a serious question to ask. Do you want to come with us? We're moving to Amsterdam."

Her face darkened and the light in her eyes dimmed somewhat. "Amsterdam? Why there? It's so far away."

"The city has a large Jewish population. Emil has an uncle there. We don't feel safe in Germany. I'd like you to come, in case things get worse here."

She looked at my hands grasping hers and then at the floor, the solid framework that had lain beneath her feet for many years. "I can't leave your father. His grave . . . the few friends I have nearby. He paid for this house. It's where you were born. I could never leave. They will carry me out in my coffin."

"I told Emil that you would never leave. I hope it's not too great a shock."

"Of course it is, but what choice do I have? Are you pregnant?" As if expecting the worst, her expression turned somber.

"No, we don't plan to have children . . . the times are . . ."

"I know. The times we live in. Who could have imagined?"

She let go of my hands and rose from the couch. "I'm making tea. Would you like some?"

"Yes."

We strolled around the yard with teacups in hand, even looking at the neighbors' flowers. We talked, but of nothing of consequence, and for the first time in my life, I felt as if I'd approached my mother as an equal, not as a child with something to hide. When we parted, she kissed me on the cheek and wished me good luck. I told her that I would call her before we boarded the train to Amsterdam.

As I walked away, I looked back at my former home. A strange combination of sadness and joy overtook me. I felt as if I had lost something, but also gained something in return—perhaps, my freedom.

I closed my eyes and turned, muttering a prayer for my mother.

On Wednesday, April 1, 1936, Emil and I left my apartment. I carried my suitcase; Emil, his bag and typewriter. We'd scrutinized our possessions, and, in the end, had carried only what was necessary. We had about fifty marks between us, enough to buy second-class tickets from Berlin to Amsterdam and have most of our money left over. The emerald and diamond bracelet also traveled with us, concealed in the secret pocket of my coat. Its future would depend on our circumstances, whether we could find work in Amsterdam, how much we would have to pay for rent. I wasn't worried about Emil. I was more concerned about how I might contribute to our income.

Late in the afternoon, we took a streetcar from the Alexanderplatz to the central train station. I'd already called my mother. We said our difficult good-byes during a restrained conversation where neither of us showed much emotion. Then I called Lotti and said I'd be leaving for some time. She was still at work and didn't have time to talk.

Emil and I purchased our second-class tickets and took a seat on the platform, watching as travelers milled about in the fading sun and slanting shadows. I observed the other passengers waiting for trains and felt like a refugee. I was, although I'm sure the others didn't suspect. Emil whispered that he felt the same. He wasn't leaving parents or close relatives behind. They were already dead and resting in a Jewish cemetery in Berlin.

I looked at the men, women, and children on the platform. Were they taking an overnight train to Amsterdam as well— a trip of nearly twelve hours? Businessmen in crumpled suits and dusty shoes read their newspapers and thought about money. Where was the next mark coming from? A woman attired in a simple dress and kerchief kept her three children close by—one, a boy of eight or so, couldn't sit still. He had a small wooden bat that he used like a mallet to knock a ball a few meters down the platform. He'd retrieve it and return to his mother's side in an endless cycle of self-amusement. Two Bahnpolizei stood by, concerned only with conversing, their eyes shifting now and then to the passengers on the platform. I wondered if any of these people were Jewish. Were they fleeing the Nuremberg Laws? If so, they hid it well. I hoped we were doing the same.

The train arrived. We walked to the second-class marker and stood behind several other passengers. After we boarded, we looked for a smoking compartment and found seats facing each other next to the window. A German couple, looking like an ordinary man and woman, joined us. They said hello and soon were absorbed in their periodicals. Emil and I looked at each other and nodded, for we had vowed to keep our interactions with others to a minimum. Traveling at night, we could feign sleep, even if we found it impossible to do so. Emil had also given me a book of elementary Dutch phrases for me to study during the trip.

After a bit of a wait, the train pulled out of the station. The city rolled past, the early spring sun on the verge of setting. The clouds shimmered with streaks of pink and blue as we headed west. Soon, we were pushing through the surrounding towns and into the countryside. The conductor knocked on the door and then stepped inside to examine our tickets. Emil had placed our luggage on the overhead rack, but left the typewriter on the floor because it took up the other passengers' space. I kept my coat, and its precious cargo, folded on my lap.

"May I put your coat overhead?" the conductor asked after examining my ticket.

I was somewhat surprised at his gesture. What if he felt the bracelet through the lining? I'd padded it as much as I could, but there was a chance he might detect it. Rather than fabricate an obvious excuse like the compartment was cold—it was warm—I folded the coat again and handed it to him. He leaned over me and placed it on top of my bag. I thanked him, as two policemen sauntered by in the corridor.

The conductor confirmed our arrival time in Amsterdam, the next morning at six. We then settled in for the long night. Emil and I drifted off as we journeyed, the train rocking us to sleep with its constant *clack* and gentle sway on the tracks. Our traveling companions did the same. I bolted awake at several stops, including Hanover and Dortmund, seeing little in the darkness except the passing city lights, the black outline of a cathedral, and the station platforms.

I wondered if there were others onboard who might be fleeing Germany. Few seemed to get off the train, but it was hard to see in the thick darkness. How difficult would it be to escape Germany in the future? If Hitler continued to amass his followers, cultivating the slavish devotion that I'd seen spreading through Berlin like a virus, the time might arrive, particularly for Jews, when it would be impossible. The thought sent a cold-blooded shiver through me. I considered myself lucky as I studied Emil's sleeping face—a man who had led us to escape with relative ease. Compared to me, he appeared relaxed, his arms folded across his lap, his legs straddling the typewriter.

About four thirty in the morning we reached the Netherlands's border. A flurry of activity broke out aboard the train. First, the locomotive's whistle awakened us from our sleep as we hissed to a stop. The window had remained opened a bit during the night for fresh air. I looked past the glaring lights illuminating a vast, treeless plain and the small platform extending from the station. The German police had left their posts on the train and were standing under the bright beams on the platform. In their place, Dutch officers came aboard and immediately began checking tickets and luggage.

Once again, my heart rose into my throat, thinking of the valuable bracelet in my coat. These officers, young men, scrutinized each passenger as they scanned the compartment. All of us were asked to remove our bags from the overhead compartment and place them on the seat for inspection. I lifted my coat from my case and dropped it on the seat, placing the bag on top of it. One of the officers opened it, rummaged through it, nodded his approval, and then left. I'd never experienced anything like it in my life; our traveling companions took it in stride.

"They're worse than the Germans," she said, and smiled, implying that they were Dutch. "It's like this every time we cross the border—and they know us, we've done it so often."

"It's my first trip to Amsterdam," I said, offering my first bit of personal information.

The woman shrugged and turned away, hoping to catch another hour of sleep before we arrived. I was wide awake now, my nerves frayed from the border crossing. The train headed northwest and through the window, I caught the first rays of dawn creeping across the green fields. Soon we would be in Amsterdam. A new life awaited us.

We arrived at the central train station about six fifteen in the morning. I was stiff from the ride and happy to be out of the compartment. We gathered our luggage, crossed through the station and onto the street. The air smelled different in Amsterdam—the wash of the tidal inlets, the murky scent of the canals surrounded us. The land was flat. Even in

Berlin, one had the sense that beyond your limited view, the country rose and fell with the hills. Here, the ground was as smooth as a piece of paper, built from earth reclaimed from the sea.

We weren't far from the Jodenbuurt, the Jewish Quarter, so we decided to walk. The buildings of Amsterdam also had a different feel from those in Berlin. Space was smaller, tighter, more compact than in my home city: stone houses of varied colors and tile roofs lay along the canals, their hues and shadows shimmering against the water. Most of them were four stories tall with pitched roofs vaulted toward the sky. Gray clouds hung over the city, and a skein of early-morning rain reflected the lights on the narrow streets like glass.

It had been many years since Emil had traveled to Amsterdam with his parents to visit his uncle, Levi Belmon. Emil had wired ahead telling his uncle when we would arrive. Apparently, accommodations had been readied for us in the upper rooms of a house on Zwanenburgwal, west of the market area. Levi had been employed in the diamond business for twenty years, but also had connections to the printing industry, a resource that might benefit Emil.

I found myself happy to be out of Germany, but at the same time saddened by what I'd lost. I wondered whether Laura would miss me, or if she would even remember me the next time I saw her, if I was gone for many years. My relationship with Rickard seemed a distant memory, as thin and filmy as smoke.

We traversed the crowded streets, crossed the canal bridges, passing people who were already up and ready for business on a Thursday morning. Emil knew the address. That, and his childhood recollection, led us to his uncle's door. The building was built like many others, a whitish stone building with rectangular windows on each side of small, central balconies. Emil peered at the buzzer set into the wood near the sturdy, paneled door. The name *L. Belmon* was listed next to a button near the top. He rang it and we waited.

Levi Belmon answered the door clad in black pants and a white shirt. A yarmulke covered the crown of his head. A small man of lithe muscle, he greeted me with eager brown eyes and a wide smile, while reaching for Emil. Levi kissed him on both cheeks and smothered him with a hug.

"Come in, come in," Levi said in German, holding the door open after he'd broken free from the embrace.

Emil took off his shoes, then touched the mezuzah before kissing his fingers. I took off my shoes, but left the mezuzah alone. Levi closed the door and we stood in a narrow hall with a stairway to our left.

"We are three flights up," Levi said. "If God blesses us, you will make only one trip up these stairs with your luggage." He turned while heading upstairs and gave us another broad smile. I liked the man and felt certain that I would be welcomed into his home.

Another mezuzah waited at the landing, but Emil didn't partake of the kiss this time. Levi opened the apartment door, revealing an open central room with a long sofa facing the balcony. A wall, holding a fireplace, cut across the center of the space. A small kitchen and dining area sat to the left of the wall. Beyond that, a sleep closet and a bathroom made up the rest of the apartment.

We dropped our luggage near the door. Levi gave Emil another hug.

"I'm not as observant as you, Uncle Levi," Emil said, his cheeks reddening as he spoke.

"I wouldn't expect you to be," Levi said. "No matter. I've not been as . . . devoted . . . since Ruth died. Keep your shoes on if you like. I wonder why God would take my wife and yet allow Hitler to live." He took off his yarmulke. "I was wearing it because I was praying . . . sit, sit . . . it's been so many years since I've seen you."

We sat on the couch, while he took a seat in a chair near the balcony. The apartment was filled with light despite the cloudy day.

"How was your journey?" Levi asked.

Emil leaned forward, bent toward his uncle, comfortable with his surroundings. He had found his second home, and it was to be mine as well. The apartment was sparsely decorated, but I got a flavor of the life lived by Levi Belmon. A set of blue drapes had been pulled aside to let in light from the balcony. Beyond the glass, the canal appeared like slate under the murky sky. Boats, built like barges, sailed the placid water on their way to the nearby Amstel River. A few paintings of a Dutch nature, flowers and landscapes, hung on the white walls. A heavy sideboard of dark wood sat against the wall, the repository for a few pictures and the objects of his religion.

The conversation between the two men continued as we moved into the kitchen, where Levi made us breakfast. His movements were quick and eager, and I could tell from the light in his eyes that he wanted to hear about what was going on in Germany. Emil was happy to tell his uncle about his troubles, including his almost coming to blows with Ludwig, his former boss at the printing shop. Crunching on a piece of toast, Emil looked at me, encouraging me to tell my story.

"I'm Lutheran," I said to Levi. The man didn't flinch. I then told him about my relationship with Rickard, the books I'd written, the birth of my daughter, the deaths at Spiegel's country home, and how I'd tried to save Laura only to have her taken by my husband.

Levi sat across from me, his eyes rimmed with tears. "I thought after my Ruth was taken two years ago, life couldn't get any worse . . . but I was wrong. I see that I'm not the only one who has suffered." He pointed to the small bed to the left of the kitchen that had been built into a space the size of a closet. "I sleep here now because I can't bear to be upstairs

where we slept. That's where you will sleep now—in peace."
He reached across the table and grasped my hand. "Years
ago, you would have been welcomed into this house, but you
would never have slept here with my nephew. Times have
changed. What is going on in Germany has changed my mind
about a number of things." He sighed. "You are welcome
here, Marie, if I may call you that."

I nodded and felt lucky to be alive. We had entered the
Netherlands with false identities, as refugees, but that didn't
matter to Levi. He was only concerned that we have a comfortable home.

"It isn't much in the attic," Levi continued, looking at the
narrow wooden stairs off the kitchen that were only wide
enough for one person to ascend. "Two single beds, a chest,
four bare walls, and a window that opens and looks out over
the canal. But the room is peaceful . . . Ruth will sleep well
knowing that you are here, Emil . . . with someone you love."

"Thank you, Uncle," Emil said.

"Thank you, Mr. Belmon," I said.

Levi held up his hand. "There will be no Mr. Belmon in
this house. You will call me Levi . . . both of you." He rose
from the table. "I will take care of the dishes while you two
rest."

I offered to help, but Levi refused. We gathered our bags
and Emil headed up the narrow passage to our room. I
handed him the luggage because it was impossible to carry it
and climb the stairs.

The room was just as Levi had described—sparse, but
peaceful. After I raised the window and the warm, damp air
filled the room, I felt a sense of serenity that had eluded me
for many years, as if I might collapse on the bed, my bones
turning to jelly. I buried my head in my hands and sighed
with relief. Emil and I were home. The concerns about jobs
and making a living could wait until tomorrow. I lay back
and luxuriated in the peace I'd found in this small room.

Emil settled next to me, equally exhausted and relieved by what we had found.

A few minutes later, Levi's head popped up in the stairwell. "Nephew, you should know that I meet with men and women regularly here. There is a gathering tonight. You should attend. After hearing your stories, I think you will both be interested."

Emil raised his head and looked at his uncle. "What is this about?"

Levi's voice turned grave. "We are preparing for war. The world is afraid of Hitler and will do nothing until he crosses a line that has yet to be drawn. When he starts the war, all of Europe will be in danger. We must prepare. It is inevitable."

Emil sighed. "All right, Uncle. We will attend . . . but can we get a few hours' sleep before the war breaks out?"

Levi smiled. "Of course . . . you are welcome to sleep." He shut the narrow door to our room.

We pushed the two beds together, and, placing my arm over his body, I faced Emil.

"We can't escape, can we?" he asked.

I took a moment to answer. "We can't escape Hitler. Your uncle is right. We have to prepare for war. What he's done to the Jews in Germany, he will do here."

Emil put a finger to my lips. "Let's rest for now. We will have time to plan later."

We kissed. He took off his glasses, put them on the floor near the head of the bed, and closed his eyes.

I watched him fall asleep and listened to the water softly lap at the canal wall.

# CHAPTER 19

For more than three years we lived in relative peace, avoiding the horrors of Germany, until the war began on September 1, 1939.

Emil found a job in a printing shop in the Jodenbuurt, and I as a clerk in the diamond-polishing factory where Levi was employed. Our days were happy, filled with work and even fun as the city became our home. I learned Dutch. We walked Amsterdam, learned the history of Waterlooplein and shopped at the market there, and wandered the tree-lined squares and boulevards of De Plantage.

But a dark current swirled beneath the ordinary lives that we tried to live. We learned through Levi and others that laws had been passed in Germany in October of 1938 invalidating all Jewish passports. After surrender to the government, a large letter "J" was stamped on the passport of German Jews. This was in addition to identity cards separating the Jewish population from the "true" German. In November of the same year, an organized rampage against German Jews was fomented by the Nazis. It became known as Kristallnacht. Many Jews were arrested while shops and synagogues were destroyed.

The meetings that Levi had mentioned when we arrived in Amsterdam occurred monthly and were more like socials until the bad news of 1938. Then the gatherings occurred weekly, every Wednesday night, with about ten men and women attending—all planning what the Jews of Amsterdam would do if the country was invaded. The conversation and interactions were formal and conducted like a business meeting, with each person assigned a different task related to the possible invasion, including reconnaissance, arms, and hiding places.

I struggled a bit with my Dutch, but I got by. If there was any translating to be done, Emil would tell me in German.

Four people stood out at these meetings—two women and two men. The women were Toos and Karin. Both were beautiful in their own ways. Toos had long brunette hair that fell to her shoulders. Her body was shapely and slender, and she carried herself in a regal manner, head held high on a thin neck, her shoulders relaxed, yet imposing, in her perfect posture. She was proud of the way she looked. She wore red dresses of varying shades that accented her body and matched the lipstick she was wearing. Usually, she sat at one end of Levi's couch, legs crossed, enjoying a cigarette, letting the smoke curl out of her mouth. She also had a fondness for whiskey, which she drank by the quarter tumbler during the meeting.

Karin, on the other hand, had hair a shade lighter than Toos and was fuller of figure. She neither smoke nor drank, but the fire beneath her eyes belied that she was no saint. One could almost hear her mind whirring as she and Toos occupied opposite ends of the couch. Karin was pretty with a pert nose and ruddy cheeks. Of all the men and women who attended the gatherings, I felt she was the smartest, as well as the most calculating and dangerous—not a woman to be trifled with.

The two men were Derk and Ruud. Derk was the scholar of the two, a serious man who rarely spoke, but like Karin had a sharp mind. His eyes and mouth shifted as plans were plotted, and I suspected that he might also be the assassin in the group, a man who would have no problem taking a Nazi's life. Like Emil, he wore glasses that he would take off at least once during the meeting and wipe clean with his handkerchief.

Ruud was a Dutch soldier, a blond, burly man with broad shoulders and big arms. He was the strategist, always analyzing every move that our group conceived, telling us why particular plans wouldn't work and what we should do to correct our errors.

And lording over us was Emil's uncle, Levi, a man with a level head who kept the group together. There were no blessings or prayers given, although every member of the Wednesday Night Club, as we called it, was a Jew except Ruud. He had been drawn into the group by his attraction to Toos. Religion was put aside for the evening in order to focus on the world's evils.

As 1938 ended and 1939 began, Emil and I realized how lucky we had been to flee Germany. Hitler had tightened his restrictions on Jews.

When the Nazis invaded Poland we knew what was coming to the Netherlands. Some believed that Hitler had pushed the world too far; he had crossed a line and would be punished. Emil and I knew the truth. No one could stop the Reich's war machine.

Communist organizations, Jewish resistance groups, and people offering housing for enemies of the Reich proliferated as the Nazi threat increased; but there was little communication and coordination among them. The Dutch Army lagged far behind the Wehrmacht in men and materiel. Ruud felt he was in an "army of children" compared to the blitzkrieg strategies employed by the Nazis. A bad economy and budget cuts had hampered the Dutch Army's efforts to rebuild a potent force after the Great War.

The Dutch always considered water, flooding their lowlands, as protection against an invasion—men and tanks would be mired in the muck. Three defensive lines were established after the war began, stretching north to south, hoping to halt the probable path of invasion from east to west.

The invasion came on May 10, 1940. Emil and I awoke to what we thought were the sounds of aircraft overhead. We went downstairs to confer with Levi and all of us ran to the windows, but we spotted nothing in the air. However, from radio reports we knew the invasion had begun. Nothing could be done, and, as Ruud had warned us, Dutch neutrality during the Great War would mean nothing to Hitler.

The next day, Emil and I witnessed from our respective workplaces the four bombs that fell on Amsterdam's center. More than forty people were killed, but we counted ourselves lucky when the surrender came three days later because the city had suffered little compared to The Hague and Rotterdam. The Germans had achieved their military goals, while the Dutch royal family and the government fled to England.

Far worse was to come.

Everyone was numb at the next meeting of the Wednesday Night Club. Levi had drawn the curtains, lit two candles on the sideboard, and turned on one lamp, which cast an anemic yellow light through the room. Toos filled her tumbler with more whiskey than usual. Karin sat with head turned, gazing toward Levi's kitchen, her chin resting on the fingers of her upturned arm. Derk, dressed in black, was more solemn than usual, and Ruud, normally bulging with strength, looked defeated and exhausted, his eyes dark from too little sleep from the sparse interaction with German forces to the north of Amsterdam.

Levi attempted to bolster the group's enthusiasm, but even his tone was grave. "Well, my friends . . . what we feared has arrived."

His words were met with silence until Ruud spoke up, his

gaze rising from the floor. "We were no match for them. They bombed the hell out of Rotterdam—there's nothing left of the city. An officer told me that Göring wanted the Netherlands . . . he needed the airfields . . . afraid they would be taken over by England." He sighed. "Utter defeat. Our defensive lines were useless. But I warned you . . ." His head sank.

I remembered my introduction to Göring at Spiegel's home and shuddered. Even then, I thought the man a monster.

Toos raised her glass in a melancholy toast. "Here's to us." She swallowed a large gulp of whiskey, her red lipstick leaving an imprint on the crystal.

"What do we do?" one of the others asked.

"Understand our assignments," Levi said. "Put them into action. Do we have places where we can shelter others . . . where we can hide?"

Many in the group nodded their heads.

"Good," Levi said. "We have weapons that can be used if necessary."

Straightening her back against the couch, Karin interrupted a mild chorus of affirmations. "I want them dead."

The air trembled and silence filled the room. A shock wave, like static electricity, traveled from person to person.

Levi, sitting in a chair opposite Karin, looked at her as if he were about to lecture a child. "Let's not forget the past, despite a bleak future. We, in this room, agreed not to honor evil, not to violate God's laws. We cannot go against Him without good reason."

Karin bent forward, thrusting a finger toward Levi, her eyes sparking with anger. "Make no mistake, Levi, the Nazis will provide many reasons to violate God's laws. Kill or be killed. I will pull the trigger, gladly."

"Let's not dwell on it," Derk said, pushing his glasses up on his nose. "We must act."

After discussing how we would deal with a Nazi occupation— rationing, restrictive measures like those passed in Germany, a Jewish registry, and threats to jobs—the meeting ended. Levi asked Emil and me to look into identification paper forgery, something he felt Emil would be better prepared to do because of his printing work. He agreed.

As the meeting was breaking up, Toos called me aside. She stood next to the sideboard, her hip thrust against the wood. She wobbled a bit from the whiskey. "How old are you?" she asked in her best German.

I wondered what she was getting at. "I'll be twenty-nine at the end of this month."

She brushed her hand against my cheek. "Young enough to get a man."

"I'm quite happy now," I said, somewhat defensively.

She parted her lips a bit, in a knowing smile. "Oh, not that. Seducing men—you're still young enough to seduce a man."

"What do you mean?"

"Ask Karin at the next meeting. She's serious about wanting them dead." She tapped me on the shoulder and left.

Soon, only Levi, Emil, and I were in the apartment.

"I'm going to bed," Levi said. "God willing, tomorrow will be better. Good night."

As we climbed the narrow stairs to our room, Emil asked, "What did Toos want?"

I closed the door and started to undress. A breeze blew off the canal, rippling the curtains. "I'm not sure and I don't think you want to know."

"If it concerns you, I want to know."

I sat on the bed and pulled off my shoes. "I think she wants me to kill Nazis."

Emil sighed and shook his head.

I turned out the light.

Levi directed me to a jeweler he knew from his work in the diamond industry. I felt it was time to get rid of the bracelet that I'd had for so many years. After the occupation, the guilder was equal to 1.5 German marks, so Emil and I decided to sell it before the Nazis got the word out in Amsterdam about a stolen piece of jewelry.

I carefully snipped the secret pocket knowing that I might need it in the future to hide documents or other valuables. I put the bracelet in my purse and walked to the jeweler during my lunch break. The shop was close to the city center where the bombs fell.

Amsterdam was under German control. The anxiety about the invasion had been replaced by a stoic understanding of what an occupation meant to the Dutch. Businesses, for now, operated as usual. The Wehrmacht soldiers often seemed polite, even queuing up at a chocolate store to buy a treat. They'd stroll down the street, as if taking a leisurely walk with weapons strapped to their sides, enjoying the spring weather, admiring the flowers, or chatting with a mother and her children. Some Dutch collaborated, even welcomed the Nazis, but most men, women, and children looked at them with fear in their eyes, knowing that the weapons the soldiers carried could be turned upon them at any moment. I had seen their faces as the German troops paraded into the city.

The small jewelry store, touting watch repair, had a glass display window cross-hatched with wooden slats. Behind it, watches, bracelets, necklaces, pins, and brooches lay on hillocks of black velvet. The afternoon sun struck the window, setting the jewels behind it aflame with color. The displayed wealth staggered me, and reminded me of the days when the Dutch controlled much of the world's commerce.

Inside, two men stood behind the counter. The older of the two sat on a stool near the back while tinkering with a watch. As I entered, he looked at me briefly and then returned to work, his gloved hands displaying the exacting movements of a jeweler.

I approached the one closest to me, a young man with an oval face and thin nose who smiled as I closed the door.

"May I help you?" he asked in his native language.

"I'm here to sell a bracelet," I said, thinking carefully about my Dutch phrases.

The young man looked at me skeptically, his blue eyes shifting as my hand moved toward my purse. "Everyone wants to sell. May I see what you have to offer?"

I handed it to him and watched as his eyes grew large from what I'd placed in his grasp. He stuttered a bit and then said, "My father will want to see this." He called out and the older man rose from his seat and walked toward us.

"Look," the young man said to his father.

The older man developed a similar expression as he held the bracelet up to the light and then examined it with a loupe.

"Where did you get this?" the father asked.

"It was left to me by my aunt," I said, repeating the story I'd told in Berlin.

He took out a velvet server and put the bracelet on it. "Your aunt was a very generous woman." The half smile on his lips faded. "Are you German?"

Somehow, I'd been caught. I had no choice but to tell as much of the truth as I dared. "Yes, but I've been living in Amsterdam for a few years."

The older man turned the piece over and pointed with a needle file to a tiny indentation in the metal that the Berlin jeweler had pointed out. "A maker's mark, identifying the piece as made in Paris." He paused and switched to a halting German. Perhaps he thought I was a spy. "You got this legally from your aunt? Do you have papers? I have to be careful now that we are . . . occupied."

My cheeks flushed. "I have no papers—I wish to sell it as soon as possible." I started to pick it up, but he stopped my hand.

"Do the Nazis know about this?" he asked.

An uncomfortable truth was coming closer. I nodded. "Yes, they do. You would be taking a chance. On the other hand, the bracelet is six hundred and fifty kilometers away from where I obtained it. I'm certain they don't know it's here."

The older man leaned over the piece again, his light-blond hair falling over his forehead. "It's exquisite, the cut and the clarity . . . magnificent. I suppose they would never know if I sold each stone separately."

"I'm sure my aunt would have no objection," I said.

"I'll give you thirty-five thousand guilders for it," the father said. The young man looked on with a pleased expression.

"Forty," I said, knowing that figure exceeded Spiegel's top estimate of fifty thousand German marks. The war had increased the price of precious stones for those who could afford it.

"Thirty-eight."

"It's yours," I said. "Could you make the payment in large and small bills?"

"Of course," he said, and walked past a curtain at the back of the shop.

The young man and I chatted about the weather for a few minutes until the older man returned carrying an envelope with the bills. "Feel free to count it," he said.

"I trust you," I said, putting the money into my purse. "If not, I'll be back."

I said good-bye and left the shop, decidedly richer than when I'd come in. Emil had readied a hiding place for the money in our room, in the base of a ceramic lamp.

The insurance policy that I'd carried for so long finally had paid off.

*   *   *

In October and November of 1940, the Nazis tightened their stranglehold. Like the restrictions in Germany, those in the Netherlands were aimed at Jews. Dutch officials were forced to swear an oath affirming that they and their family members weren't Jewish. A month later, Jewish civil servants were dismissed from their jobs. The Wednesday Night Club took note of these new decrees with renewed trepidation. A few believed that these measures were an inconvenience at most and that Germany would soon be defeated. But there were others, including Emil and me, who dismissed those false hopes.

Toos, Karin, Derk, and Ruud stayed late one night after the others had left. Together we formed the core of the group most likely to resist the Nazis. Levi sat in his usual spot, fidgeting with his gold pocket watch, studying us as if we were foolish children.

"Violence will only get more Jews killed," Levi cautioned. "The Nazis will take their revenge. They will not hesitate."

Karin shook her head. "But if we take them down one by one by making a list, finding those leaders who have no wives or children . . . shouldn't they be marked for liquidation? At least we've limited the damage."

I was stunned at Karin's calculating mind—a pretty girl with the intellect of a killer.

"You're planning to kill by prescription?" Levi asked, putting a hand to his forehead as if he had a headache. "You think that will make it better, somehow, because they have no children—that the murder will be less offensive to God?"

Karin nodded. "It's the best I can offer."

"We have to do something," Derk said. "The Nazis must be punished. They must feel the pain they've brought to others. If not, we might as well be slaves."

Emil pulled a sheaf of papers from behind his back and placed it in the center of the room. "This is what I've been doing after work hours. I started this in Berlin, but I've been even more careful here. My boss is Jewish, and he doesn't want to get into trouble." He untied the twine holding the papers together, pulled a bundle from it, and passed it to Karin. Soon, the flyers had circulated around the room.

Ruud whistled. "This will get their attention." He pointed to the stick figures on the page, their helmets and caps painted with swastikas. "Citizens of Amsterdam—of our beloved Netherlands—resist the Nazi pigs," he read. "They've destroyed our country and they will come for you." He snickered and tossed the flyer to the floor. "Well, I will say this, Emil. Your execution is as certain as if you'd shot a Nazi in the head. I'd rather cut their throats than play games."

Toos put a finger to her painted lips. "Save that thought." She paused and turned to me. "Niki, would you like to be part of our little group? Karin and I have decided upon a plan. Derk has offered to help us out." By this time, they all knew me by my nickname.

"You'll have to explain," I said. Emil's gaze shifted toward me and I could tell that he wanted me to have no part in whatever they were planning.

Toos sipped her whiskey and leaned back coolly on the couch. "It's simple really. We make the list, take an officer under a canal bridge or into the park woods and seduce him. They're men, alone in a foreign city, without their wives or girlfriends. We have to kiss the monsters, maybe go a little further, unbutton their uniforms, unbuckle their belts . . . and Karin or Derk finish the job. One quick cut, one shot, and it's over."

I had been right about my suspicions. The killers in the room were Karin and Derk. Emil took in a few quick breaths and rose from the floor. "No! Niki won't have anything to do with this—I won't let her." His voice rose. "It's ugly . . . evil!"

Levi grabbed his arm and forced him to sit. "I understand, but calm down. We don't want everyone in Amsterdam to hear what we're planning." He looked at the pile of printed pages on the floor. "Perhaps you should let Niki decide, since you've taken your own stand against the Nazis. I don't condone killing, but, after all, one mistake with your flyers and we could all be dead."

Beneath his glasses, Emil's eyes widened. "No, don't do it. Please don't. It's too—"

"Too what?" Karin asked, the question bitter in her mouth.

Emil put his hands on the pages and shook his head. "I'm not killing people. I'm pointing out the truth."

"It's the same," Toos said. "Let Niki decide." She pursed her red lips and stared at me.

"I can't," I said after some time. "I have to honor Emil's wishes."

Toos lit a cigarette and then smiled. "We're here if you reconsider." She blew smoke in my direction. "I think you'll come around. Karin and I have decided."

The group soon disbanded, and Emil and I found our way to our room after saying good night to Levi.

We collapsed into bed, crawling under the sheet. A warm, damp breeze drifted into the room, reminding me that the canal was only a few meters from the building. I shifted next to Emil. He had turned away from me, toward the chest of drawers and the lamp. I touched his shoulder and he shuddered violently, sobs wracking his body.

"It's all right," I said, wrapping my arms around his chest. "I won't kill anyone."

He turned toward me. In the dim light, I saw the tears glistening in his eyes. He pulled me close, so close that we were entwined. "My God, if I lost you, I don't know what I'd do. We've been through so much. Can we go to England . . . to America? I don't care—any place that's far away from the Nazis."

"I'm afraid it's too late," I said. "We didn't think it could happen here. We didn't know how weak we were."

He kissed me, his cheeks wet against mine. "And now we have to be strong . . . again. How long will this go on?"

I shook my head and listened as his breathing grew shallow and his tears dried.

I woke up a few hours later, sweating and shivering, with Emil still near me, but my mind reeling from the images of a nightmare.

I was kissing a German officer, my hands on his chest, his hands cupping the small of my back. Suddenly, he gasped for air as his throat was cut, the flash of the knife coming from behind. The blood ran red and deep down his throat and chest, blackening his uniform.

I screamed because I wasn't in Amsterdam.

I was surrounded by the fires of Hell.

# CHAPTER 20

In January 1941, Jews were told they must register with the Nazi government. The news, delivered blithely by uniformed officers on the street corners, also was posted in newspapers and printed on flyers much like the subversive tracts created by Emil. So far, he'd escaped detection, but the Wednesday Night Club knew the SS was tracking down every lead in order to quash dissent.

On a snowy, late-December morning, I listened as the decree was issued by a German officer who stood in front of a bakery not far from Levi's apartment. The location had been selected with care, for the Nazis knew that a crowd would be gathered to buy pastries for the day.

"Listen, Jews," the officer said. He was tall, as tall as the Dutch men surrounding him. His eyes shifted from the piece of paper he held to the crowd. I couldn't tell much about his personality—he was another uniform among many, his face decidedly Germanic, but neither cruel nor saintly. He seemed intent on his job, espousing the Reich's power to enforce the new "law" at any cost. If nothing else, he projected authority.

"You must register as a Jew by . . ." his voice droned on in Dutch with no emotion behind it. The Christians in the group hurried away, foregoing their morning purchases. A few men and women lingered behind, perhaps convinced that

this was another annoyance foisted upon the Dutch Jews—
something only to be marked in their datebooks.

A man emerged from a dark stairway at the side of the
shop, holding a large dachshund in his hands. The short-
haired creature erupted in fevered barks as the officer spoke.

"Silence that dog," the Nazi said.

"Yes, officer," the man said. "We were going to take a
walk. He clamped his fingers around the dog's snout and
clutched its blue collar, but it squirmed and wriggled until it
was free from his grip. The dog continued barking as the man
struggled to control it.

The German gave the stout Dutch man a withering look
and held out his hands. "Give me the dog."

"He's not friendly, officer," the man replied. "I don't think
you'd like his bite."

"I don't like him at all," the officer said. "Go on, get out
of here."

The man scooted to the curb, placed the dog in the street,
and started to walk away.

"Halt!"

The man stopped, turned, and looked at the officer.

The German withdrew his pistol and shot the dog. The
animal screamed as the bullet entered him. It fell in a heap
near the gutter, bleeding on the stones.

The dog's owner fell to his knees, crying over the animal's
body, caressing his fur and lifting its matted head. "Why?
Why did you do that?" the man implored, blood streaking
his fingers.

"Because it wouldn't shut up. This is a lesson in manners.
You've learned to respect German authority. You Jews think
you can get away with anything."

"I'm not a Jew," the man said, and lowered his head.

The officer scoffed and gave the flyers to another man near
him. "Make sure everyone reads this. Your day will come."

He holstered his pistol and strode away as if nothing had happened.

I walked to the dog's owner, who was still kneeling in the gutter. "I'm sorry." I put my hand on his shoulder.

"I lied because I didn't want him to touch my pet. He was a good dog. He never bit anyone. Why would he kill him?" He looked up, the painful loss searing his blue eyes.

"Because the Nazis are cruel and care for nothing but themselves."

"Now, I have to bury him. He was my friend."

There was nothing I could do but offer another expression of sorrow and walk away. I returned to the apartment, shaken and late for work. I sat on the couch and looked out the balcony window toward the canal. The gray clouds threatened snow. The day was as bitter as the feelings in my heart.

Perhaps Toos and Karin were right.

*Perhaps we have to kill in order to live.*

A few weeks later, as I bicycled to work, I stopped at an intersection crowded with people. Light the color of slate covered Amsterdam as winter clutched the city. A mother and two children stood by a wall that bordered a half-frozen canal. In front of the terrified children, a man pointed a pistol at the woman. He wore a dark double-breasted coat and a hat bearing a triangular patch of red and black. The patch was split by a National Socialist symbol that looked like a lightning bolt.

A man from the edge of the crowd rushed toward me, thrusting out his gloved hands, urging me to stop, to go no farther until the commotion was over. I couldn't imagine what kind of offense involved a mother and two small children.

I looked at him with that question in mind.

"I don't know, but she's rumored to be a spy," he whispered to me. "He's Dutch SS, the NSB, the National Socialist Movement, the ones who have fallen in with the Nazis."

"What if I'm a member of the NSB?" I asked.

The man's eyes widened in shock and he recoiled, ready to slink away.

"Stop," I said, as he turned. "Don't trust anyone. Be careful what you say."

"I should have kept my mouth shut," he said. "I'm so upset. The children . . ."

The man was right. A small boy and girl, clad in their winter coats and boots, stood on each side of their mother, their eyes peering out from under their caps. The boy held two fingers in his mouth. The mother protested her innocence while the man shouted at her. With each scream the children shook and drew closer to the woman's legs.

I got off my bicycle and pushed it forward. The crowd around the SS man seemed hypnotized by the scene. The individual expressions ranged from concern and indignation to curiosity, many acting as if they had stumbled across a grisly accident they couldn't look away from.

"You're a spy," the SS man shouted. "We know what you've done—distributed literature against the Occupation, given the enemy the location of troop movements, worked to undermine the NSB with your false accusations."

"False accusations?" the woman asked, lunging forward. "Look around. You've destroyed our country, enslaved our people."

I gasped, for I knew the woman had gone too far. Even though I was a few meters away, I could see the rage boiling in her accuser's eyes.

"Your people? You are a Jew." He stepped closer to her. "Which one of your children do you love the most?"

The woman stumbled back to the wall. "I love them both equally."

"If they grow," he said, shaking the pistol in her face,

"they will produce more Jews and that is against the law. Which one of them is to die?"

Some in the crowd moaned. The chill in the air was nothing compared to the paralysis that filled my body and froze me to the spot. I wished I'd carried a gun—I would have killed him on the spot.

The children screeched and the mother wailed, asking the man to take pity on her offspring. A member of the crowd moved toward him. Turning, the SS man swept the pistol in an arc toward us. "I'll kill anyone who takes justice from the NSB."

Another man wearing an identical hat appeared from around the corner. What was unfolding in front of me seemed like the climax of some hellish tragedy. The colorful buildings with their pitched roofs stood as a backdrop unflinching in their history; the greenish-gray water flowed under the ice in its never-ending mix with the sea. The city stood timeless, holding its breath as Death showed its prescient face once again.

The second SS man held the mother and son. The first took the girl, who struggled and cried out in his arms, then grabbed her by the ankles and swung the child into the wall. Her head smashed into the stone with a bitter crack. The child's cap turned a sickening red as she dangled from his hands. He dropped her like a sack of potatoes onto the walk.

The mother screamed and fell to her knees in front of the dead girl. The SS man shot her in the back of the head. The boy ran, but the other one caught him by the arm and threw him backward.

"Into the canal with him," the first man said.

The second lifted the boy, pushed through the crowd, and then, standing at the edge of the canal, heaved the child into the water. The boy hit the ice, cracking it, yelling, screaming for his life, as his boots and clothes sucked up the water and dragged him under. His young hands stretched above the ice for a moment, his head bobbing before it disappeared in a wreath of bubbles.

My soul left my body, as empty and lifeless as the hollow sky. The loyal Dutch in the crowd stood silent for a time before moving. Like me, they were shocked beyond belief by what they'd just witnessed.

Satisfied that their cruel justice was finished, the NSB men left the bodies at the wall and walked away. I looked at the canal, hoping that the boy might somehow swim to safety. But the turbulence in the water had died and the fractured ice had begun to cover the hole.

I pedaled to work, knowing that I couldn't desert my duties; otherwise, I might lose my job. The rest of the day, I fulfilled customers' orders and filed, often wiping away tears.

The clouds had broken a bit by the time I left work. The western sun slanted across them, painting their pearly tips crimson. I thought of the Dutch man's dead dog, the murder of the mother and her two children I'd witnessed this morning, and what Toos had said to me while discussing the assassination of German officers.

*I think you'll come around.*

Toos was right. As I rode home, a terrible hatred consumed me, rising from my stomach into my head, blinding my vision as if I was looking into the sun. The Wehrmacht men who stood on the streets of Amsterdam were as dead to me as the murdered woman and her children.

I wanted to kill.

Only Emil and Levi stood in my way. Did they have to know?

Toos's apartment was a few blocks away from Levi's, off the center of a congested street. She lived in three small rooms that got little light because of the dense cluster of buildings surrounding them. One evening after the murders, as the day grew dark, I went to see her.

In contrast with the reds that she favored for dress, her apartment was decorated in shades of delft blue and white. The colors made the space seem larger and brighter despite its lack of natural light.

She welcomed me and offered me a drink of expensive scotch whiskey, which I accepted. My nerves rattled underneath my skin as I thought about what I had to say. I sat in a chair near a tiny window facing the street and wondered how to begin.

Toos made it easy for me. "I knew you'd come around." Her eyebrows lifted in an *I told you so* gesture. "Would you like a cigarette?"

I nodded.

She handed me an ebony cigarette case from the center table. She took her place on a small couch, positioned her feet underneath her legs, and stretched the fabric of her blue dress down to her calves. She looked confident and serene, but her faint smile unnerved me because she knew why I'd come.

I lit the smoke and settled back in the chair. "I saw an NSB man murder a woman and her two children. The killings made me sick and angry, and made me feel helpless because I could do nothing to stop them. It brought back memories of the night my daughter was kidnapped by SA thugs."

"I didn't know you had a daughter." She paused. "I heard about the murders. The Nazis are butchers."

"I think about my daughter every day. She's part of the reason I want revenge." The inner barriers I'd created broke like a flooded dam and I told Toos everything about my life since I'd met Rickard, including how the SS had murdered Spiegel. The only details I left out were the theft of the bracelet and its sale.

"I want to help you and Karin. It was different with Spiegel. I didn't like him, but this woman and her children . . . I'm driven by revenge."

"Have you told Emil?"

I shook my head. "Not yet . . . but I will. As Levi pointed out, what Emil's doing could get us killed just as easily."

Toos looked at her nails and then at me. "Karin surprises me at times. She makes it all sound so simple, as if taking a life is like picking a flower. Have you ever killed anyone?"

"No. Have you?"

"I had an illegal abortion . . . some people consider it murder." Her dark eyebrows rose. "I was in bad straits. My parents had died the year before. A short time after their deaths, I had a passionate affair with a man who said he loved me—for three months—then walked out of my life . . . with me carrying his child. I got a little money from my parents, but not enough for a life of ease. For a time, I made money the way women have for centuries. That's a polite way of saying I was a prostitute." She reached for a cigarette. "Are you certain you want to do this?"

"Yes. I was never very good at seduction. Mostly I was looking for a meal and a place to stay."

"I'll teach you." She laughed and then her smile dimmed and her voice darkened. "Ruud has selected a German officer, about twenty-eight years old, named Miller. We don't know if he's married or has children. Why should we be concerned about that? Because we're Jews and we want to limit the life we take, the lives we affect? That's nonsense coming from Levi, as far as I'm concerned. Does he think the Nazis have any hesitation about killing us?" She studied me, judging my thoughts.

"Miller likes to drink and often has a few beers when he's off duty at a pub, a *kroeg*, across the canal," she continued. "He loves women even more than he likes to drink. Ruud and Derk have been watching him for weeks. His pattern is consistent, and because of his rank, he doesn't often socialize with the men below him. He's escorted a few women, whom we've marked as collaborators, to a hotel. Miller's been seen leaving the hotel early in the morning with his chosen ones. They go their separate ways. He's perfect for us."

"How do we kill him?"

"There's a canal near the pub. We entice him—seduce him—and offer him favors by the canal—as soon as we can—maybe next Tuesday night. If he wants to go to a hotel, we have to change his mind. We'll tell him that we have something special planned outdoors, that we don't like hotels. We make sure he's had a few drinks—that he's loose and ready. Karin or Derk will be waiting—with a knife. Tuesday isn't a big night for the pub. Get him ready to pop and then . . ." She raised her hand, positioning her fingers as if she was gripping a blade, then slashed it across her throat. "Weight the body, dump it in the canal, and we're done. Miller's deserted his men, never to be found."

I asked for another cigarette. My hands trembled as I lit it.

"Scared?" Toos asked. She shifted, sliding her long legs to the floor.

"Of course . . . but, we're doing something, aren't we? What we're doing might not stop the Nazis, but if we do nothing, then we wait for them to kill us."

Toos nodded and crossed her legs. "It's revenge . . . our way of fighting back."

"We could die as well."

"*Liebchen*, it doesn't make any difference," she said, resorting to a German word meaning "sweetheart." "Death will come no matter what we do. Death will come until the fascists are wiped out or until Hitler rules the world and has no one left to kill." She tilted her head toward my glass. "Another drink?"

"No," I said, placing the empty glass on the table. "I should be going. Emil will be worried and there will be liquor on my breath."

"He'll understand."

"I'm not so sure."

I got up and Toos followed me to the door. "Come here next Tuesday at seven, unless you get a message telling you not to come. I'll make you up."

"I'll need something pretty," I said.

"I've got dresses."

We said good night and I left. When I got to the apartment, Emil and Levi were having supper at the kitchen table. Emil smiled and asked me why I was late.

"Nothing much," I said. "I'll tell you later."

Levi's eyes took me in.

I was certain he knew where I'd been.

# CHAPTER 21

I didn't talk to Emil that night. The next evening, after Levi had gone to visit friends, I decided to open up.

Emil and I sat on the couch together, looking out the window toward the canal, which glittered under a nearly full moon. I expected to cry during my confession. That morning, I'd told the two men about witnessing the murders, but didn't mention how that awful event had changed my mind about the Wednesday Night Club's plans. Laura and Rickard were in my thoughts as well. At that moment, the war was going so well for Hitler that world domination by the Nazis seemed a real possibility.

"I'm going to work with Toos and Karin," I told him, crushing the handkerchief between my palms.

To my surprise, Emil took off his glasses, rubbed his eyes, and then looked at me as if the world had opened before him. "When Toos asked, I knew you'd eventually join them. I could see it in your eyes. You've been through so much, seen too much to roll over like a dog." He motioned to me. "Give me your handkerchief."

I handed it to him. He cleaned the lenses of his glasses before hooking the pair over his ears. "I'll hold on to this," he said, holding it. "There's no need to cry."

"I've been so scared to tell you—I thought you would be angry—forbid me to do it."

He turned to me. "I've changed, too, since the murders. I'm still printing flyers, resisting in my own way. The Nazis could come for me at any time. Jews are beginning to disappear. There's a rumor circulating that the Germans will confine us to the Jodenbuurt. God knows what will happen after that. It's too late to escape. We have nothing to offer but our lives."

"I'm not going to kill the man," I said. "I couldn't do that."

"But you are killing him. You're justifying your action by saying you're not."

"Please, at least let me believe that I'm not."

"You're not a killer, Niki. You're a writer—an artist." He kissed me on the forehead. "When is this supposed to happen?"

"Next Tuesday . . . if everything goes as planned."

Emil rose from the couch, walked toward the balcony, and looked into the sky. The wide windows were closed to keep out the cold air. "We left Germany and they followed us. Now we have to fight."

I nodded and looked at his body outlined against the glass. He clutched my handkerchief in his right hand. I thought he might cry, but no tears came.

We had no idea that Tuesday, February 11, 1941, would be a turning point for the Jews of Amsterdam. The restrictions put in place since the Occupation, and the Nazi threat of forced labor in Germany for Amsterdam's shipyard workers, escalated simmering tensions.

Uncle Levi and I had bicycled home from work in the late afternoon. Wild rumors were circulating that a fight had broken out between the paramilitary wing of the NSB, the Weerbaarheidsafdeling (the WA), and Jewish defenders in the nearby Waterlooplein. I was already in an agitated state because of what I had planned for the evening.

Toos had sent me a message at work, in coded language, stating that the plan was going forward. It read: *Nice evening. Meet you at my apartment for that drink tonight.* She'd hoped for rain and clouds to hide our actions—the full moon could present a problem—but the WA fight on the Waterlooplein meant that reprisals might soon follow. It was better to act now than to face another Nazi crackdown. I burned the note in the water closet and flushed the ashes down the toilet.

As I readied myself in our attic bedroom, the door burst open below. Levi shouted and a *thud* echoed through the apartment. I rushed down the narrow stairs to find Emil sprawled on the floor, blood seeping from a cut on his cheek, his clothes spotted with crimson.

"I ran back," he said. "The cut's not as bad as it looks." Looking dazed and flushed, he lifted himself on his elbows. "The blood on me is from someone else."

"My God, what happened?" I asked, kneeling beside him. "Levi, get a cold washcloth." Dashing to the bathroom, he did as I asked.

"I saw members of the *knokploeg* run by the shop," Emil said, still trying to catch his breath.

I knew he was referring to a Jewish defense group.

"One of them popped his head in and said that the WA men had entered the square and were threatening Jews and looking for a fight." He exhaled and lay back on the floor. "I didn't even think about it. I took off my apron and ran after them."

Levi returned with the wet cloth. "This is a nasty cut," I said, as I swabbed the blood away, then pressed the compress against the wound.

"There must have been forty of them," Emil said. "Soon, fists, sticks, and clubs were flying. It turned into a riot. One of the WA leaders—a man named Koot, I think, got hit in the head with a club. He went down and his compatriots rushed to him. The fight broke up. They carried the wounded man away. I decided to get out while I could."

Levi, who'd been bending over Emil, straightened and paced around the room. "I knew this would happen. Violence begets violence. It will be terrible now. The Nazis will call out the dogs. A flyer is one thing, but a fight . . ."

Emil pushed himself off the floor, groaning, while pressing the bloody cloth against his face. "One of those thugs got me with his knuckles. He missed my eye."

Levi moaned and settled on the couch.

"Uncle, calm down," Emil said. "We've known for almost a year that this was coming. No one ever said the Occupation was going to be a picnic."

"Watch," Levi said. "See what happens."

"I'm going to clean up," Emil said, swaying toward the bathroom.

I wanted to tell Levi that I was on my way to help kill a German officer. I wanted to prove that I was *doing* something, not just printing words or planning where to hide. I said nothing, however. He would find out soon enough.

I followed Emil. He washed his face and then put a bandage over the cut. I kissed him on the forehead. "I'm going now."

A purple bruise had blossomed around the wound on his cheek. The right earpiece of his glasses had been bent in the fight. He took them off to mend the damage. "This is not what I need. I can't afford a new pair."

"Did you hear me?" I asked. "I'm going."

He turned his bruised face toward me, his eyes dim and watery. "I know. Please be careful. Are you certain you want to go through with this?"

"Toos and Karin need me, just as the *knokploeg* needed you today."

He nodded. "I'm not going to think about it. I'm going to have a drink and keep Uncle Levi occupied . . . and when I'm in bed, I'll dream that you return safely home." He pulled me into his arms and kissed me. "You will return to me." The words came out with confidence and ease.

I gathered my coat and said good-bye to Levi. His eyes drooped with sadness as I closed the door.

Toos was waiting when I arrived at her apartment.

She was ready, dressed in a darker shade of red than I'd ever seen her wear. She'd heard about the fight, but didn't know that Emil was involved. We didn't talk much about it, for we had more pressing plans.

"With your skin color and hair, we're going with black and a bright red lipstick." Toos took me to a wardrobe in her bedroom, opened it, and took out a dress that somehow shimmered in the dim light. "I think it will fit. Try it on."

It did fit, along with a pair of black shoes that Toos fished out of her closet. I applied the lipstick at the small dresser and mirror and studied my reflection. I looked good, but the image shocked me. The woman who stared back at me was one of the world, much more confident than my heroine in *The Berlin Woman*. The reflection wasn't my past either: a woman escaping her mother, going from man to man, depending on Rickard, or even dancing around the Nazis. No, she was strong, knowing that what she had to do was right despite any outcome. Leaving Germany, living in Amsterdam, had changed her.

"You look beautiful," Toos said, "but there's one more thing." She stood behind me, combed my hair back, and then fashioned it in a knot on the back of my head. "There. Perfect. You're a Dutch woman ready for a night on the town."

"Thank you. I feel strange, though."

"That's to be expected. Follow what I do. That's all you need to know. You can do it—killing may become your game. Keep your head on straight, don't drink too much, and remember what you're selling. Let's go."

We grabbed our coats. Toos extinguished the apartment lights and we stepped into the chilly air. The moon rose in the east, but clouds had dimmed its light considerably. We were glad.

The pub, De Vier Drankjes, was across the canal from Levi's apartment on Zwanenburgwal. We walked past my Amsterdam home and I looked up. The curtains to the balcony had been drawn. I pictured Emil stretched out on the couch, nursing his throbbing head, a drink in his hand.

As we crossed the bridge, Toos peered into the inky water. She said nothing—the movement was brief, and soon her gaze was directed to the buildings opposite the canal. I realized that in my time in the city, I'd never paid attention to the canal bridges. I'd always taken them for granted as one often does with something seen every day. Toos's attentiveness to the water made me think. There was no place to hide under the bridge unless you were a fish. There was no bank sloping toward the water as I'd imagined.

I walked beside her. "How is this going to work?"

"Cold feet? Don't worry about the details."

"Does the pub's name mean what I think it does?" I asked.

She slowed her pace for a moment and tilted her head. "That's it on the corner. The Four Drinks. Legend says that the number is one more than the number of drinks that it takes to get you drunk in this pub. It's been around for a couple of hundred years. Always popular—the Nazis like it, too." She stopped and placed her hand on my shoulder. "If you don't want to go through with this, or think you can't, make the decision now. Once we go inside, you're committed. You can't leave—it will look suspicious."

I shook my head. "No—it has to be done."

"All right." Toos walked ahead of me. "Your life is in God's hands. Let me judge if it's safe. If not, I'll ignore Miller—if he's there. We'll have one drink and then leave. If we're not by the bridge by eleven, Karin and Derk will know the plan's been called off."

It was a few minutes past eight. De Vier Drankjes's door was heavy, much like the one at Spiegel's country home, but without the carved decoration. The yellowish-orange light that shone through the ancient frosted glass windows gave the impression that I was stepping into something much older than two hundred years. The building looked as if it had been standing since the Middle Ages. The warmth inside contrasted with the cold seeping into my limbs. I shivered and pushed down the urge to turn back, keeping Toos's advice in mind.

She opened the door and I followed.

The air smelled of smoke, beer, and ancient wooden beams. I looked around, certain that there were no Jews out after the day's fracas. Toos took her time, slinking past the tables with precision.

Three German officers stood at the end of the long wooden bar. I had no idea of their rank because I'd never learned the significance of their insignias, but I assumed from the SS runes, service ribbons, and Iron Crosses on their uniforms that they were important. Miller was surely one of them.

A man near the back gave me a brief look. He was sitting with a woman I recognized from the Wednesday Night Club. When we sat down at a nearby empty table, Ruud looked at me once again. I did nothing, and refocused my gaze on Toos.

"Would you like a cigarette?" my companion asked.

I nodded because, after the incident with Emil, I'd forgotten mine. She lit one and handed it to me, the white paper circled with her lipstick. The gray smoke snaked to the ceiling, dispersing under the aged roof.

"I'll get us drinks," she said. "I'm not waiting for service. What would you like?"

I thought a moment. "Brandy."

She rose like a graceful swan from her chair and stepped

behind the three officers. They turned their heads to look at her, but the man in the middle of the group gave her a thorough inspection. He studied every curve of her body as she placed the order. Toos maneuvered herself next to the man and stood for several minutes, flirting and laughing.

Ten minutes later, Toos returned with the drinks. She placed two brandies on the table and we toasted each other. She leaned toward me. "Miller's the one who looked me over. Ruud was right. He likes his women."

I glanced toward Ruud's table, but he and the woman had slipped out of the pub. Another couple sat there now.

We sat for another hour, I sipping my drink. Toos finished hers and ordered another. The two officers accompanying Miller left, leaving him alone at the bar. A few minutes later, he found an empty chair and pushed it to our table.

"How are you, ladies?" he asked in German.

Toos was the first to answer. *"Wunderbar. Die Nacht wurde einfach besser."*

She was playing with him, telling Miller that the night had just gotten better since he arrived.

*"Du sprichts Deutsch?"* he asked, apparently impressed by Toos's command of the language. I decided to keep my conversation brief, to the point, and in Dutch.

*"Ein bisschen,"* she responded.

"Enough that we can communicate," he said, continuing in German.

I let Toos take the lead, the brandy and the adrenaline going to my head. I hoped that my face wasn't too red or flushed from the hormone surging through me. Toos's fingers crept to Miller's hand as the night passed and the officer enjoyed the attention. After a time, he got up and ordered another round of drinks.

"After this one, we go to the bridge," she whispered to me after he left.

I nodded.

She patted my hand. "Good job. Keep looking at him—throw him a bone. Speak some German. Smile and look sexy."

It wasn't until Toos said those words that I truly realized what I'd gotten into. Not only was I about to help murder a man, but on a lesser scale I was prostituting myself. The thought made me feel dirty. But then the murders of the woman and her children played again in my head and I realized that this evening was about much more than me. I was a pawn in a larger game that had nothing to do with my feelings. The Nazis cared nothing for my feelings. They were killers, and unless they were stopped there would be no end to their destruction. I had to divorce myself from useless emotions in this terrible war. I'd already suffered terror and loss. I might have a hand in Miller's death, but the true murderer was a demented dictator who considered the world his personal dominion and the people who inhabited it his slaves.

Miller swigged another beer. I didn't know how many he'd had, but his eyes took on that sleepy look and his head lolled from side to side. He'd taken off his cap and opened the top button of his uniform jacket. Toos kissed him on his cheek, being a little more aggressive. Miller turned to me while Toos ran her hands up his arm. I smiled and kissed him on the other cheek.

"Ah, two for the price of one," the officer exclaimed.

Toos reacted with mock horror. "Nothing as crass as that . . . but we *can* make you happy." She grasped his hand. "Let's go. My friend will join us."

Miller smiled and put his hand on her cheek. "My cup runneth over." He rose from the chair, knocking the table to the side a bit as he got up.

As we put on our coats, he grabbed Toos's right arm. "You're going to have to help me a little."

"Certainly, General. Whatever you need."

His head dipped back in a boozy laugh. "I'm not a general . . . I'm a captain."

Miller walked between us as we left the pub. The temperature had dropped; a thin band of clouds still covered the moon, a pearly sheen of light surrounding it.

"I know a hotel near here," Miller said, donning his cap. "I'll take you there."

"Too conventional," Toos said. "Aren't you up for something more exciting? Why wait—we can't be bothered."

Toos stopped under a streetlamp and kissed Miller. "Vixens," he said, breaking away from her embrace.

Toos dragged him out of the light and into the darkness a few meters to the left of the bridge. "Let me show you how it's done."

"Not here—in the open," Miller said in a sudden burst of clarity.

"My friend will watch." She walked with him down the stone walk as I followed. "Here."

She turned him so his back faced the water and she began to kiss him, running her hands over his jacket and down to his belt. Few people were out, the exception being two couples who had already passed us.

"Wait," Miller said, wrenching her hands away.

I looked across the bridge and then both directions down the walkway. "There's no one about," I said in German.

Toos pushed the officer off the ledge. The force was so sudden and surprising, Miller had no time to react.

She called me over. "Take a look."

Toos had thrust the officer into a flat-bottom boat moored at the side of the canal, as planned. The drop was steep enough to knock the wind out of him. The German's arms and legs flailed for a moment as he tried to recover. Stunned, he wasn't fast enough and the blanket that Derk wrapped around his head muffled any cry for help. Karin slashed the knife across his throat and the murder was done. They covered the body with a tarp and cast off from the canal. The liquidation had taken less than a minute.

Toos took a handkerchief from her purse and wiped off her lipstick, the red staining the white cloth. "I don't want him on my lips," she said, and then spit on the stones. We walked away.

"I didn't know how this would be done. What's going to happen now?" I asked when we were in the middle of the bridge away from everyone. The boat drifted off into the darkness.

"The body will be weighted and dumped into the Amstel. The bloody tarp underneath him will be scrubbed and everything will go on as before. One dead—many to go."

We stopped in front of Levi's apartment.

"Are you all right?" she asked, as we stood in front of the dark building.

"Yes, it was over faster than I imagined."

"Yes . . . have a good night."

She walked away as if nothing unusual had happened. I opened the door and climbed the stairs, hoping that Emil was asleep because I didn't want to relive the murder. It had been so quick and easy. For an instant, I recalled the German's blood in the boat and I reveled in it, just as Spiegel had done that day at Passport Pictures.

By the time I reached the top of the stairs, I knew I could kill again.

# CHAPTER 22

The German reprisal for the fight that had broken out was swift.

The Jodenbuurt was closed off from the rest of the city. Non-Jews were forbidden to enter; those leaving had to present their papers. The Dutch police helped the Nazis cordon off the area. We watched as the barbed wire went up, strand by strand, and police checkpoints were established near the bridges. We heard rumors that a Judenrat, a Jewish Council, was to be established to "control" Jews.

Levi and I wondered if we'd be able to leave the Jodenbuurt for work. Emil's print shop was located in the neighborhood, so getting to his job wasn't an issue for him. My identification papers would be checked and I'd have to rely on my fake German passport, which created a big problem. Why was a German woman living in the Jewish district? I couldn't use the excuse of marriage either. The surname given on my forged passport wasn't Belmon.

I assumed the Nazi action was taken because of Miller's murder. Perhaps his body had been found and the furious Germans had decided to punish the Jews for his death. I found out later in the day that the "ghetto" had been formed in response to the WA fight in the Waterlooplein and had nothing to do with a missing Nazi officer.

Hendrick Koot, the WA man who had been injured, died on February 14. His funeral took place three days later, and although we weren't there to witness it, Ruud reported the ceremony to Toos.

"It seemed the whole city turned to fascism to honor this thug. His casket was carried on a horse-drawn carriage for all to see. Flowers were strewn in its path, while women wept and men gave the Nazi salute. Thousands of National Socialists, complete with a marching band, escorted this man to the afterlife. The NSB flag waved proudly and its symbols were placed on his grave."

When we heard this, Levi scheduled an emergency meeting of the Wednesday Night Club, calling for those of us living in the Jodenbuurt to attend. Ruud could no longer get into the district because he wasn't a Jew.

Sadness was the order of the day as six of us gathered early one evening. At previous meetings, flickers of hope had burned through our collective gloom. Everyone, Karin included, looked forlorn, as if they had suffered a great loss. No one had slept well since the ghetto had been established.

"Did you hear what Rauter said about Koot's death?" Derk asked, referring to a high-ranking SS leader in the Netherlands.

Everyone shook their heads.

"It was in the *Volk en Vaderland*, the NSB newspaper," he explained. "Rauter said ugly words—a Jew had sucked the blood from Koot's body . . . he had ripped open an artery and feasted on Koot's blood."

Quiet fell over us. I remembered Spiegel's actions at Passport Pictures, kneeling over the beaten body of director Anders Pechstein, the Oberführer sucking on his fingers drenched in Anders's blood. The thought made me shudder, the images too similar, but now the Nazis were accusing us of being the vampires.

"I need Jewish identification papers," I said, trying to rid my mind of the memory. "I have to be able to leave the ghetto or I'll lose my job." Emil and I still had plenty of money stashed in the lamp in our room, but I wanted to be working—able to bicycle through Amsterdam—not be a prisoner in the ghetto.

"I'll handle that," Karin said. "You'll have it in a few days."

Emil looked at me, sadness drifting in his eyes. Like me, he still had the forged non-Jewish German passport; yet, I knew what he was thinking. He no longer wanted to deny that he was a Jew. He was willing to stand against the Nazis no matter the consequences. The battle had been brought to our front door. I told Emil a German officer had been killed the night I went out with Toos, but he didn't regret it. I filled in the details that he had imagined. We had become hardened in order to survive.

As the meeting broke up, Toos came to me. "The establishment of the ghetto has changed everything," she said. "We've had to postpone the actions we had planned. It's too dangerous."

"I understand," I said, feeling some relief.

Everyone left, and Levi went to bed.

As we climbed the stairs to our room, Emil said, "I'm proud of you." He paused and took my hand. "God will forgive us."

We went to bed that night, still worried about our future despite any prayers we offered to heaven.

On February 19, a week after the ghetto was established, I was still waiting for my new papers. A thin layer of dull clouds hung over Amsterdam, but no rain fell. The day was cold and melancholy.

I was at the market when another rumor spread like lightning from stall to stall. A fight had broken out in an ice cream parlor between German police and Jews. Some of the police had been injured.

Other clashes broke out and by Saturday, the 22nd, the Nazis had had enough.

To get some exercise, I had gone for a bicycle ride in the district as Emil and Levi celebrated the Sabbath. I returned late morning to find the door open and the dark cavity of the stairwell looming in front of me. I tamped down the anxious alarm prickling through me and carried my bicycle inside. The hall was quiet, the only movement being my steps on the stairs.

As I ascended, I saw that Levi's apartment door was open. When I reached it, I held my breath.

The room had been ransacked. The couch and pillows were ripped open and strewn about; the stuffing lay scattered on the floor. Books and papers had been scattered across the room. Every drawer was open, every piece of furniture moved to a different spot from its original location in the house.

Panic rose inside me. I wanted to yell, to scream—instead, my weak voice called for Emil and Levi. No one answered.

I turned toward the kitchen and Levi's sleeping nook. The Nazis, I assumed, had done this as well—the back of the apartment showing the same disorder as the front. Turnips, carrots, and beets lay on the floor, the pantry shelves in shambles from the search.

I climbed the stairs to our room. The mattress had been overturned, the pillows slashed, our clothes pulled from the chest, and the drawers emptied. The lamp containing the money rested on its side on top of the mattress, its ceramic base unbroken.

Taking in the destruction, I knew that Emil and Levi had been arrested. A small scream escaped from my mouth as I gripped the sides of my head. Stunned, not knowing what to do, I collapsed on the disheveled bed.

Footsteps knocked me from my stupor. "Who is it?" I

called out. There was no way to escape if Nazis were in the house.

"Niki?"

I recognized Toos's voice. I rushed down the stairs and into her arms.

"Oh, God, tell me that they're all right," I said, and sobbed against her shoulder. "What has happened?"

"They're rounding up young Jews," she replied. "Hundreds of them . . . but I think they've arrested Emil and Levi for treason."

"The Wednesday Night Club. . . ."

"Yes, if they found materials here—the flyers that Emil printed—their fate is sealed."

"What can I do?" The question sounded as if I was begging for my life. I sat on the tattered couch.

"Nothing," Toos said. "Who knows where they are or where they'll be taken. Unless they've broken Emil and Levi, you're probably safer here than anywhere. They've searched the apartment and taken what they needed." Her eyes blazed for a moment. "Do you still have your German passport . . . is it gone?"

"It's in my purse." I'd left it in the hall near my bicycle. I sprinted down the stairs, found it next to the bike, and fumbled through it as I ran back. The passport was still there, residing behind a leather flap. I waved it at Toos.

She looked around the room. "Let me help you clean up. You have food. Is there somewhere to hide if they return?"

Unlike the secret closet at my mother's house, there was nowhere to hide in Levi's apartment. I could rig a curtain at the back of the sleeping nook, but it would offer little protection in a thorough search. "No—not unless something like a false wall was constructed in the garret, but it's too late for that." Needing something to do, I gathered a handful of books from the floor.

Toos watched and then sat on the edge of the couch. She was thinking with a clearer head than mine.

I threw one of the books to the floor in a rage. "I need those Jewish identification papers. Why hasn't Karin gotten them to me?"

"It takes time," Toos said calmly. "Forgeries require time and patience in order for them to pass inspection. She's working with a new picture, a new name. She's offering you a way out of Amsterdam." She picked up the ashtray that had been tossed into the corner and lit a cigarette. "Do you know what I would do?"

"No, what?" I was in no mood to play guessing games.

"I'd leave and go back to Germany."

I sighed, scoffing at her suggestion. Only once after the invasion, because I had a brief bout of homesickness, had I thought of going back. But never alone—the dangerous journey always was with Emil. "Give up? Leave the man I love and walk out of Amsterdam? I've already left my mother and my daughter. I'm not doing that again."

"You may have to—in order to find them. You have a false German passport that got you into the Netherlands. It can get you out."

I walked to the window and looked out at the gray canal and the equally dreary city. Below, a few people walked bundled against the chill in their coats and scarves. The sound of gunshots echoed from somewhere in the district.

"I can't think now," I said. "I need a plan—I need to know what's happened to them."

Taking the ashtray and the cigarette with her, Toos walked to the kitchen. "I'll clean in here. You can spend the night at my apartment if you want, but I'm not sure that's the safest thing to do. They may come for me, if a club member talks."

I walked to the door, closed it, and checked the lock. It worked, and I still had the key.

Toos cleaned the kitchen as I stood near the couch fighting back the tears I'd been holding.

"Toos?"

She looked at me.

"I'm glad you're here." I picked up a pile of stuffing and pushed it back into a torn cushion.

Although Toos and I cleaned the apartment as best we could, nothing could sweep away the feelings of violation and despair. My suffering, surely, was nothing compared to that of Emil and Levi. As the weekend passed, I still had no idea where they were; however, rumors circulated that the men had been taken to a Nazi concentration camp near the village of Schoorl, more than fifty kilometers north of Amsterdam.

If I'd been able to get out of the ghetto, I considered bi-cycling north to find Emil. How ridiculous that would have been! Every action the Nazis took was designed to break, to destroy, to make freedom impossible for anyone other than their own kind. Riding my bike to the camp would achieve nothing, and only open myself to interrogation and arrest.

On Monday, the 24th, a rally was held protesting the Jewish arrests. The next day, a general strike spread through the city and locations beyond Amsterdam. The Communist Party of the Netherlands, deemed illegal by the Nazis, had circulated a tract calling for the strike, or *Staakt*. Everyone in the Jodenbuurt was pleased by this action, but we knew a German crackdown would come—and it did, two days later. Still, it was a miracle—a mass protest organized by non-Jews against Nazi atrocities.

I kept to myself during this time, still waiting for my Jewish identification papers, so I could leave the ghetto for "my work." No word came about the fate of Emil and Levi. My boss at the diamond shop left a message saying he'd heard what had happened. Another worker had volunteered to take over my job until I returned.

On Thursday morning, someone knocked on my door—most likely someone I knew rather than the Germans who would have broken it down.

"Yes?" I asked.

"It's me—Ruud."

The burly Dutch soldier walked in. His blond hair had been ruffled by the wind, and his cheeks were flushed from the cold. He took off his coat and sat on the mangled couch.

"Would you like tea?" I asked. "I have a few bags left and I can boil some water."

"Yes, it's a cold day."

I closed the balcony curtains for privacy, turned on the light, and headed to the kitchen. It took a few minutes for the tea to brew and for me to return to the room. Ruud smiled as I handed him his cup on a saucer. He took a sip and put it on the floor. I sat in the chair across from the couch.

"Karin tells me you had an adventure at the pub," he said, and then held up his hand. "You don't have to tell me anything; in fact, it would be better if you didn't. I'm just happy that my plan worked out—I did have something to do with it."

I thought of how Ruud, the strategist, might have suggested the operation—pushing Miller off the bank into the waiting boat below, to have his throat cut by Derk. The body, afterward, dumped into the Amstel. The murder was anything but a lark, but I could picture Karin telling Ruud that it had been an "adventure."

"Yes, it was a success." That was all I wanted to say.

"I have something for you." He reached into his coat pocket, withdrew an oversized envelope, and handed it to me.

I knew from the ridges, the shape—its outline almost embossed on the paper—that it was my Jewish papers. I opened it and found yet another identity—I'd had so many since Lotti had named me Niki—the recently taken picture, the appropriate documentation would get me out of the ghetto. "Thank God," I said. "I was about to give up hope."

"Never give up hope," Ruud said.

"It's just an expression," I replied, somewhat taken aback by his implied criticism. "I've never given up hope. It would be easy to do, but I've been through too much . . . how did you get into the ghetto?"

He rubbed his thumb over his fingers. "It helps if you have a few guilders to hand out and you know a Dutch policeman. He didn't ask questions—but he told me to make my visit quick." He lifted his cup and took a sip of tea. "What are you going to do?"

"Have you heard anything about Emil and Levi? Can you tell me where they are?"

He nodded. "Levi is being held by the German police in Amsterdam. You shouldn't visit him, it would be too dangerous, too incriminating. He'll probably be tried for associating with a seditionist and operating a terrorist group—if someone has talked. The Wednesday Night Club is dead." He paused and then looked at me with a frown. "I'm afraid the news about Emil isn't as good. A group of young Jews were held at Schoorl, but they've been moved."

I leaned forward, eager to know. "Moved? Where?"

"No one knows for sure, but two concentration camps have been mentioned—Buchenwald and Mauthausen. I can't be certain."

I felt myself slipping into a crevasse, the future darkening with Ruud's words. "I'll leave Amsterdam. I have to find him."

"There's nothing you can do," he said, shaking his head. "Keep your wits about you. Toos thinks you should go back to Germany, and I agree. No matter who wins the war, you might be able to find your daughter. At least make a life with her. Maybe Emil will make it out. . . ."

"She turns ten this year . . . I'm not going to abandon her or Emil. I have connections." A chill skittered over me; gooseflesh rose on my arms. If Rickard was still in step with the Nazis, and I could find him, would he be able to get Emil out of a camp?

Ruud finished his tea and then looked at his watch. "I'd better go—as my policeman friend suggested."

I walked him to the door, wondering if I would ever see him again. "Thank you." I kissed him on the cheek. "I don't know that we'll meet again."

"I wish you luck, Niki. I hope the war ends soon." He grasped my hands and squeezed them.

With a few deft steps, belying his ample frame, he was out the door and on the street. I truly didn't know whether I would see any members of the Wednesday Night Club again, but with each passing minute in Amsterdam I felt my life was in danger.

I picked up the saucer and tea cup and walked to the kitchen. I put them down and sobbed over the sink, remembering how lovely my life had been in Rickard's grand apartment, how Laura's birth gave me happiness through the dark times of the growing Nazi movement, and my frantic, yet beautiful time with Emil. Everything good in my life had come to an end.

Now it was time to kill myself.

# CHAPTER 23

I met Toos at her apartment one more time before I left Amsterdam for Germany.

"You should leave while you can," she said. We sat in the dim room facing the street the last evening in February 1941.

"I'm going to kill myself," I said.

A smile broke out on Toos's red lips, and her long brunette hair shook around her face as she laughed. "Don't be ridiculous. If you'd said the Nazis were going to kill you, I would have believed you. You have too much to live for."

"Do you have a cigarette?" I asked.

Toos complied and leaned back waiting for my explanation. "I'm going to kill my former self. For a brief time, I was a sensation in Berlin before the Nazis banned my books and put my publisher out of business." I puffed on the cigarette, but the smoke burned my throat and I coughed. "I've thought about this since Emil and Levi were arrested. I'm wanted in Germany and unless my former husband would step in to save me, I'll end up in a concentration camp—"

"As you would if you stayed in Amsterdam," Toos said. "We're all treading water, scared to death of what's going to happen. Derk called me—we had to speak in generalities because we fear the telephone lines are tapped—and he's certain that their next step will be to confiscate Jewish property."

"They are methodical in their madness." Hooves sounded on the street, followed by a car blowing its horn. I peered out the window, but nothing was amiss. "I have to kill Marie Rittenhaus—I have to kill Niki."

"I understand . . . I think," Toos said, stretching her long body across the couch.

"The Nazis must believe that the woman who wrote those novels ten years ago is dead. My death must be accompanied by the revelation that Niki, Marie Rittenhaus, wrote those books under a pen name, and now she's dead."

"How are you going to do this?" Toos asked. "What about a body?"

I returned Toos's faded smile. "I learned from our 'adventure' at the pub. The canal is only a few meters away from the entrance to Levi's building. I'll leave a note explaining what I've done . . . but I need your help."

Toos tilted her head. "Go on."

"Do you know anyone who works for an international newspaper? Not a local reporter, but someone who might work for—British Broadcasting, for example."

Her lips pursed. "I don't. No man ever admitted to me that he was a reporter while in my arms . . . but Derk might know someone. He has scholarly connections."

"Then tell Derk to visit Levi's apartment on Sunday morning after eight. By that time, I'll be on a train to Germany. The door will be unlocked. I'll leave a note on the couch and the key stuffed in one of the ripped cushions. If he can get the news out about my death, I'll be grateful."

"What about your mother and Rickard?"

I sighed. "I'm worried about my mother, but somehow I'll contact her. Rickard might be relieved that I'm dead."

"You have it all planned," she said with a tone bordering on jealousy. "I wish I could go with you, but I'll take my chances here. At least you have a fake German passport at the ready."

We talked for a few more minutes, but I couldn't stay long because I had much to do before I committed suicide. Both of us were numb from the recent turmoil in our lives, so we hugged without tears and said our good-byes. My final words to the brave woman were wishes for good luck and a long life.

As I walked back to the apartment, I looked at the stars and marveled that they hadn't changed. They lay silent, cold, twinkling in the black sky, their light coming from untold distances, falling into my eyes like gifts from heaven. They endured, steadfast, unchanged, while the earth descended into chaos.

Only two more nights remained in Amsterdam, both of them without Emil.

I never knew how much blood was in a rat until I'd killed one and spread the fluid on the floor near the apartment door. I doubted that the Nazis would bother to test the blood. They'd only see it as the liquid of life and cheer that another enemy of the state had been eradicated.

My suicide note was short, to the point, stating that I, Marie Rittenhaus, also known as Niki, had been hounded by the Nazis and could no longer go on with my life—I was the writer of two books that had been banned by the Third Reich. My income, my creative drive, had been appropriated by an outlaw regime—I'd fled Germany for Amsterdam, but now realized that there was nowhere to hide, and that my sympathies fell with the Jews of Amsterdam against the fascist Reich. I'd cut my wrists, wrapped them in a towel, and jumped into the canal in the middle of the night. I'd put rocks in my robe to weigh me down, but not enough to keep my body from floating to the Amstel. I'd made doubly sure that I'd die—by loss of blood and drowning.

When I left the apartment, everyone in the building was asleep.

With my Jewish identity, I'd had no problem leaving the

ghetto under the eyes of the bovine-like Dutch guard on the bridge, telling him that I was on my way to an early shift. Then, after all of Karin's work, I tore it to pieces and tossed it into a canal. I would have been arrested had those papers been found on me while traveling to Germany.

At seven in the morning—an hour before Derk was to find the note—I was waiting to board a train to Berlin. I'd purchased a first-class ticket. The German and Dutch police at the station inspected my German papers with breezy looks, ushering me, a nicely dressed woman who smiled at them, through the gate with far more gusto than someone who looked as if she was slinking out of the city.

The guilders rescued from the lamp resided in my secret coat pocket, the one that had carried the bracelet to Amsterdam. I carried nothing suspicious in my suitcase—the authorities were welcome to inspect it. I'd left the typewriter behind in the apartment.

As the train pulled away, I thought of Levi, whom I presumed was still under arrest. How I wished I could have set him free. What had happened to Emil? Was he in a concentration camp in Germany? These questions dampened my mood as we left the city.

The train rattled along. We had no fear of attack from a neighboring country because they'd all been conquered. British forces were confined to African campaigns, and the United States had yet to enter the war. I was filled with a strange mixture of emotions as the countryside slipped by—excitement, fear, regret, and sadness. No paper or magazine held my attention. A former passenger had left a German novel on the seat; the pages turned into a blur of words as I tried to read. I twitched in the seat, closed my eyes, hoping to relax, but I was never able to sleep even though I was exhausted.

Carrying my suitcase, I arrived in central Berlin about twelve hours later without a place to call home. I first thought of my mother's, but then decided that Lotti's might be a better choice if she still lived in the same apartment. About an hour later, I arrived at her place between the Berliner Dom and the Alexanderplatz.

The buzzer rang with its usual metallic hiss. I recognized Lotti's voice through the box and I sighed with relief.

"Who is it?" she asked, sounding somewhat annoyed.

"An old friend," I said. An audible gasp burst through the box and in a few moments Lotti came rushing down the stairs in her robe.

"You . . . you, of all people," she blurted out as she opened the door. "I never expected to see you again. It's been almost five years."

"I'm back, for a little while," I said, depositing the suitcase on the tile. "Is there any chance—"

"You don't even have to ask," Lotti said, interrupting my question. "But you'll have to sleep on the couch."

"Oh?"

"I have a gentleman friend," she said. "He's here now— Egon. He's a National Socialist."

While reaching for my suitcase, I froze to the spot.

"Don't worry—he's *not* that kind of National Socialist."

"Lotti," I whispered. "I'm a hunted woman. I can't have tea with a Nazi. Do you trust him?"

She picked up my suitcase and started up the stairs. "Of course. His father made him join the Party. He hates it all— the book burnings, the military service, the Jewish laws— he's only here on a few days' leave and then he's headed for Poland—maybe even farther east."

My brain told me to flee. "How long have you known him?"

"Since the war started. He served in France. He saw what Hitler and the Wehrmacht can do, but he keeps it inside. Sometimes, I think he'll pop."

"That's what I'm worried about. He'll pop and you and I will be dead."

"He loves me, and I . . ." The pause marked an uncertainty. "Well, more than any other man I've been with. I met him at the Leopard Club. Rudi approved—but he's been called up as well—to Africa I think."

I stopped Lotti and told her to look me in the eyes. "You swear?"

"Yes."

I had only one other choice and that was to go to my mother's, but Lotti looked so content and assured that I cast that thought aside. My friend had gotten the best of me, and I wondered what it might be like to have a National Socialist on my side. Perhaps a Nazi infiltrator who could help me find my daughter and Emil.

Lotti opened the door. The young man who'd captivated her was sitting on the bed, his back against the headboard, his chest bare, except for the suspenders that crossed his shoulders and held up his uniform pants. Egon could have posed for a Hitler Youth poster. He was probably twenty-five, blond, with eyes as blue as a spring lake, wispy eyebrows, a sharp nose, and a pleasant smile. His chest, arms, and shoulders were muscled from his army training; he exuded sexuality without even trying. No wonder Lotti and Rudi approved—but could he be trusted?

He swung his legs off the bed and took a swig of something brandy-colored resting on the nightstand, before standing to greet me.

"I'm Egon," he said. "Lotti's told me about you and what you've been through."

I looked at my friend. She had given Egon my life story long before I arrived.

"Did she tell you my name?" I asked, placing my suitcase by the couch.

"Niki," he answered, with no surprise in his voice.

"I guess we have no secrets."

He hopped backward, landing on the bed, his legs flipping

onto the mattress. The maneuver seemed like something a teenager might do. Lotti joined him and the two spooned together, facing me as I sat on the couch. Their intimacy made me feel like an awkward intruder. Egon stared at me, with a rather inviting and lascivious look, showing moist teeth and red lips. I wondered if they were inviting me to their bed. I had no intention of going.

"Lotti—I don't think this is going to work," I said.

"Don't worry, I won't be staying," Egon replied. "My parents want me at home once in a while. They believe that their son, old enough to be killed in action, is too young to spend the night with a woman."

Lotti slapped Egon's arm. "I guess there are no secrets."

"I'll let you two reminisce," he said, prying himself free from Lotti's arms. He turned, pressed his lips against hers for a long time, and then asked, "Tomorrow night? I only have a week before I head east."

She nodded and smiled.

Egon slid off the bed, grabbed his undershirt from a chair, pulled down his suspenders, and put the garment on, tucking it carefully in his breeches. In nearly a swoon, Lotti stared at him as he finished dressing, tugging at his uniform jacket, slipping into his boots, and clutching his gray field cap. He kissed Lotti once again and headed for the door.

I called his name. "Are you going to have me arrested? Hitler, Goebbels—they want me. If you're turning me in, would you at least give me a chance to save myself?"

He walked to the couch and clasped my hand. "Why would I do that? Why would I hurt any friend of the woman I love?" He turned and left.

For some reason—perhaps it was the tone of his voice, the way in which he spoke, a kindness that emanated from his spirit—I believed him.

Besotted, Lotti breathed a rapturous sigh and pulled a pillow close to her.

"I can see that you're in love," I said, "but Nazis can be charming if they want to be."

Lotti's smile soured. "Egon's not like that. He's a good man. He hates what the Nazis have done. He's only fighting because he has no choice. We've talked about how hard it is to point a weapon at another man. In France, he aimed to miss. The officers never knew or suspected because the country fell so quickly. He wants out, but what can he do? I fear for his life if he goes east. Who knows what Hitler is planning?"

"I must get something to eat," I said, rising from the couch. "I'll be back soon."

"I can't wait to hear what's happened," she replied, lifting herself on one elbow. "You look sad. Are you all right, Niki?"

I sighed. "No, I'm not all right. I'm on the run and I've lost two people very dear to me because of the fucking Nazis." I rarely swore, and never in front of my mother. The word made me blush—from anger and my inability to do anything for the people I'd lost. The New German Woman I'd written about was disappearing in front of my eyes. "My life can't get much worse . . . although it might if Egon can't keep his mouth shut."

"He will," she said without a quiver or a crack in her voice.

"I hope so." My stomach growled. "Do you have some marks, all I have is guilders. I'll have to have them converted."

She opened the nightstand drawer and handed me the money. "Hurry back. I want to hear everything."

"It'll be a long night," I said, and closed the door.

For the next several days, I talked to Lotti about what had happened since Emil and I had left for Amsterdam. My real attention was directed at Egon, however. Like Hermann, the young man who had taken me to Spiegel's country house to meet Rickard, Egon had a car. It was his parents', but they allowed their son to use the vehicle.

I took walks in the early evening, leaving Egon and Lotti alone for their conjugal visits, respecting their privacy. I knew my arrangement with Lotti couldn't last and I would, once again, have to get my own apartment. However, I suspected that Lotti would be depressed after Egon left for duty. She would be lonely and out of sorts, maybe even wanting my company.

The three of us would talk late into the night, after supper. The only barrier that stopped us from staying up until dawn was Lotti's job. A few days before Egon was to report for duty in Poland, I asked him for a favor.

"Will you take me to Buchenwald?"

Lotti was somewhat aghast at my request, but she knew what I wanted. I wanted to see the concentration camp where Ruud said Emil most likely had been taken.

Egon surmised my intention as well and looked at me with sympathetic eyes. "You won't see him. The camp is heavily guarded. I'm not even sure we'll be able to see it from the road—if we go."

"I know," I said. "I want to see the lay of the land—see for myself if there's any chance for Emil to escape." Those reasons were true, but I was hiding the emotions that welled up within me. As far as I knew, Emil was back on German soil, and I wanted to be near him, even if it was only by a few kilometers separated by walls and electrified barbed wire. I didn't know how else to explain it other than I had not given up, at least I was trying to reach him.

Egon shrugged. "Of course. A little adventure before I go back to war. You'll have to pay for fuel. I can't expect my parents to subsidize that."

I nodded, knowing that Egon was humoring me, indulging my wish.

Volker, the owner of the Leopard Club, had been exchanging my guilders for marks, bit by bit. Lotti had suggested it, and Volker, not a National Socialist admirer by any means, particularly after his doorman had been beaten by the SA so long ago, was happy to help. It was safer going through Volker than at a bank. That kind of exchange would have raised eyebrows.

With three days left before Egon was to leave, he picked me up for the journey to Buchenwald, near Weimar. We set out in a gray dawn for the nearly three-hundred-kilometer drive. Egon, dressed in his uniform, smelled of a lemony aftershave. The car's heater blew warm air, and, oddly, I felt quite at ease with the young soldier. Over the few days that we'd spent together, I'd begun to trust him, and the fear of arrest had left my mind. He seemed to know things, be aware of "secrets" that in my limited civilian knowledge I could never have known.

As we drove south from Berlin, he tossed me a map outlining our route. We were headed southwest, past Potsdam, past the winter fields, through the rolling hills, past Wittenberg, until we connected with a road just north of Leipzig. From there we would continue our southwest course to Buchenwald.

We'd been traveling for about an hour, when Egon took his eyes off the road for a moment, turned to me, and asked, "You're very much in love with this man, aren't you?"

I faced him as he returned to driving. His question triggered a cascade of emotions that I'd stored in my body since leaving Amsterdam. A lump formed in my throat and I found it hard to speak for a time. When, at last, I could, a tear had fallen upon my cheek.

"I've lost my daughter and my lover to the Nazis," I said. "Emil saved me at a time when I needed to be saved. Laura's father is an opportunist. He'll use the Nazis as long as he can. Most of the time I feel . . . resigned . . . to the way things are. I can only change the way I feel about what I've lost. Now, I suppress my feelings of anger and sadness . . . and revenge."

"You're brave," Egon said. "I admire you. I don't know if Lotti and I could ever be as brave as you."

"Lotti was pummeled by Spiegel and his thugs, the night Laura was taken. She managed to survive." I opened my purse and rummaged through it looking for a cigarette. I took out a Juno—easier to buy than my usual brand—and offered one to Egon.

"I don't smoke," he said, shaking his head.

"Do you mind?"

"No."

I lit the cigarette and smoke filled the interior. I lowered the window a crack, the smoke flowing out in a gray silky ribbon.

"You spoke of revenge," Egon said. "I still have three nights."

I studied his calm profile. His hands were steady on the wheel, his blue eyes focused on the road, his complexion as smooth as cream. One could almost hear his heart beating, calmly, steadily, in his chest.

"What do you have in mind?"

"I was called up so fast—one day a civilian and the next in service to the Reich. The Nazis are like efficient machines, any disruption sends them reeling. The most effective way to hit them is with blows to their order, their organization."

I understood what he meant. The Wednesday Night Club had discussed a similar tactic. "When I was in Amsterdam, we talked about burning the passport offices, the ration card offices, the Nazis operational headquarters. Is that what you mean?"

"Exactly," he said, glancing toward me again. "I'm not talking about the Reich Chancellery or Gestapo Headquarters. I know the recruitment offices, the bureaus on side streets, the small spaces in Berlin that would make a difference—that would make them think. They won't be expecting it in the heart of Berlin. If we hit hard and fast, even for one night, it'll put a fear in them, and ordinary Germans will know we are striking back. The Nazis hate being despised. It drives them mad."

I thought for a moment as we sped through an area of wooded hills. "Emil used to print flyers. I suppose they were effective, but, in the end, they didn't hurt anyone but the printer and National Socialist feelings. It's like sending a postcard, letting people know what you're thinking. Destroying something is a whole different matter."

"One that's effective."

Plotting our targets, we drove for another two hours before we came to the road that veered toward Buchenwald. The land was thick with trees, cleared in spots, dense in others. We seemed to be on a road that ended at one destination. Warning signs came into view. *Verboten. Achtung.* Egon stopped the car on the side of the road and we both got out.

Over a crest of trees, I spotted the top of a clock tower. Somewhere near there, Emil was being held prisoner—if he was still alive. I didn't want to think he was dead. I only wanted to believe that he was waiting for me, waiting for someone to rescue him from this camp.

"This is as close as we can get," Egon said. "We risk getting arrested if we go farther."

I turned away from the tower and looked in the opposite direction toward the sprawling fields and villages that lay to the west. The feeling of resignation that I'd described to Egon came over me. There was nothing I could do but look and wonder what lay beyond the trees.

"I don't know why I made you do this," I said. "I wanted to be near him . . . that's all. Maybe it was to say good-bye. Does that make any sense?"

Egon put his arm around my shoulders. "Of course. This must be rough." He swept his free hand in a broad arc. "I wonder about the Germans who live nearby. Do they know what's happening here? Do they care? Or are they happy that a camp has been constructed to enslave communists and others that the Reich deems a threat? Misfits? Degenerates?"

He walked to the car and leaned against the door. "When you first met me, you didn't trust me. Isn't it sad that we have to live this way?" He bunched his fists. "They want us to turn each other in, to live like fighting dogs. It's the only way they can achieve control—if they pit us against each other— squash those who disagree like bugs underfoot."

"Destroy all threats," I said.

"So, we must destroy them. And we should start tomorrow night."

I turned once more toward the distant tower, fidgeting with a cigarette, but the sound of a fast-approaching motorcar interrupted us.

"Quick, into the car," Egon said. "Put the map in the glove box."

I ran to the car, slipped into the passenger seat, and crammed the map into the box. As soon as I shut the door, I caught the gleam of an approaching black sedan in the side mirror. I brushed my hair with my fingers, took a deep breath, and relaxed in the seat. Egon kneeled in front of the car inspecting the front tires.

In a few moments, the sedan pulled up beside us and an SS man and a German officer got out of the car. They were armed and scowling. The driver stayed at his post.

Egon stood and saluted the two men, who, apparently annoyed by the interruption in their journey to the camp, returned the gesture half-heartedly.

"What are you doing here?" the tall SS man asked, putting one hand in his coat pocket.

"The car was vibrating, sir," Egon replied. "I thought we were getting a flat."

The SS man peered into the car at me. I said, "*Guten Morgen*," and smiled.

He turned back to Egon. "What are you doing on this road? Didn't you see the signs?"

"Yes . . . but isn't this the way to Ottstedt am Berge?" Egon asked.

"The other man shook his head. "No, you've taken the wrong turn. The village is to the west."

"I'm sorry, Captain. We'll go back immediately."

"Papers—including those of your passenger." The SS man held out his hand.

Egon retrieved his from his uniform jacket. The captain came to my side of the car, peered into the vehicle, and then inspected my identification—the fake German passport manufactured by Emil.

"Open the trunk," the SS man said.

I heard Egon twist the lever that opened it. After several minutes of rooting around, the two men seemed satisfied.

"Return on this road and then turn left," the captain said.

"Yes, sir." Egon saluted the men again, slid into the driver's seat, rolled up the window, and turned the car north. The black sedan remained parked until we were out of sight.

We turned left as instructed, but pulled off the side of the road to see if the men had followed us. After fifteen minutes we were on our way back to Berlin.

"I'm sorry we didn't have more time," Egon said. "We were lucky I was in uniform. That inspection could have been unfortunate."

I lit a cigarette. "Emil made my passport. He would be pleased to know that I'd duped the SS only a few kilometers from the camp."

"You were steadfast under pressure."

I looked at him. "It was nothing compared to the time I helped murder a man."

His head jerked toward me. "Repeat that, please."

"A captain in Amsterdam." I drew a finger across my neck. I told him of my time in the Netherlands and my alliance with the resistance.

Egon glanced at me with amazement. "We really must work together."

On the way back, we talked about the locations that Egon felt were most vulnerable and would give us the best chance of making a fiery point. We stopped to eat, then continued our journey and arrived back at the apartment after four in the afternoon.

Egon and I were sitting on the couch when Lotti opened the door, looking rather glum as she shed her coat. She tossed a newspaper to me, a Nazi propaganda mouthpiece she'd purchased during the day.

"Look at the front page below the fold," Lotti said.

I immediately spotted the headline.

### The Berlin Woman
### Found Dead
### In Amsterdam Canal

The story went on to say that the body of Marie Rittenhaus, the author of *The Berlin Woman*, also known as Niki, was found in an Amsterdam canal. The Nazi paper had picked up a story originally reported by British Broadcasting. Derk had done his job, but I wondered what poor soul had taken my place in the murky waters. I also thought of my mother, who might have heard the news. I needed to contact her.

"Good to know I'm living with a corpse," Lotti said.

"Don't you feel safer?" I asked. "The Nazis think I'm dead."

"All the better," Egon said, with a wink.

He was plotting our next "adventure."

# CHAPTER 24

Fortunately, my mother, having little interest in politics, hadn't seen the report of my death by the time I came calling the next morning. I was also surprised that a neighbor hadn't seen the news and come to tell her. She was, however, somewhat startled to find me at her front door.

She'd lost weight, from worry about the war and, possibly, me. Her usually red cheeks were muted, less taut, and the auburn highlights in her hair had darkened to brown. The condescending smirk she often carried on her face had molded itself into a thin scowl.

There was no scream of joy when she opened the door, no hugging, merely a stony expression that indicated mild disbelief. It seemed as if she'd expected to see me again, counting off the years until she could chide me for another failed relationship, my lack of money and initiative, and for being the wayward daughter who always failed to build a responsible life.

Frieda wasted no time in ushering me inside, gazing at the neighboring houses and street before closing the door. Little had changed in the years I'd been away. I'd interrupted her reading on the couch—of the Bible. A crumpled afghan lay across the cushions. She picked it up and made room for me to sit.

"Have you come home? Have you been followed?"

"One at a time, Mother," I said. "No, I was careful, but you must understand . . . your daughter, Marie, is dead. The woman who wrote the books that infuriated the Nazis is no longer alive."

She bunched up her face, looking at me as if I were mad. "What do you mean?"

"The papers reported me dead yesterday. I faked my own death in order to leave Amsterdam."

From her shocked look, that bit of information didn't sit well. We talked for an hour in the cold room and I told her everything that had happened in the Netherlands, but divulged nothing about the German officer's murder or what Egon and I had planned for the evening.

"Are you pregnant?" she asked, always looking for a way to broach the subject of my faults.

I shook my head, not wanting to go into details of my personal life. "I wanted you to know that I was alive. I'm staying with Lotti, but I'm finding my own apartment as soon as I can. When I find a place, I'll let you know."

"Do you have money?"

"Yes, you don't need to worry . . . do you need money?"

She shook her head. "I'm fine . . . I'm worried about the war."

"All good people are."

She lowered her head, and I felt that she was about to cry, a rarity for my mother. Haltingly, she asked, "Have you seen Laura?"

The question was like an unexpected punch in the gut. Equally reticent, I answered. "I don't know where she is . . . I assume she's still with Rickard, but I haven't seen or heard from him for years. If he's still serving the Nazi Party, Laura will be fine." In fact, the last time I'd seen my daughter was the night of Spiegel's murder, another terrible event not revealed to my mother.

"I'd like things to be different," Frieda said. "I wish you

could stay here . . . I wish we didn't have to worry about bombs or death."

"I'm in Berlin now. I'll never be far away." I grasped her hand. "All you have to remember is that Marie is dead. She died in Amsterdam and her body was found in a canal. When you talk to someone about my death you need to be sad."

"I will . . . be sad. I'm sad about Laura, too."

"Finding Laura is the most important task in my life. I'll never give up until I've found her."

She let go of my hand and hugged me, a rare gesture of love. Our lives had changed and we were starting again. I found it in my heart to admire her courage: living alone, without a husband, making her way in the world. Although it was hard for me to admit, she possessed some of the qualities of the Berlin woman I'd written about years ago, only without love and men in her life. To me, it didn't make that much difference—my books were about survival. They had always been about survival.

If she saw something new and changed in me, she made no mention of it.

When we parted, we kissed each other good-bye. Walking under a somber sky, I left her home in Rixdorf, the street where I'd grown up, the formative realm of my youth. As I made my way to a tram, I knew I'd transformed into something quite different from the little girl who'd lived here.

And in a few hours, another transformation would be happening.

I was taking another direct action against the Reich.

Living under Nazi rule was always a charade for people like me. Another lie, another secret held in order to endure. Egon and I decided that Lotti didn't need to know about our plan for the night. Discretion was always better than knowledge in order to protect your family and friends. The SS remained a jackbooted step away. The Gestapo lurked on every corner.

Egon made his excuses to Lotti for the evening, telling her that he needed to spend one of his last nights at home with his parents. We'd made plans to meet at nine at Die kleine Rose, the *biergarten* near the Alexanderplatz, where my publisher and I had met after the banned book trial.

I told Lotti that I was going for a walk and not to wait up for me—I needed some time alone to think about what to do with my life.

Egon and I had picked a small Nazi recruiting office on a dark street near the *biergarten* because of its location—not on a main street—and the high potential for a safe escape. The street was open on both ends, but not well lighted. Sporadic Allied bombings of Berlin since June of 1940 had led to blackout rules. The lights I'd enjoyed from Rickard's apartment had dimmed.

Egon and I hoped the operation would be quick, sending us back to our respective homes, after completion of our task.

The damp cut through my coat and scarf and sent me shivering on the short walk from Lotti's apartment to Die kleine Rose. The triangular patio was closed for the winter. The tables, chairs, and umbrellas were stored next to the surrounding hedges, now semi-brown from the cold weather. The patrons laughed and drank inside the warm confines of the *biergarten* on this cold night. Slices of yellow light shone past the curtains, and shadowy forms drifted back and forth in the slight illumination.

I wrapped my arms around my chest and waited, trying not to look conspicuous as people entered for a drink, or departed, consumed by alcohol. My watch read ten minutes after nine. I was thinking that something must have gone wrong, when a finger tapped my shoulder.

Egon stood there, smiling, in his uniform. I clutched his hand, as if we were a couple on a date. In a way, we were.

"I thought you weren't coming," I said—words any woman might say to a man.

"Let's go," he said, his voice calm and steady.

We left Die kleine Rose, walked a block, and then turned left on the darkened street. I saw no one, no other living thing except for a stray cat, in front of us. About halfway down the street, Egon pulled me into a small space cut into the rear of two buildings, a holding place for trash bins.

"I had to deposit these before meeting you." He lifted one of the lids with his gloved hands, pointed to a bag inside the container, and then opened it. Two glass bottles filled with petrol sat inside. "That should do it." He tilted his head toward the recruiting office across the street. A foggy mist covered its stones. A huge Nazi flag took up most of its cross-hatched window. Books and propaganda papers filled in the surrounding space. No light came forth from the building.

"What about the structures around it?" I asked. "I didn't think of that."

"No apartments, only businesses—a dry cleaner's that should add fuel to the fire, and a cloth merchant." I imagined the gleam in Egon's eyes, although I couldn't see them. He was enjoying what we were about to do.

He stuck his head around the bricks and then pulled me close. "Kiss me," he whispered.

A man and woman walked by, in front of our target. I observed them, strolling casually, as Egon put his lips on mine. His kiss was cold, not one of passion, but one designed to conceal the true intention of our meeting. Soon, the couple had passed by, apparently paying no attention to our romance in the dark.

He broke away and was immersed in our operation in moments. He lifted the bag from the bin and clutched it with one arm against his chest. "The building may be alarmed," he said. "If it goes off, put the bag down and run." He handed the fiery cocktails to me.

We crossed the street, stopping in front of the recruiting office. I watched the street as Egon leaned toward the door, listening for any noise inside, scanning the frame for wiring. He nodded and withdrew a small crowbar he'd concealed under his uniform jacket. With a quick slash, and a small crack, the door swung open. We hurried inside and Egon shut the door. No alarm sounded.

He dropped the crowbar on a desk and withdrew a small electric torch from his pocket. The light revealed two desks and accompanying chairs, like one would find in any office, and rows of bookcases and filing cabinets. A portrait of the Führer hung over a back door, looking down upon his favored disciples.

"Let's see what's here," Egon said.

I watched as he shone the beam across one of the desks. He scattered neatly stacked piles of papers, holding a few pieces up to the light. They were mini-dossiers: notes on recruits, their psychological profile, their ability to serve, what they would be most suited for, where they might be sent, and probably their first military pictures, taken on-site and clipped to the form.

"Beautiful," he said. "What a fire these will make." He stopped for a moment and clicked a cigarette lighter he'd taken from his pocket. A flame leaped from the wick. "From the front door—we make sure no one's in sight, then we light and throw."

I crept toward the door and opened it a crack. No one was in sight and I heard no footsteps as I craned my head around the frame. The street was clear.

Suddenly, the metallic ring of a bell blared in the office. Egon's torch fell into the desk drawer he'd opened. It had tripped an alarm. The beam jutted up for a moment, striking his shocked face. The lighter went out.

"Shit," he said, wrangling with the torch. "We'll have to go out the back. Quick! The bag!"

I put it on the desk, as he ordered me to check the back door. It was secured, but the key was in the lock. I opened it and thrust my head into an alley, looking both ways. No one was in the dark corridor, but it presented its own problems. One way led to the dead end of a high brick wall; the other to a large wooden gate. I had no idea what was on the other side.

"There's a gate at one end," I said. "The other is impassable."

"It's the only way out, now. Hold the lighter."

He grabbed one of the containers from the bag. I held the fuel-soaked cloth to the wick. It burst into flame and Egon pitched it into a corner. The glass shattered and the room turned orange with fire. The flash, subdued at first, jumped up the wall as recruitment posters caught fire. I lit the second and Egon threw it into the window nook. The Nazi flag ignited, and, within seconds, the display was consumed.

Egon grabbed the crowbar and we ran as fast as we could to the gate, which stood about two meters tall. From the building we could hear shouting and cursing. Time was growing short for us to make an escape. Egon worked at the gate's padlock with the tool, but it wouldn't budge.

"I can't climb over that," I said, knowing that my coat, purse, and dress would make it impossible to get over.

"I'll go first and hoist you over," he said. He tossed the crowbar and it landed with a *clang* on the other side. Egon jumped up, grabbed the top of the gate, kicked himself into a straddle over the wood, and reached down for me. "The alley leads to the street. I'll pull you up. Grab my hands."

I tossed my purse over the gate. Egon maneuvered himself over the fence, until I could only see the top of his head and his arms.

"Dig your feet into the wood! Kick!"

I followed his instruction and soon half of my body was over, my face looking into his as he stretched above the alley. I heard voices and glanced over my shoulder. A man, coughing and sputtering, rushed toward me.

I pitched forward and Egon dropped to the ground, pulling me with him. We landed in a heap on the other side. He didn't need to order me to run. He grabbed the crowbar and stuffed it in his uniform jacket. We sprinted to the street and turned the opposite direction of the recruitment center. Behind us, the man pounded on the gate and cursed.

We slowed to a walk on the street in order not to arouse suspicion. Eventually, we found ourselves at the Alexanderplatz, not far from Lotti's apartment. My legs felt scratchy and sore from our fall on the stones. In the distance, fire service sirens rose in the night.

"You're bleeding," Egon said. "You cut yourself."

"Oh, hell," I said, opening my coat a bit to look at the bloody lines on my legs. "Lotti will be furious."

"Perhaps we should both tell her," Egon said.

"No, she'll find out sooner or later. She'll read it in the paper."

"I'm heading back to the car. Be careful."

We said our good-byes with no plans to try another adventure on his final evening in the city. When I arrived at the apartment, I found Lotti curled into a comfortable position on the couch with a magazine in her hands.

She looked at my legs and turned back to her reading. "You need to clean those wounds. They could get infected."

I sat beside her. "Lotti . . ."

She held up her hand. "I don't want to know . . . you smell like petrol."

"All right," I said, and then stripped down to my underclothes. "I'm taking a bath."

"Good. I'm going to bed soon."

Lotti was right. As I soaked, the odors of gasoline and smoke, released by the soapy water, filled my nostrils. I sank into the tub, my body numb, my limbs weak from exertion, exhaustion settling in. The man who was after me didn't get a good look at my face, but I remembered his, cheeks reddened by heat, his lungs trying hard to expel the smoke that swirled around him. I wondered if he'd made it over the fence or had retreated back to the blazing office. Maybe the fire had been put out quickly.

From the bath, I heard Lotti slip into bed.

I splashed water on myself, soaked a half hour longer, and then dressed in my nightclothes.

As I stretched out on the couch and closed my eyes, all I could picture was the Nazi chasing me, a swastika banded on his left arm.

# CHAPTER 25

The next afternoon, I looked for an apartment. I found one not too far from Lotti's and signed a lease on the spot using my false passport as identification. My good luck was the result of an unfortunate event for another—a man who had escaped conscription previously was leaving Germany for service with the Wehrmacht. I also paid the first month's rent. Fortunately, I still retained a stash of guilders that could be converted into Reichsmarks. The elderly landlord seemed happy to get a woman as a tenant—even one who wasn't married.

Lotti came home from work late, holding another Nazi paper. A banner headline told of an attack on a recruiting office carried out by a man in uniform and a woman, both escaping the custody of two Gestapo agents. *Thanks to the quick action of the fire brigade, the damage to the office was minimal,* the report read. *Those responsible should be arrested immediately and punished for this heinous crime. The Reich will not be swayed by cowards.*

Lotti scoffed as I read the account. "Egon and I are going out tonight," she said. "I convinced him that if he ever wanted to see me again, he would take me out to dinner and not cavort with friends on his last night in Berlin. We have a room."

I put down the paper. "Please understand—"

"I'm not a fool. I know what you did." She stood near the window and looked at the dark street. "I'm not angry about what you did—I'm angry because you could have been killed. It was a stupid thing to do . . . I love you both."

"On the way to Buchenwald . . . the idea came into our heads and we decided to burn the office. We were rash, but for the second time in my life, I struck back at the people who stole my daughter. I'd do it again . . . that's why I can't stay here."

Lotti pivoted toward me. "The second?"

I nodded. "I can't tell you about the first—I shouldn't tell you."

We both sat on the couch, staring at each other, Lotti as uncertain about the future as I was.

"I'm moving out tomorrow. I won't be here when you get back from work."

Lotti's face soured. "Egon's leaving . . . you're leaving."

"My apartment isn't far. We can see each other. I don't want the Nazis to connect you to me. It's safer for both of us."

She got up from the couch and headed toward the bathroom. "I have to get ready." She stopped and then turned to me. Lotti had matured and I could see it clearly now. The girl I'd met years ago, with the blond hair that was often braided across her head or fashioned into pigtails, had become a woman who knew what she wanted, despite the war. She still visited the Leopard Club, enjoyed a night out, and relished her relationship with Egon, even though I, in some ways, seemed to know more about his thoughts than she did. I understood that the war was weighing on her dreams of marriage, of starting a family. Those personal considerations were foremost on her mind, all of them rendered uncertain by a madman named Adolf Hitler.

I had changed, too, finding that love was more than passion. Life had shown me that love must be accompanied by the handmaidens of truth and trust in order to be constant. Love wasn't Rickard and the trappings of his former Berlin apartment, or the glitz and glamour of his life at Passport Pictures. Love was loving someone who could change your life with a smile, who could lift your spirits with a touch, someone who would always be there for you no matter how dire the circumstances. That was love. Emil had shown me the way and then was torn from my life, like my daughter.

When Lotti left we kissed each other good-bye, not knowing when we would see each other again. She carried a small bag, with a change of clothes, allowing her to go from the hotel to work the next morning. I envied her relationship with Egon, but I suspected that it might not last forever. He had already reached far beyond what she could conceive.

She closed the door and I sat alone on the couch.

The next morning, I ate a small breakfast, packed my case, and walked to my new address. The day was pleasant for late March, warm sunlight on my shoulders, but my thoughts flashed to my daughter, Emil, and the people I'd left behind in Amsterdam.

My apartment, small and somewhat dark, was on the ground floor at the back of the building. My one window looked into a square that bordered the street. Several large trees spread their gray branches into the air. In the summer they would be loaded with leaves, filling the room with shades of green.

I spent the remainder of the day purchasing a small desk, a chair, a dresser, and typewriter. An icebox and a second-hand bed and mattress had been left behind.

I'd decided to write when I could—when my energies weren't directed at temporary jobs, or finding Laura and Emil. More than anything, I needed a contact like Egon, someone I could trust who would bring me the world's news.

Western newspapers were censored or banned. The only news came from Nazi papers or the state-controlled radio. The Reich airwaves vomited a constant retch of propaganda, military songs, and approved classical music. Those were the extent of our entertainment. One dared not listen to foreign broadcasts that might happen to get through, the penalty being arrest and imprisonment.

A few days after I moved in, on a Tuesday, I walked past a café on Unter den Linden and spotted a man from my past. Wrapped in his Wehrmacht coat and smoking a cigarette, he faced me while sitting at an outdoor table. I recognized his bent form instantly and wrapped a scarf over my head, partially concealing my face. I didn't want him to recognize me. It was Wolf, the man who'd played the Vampire King and, later, the old Jew in the propaganda films.

I was somewhat shocked to see him in military dress, for he'd professed no sympathy for the Nazis. However, those objections were of no matter when the Reich came calling. He looked like a normal soldier, although he was drinking at ten in the morning. He had that inebriated, dazed look that followed him from our first meeting, and I wondered if the Nazis had relegated him to a desk job rather than put him on the front lines. With his stoop and clawed hands, Wolf had a much better chance of remaining alive in an office rather than a trench. I chuckled at that thought because I knew the Nazis really didn't care whether Wolf lived or died.

I strode past, hoping that he didn't recognize me. I was dead to everyone except Lotti, Egon, my mother, and Volker at the club. He gave me a quick look, but I avoided eye contact and was soon past him.

He didn't call out after me and I was glad.

The days, weeks, and months dragged by.

I found myself isolated from Lotti and my mother while

working temporary jobs under my assumed identity. I also had learned nothing about Laura or Emil. During 1941, most of my news about the war came from Lotti. She often gossiped at the Leopard Club with young soldiers on leave. We learned that Egon had been sent to the Eastern Front as part of Operation Barbarossa, the Nazi invasion of the Soviet Union on June 22.

Lotti and I were overwhelmed when we heard the news, but the Reich propaganda mouthpieces assured us that a "decisive and quick" victory was at hand. I didn't believe anything that came from Goebbels, Göring, or Hitler. What had happened to our friend Rudi was less clear. Lotti had heard he was in Africa, but even Volker, the club manager, knew nothing of his whereabouts. We feared the worst—that he had fallen in North Africa.

Eventually, I found a job as a secretarial clerk at a bank not far from Rickard's old apartment on Unter den Linden. Although I still had money, I didn't want to deplete my savings any more than I had to. About half the funds remained from the sale of the bracelet.

Because I worked close to where I'd lived with Rickard, I often pictured him walking up the apartment steps with Laura by his side. Those cogent dreams broke my heart. One day, after work, when it was still light, I drank two brandies at the club and then took a taxi to within a few blocks of Passport Pictures. Every time I returned to the studio, little had changed, and every time the result was the same, except for this particular evening.

The studio door opened and he, attired in a dark double-breasted suit, walked out with a young girl by his side—Laura. The guards were there, the entrance was as fortified as it had ever been since the Nazis had claimed it as their own. The late-afternoon sun cast long shadows on the wide lot where Anders had been beaten. Laura, almost ten, held on to his hand, laughing, practically skipping to keep up with his longer stride. She wore a fancy dress, a creamy shade of velvet, shimmering in the rosy light. At one point, Rickard bent over and kissed the top of her head. This loving moment stopped my breath and made my stomach quiver. They got into a chauffeured car and pulled away. I stepped behind a tree across the road as they drove out the gate. They never knew I was there.

The liquor roiled in my stomach and I retched at the base of the tree. I wiped my mouth and walked with uncertain steps to a tram stop. Soon, I was back in my apartment, lying in the dark, wishing I'd never gone to look for my daughter, sorry that I'd seen the display of affection with her father. In a way, I thought Laura lucky because she was privileged to lead such a life while so many suffered, but I feared that her father would ultimately destroy her future. Would she join the Jungmädelbund, the Young Girls' League of the Nazi Party? Would Rickard, who had never been an ardent supporter when we were together, instill the party ideology into our daughter? Certainly she would be influenced by those who lived and breathed Nazi politics. What would happen to her if Germany lost the war? I writhed on the bed, my fevered mind seeking the answers to those unknowable questions.

Unable to sleep, I went to my desk that I'd positioned in front of the solitary window. The curtains were drawn, but a sliver of gray light pierced the meeting of the fabric. I sat down on the cold metal chair, turned on the desk lamp, took a piece of paper, and rolled it over the typewriter's platen. I began rewriting *Einsamkeit*, *Loneliness*, the novel I'd started after I'd met Emil. I'd destroyed the few pages I'd written before we left for Amsterdam.

I revived the character of Martin from *The Berlin Woman*, a man the heroine had deserted because her life had gotten too comfortable.

*I search for him as I search for everything in life. Sometimes an orange or an apple that I find at the fruit and flower stand become the joy of my day. Everything is heightened by the sadness I feel. Colors. Soft, pink clouds, a red sunrise, stars that sparkle against the black veil—they're inflamed by what I've lost and can never be found. Sounds. Aching strains of music that tug at my soul, pulling me into the abyss.*

*How I miss Martin. I believed that I couldn't love a man who was kind to me. I'd misunderstood his attempts to shelter me—his trust, his love, his passion. Those wondrous attributes became suffocating instruments because I didn't understand them. Other women would sneer at my inability to return his affection, to desire his smile, to sink in the depths of his flashing brown eyes, or the warmth of his arms.*

*To live in a country that one is free to walk in, to love as one pleases, to worship the God one chooses— that would be bliss. But that paradise is so far away, so unattainable that my heart sinks with each sunrise and dies at each sunset. How will I find him? How will I find the happiness I threw away?*

*I live the life of the lonely.*

I wrote until I could work no longer. I stumbled back to bed and slept until the alarm clock woke me at six. I had to be at work by eight; if not, my tardiness would count against me.

The bombings of Berlin began in earnest in November 1943. Bombs had fallen on the capital for more than three years, but the attacks had been sporadic with limited damage. Lotti had seen Egon twice in the two years since he'd left for the East. I left them alone so they could spend their limited time together, but I talked to him briefly on the phone.

He told me to "watch for a surprise." As the months drifted past, nothing happened, and I forgot about his words.

When the German armed forces were defeated at Stalingrad in January 1943, Lotti came to me with tears in her eyes. I offered her my support, knowing well what she was going through. She'd heard nothing from Egon and had even taken the bold step to contact his parents, who were not in favor of their son's relationship. He had disappeared and we feared that either he was dead or had been captured by the Red Army.

In the late summer of 1943, I was awakened in the middle of the night by a rattle at my window. At first, I thought it was the wind, or some creature, a squirrel or a bird, brushing against the glass, but the intrusion ended with a definite knock.

My nerves on edge, I slid out of bed and padded to the window. I picked up a pencil on my desk and slid the curtain back a few centimeters, fearing that I might find a face staring at me. Instead, in the dismal light, I spotted a brown envelope leaning against the glass. The dark figure of a man weaved through the trees, gliding toward the street and a waiting car. He was in no hurry and even looked back at me before climbing into the vehicle. I couldn't see his face, but he was clothed in a Wehrmacht uniform.

I sat at my desk a few minutes, the curtains parted, to make sure no one would jump me if I grabbed the package. Satisfied the apartment grounds were deserted, I lifted the sash and seized the envelope. I closed the window, drew the curtain, and sat in my chair, my heart pounding.

The envelope was larger than average, with no address, stamp, or return. I lifted it to my nose, but it only smelled like paper. I wondered if this was the "surprise" that Egon had promised.

After settling down, I turned on the light, ripped open the flap, and studied the contents. A small yellow note had been clipped to three pages of Nazi stationery—the Reich's eagle proudly spread its wings across their tops. On the note were the words: *Von einem Freund von Egon*, From a friend of Egon.

I reached for a cigarette and forced myself to read the pages despite my fear of the bad news they might bring.

The first page contained an account of the fighting on the Eastern Front: the relentless bad weather, the horrible food, the low morale as the troops waged battle against the massive Red Army. I was sure that Egon had made a show of fighting for the Nazis, but that his heart lay more with the oppressed than the oppressor. He was on the side of freedom, wherever that might be, not on the side of political parties. The page ended with notes about starvation, surrender, and the incompetence and interference from Hitler that had doomed the operation to failure. Everyone considered the Führer's military acumen a joke.

Because I'd told Egon of my time in Amsterdam, the second page was a listing of the atrocities committed by the Reich in that city. I'd left in March 1941, just before the Nazi government confiscated Jewish property. From that time forward, a planned timetable of restrictions and harsh measures had been laid out against the Jews. In April, German identification cards had been issued to the Dutch; in July, the Nazis had decreed that all Jewish identification cards must be marked with a red "J"; in August, Jewish children were barred from attending trade schools, and only two hundred and fifty guilders were allowed to Jewish property owners.

Labor camps had been constructed early in 1942, and, that May, Jews were ordered to wear a yellow star and observe an 8:00 p.m. to 6:00 a.m. curfew. No telephones were allowed, and Jews could shop only from three to five in the afternoon. In July of that year, the roundup of Jews began. German trains took the Jews away. Once people disappeared, they were never seen in Amsterdam again.

The last page contained the shortest description, but it tore at my heart. In June 1941, shortly after Egon and I had made the trip to Buchenwald, most Jewish prisoners arrested during the Amsterdam fights and the February strikes of that year had been transferred to another concentration camp called Mauthausen. I didn't even know where the camp was, but I suspected it might not even be in Germany. The page ended with the words: *Casualties are high among those taken, with little chance of survival.*

I stubbed out the cigarette and threw the pages on my desk. I didn't know whether to rage or cry. But, in the end, it made little difference.

Two months later, Berlin was pounded and punished from the skies.

A battle for the city had begun.

# CHAPTER 26

On the evening of November 22, 1943, Lotti stopped by my apartment to swap ration cards—something that was routinely done during those years. She left shortly after eight, and I looked forward to getting into bed early because Berlin had been under attack by British bombers for three of the last four nights.

Instead, a few minutes later, she returned, pounding on my door and screaming. I rushed into the hall to find a gallery of frantic, terrified residents rushing in and out of the building wondering what to do. Would the next bomb land on us? The air raid sirens blared.

"Come look," Lotti said, her gas mask in hand. No one traveled without one. She grabbed my arm and pulled me out the door, past the sandbags, to the curb. The lights of Berlin were dark under blackout restrictions. Red and green flares dropped through the clouds, illuminating the skies and the bombs' targets with their steady light. The flares were effective. Many contained explosives to stop the fire brigade from extinguishing the flames.

"Should we go to the U-Bahn?" Lotti asked, still grasping my arm. A man who lived in the building rushed up to us with a printed list of shelters.

Lotti was as terrified of the bombs as I was of being buried by a blast. We had two options—either sitting in an apartment waiting for the bombs to fall, or squatting with hundreds of others in an underground railway station. Neither choice offered much comfort.

"Let's see what happens," I said. "Maybe it'll be nothing." Oddly, despite my fear of being smothered, I felt somewhat relieved that the bombs were falling. The Luftwaffe's response to the sorties had been marginal, not strong enough to deter the British attacks. For the first time, as we nervously awaited an uncertain fate, I believed that Hitler might be *vulnerable*—that the war might come to an end—but at what price to Germany? If the Führer surrendered, he would save countless lives and the destruction of the capital. If he continued in his mad drive for world conquest, the nation would be destroyed and National Socialism and the German people would shoulder the blame. Those of us who resisted could only look on in horror as the war played out.

The bombs soon rained down, and Lotti rushed to the U-Bahn station as I stood near the curb defying the prohibition to remain outside during an attack. Traffic on our busy street had come to a stop. I rubbed my hands over my arms, warming them, as the cool, night air settled upon me. Searchlights swept across the gray clouds, and flak from the antiaircraft guns burst through the overcast, creating a strange and deadly dance of flashing lights in the sky.

Those who rushed around me must have taken me for a fool, or someone possessed, as I watched the explosions and felt their shudder under my feet. Much like my relief that the bombs were falling, I was aware that my life could end at any moment and I would be lucky to die—spared from the horrors to come. Perhaps fate had other plans for me, though. Perhaps my time on earth hadn't come to an end. I didn't fear for Laura. I was certain that she would be protected by Rickard. He and our daughter would be shuffled off to some secure location where they would survive the bombings. Laura was twelve now, old enough to know that what was transpiring over Berlin wasn't a game. A younger girl might have considered it so—to hide with her father, who would assure her that they were escaping from the "bad people," telling her in a soft voice, *All will be well once this passes.*

Emil, if he was still alive, would be saved from the attacks as well. The Allies would spare the concentration camps, the fetid homes of those who opposed the Reich. Ironically, many of those prisoners probably wished that their lives would end in a quick blast rather than spent suffering in the grueling camps.

Most of the bombs had landed to the west of my apartment, near the Tiergarten and beyond. The fires, a blazing line on the horizon of yellow and orange flames, and billowing columns of black smoke that piled against the clouds, combined into one raging firestorm. I shook my head, not believing what I was seeing, the destruction of my city—the capital of the Reich was burning and Hitler could do nothing to stop it. The war had come to the people, and we would suffer. As I stood there, my feet seemingly unable to move, I heard screams, the cries of people burning alive.

I wondered if I'd feel the pressure of a bomb dropping toward me, or hear the shrieks of tons of ordinance falling on my head. For what seemed hours, I watched flames ripping toward the sky. Often I would hear the sound of flak and then see a burst of light and an explosion, as if a bomber had been blasted from the sky. Black pieces of wreckage—part of a wing, a flaming engine, fell through the searchlights, smashing into the earth not far from where I stood.

When I next looked at my watch, almost forty-five minutes had passed and I caught movement from the corner of my eye, as if a shadow had passed. I stared into the darkness toward the bare trees spread across the apartment grounds. In the corner, near my window, a figure melted into the gloom.

I wondered if it was someone scared or hurt by the bombs.

I crept forward, weaving through the tree trunks.

A man huddled in the corner. He was young, attired in clothing not worn by Berliners. He held a gun in his shaking right hand.

"*Bleib zurück,*" he said. *Stay back.*

I could tell from his accent that he wasn't German. There appeared to be a uniform under his fur-lined jacket.

I held up my hands. "Friend," I said in English, one of the few words I knew.

He shook his head and repeated his command.

A black stain dripped from his left hand. "Blood?" I asked.

"Hurt," he said. "*Schmerz?*"

"*Schmerz.*" I suspected that he was British. I lowered one arm and pointed to the window. *Bleibe.*

He seemed to understand—I'd said *Stay*, a word he knew. A man was hurt and I wanted to help. The hall was quiet . . . a few neighbors had stayed inside. Most had taken shelter, like Lotti, at the U-Bahn station.

I locked my apartment door and rushed to the window. I wondered if he would still be there, but he was, a dark lump against the stone. I pushed my desk back, opened the window and curtains, and waved my hand for him to come inside. He pocketed the gun and, using his right arm, lifted himself over the sash. In a few seconds, he was inside my apartment, staring at me like a lost animal. I closed the window, drew the curtains, and turned on the desk lamp.

He was younger than I expected. I had turned thirty-two in May, but this man was probably twenty, perhaps younger. His face was white, possibly from loss of blood, and his blue eyes bulged from shock. A curl of wavy brown hair lay across his sweating forehead.

I put a finger to my lip, signaling him to be quiet. He understood and sat in my desk chair. Kneeling in front of him, I looked at the blood dripping down his left hand to the floor. I put a newspaper under the chair to catch it.

We communicated as best we could without words. I motioned for him to take off his jacket and he did so, wincing in pain. He wore a blue uniform with a propeller insignia on the right shoulder. His left arm was stained with blood. An irregular gash cut across his left bicep, causing the blood to flow. While the wound might not lead to his death, it was painful and needed tending.

He studied my movements as I knelt in front of him. His eyes fluttered now and then and his head lolled to one side. Then, he would snap out of his stupor and sit stiff and still in the chair.

"Friend," I tried to reassure him in English. "Resistance."

That brought a smile to his face and his body sagged a bit in the chair.

"God bless you," he said. "I need to wash up."

I led him to the sink, doused the wound with soap and water, closed the cut with tape, and wrapped it with an old, clean towel.

"Bomber. Gunner. Parachuted." I made some sense of what he was saying, but couldn't imagine the trauma that he'd suffered—the plane exploding around him over Berlin and then jumping for his life, drifting through the clouds, hoping to avoid being shot in the searchlights. And what of landing on a deserted street or a park as the bombs fell around him? Most of the men hit at ten thousand feet either died or faced capture.

The bleeding appeared to have stopped, and I motioned for him to sit on the bed.

Then, someone knocked on my door. I looked at my watch. It was after ten thirty. My British guest jumped for his coat and gun. I shook my head, but he grabbed it anyway. If the SS or the Gestapo had come, neither one of us stood a chance against their organized firepower.

"Who is it?" I asked.

"Lotti . . . let me in."

"Are you alone?"

"Of course . . . please let me in. I'm scared to death."

I opened the door a bit and peered out. Lotti, her face flushed, stood alone in the dark hall.

She stepped inside and, at first, didn't see the man sitting on my bed—the man with a gun pointed toward us. A little squeak came out of her mouth.

"This is Lotti, my friend," I said in English.

The weapon didn't drift from us.

"Lotti," the man said. "*Willkommen.*"

She stumbled toward my desk chair. "Who is he? How did he get here?"

"I don't speak much English and he doesn't speak much German, but I think his bomber was hit, he parachuted out and, in the confusion, found his way here. He was wearing a jacket and uniform. He's been injured. I imagine he's hungry."

Lotti spoke more English than I did because of the various clients she served in her office job. "Let me try," she said.

The young man and Lotti spoke in whispers for a half hour. Chester Osgood was his name and everyone called him "Chet." He was from London. His Lancaster bomber had been hit and was limping over Berlin in a mission to drop its payload when it began breaking apart. He and the rest of the crew parachuted out, but he'd lost them in the clouds and smoke, only to find himself on the edge of a large wooded park—the Tiergarten, we thought. Chester discarded his parachute and made his way east toward the Berliner Dom, when he saw me standing at the curb. Avoiding everyone he could, he darted through the trees.

"Would he like something to eat?" I asked Lotti.

Chester nodded and I heated some leftover soup on my hot plate. The electricity was still on, and in the distance we heard the faint wail of the all clear.

The young man ate as if he'd never seen food in his life, and soon the adrenaline in his body began to subside and exhaustion set in. "You've been very kind," he said, "but I can't stay here for any length of time. You'll be in danger. I need clothes. *Deutsche* clothes."

Lotti translated and we agreed that he should sleep here and then leave the next evening. Another attack was planned for the following night and others after that, he told us. The RAF was determined to destroy the city.

"There's a men's clothing store near my work," Lotti said. "Egon left a few things at my apartment. I'll bring those."

"Let me give you some money," I said.

"Pay me tomorrow." She slipped out the door and we were left alone—the only noise outside was the sound of the fire sirens to the west.

"*Schlafe*," I said, for I was growing tired myself.

"I'll sleep facing the door," he said. I wasn't sure what he meant, but he shifted on his side, still clutching his gun, looking toward the window and the entrance to my apartment. I pushed the desk back to the window and turned off the lamp. I had to work in the morning as well. Chester would have to spend the day alone until we could get him clothed.

I slipped into bed fully dressed. I pulled a blanket over his shoulders, startling him a little. His breathing slowed. "*Danke*," he said.

"*Gut schlafen*," I replied.

I slept with one eye open most of the night. My skin itched from raw nerves. Chester didn't move during the night.

When I woke up, he was sitting on the edge of the bed staring at the door.

I told him to wait inside, make no noise, and when Lotti arrived with the clothes, he could leave as darkness fell.

He agreed. I said good-bye and left for work.

Because it was December, darkness came early to Berlin. Lotti and I arrived at my apartment about the same time. She carried a bag of clothes. I'd picked up a supply of bread and cheese for Chester, using some of the coveted ration cards in order to get the goods.

"I found this coat and jacket at a second-hand store," Lotti said, pulling them out of the package. She also provided Chester with a white shirt, dark pants, and shoes, which he put on as we looked away.

During the day, he'd shaved using a sharp kitchen knife and slicked back his hair with water and a bit of cooking oil. With his new clothes and appearance, he looked like any German young man. Unfortunately, we had no forged documents to give, so he was on his own.

Chester holstered his gun and, using the bag Lotti had brought, wrapped the gifts of bread and cheese into a neat package. I gave him twenty-five marks because he had no money.

Everything else he left with us needed to be destroyed. We planned to pack his clothes in a box and throw it into the nearby Spree River.

I looked into his blue eyes as he readied himself. They displayed a strange mixture of resolve and nerves. I relished his bravery, but feared for his life. If Berlin was bombed again, he might be able to slip out of the city into the countryside, but his chances of getting out of Germany weren't good. He mentioned something to Lotti about going north and somehow catching a ship to Sweden.

We turned off the lamp. He crept in the shadows toward the door.

"Friends . . . for life," he whispered.

"*Freunde . . . fürs Leben*," Lotti replied.

"For life," I repeated in English.

And he was gone.

# CHAPTER 27

The Royal Air Force campaign against the city continued until the end of March 1944. Often the bombings were successful, many times they were not, but the casualties mounted in the air and on the ground. There were other bombing targets as well: Frankfurt, Stuttgart, and Leipzig numbered among them. In February 1945, Dresden was obliterated by bombs and the resulting fires.

Berliners were suffering before the war ended, but the worst was yet to come as the Red Army approached in April 1945. Much of the city lay in ruins. Death came in numerous ways: missiles, bombs, and artillery fire; the conflagrations; drowning in the U-Bahn shelters as pipes burst; from disease as life became a continual struggle for survival. Yet, Hitler and his officials continued to urge every German to fight to the end, to willingly give their life for National Socialism. Many continued to believe the Führer's rants about the war—that all was not lost—that Germany would reemerge stronger than ever from its fight against its enemies.

The business where I worked was destroyed in early 1944, putting me out of a job. Lotti's office lasted a bit longer. We often spent time at my mother's house when we could find transportation. I packed a few clothes, some necessities, and my typewriter and took them to Rixdorf because it had been spared from the worst of the air attacks.

My mother, in her wisdom, had planted vegetables to supplement her diet and was happy to share her meager meals with us. On days when we felt the bombs wouldn't fall, we decided to stay in the city.

In the month before the war ended, we took shelter at my mother's home again. Lotti and I often looked to the north as Red Army missiles and artillery pulverized the city. We saw the smoke from the fires, witnessed the explosions that rocked Berlin. I imagined that there would be nothing left of Unter den Linden and Rickard's former apartment, or anything to do with the National Socialist government—the Reichstag and Hitler's Chancellery in particular.

The Leopard Club had closed its doors at the beginning of 1945. I'd rushed to the club to trade in the rest of my guilders for Reichsmarks. Fortunately, Volker obliged, but took a higher cut, telling me that he had little use for guilders now that the banking system was under stress and likely to fail. He was right and I thanked him for offering me a service that had kept me alive.

Egon and Rudi were still missing and we'd heard nothing about them. No "surprise" envelope appeared at my apartment window again. We assumed that both had been killed.

I learned that Passport Pictures had been bombed and that the resulting fire had destroyed the studios. I was concerned about Laura, but with the destruction of Passport, my hope of ever seeing her again diminished. Frieda, my mother, prayed every night that death would spare us. Lotti and I were grateful for her prayers, but we knew the Red Army, the French, the British, and the Americans had other ideas for Germany.

And then, in May 1945, it all ended. Everyone knew that Hitler was dead. Before he committed suicide, he blamed his generals and the German people for the defeat, never taking any responsibility for the world war he'd created—the deaths of millions rested upon his bloody hands.

I decided to walk to the city. Lotti had already left to see if anything remained of her home.

The city that was Berlin had become a surreal canvas of death and destruction. People often describe destructive events of war and nature with the words, "I can't believe what's happened. I've never seen anything like it." It was too horrible to believe. My eyes had to convince my brain that what I saw was real.

Of course, my mother cautioned me about going into Berlin at all. She feared the Red Army, for she'd heard that its soldiers raped women—butchered children and animals— how the men destroyed everything in their drive for revenge. I told her that I would be careful, always mindful of what was going on around me. I had to see what had happened, to know if my apartment remained standing.

I put on a coat, gathered a few late-blooming tulips from the garden next door, and prepared for the walk into the city. No transportation was operating. The tulips, I thought, would go into the hands of Red Army soldiers if needed, a gift from a grateful German. The flowers were a slim measure of protection against unwanted aggression. I walked northwest toward the Brandenburg Gate, preferring an inland route rather than one along the river. I assumed that all the bridges crossing the Spree had been destroyed.

The walk was almost nine kilometers and a normal trip would have taken more than two hours. As I got close to the city center, walking became more difficult, more hazardous, as the streets presented their own obstacles. The corpses of destroyed military vehicles and collapsed buildings littered the landscape. Smoke filled the air, often choking me as the rancid odor of burning fuel entered my lungs. The smell of death also struck me at times, sometimes faint, often overpowering and retching in its violence. Berlin had become hell, a nightmare that one hoped to wake up from.

Those who had emerged from their hiding places, from sanctuary below ground, from anywhere they could take shelter, looked like ghosts—wan, stick figures with dark eyes and skin blanched by war. Water, food, electricity, and transportation had been destroyed in the final throes of battle. Berlin's recovery, if at all, would be long and costly. I wondered if Hitler would have cried or taken pity on his deluded followers if he'd lived long enough to see his precious Third Reich in ruins.

Red Army soldiers milled about on the streets and I avoided them. I passed through an otherworldly landscape, traveling alone as most war-battered Germans kept to the shadows. The Brandenburg Gate came into view, still standing, its columns pockmarked by the powdery gray holes of bullets and shrapnel. Only parts of the Quadriga, the victory chariot crowning the gate, remained. Surrounding it were the metal cadavers of destroyed vehicles, also blasted by explosions and gunfire. Through the wreckage, the splintered trees of the Tiergarten and the ruined dome of the Reichstag came into view.

I turned on Unter den Linden, toward the Berliner Dom and the Alexanderplatz. What I saw took my breath away. All that remained were shells, the thrusting needles and spires of the once-beautiful buildings that had lined the tree-lined boulevard. The sight reminded me of a painting of interconnected lines and charred, blocky shapes, crisscrossed by fallen lamp poles and electrical wires. The remains of wrecked cars and destroyed military vehicles lay in ruins as far as the eye could see. This testament to death and destruction brought tears to my eyes. Nothing remained of Rickard's building but the front wall and the shattered steps. Looking into the soulless eyes of the windows of the once-opulent apartment, I saw nothing but patches of a cloudy sky.

290 V. S. Alexander

The conquering troops of men and women gathered in groups, dancing and singing to victory songs played on an accordion. One of the soldiers saw me and approached. His face was sunburned and covered in grit, his uniform blackened with dirt and grease, a rifle slung over his shoulder. He asked for my identification papers, which I withdrew from my purse. I handed him the documents and a red tulip. I wasn't afraid because women of the Red Army were nearby. I suspected they wouldn't let me be harmed.

He looked at the papers, spoke in Russian, handed them back to me, and waved me on. He broke the tulip's stem, stuck the bloom in his uniform pocket, and returned to his group. I was glad that I'd carried the flowers with me.

Destruction accompanied me, no matter where I turned. The Berliner Dom sat in shambles, its once-proud façade blackened. The Lustgarten, the site in front of the Dom, where so many Nazis had gathered at the height of Hitler's power, lay scorched, the trees shattered and burned, and the flagstones jumbled in broken disarray. The chanting, the proud display of Nazi flags, the Germanic theatrics, had been silenced by the Allies.

Not far away, only a shell remained of Lotti's apartment building. I noticed smoke coming from a makeshift chimney protruding from a broken window in the building's basement. I peered into the darkness, my eyes adjusting to the murky light. Candles burned, but offered little to view except shadows that drifted across the space.

I called her name into the void.

An older woman with a blue-and-white scarf wrapped around her head came to the window. "I'm looking for Lotti," I said.

"She isn't here," the woman replied. "She's searching for water. We have to take it from the Spree. Boil it."

I turned away, revolted by the thought of drinking wa-

ter from the polluted river, boiled or not. I'd seen the army
tanks that had fallen into its waters, the shells that exploded
near its banks, the chemicals that floated downstream. We
were lucky in Rixdorf to have access to well water, as yet
unspoiled.

"Please tell her that her friend was here," I said. "She can
come to Rixdorf anytime she wants."

The woman sniffed and turned away.

*Everyone is sad*, I thought.

In a short time, I arrived at my former apartment. A shell,
or some other weapon of destruction, had landed near the
corner of the building. The trees that had shaded the structure in summer were reduced to burnt sticks. A large hole
existed where Chester Osgood, the Royal Air Force man, had
tried to hide. I stepped through the opening—no one stopped
me, for, like much of Berlin, the building seemed deserted.
Had everyone fled to the country in anticipation of the Red
Army victory?

Little in my apartment had escaped damage. My desk was
broken into pieces—I'd left no papers of importance behind,
including the mysterious letter I'd received from the "friend
of E." My bed and the few remaining clothes were scorched
beyond use. A cool wind blew through the opening. A dead
bird, its black-and-gray feathers splayed, lay near the door.
There was nothing for me here. I'd live with my mother until Berlin could be rebuilt, and no one knew how long that
would take.

A scream filled the air and I stepped through the damaged wall. Several women ran down the street, some carrying
pails. Lotti, her curly hair bouncing against her neck, was
one of them. I yelled and she pivoted toward me, leaving the
others to race on. She rushed into my arms.

"They're after us," she panted.

"Who?"

"The soldiers . . ."

I pulled her inside the ruins of my apartment and we peered around the shattered wall.

"There," she said. Three Red Army soldiers raced toward the Berliner Dom. Lotti grabbed a breath. "We were gathering water when a group of them came up behind us. One of them grabbed a girl and pulled off her blouse—right in front of us. They told us to watch as they stripped her . . . they called her a 'dirty German whore.' Then, the one who'd grabbed her pulled down his trousers. We swung our pails at them, dousing them with water, and they shouted they would shoot us . . . we understood that much . . . I and a few others ran away."

Sobbing, Lotti fell into my arms. "I have no home, no food, no water . . . what will I do, Niki? What will any of us do?"

I stroked her cheek. "You can come to Rixdorf with me until things settle down. It's too dangerous here."

She shook her head. "I can't. What if Egon comes back . . . the war is over . . . what about Rudi? They won't know where I am. I don't want to lose everyone I love."

"Lotti, look around. There's nothing left."

She wiped away a tear. "I know, but we have a shelter under the building. If Egon comes home, he'll look for me. A few men live there, too. They're older . . . they really can't protect us, but I feel better knowing they're there."

I thought of my daughter and Emil and wondered if they were still alive. Had Rickard and Laura lived through the bombings? Emil must have been liberated from Mauthausen. Only my efforts to find the truth would answer those questions. Germany had become a puzzle. The torn pieces had to be put together again, and we had new masters now: the Red Army and the Allied forces. Would they be kind or treat us as war criminals? No one knew. Maybe each victor would behave differently toward us.

I carried my two tulips, now withering, in my hands as I

retraced my steps toward Rixdorf. I felt more comfortable going through the city rather than walking by the Spree. I left Lotti, promising her that she would be welcome at any time at my mother's.

By the end of August 1945, the Allies had divided Germany and Berlin. The Potsdam Conference laid out the four zones, each victor receiving a piece of the country: Great Britain in the northwest, known as The Industrial Ruins; France in the southwest, The Wine; the Soviet Union in the east, The Food; and the Americans in the south, The Scenery.

Berlin, deep within Soviet territory, also was divided into four sectors with each power taking its share of the city. The Soviets took Unter den Linden and most of the city center east of the Brandenburg Gate. My mother's home and Tempelhof Airport, including the ruins of Passport Pictures, fell within the American zone.

At first the four sectors of Berlin cooperated in a shaky truce, all the victors congratulating each other on their success. Fraternization with German nationals—men, women, and children—was forbidden. Eventually, that barrier broke down as GIs and the occupying soldiers, separated from their wives and girlfriends, sought the company of German women. The goal of the occupation was to root out the remaining Nazis and prevent the rise of another fascist movement, one possibly more rabid than the one that had just been destroyed. At first, the divisions, political or otherwise, mattered little to Berliners. Survival had once again taken precedence over politics. The few times I ventured into the city, I saw what had become of "ordinary citizens."

The Wehrmacht had been disarmed. The Allies paid special attention to the capture of high-ranking SS and Gestapo officers. Most were arrested, but some evaded capture.

Berlin streets had to be cleared, the roads opened for traffic. The rails and bridges needed to be rebuilt, including the metal taken by the Soviets as war reparations. Women swept the sidewalks or worked in makeshift assembly lines removing piles of debris, brick by brick, sometimes aided by older men. The Allies filmed the Berliners at work. Sometimes the women smiled. Often they smirked or thumbed their noses at the photographer. Men and women gathered around the few working water wells in the city, men pumping the handle for those who couldn't. The work was backbreaking and demoralizing for a country that once had been the strongest in Europe, a cradle of civilized discourse, music, and art. All that had been destroyed. Many of us, myself included, believed we deserved the punishment that had rained down upon us. We knew who to blame. He was dead. Now we had to survive.

And, once again, I yearned to find out what had happened to Laura and Emil.

# CHAPTER 28

———◆◆◆———

His name was Viktor Volkov and he was a senior sergeant in the Red Army.

About a kilometer east of the Brandenburg Gate, a jail had been constructed, hastily, by the Soviet troops in the fall of 1945. This was the beginning of my renewed quest to find my daughter. The jail was housed in a small building that had somehow survived the bombing mostly intact. The troops had reinforced the walls and added bars across the windows. I surmised that prisoners were held only for short periods before being transferred to another facility in Germany, or for possible deportation to the Soviet Union.

A monument to Stalin had been constructed beyond the Gate, announcing to the world, and anyone who entered the former Unter den Linden, that you were stepping into Soviet territory. I had done the improbable and asked a Red Army soldier patrolling near the Gate if there was a prison nearby. I had learned the Russian word for just this occasion. He pointed east, gave me an address in Russian I didn't recognize, and then pointed to a sign printed in Russian, French, English, and German that pinpointed the jail's location. I found it easily.

I had no idea who was in command, but soon found out through a corporal, who spoke German and acted as the translator for the senior sergeant, that Viktor Volkov was in charge. I asked to speak to him. The corporal shrugged, as if I was only one in a long line of people seeking missing spouses or relatives.

Visitors were taken by guard through the main door to a small waiting room containing one chair and a diminutive oak table. A large steel door cut a short hallway in half and kept the captives apart from the senior sergeant and his sole supporting member, the corporal.

I knew this would not be easy, for many believed that the Soviets hated the Germans absolutely, wanting nothing but the total destruction of the country. The British were cold and all business, the French out for blood as well. The Americans had the reputation of being the most genial of the victors. Survivors had fled to the American sector for that reason, but many wouldn't leave their lifelong homes. Even some Wehrmacht soldiers had raced to surrender to the Americans, believing they would be better treated by the GIs than if they fell into the hands of the Red Army.

The corporal left me and I sat alone for about thirty minutes before he returned. He led me to another small room near the steel door. Volkov was seated behind his desk, smoking a cigarette and reading a file—one of many piled on his desk. He was attired in a brown uniform with solid red bands on his epaulets. Medals displaying the hammer and sickle and the Red Star were pinned to his chest. He looked bored and then annoyed when I entered the room. A Red Army flag was pinned to the otherwise bare walls. A dismal, grainy light entered the barred window behind him.

Volkov spoke some harsh words in Russian.

"He said you have five minutes." The corporal remained in the room with us.

"I'm looking for a man," I said. "I'm trying to find my daughter." I hoped that the words elicited some sympathy from the cold man sitting in front of me.

Volkov leaned back in his chair, his brown eyes dissecting

me. "You and every German in Berlin are looking for some-one. Have you seen the posters plastered on every wall? What is his name?"

"Rickard Länger," I said. "We're still married, but we've lived apart for many years."

The sergeant pointed to a black file cabinet against the wall and the corporal began a search. In a short time, a sheath of papers lay on Volkov's desk.

"Would you like a cigarette?" the sergeant asked me through his interpreter. I was dying for one, no matter the brand. Food, liquor, and cigarettes had become hot items on the black market. Everyone paid dearly for these luxuries— even the troops in the four sectors bartered among them-selves.

I gratefully took the cigarette and thanked him. The smoke was cool going down my throat. It was menthol.

Volkov crushed one in an ashtray and lit another. He stud-ied the file in front of him for a few minutes and then spoke. "Were you a member of the Nazi Party?"

I shook my head. "No, I worked against them." There were many significant details that I didn't want to divulge, but I added: "I was a writer. The National Socialists banned my books and I lost my living and my daughter to them. I fled to Amsterdam and then returned."

"What is your name?"

Volkov had maneuvered me into a corner. I could present my falsified German identification papers, or I could tell him my real name. Sitting in front of this forceful man with the in-tense brown eyes and the strong, broad face, I felt I should tell the truth. Besides, the Nazis were gone—for the most part.

"Marie Rittenhaus. Länger was my married name."

The sergeant ran his finger down a column on the page. His lips tightened, giving him a smug look. "He's been arrested and charged with aiding the Nazis, producing propaganda, defiling the character of a race . . . and related war crimes."

The charges didn't surprise me. Rickard had known what he was doing when he made the devil's pact with Spiegel to save Passport Pictures. Certainly, I didn't want to see Rickard dead or tortured—I'd loved him, for a time. I'd survived off Nazi wealth when I shared his home, but that association had driven me away. I pushed down the shame I felt about our relationship, but my real concern was for my daughter. "Is he here?" I asked. "May I see him?"

Volkov closed the file on the desk and motioned for the corporal to return it to the cabinet. "He was here, but has been transferred to a special camp opened by the People's Commissariat for Internal Affairs. From what I've seen, he'll be spending a long time in confinement."

I'd also heard the Commissariat referred to as the NKVD. "Can you tell me where he's being held?"

Volkov shook his head. "I don't give solace to war criminals. I don't care if he's garroted, hanged, or shot."

"I want to ask him about my daughter."

He sighed and then smiled at the corporal who was still interpreting our conversation. "Do you know how many requests I get every day to see the most hardened Nazis? We are doing the world a favor by holding these animals until they can be . . ."

"Executed?"

"I deny most requests because they do nothing for our Party." He leaned forward. "Otherwise, let the punishment fit the crime. I believe those words come from an Englishman. *The Mikado?* Or perhaps it's Roman."

I didn't know and I had no desire to debate him. "Rickard is the only person who knows where my daughter is." I extinguished the cigarette in the desk ashtray. He held out the pack. I declined, not wanting to push the limits of his good will.

He placed the cigarettes near one of the piles on his desk and leaned back in his chair. I could tell that the end of my visit was near.

I got up. "Thank you for your time."

"Sit down, if you would . . ." The corporal took hold of my arm while the sergeant spoke.

I followed his order.

Volkov threaded his fingers together. "You said you worked against the Nazis. What did you mean?"

"Will you have me arrested if I tell you what I've done?"

He laughed, his lips parting, his cheeks flushing a bit. A few gold teeth showed in his smile. "I might arrest you if you don't. If you tell me the truth, I might give you a medal like the one on my chest." He tapped the Red Star.

My face reddened as I thought about what I might have to tell this officer. My heart thumped in my chest. What if he was lying about arresting me? Then, a memory of Laura flashed into my mind—the night she'd gotten into the car with Rickard after Spiegel had been executed. I'd held her close and cried, not knowing if I'd ever see her again, knowing there was nothing I could do to keep her from her father. That memory gave me the courage to face the man in front of me.

I recounted my stories through the interpreter: I told Volkov how I'd stolen a Nazi bracelet and exchanged it for guilders in Amsterdam; how I'd published books that had been banned and how my publisher had been roughed up at the hands of the SA; how I'd witnessed the execution of Spiegel and his wife by the SS; how, after Rickard had taken my daughter, Emil and I had fled to the Netherlands, where we witnessed more killings and Nazi persecution; how I'd faked my own death in order to get back into Germany; how I'd set a Reich recruiting office on fire; and, finally, how I'd been an accomplice to the murder of a German officer in Amsterdam.

By the time I finished, Volkov's expression had shifted from a cynical turn of mouth to one of astonishment. He lit another cigarette and said one word: "Impressive." Then, he added, "I know high-ranking officers in the Red Army who have done less than you in the fight against the fascists."

"I'm happy you're not going to arrest me, but your own troops have not been without blame when dealing with my people."

He ignored my comment and picked up a pen. "I'm going to write your name—Marie Rittenhaus. It's one I will remember. Come back in two weeks. I will find Rickard Länger for you. Perhaps, I can arrange a meeting."

"Thank you, Senior Sergeant Volkov. I will come back." I rose, but the corporal snagged me again on his superior's order.

"One last request," Volkov said. He pointed at the Red Army flag pinned to the drab wall. "If you work for me—if you find those who must be punished and turn them in to me—I may be able to find not only Länger but the man who accompanied you to Amsterdam—if he's still alive. What was his name?"

"Emil Belmon. I was told he was transferred from Buchenwald to Mauthausen."

He scribbled another note on the pad. "Good day, Marie Rittenhaus."

The corporal escorted me to the door and I stepped out into a fine mist falling from the overcast. I pulled my collar close to my neck and breathed deeply of the Berlin air, now somewhat devoid of the stench of war. For the first time in years, I felt free. A sensation like euphoria flooded my body. Had everything I'd been through been worth it?

The clouds seemed immovable with little wind to guide them. The city lay in ruins, but my soul was buoyed by hope and the realization that I might be able to see my daughter and Emil again . . . if everything fell into place.

I walked home and told my mother what had happened.

She gave me a message from Lotti.

A soldier had returned from the war.

# CHAPTER 29

I rushed into Egon's arms as he hurried up the path to my mother's house in Rixdorf. Lotti was by his side.

"My God," I said, "I thought you were dead—killed at Stalingrad."

"I never made it to Stalingrad," he explained, wrapping his arms around me. "I was on its outskirts as a courier, delivering messages back and forth from the Front to East Prussia." He paused. "We have a lot to talk about."

"Come inside," I said. I introduced Egon to Frieda, whom I'd convinced to work in the back garden in order to give us a few minutes of privacy. The weather was cool but manageable, and much needed to be done in the fall for the spring growing season ahead.

Sunlight fluttered into the house in flashes, striking the couch and casting its sharp rays upon Egon. I studied him. He looked older now, his blond hair a little darker, the creases around his blue eyes underscoring the stresses of war. The fire and determination that had made him the likeness of a poster boy for the Hitler Youth when I met him had diminished. He seemed reserved. I couldn't imagine either of us embarking now on a mission like the one to the recruitment office we'd torched. The death and destruction Egon had witnessed at the Front had tempered him, but, I hoped, left his resolve for a better world unchanged.

I sat across from them. Lotti clutched Egon's hand as if she never wanted to let go.

"I can't believe you're alive," I blurted out.

He frowned.

"I'm sorry," I said, lowering my gaze, ashamed of what I'd said. "I'm just so happy to see you. I should have said, 'I'm so glad you're home.'"

Lotti smiled. "We all are."

Egon talked about his time in the Wehrmacht and then seemed to tire of the subject. I was eager to ask a question, but it came with difficulties.

"How do you feel?" I asked him.

His blue eyes studied me, searching for something deeper. "What do you mean?"

"Are you strong enough to help me, to take on something that has real consequences?"

"It depends," he answered. "There's no need to burn down Nazi buildings." He ended his words with a slight smile.

"I'm talking about revenge."

Before he could answer, Lotti gripped Egon's hand even tighter and scooted closer to him. "Don't ask him to put himself in danger," she demanded. "Don't you think he's been through enough on the Eastern Front?"

"Yes, but let me explain," I said.

He put a finger to Lotti's lips. "Don't worry. I'm safe now. I spent four months at a camp for German prisoners of war. I got out because I was a lowly courier—not an officer. No one is after me."

I sighed, thinking of what I was asking. Something terrible was tearing at me and it came down to one question. Did the Nazis, who had made life hell in Germany for a dozen years, deserve the sword of justice against their necks—to be tortured or killed by the Soviets for their crimes? The Red Army wanted blood. Or was it up to me, and others, to forgive? I was wracked with doubt. Could I put men to death because I wanted to find my daughter and Emil?

To an irrational mind scarred by war, the answer was easy. *Yes.*

To a mind grounded by the prospect of death, the answer wasn't clear. *No?*

"Just consider what I'm asking. It's for Laura and Emil." I told them about my meeting with Viktor Volkov and what the senior sergeant wanted of me. *Bring me the Nazis who committed war crimes.* I told them that Volkov had offered me a chance to meet with Rickard and to find out what had happened to Emil.

"You're playing with the devil," Egon said. "I don't know how I feel about this. The war is over. Others, with more power, should fight for justice."

"I'll understand if you don't want to do this," I said. "I want nothing to stand in the way of our friendship."

"Nothing will," Egon said, reaching for my hand. Lotti nodded as Egon looked out the open back door at a sudden shower. "It's raining."

I looked at my mother, bent over, pulling up the late-summer weeds that still lingered in the garden, clods of dirt dangling from brownish sprouts. The moist black earth turned over as Frieda plunged the hoe into the ground. She had survived as well, and my respect for her had grown enormously. I'd told her some of what I'd been through, but I knew that a complete revelation might throw her into a panic about my eternal soul. Some secrets were better left unsaid, and, because of that, I think she felt more love for me now than she ever had.

I slept in my old room and was grateful that I had a bed, for the scenes in Berlin were very different. Like Lotti, people lived in the ruins, chopping wood for fuel, finding what they could to burn, trading what they could for bread or soup.

Meat had disappeared—only the occupying troops were af-
forded the luxury of dining on beef or chicken.

Some survivors lived in the ruins of their upper apartment
floors, even though the building might be in danger of collapse. Seeing these people was like looking into a painting,
the frail outline of the walls serving as the frame, the image
burning into one's mind like a picture. The furniture was arranged, the dining table and chairs overlooking a precipitous
drop to the street, the red tablecloth flung and draped over
the oak surface. Sometimes even a bed was visible from the
street. The survivors could live there during the summer, but
the winter was coming on. None of us knew how we would
survive the years ahead, but my mother and I were luckier
than most.

The changeable fall clouds had covered the sun. My
mother propped the hoe against the house and stepped inside, brushing the rain from her coat. She smiled at Lotti and
Egon. "Would you like something to eat? Not a feast, but I
have bread, cheese, and soup."

They both smiled. "That sounds wonderful," Egon said.

We sat at the small kitchen table and talked about the war
and planned for the future.

Of all the decisions that I'd made in my life, grappling
with Viktor Volkov was the most difficult. Everything I'd
told him, I'd done . . . but the war was over and I wanted no
more killing. But the senior sergeant had offered me a door,
one that I might pass through to find my daughter and Emil.
The horror of that passage lay in the possible bloody consequences to follow.

I spent many fitful nights after Egon and Lotti left my
mother's home. I even talked to Frieda about the dilemma
I faced—knowing that she wanted to see her granddaughter again. As she'd stated before, she had no love for men in
power and believed that the Nazis should be punished. "They

brought this upon Germany and themselves. Anyone stupid enough to put their faith in Hitler was a fool," she declared. Despite her Protestant beliefs, my mother made her choice after hearing my story. She believed that our family was more important than the lives of war criminals.

Finally, as the deadline for my next visit with Volkov neared, I sought out Egon and Lotti and found them living in the basement of another building still in the Soviet sector, but closer to the Brandenburg Gate. He was dressed in civilian clothes, wearing a coat, as we all were, and huddled around a crude woodstove. He picked up a scrawny stick, opened the grate, and tossed it into the fire.

"I've made up my mind," I told them. "The Nazis deserve to be brought to justice for what they've done. No more excuses, no more letting the past slip by."

Egon looked at me. Waves of heat curled around his face as the fire flickered through the stove's grate. "Lotti and I have decided the same—as long as I can remain removed from the proceedings." He glanced at her before continuing. "We will never burn a building again, but I will give you information that you can pass on to . . . what was his name?"

"Volkov. The jail isn't far from here."

He handed me a folded piece of paper.

I opened it and looked at the name written upon it, along with an address in the borough of Tiergarten. "Who is he?" In a way, I didn't want to know. Learning about the man listed on the paper made him too real, too much of a human being.

"He's in the British sector. I don't know if the Soviets can arrest him or if they'll have to bargain with the British."

"What did he do?"

"He was a *wächmann* at Sobibor in Poland—only a guard, but one that oversaw much of the killing at the camp. He knows others . . . and where they're hiding."

I hadn't heard of the camp, but I knew it must have been

terrible if it was anything like Buchenwald. "You're certain that he was at Sobibor?"

"It was an extermination camp. A friend of mine, who survived the Eastern Front, talked with him. This *Wächmann* bragged about escaping the Red Army and told my friend where he was going to live after he got back to Berlin. Typical Nazi bluster."

That was enough evidence for me—at least enough to present to Volkov.

I thanked Egon, kissed them both, and then decided to finish my task for the day. I was riding a bicycle that I'd found discarded near a pile of rubble in Berlin. It made getting around the city easier now that the streets were being cleared.

This time, I didn't have to wait long to see the senior sergeant. The corporal who had translated before was still there. I handed Volkov the paper containing the name and address of the man, and recounted the history that Egon had told me—without naming the source.

"Interesting," Volkov said. "Thank you."

I stood in front of him, waiting to be rewarded for my efforts.

The sergeant looked at his desk, moved a pile of papers, and then handed me a note of his own. Written upon it were Rickard's name and an address in the northeastern section of Berlin, specifying the location of a "camp."

"Länger doesn't know you're coming," Volkov said. "However, I've informed the authorities. Go soon. I had to beg the colonel to arrange a meeting with this man. The policy is for total isolation. The fifteen minutes you have with him will be your last."

"Do you have any information about Emil Belmon?" I asked, wondering if I should have been so bold.

"Nothing. Would he have used another name?"

I nodded. "Perhaps he used his German identification." I

told the sergeant Emil's false passport name and held up the note. "Thank you for this."

"It's nothing," Volkov said, with a glint in his eye, pointing to my information from Egon. "You're still working for me. We will pay a visit to the Tiergarten."

It was too late in the day and too long of a trip to get to the camp where Rickard was held. I decided to go the next day.

I barely slept that night as memories of Laura drifted through my dreams.

The camp, as Volkov had called it, was about twelve kilometers from my mother's house. The trip would require crossing the Spree and traveling through war-ravaged Berlin neighborhoods until I reached Hohenschönhausen. The camp was located somewhere near Genslerstrasse.

Dawn's murky light spread through an overcast that held rain, shifting between showers and downpours. The clouds covering the city ranged from milky gray to purple depending upon the moisture in them. I decided to walk rather than ride my new-found bicycle because it would be less messy. Going by foot would take at least three hours on a dry day, so I gave myself extra time.

I wore a raincoat and hat, to protect against the chill, and began my journey about seven in the morning after breakfast. My mother wished me luck. She was as anxious about Laura's whereabouts as I was.

The walk seemed to go on forever as I made my way across a shakily reconstructed bridge over the Spree and then through districts where the damage was much less than in obliterated central Berlin. About ten, I found myself standing in the rain outside a gate and high stone wall that, by all appearances, made up the camp's borders. Beyond the top of the wall, I spotted part of a large redbrick building.

I knocked on a door beside the gate, and in a few seconds, a

Red Army soldier answered, a young man with ruddy cheeks and intense eyes. He looked me over from head to toe; his rifle hung loosely at his side. I sensed that he knew how to use it and that any provocative move by me, or anyone else calling at the camp, would be met with deadly force.

I screwed up my courage because I found myself wondering what would happen once I stepped inside. "I'm here to see Rickard Länger," I said in German.

The young soldier looked at me as if I were mad and started to slam the door in my face. I stopped him with the words, "Orders of Senior Sergeant Viktor Volkov."

That he understood. He opened the door, revealing a small office that he shared with another soldier who sat behind a table.

"Volkov," the first soldier said, and his companion reached for the desk phone. The young soldier indicated with his gestures and the barrel of his rifle that I was to wait outside in the rain until the gate opened.

I did so. After ten long minutes of water dripping off my hat into my eyes and onto my cheeks, the gate's large wooden doors finally opened, revealing another fence beyond. From there, two soldiers escorted me around the brick building to a drab courtyard and ordered me to wait until the "prisoner" appeared, along with other instructions. They took their places at both ends of the rectangle and watched me as I shifted on my feet. After seeing this camp, I wondered how it compared to those that had been constructed by the Nazis. There were no beautiful woods surrounding it, like Buchenwald—woods that held the mass graves of those who had been murdered by Nazi hands. No streams ran nearby, no mountains were in view, only brick, cobblestones, tiles, and the roofs of nearby houses. Bars covered all the camp windows, large and small. I imagined the cramped cells, the dismal light, the days of darkness and isolation with no visits from family members or relatives.

A door swung open, from the cells surrounding the uninviting courtyard, and Rickard appeared. Clad in a gray uniform, his head bowed, his bare feet sloshing across the cold concrete pebbled with stones, he slowly made his way toward me. He was sandwiched between two soldiers. One of them punched him in the back and he looked up.

His eyes, distant at first, as if they were looking through me to some unknown destination, then flickered in recognition. He stopped. The soldiers urged him on. In a few seconds he was standing in front of me—a man whom I hadn't seen in nearly a dozen years. The memory of our first meeting flashed through my mind—the handsome man, wearing an expensive black suit and leather shoes, sitting in a booth at the Leopard Club. His luminous blue eyes had captivated me in the dark. Rickard's profuse slick-backed hair was cropped short now, stubble really, gray on the sides.

He shivered in the rain, and despite all our differences, the terrible history between us, I felt sorry for this beaten man. His skin was chalky white, his lips nearly as purple as the clouds, his body thin and wasted. I would never have recognized him on the street—he had changed so dramatically since I'd seen him last.

One of the guards told me "*Zehn minuten*," and then stepped away with the other to the unoccupied sides of the rectangle. The four soldiers, one in each corner, watched as we stood there, the clock clicking down on our ten minutes.

"Niki?" His voice squeaked. "Niki? I thought you were dead." A tear ran down his cheek . . . or could it have been the rain?

"What have they done to you?" I asked.

He looked up and stuck out his tongue, the water catching on the purple flesh. "I'm so happy to see the sky. I'm glad it's raining—I don't know if I could have stood the sun. I've been sitting in the dark for months now . . . or sitting in water, when they flood the cell."

As much as I hated—regretted—the pain he'd caused me, I wanted to hold him, embrace his thin body. The guards had warned me not to touch him.

"Look at me," I said. "Where's Laura? I need to know. Is she alive?" I held my breath.

He nodded. "I last saw her in late April as they . . . entered the city." He tilted his head toward one of the guards. "I knew what they did to women and young girls—she's almost fourteen. I didn't want her to suffer. I sent her away with a housekeeper, Anna Becker, and told her never to reveal where she was staying or Laura's real name. I was afraid of what the Red Army would do to her. . . ."

"Where did they go?"

He shook his head. "The woman had relatives near Leipzig—somewhere in the country—there are hundreds of farms near there. Everything was so chaotic . . . but Anna also worked at my apartment in Prenzlauer Berg near the Helmholtzplatz. That's where we lived after I left Unter den Linden . . . the street northeast, bordering the park. Number 22."

Rickard broke into a fit of violent coughing. He covered his mouth and nose with his hands and when he took them away blood spotted his fingers. He smeared the gore on his thighs, staining his uniform.

"I'll be in trouble for that," he said, shivering again in the rain. "They make me sit in filthy water. They don't care if I shit my pants, but they'll take it out of my skin if the uniform is dirty . . . it doesn't make any difference—I'll be dead soon."

"Don't say that."

"You know it's true. I have nothing to live for. My daughter is gone, my business is destroyed. You're still my wife, but few people know it. Our relationship is over. The Soviets believe I aided the Nazis with my heart and soul." He paused. "Look at me and know that I'm telling the truth. What I did, I did for you and Laura, as well as myself . . . but I was blinded by my own desire to live . . . to succeed."

"I know, Rickard. So was I. I'm sorry for us both."

A tear melded with the rain on his face. "But you escaped with your life . . . it's my fault. I shouldn't have taken their favors, but I couldn't see another way. They were too powerful. I shouldn't have tumbled into the trap. Once I'd fallen, I couldn't escape. All the time, you knew, Niki. You wrote about survival. You did it."

One of the guards looked at his watch. Time was evaporating. "I was weak, too, then. I should have forced you to get out."

"I wouldn't have done it, Niki. You needn't feel guilty about that."

I nodded while looking at his rain-soaked figure. "I'm living in Rixdorf with my mother. You've been there. I'll talk to the Senior Sergeant Volkov about your situation."

A faint smile broke out on his face. "So, that's how you got in here. No one is allowed to visit. You've fallen in with the Red Army just like I fell in with the Nazis. I don't feel so bad now."

"I'll do anything for my daughter," I said.

"Our daughter," Rickard replied, sadness tingeing his voice. "I hope you find her and give her all the love you were denied. It's my final wish for you."

We stood for a moment, staring at each other as the guards walked toward us.

"Find her and give her my love—from her father."

My breath caught in my throat and I choked, fighting back tears. Two guards grabbed his arms, herding him back to his cell. He looked back over his shoulder. "Good-bye, Niki. This is the last time we'll meet on this earth."

"Good-bye," I whispered, as the two soldiers who had walked me to the courtyard approached.

A few minutes later, I was outside the camp, watching the water slide in gray streaks down the gate.

As I walked to my mother's, the rain beat hard upon my coat, and the feeling that I had somehow betrayed Rickard weighed upon me. Questions tore at me. Had I done enough to convince Rickard to leave the National Socialists? Did I try hard enough to keep the family together, to convince my husband to abandon Passport Pictures and the Nazis who supported it? I was young then and interested only in survival, the theme of my books. I had poured my soul into a plot that I carried out in life. I felt disoriented, hardly able to walk in a straight line. Nothing seemed right.

In the past, I was the New German Woman I wrote about, needing no one but myself. Rickard said he'd been blinded by the Nazis, but I was as well. A tyrant had caused Germany to lose its sight. Rickard and I each wanted to survive in our own ways—and the cost was high.

I tried to stop the feelings swirling inside me. The steady, calm, and determined voice of Emil came into my head, telling me to be strong—that I'd done nothing wrong, that I'd done my best at the time.

I stopped near a bombed-out building near the Spree and cried. I was no closer to finding Laura or Emil. At least it seemed likely that Laura had survived the war.

When I arrived home in the midafternoon, my mother was sitting by the stove eating bread and a bowl of soup.

I couldn't talk about what I'd witnessed at the camp, and, somehow, she understood that. I took off my wet coat and dress and put on warm clothes. We sat in front of the fire, warming our legs and sipping soup.

# CHAPTER 30

For more than two years, as Berlin slowly rose from its grave, I searched for Laura. Number 22 was near the end of a long two-block stretch of apartments bordering Helmholtzplatz. Many of them had been damaged, one end of the row had crumbled after a bomb or artillery shell had struck. That roof lay open to the sky, pigeons and starlings flew in and out of the deserted rooms. Torn curtains waved in the wind, their tattered pieces often catching on shattered glass.

I visited the address every month looking for my daughter—in the warmth of spring, the heat of summer, as the first snow fell—I was there waiting . . . and hoping. Rickard's name was on the buzzer, but no one ever answered. Sometimes the residents, who had remained in this Soviet sector and managed to piece together a life, let me into the building. Never was there an answer. The door was always locked and my knock sounded hollow. After a time, I gave up hope of ever seeing my daughter again.

I gave Volkov the name of one more "secreted" Nazi— a man of interest the Soviets might want, the information again provided by Egon. The senior sergeant seemed preoccupied and unwilling to see me for more than a few minutes. He mentioned his own transfer to a special camp at a location he couldn't disclose, and offered nothing about Emil or

Rickard, only to say that commanding officers above him had ordered that camp prisoners could see no one, or contact anyone, no matter how dire the circumstances. That meant if a prisoner died, the family would not be told. Rickard had been correct when he said that our one meeting was the last time we would see each other. People were disappearing in the Soviet sector never to be heard of again—as if the Red Army had copied, or perhaps improved upon, Nazi interrogation and imprisonment tactics.

After our last meeting, I wanted nothing more to do with Volkov.

Living in Berlin was like living in four different cities controlled by four distinct cultures: French, British, American, and Soviet. All the sectors were different, but in the few years after the war, Berliners mixed with the occupiers in an uneasy dance. The Soviets had taken most everything of value in their sector and shipped it to Moscow as war reparations, making the people living there dependent upon their occupiers. The other conquerors tried to build the city again, but the work was slow and life was hard. Food and money were difficult to get, power and transportation needed to be restored, and distrust grew between the eastern and western sectors.

I got a job cleaning at Tempelhof Airport in the American sector, near my mother's home. I was even put to work constructing and repairing runways. The job was hard and I was exhausted at night, but the Americans were friendly and gave us extra rations for our trouble. For a time, I felt like the New German Woman of old again, able to fix my makeup, flirt a bit, give a smile, and say a kind word now and then in English. They were men who missed their wives and girlfriends even as the non-fraternization policy remained, although it was slipping into obscurity. The Americans appreciated the kind words from Germans, for many in my nation had looked suspiciously and with contempt upon all the victors. Many were unwilling to believe that Germany had lost the war, or that they had been duped by Hitler. Never a Nazi, I was more than willing to be friendly.

In the spring of 1948, on one of my journeys to Number 22, I met a woman who knew Anna Becker, Rickard's housekeeper. She was standing outside, enjoying the sun and talking with a neighbor on a warm May afternoon. Like most German women, the dress and shoes that she wore were old, probably purchased about 1941, before the tide of war had begun to turn against the Reich. Her blue dress with the white collar had been taken in at the waist and mended at the hems. Her black shoes, although shiny, showed nicks and scratches.

I introduced myself as Marie Länger and told the woman I was looking for Laura. My daughter was soon to be seventeen; I was about to turn thirty-seven.

"I know who she is," the woman replied in a tone that one might use with a stranger.

I leaned toward her, eager to hear anything about my daughter. My quick action surprised the woman and she backed away. Her black hair, pinned at the sides, was streaked with gray. Her mouth puckered at my zeal.

"Do you know where she is?" I asked, wanting to shake the truth from her.

"No. I know Anna Becker. She took Laura to Leipzig, but that was three years ago. I got a letter from Anna about a year ago, saying they were still there. There was no return address on the letter, and Anna said she had been sworn to secrecy by her employer. She gave me a key before they left and asked me to check on the apartment . . . when I could."

"You've done that?" I asked. "You have a key?"

She gazed at her purse, which she'd placed on the stairs. "Yes . . . who are you again?"

I didn't know the woman's politics. For all I knew, she could have been a former Nazi or a sympathizer. She seemed interested in the information I offered about Laura.

"I last saw her many years ago," I explained, without offering details that might put the woman off. "Rickard and I separated after the war started. He was too involved with his job." That was the most I dared offer, but I added, "He worked for Passport Pictures."

That piece of information seemed to satisfy the woman, and her eyes came to life. "He won awards for his work. There are trophies in the apartment."

"May I see?" I asked.

The other woman whispered to her friend.

"She's seen you here before," the woman in the blue dress said. "We can go up for a few minutes."

"Thank you," I said. "I've been searching for my daughter since the war ended."

The woman's red lips pressed together; then she said, "We've all lost someone."

We left the other woman and walked up the three flights of stairs to the apartment that faced the street. "What's your name?" I asked as she opened the door.

Surprisingly, she said, "It doesn't matter . . . a friend of Anna Becker's—that's what you can call me. I think it's better these days if the Reds don't know your name."

I nodded, as she fitted the key in the lock and opened the door.

Rickard, or Anna, had drawn the red drapes that covered the two large windows facing the street. An eerie light, like a smear of blood, filtered through the windows and splashed on the wooden floor. The apartment smelled musty, the dust in the air scratching my nostrils.

I recognized a few pieces of furniture that had come with Rickard from the apartment on Unter den Linden—the V-shaped chairs, the cocktail bar, were three of the pieces that had survived the move. A floor-to-ceiling bookcase covered the width of the wall to the left of the door. Rickard's books on film and art made their home there, along with the awards that Anna's friend had mentioned. A desk sat near one of the windows, and part of the array of objects on it included the typewriter on which I'd written my two books. I looked at the piece of paper curved over the platen. Nothing was written on it.

"Do you mind if I open the drapes?" I asked.

"No, go ahead. I never touch them . . . be prepared to sneeze."

I walked to the windows and pulled the coverings apart, and the blood-like light turned a dull white. Dust fell in clumps from the material, sending motes swirling through the air. The woman was right—we both sneezed from the disturbance.

I circled the room, wanting to take it all in, imagining my daughter, who had lived here for so many years, walking upon these floors. This had been Laura's home while I was hiding in Amsterdam, and even after I'd returned to Germany. She had played in these rooms, dressed in her bedroom before going to school. Perhaps she'd joined—with the encouragement of her father—the Nazi's groups for girls and young women. That seemed likely, knowing Rickard's slavish ties to his benefactors.

I swiped my hand across one of the awards that had been given to him. The dust came off in gray piles on my fingertips. "Service" commendations had been given for the films he'd produced on behalf of the Reich, all propaganda, each one promoting National Socialist "values." Four brass swastikas adorned the plaques. I marveled that the Soviets hadn't ransacked the apartment, leading me to wonder if Rickard had been arrested on the street, or perhaps he'd turned himself in, wanting to spare Laura the trauma of seeing her father arrested.

I thought to ask Anna's friend. "Why haven't the Soviets come to this apartment?"

"I don't know," the woman answered flatly. "Herr Länger

sent his daughter and housekeeper away near the end. Then, he disappeared—with some money, Anna told me. Perhaps someone turned him in. I guess the Soviets never knew where he lived. Maybe he gave them the old address on Unter den Linden. That building was destroyed. They would never know the difference. We can be quite tight-lipped if we have to be."

*We . . . we?* I knew then I was dealing with a Nazi Party member, or, at least, a sympathizer. My guard went up. "I understand," I said, letting the subject drop.

A picture in a white frame near one of the plaques caught my eye. It was Rickard and Laura, probably taken about 1943. Rickard was dressed in a suit, smiling, happy, his arm around his daughter. She was attired in a white blouse and black skirt, a dark tie running down the length of the blouse. A boy I didn't know stood behind her, his blond hair parted to the left, his black uniform contrasting with his white skin. A lightning bolt insignia was attached at the elbow of his left arm.

I cried—not because I'd seen a picture of my daughter, but because I'd seen what she'd become under Rickard's guidance. Laura was now of the age that she could make up her own mind about politics, the war, and its outcome, but could I accept her views? Could I love my daughter if she'd become a Nazi—a believer in fascism with no regrets? Did I have a choice? The sight of the picture and the questions it precipitated roiled my stomach. I pressed my hands into my belly and sat in one of Rickard's leather chairs.

"Are you all right?" Anna's friend asked, as she rushed toward me. "I know we've all been under stress, but you must get hold of yourself."

I took a few deep breaths and swiped at my cheeks with my hand. "I'll be fine," I finally said. "It's overwhelming to be here where my daughter and my husband lived. I want to find her."

Still clutching the key, the woman sat across from me on

the couch. She gave me another look and sighed. "She might come back. . . ."

"Yes, but I won't be here, and Laura could be anywhere."

She held up the key. "This is not an easy trip for me to make—across Berlin on the outskirts of the Soviet sector— and frankly, I'm tired of it. I can see how much this means to you . . . to be here."

I nodded, while thinking that something unexpected was about to fall into my hands. "This apartment connects me to my daughter. I haven't felt like this in years, and you're right—she might come back! How wonderful that would be!" I didn't want to act like I was in a play, but the woman was right. Laura might return from the countryside near Leipzig—she might return to her childhood home.

The woman extended her arm toward me, offering me the key. "Here . . . you'd be helping me out."

I took it and leaned forward, almost hugging her but then thought better of it. "Thank you. You've been so kind. I will take good care of the apartment."

"Yes, keep the Reds away. They don't need to know how much good work Rickard did for the Reich."

We stood up, ready to leave. I closed the drapes, once again filling the apartment with the strange red light. I took a last look at the photo before we locked the door.

As we walked down the stairs, the woman said, "If I hear from Anna Becker, I will let her know that you have the key. Where do you live?"

"In Rixdorf, in the American sector."

Her lips parted in a faint smile. "Oh, lucky. The Americans are too stupid to know what they have. They're just— what are they? Cowboys? Gunmen? Boys with guns. *We* knew how to use them."

I left her and walked back to my mother's house. Although Rickard's apartment was in the Soviet sector, I felt it might be time to leave Frieda again and strike out on my own. I'd wait for my daughter's return in an apartment the Nazis had provided for Rickard.

There was some justice in that.

Fortunately, I hadn't left Rixdorf by June 24, 1948, when the lights suddenly went out and the Soviets closed the western sectors of Berlin to the world. The "Berlin Blockade" had begun. All rail, roadway, and canal accesses to the city were closed, and the world teetered on the precipice of war.

Politics had taken precedence over human lives once again, as the Soviets tried to convince the Americans, British, and French to abandon their claims to a city deep within its territory. Berliners, for the most part, were unaware of the behind-the-scenes political maneuverings, but were acutely aware of the staggering effects upon their lives.

Panic once again gripped the other sectors, as people bargained for the short supply of ready food and energy. The rumor circulated that only three weeks of food remained in the western sectors. Then, starvation would set in. The Soviets, meanwhile, fed their own. It was all over money, they said, and offered to end the blockade if the Allies removed the new Deutsche Mark from circulation, which had undercut their own currency. A counterblockade developed, putting pressure on the Soviet sector. Steel and coal shipments to the east ended.

I worked at Tempelhof during the blockade, never setting foot in the Soviet sector or checking Rickard's apartment while it was in effect. The Americans flew from their bases in southwest Germany to Tempelhof in one of the three air corridors in and out of the city. We Germans watched with our eyes to the sky, climbing street signs, perching upon makeshift risers, as transport plane after transport plane—one every three minutes—landed with milk, flour, coal, medicine, and other goods. The roar of the planes never ended over Berlin regardless of weather or the time of year. The sound of the engines thrilled our ears.

One astute officer noted that unloading planes at Tempelhof took too long. The crew would linger on the airport grounds, thus delaying the shipments and the return to the home base. Therefore, I and other German women were recruited to work beverage trolleys, offering the crews food and drink by their planes. We offered refreshment, a smile, kind words, and thanks for all they were doing to save the German people. Those of us who worked found ourselves with extra rations as payment.

German children even got treats from American pilots. One in particular dropped candy by handkerchief-parachute from his transport. He was known as "Uncle Wiggly Wings" because he rocked the aircraft's silver wings before releasing the candy. The rocking motion raised a chorus of shouts, as well as smiles, from children and adults. As the news spread, the crowd grew ever larger to catch the treats. Other planes followed and were named "Candy Bombers" by the grateful children.

The Soviets finally realized they couldn't defeat the airlift, which in its way became the most efficient transport of goods that the city had ever seen. The Soviets had the military might, but lacked the infrastructure in devastated East Berlin to wage a fight. They also lacked the atomic bomb. By September of 1949 the last flight was over. The Soviets had been defeated by the combined power and will of the Allies, and the willingness of the German people to accept their offerings with open arms.

One could still travel between East and West Berlin after the blockade. People had been escaping to West Germany by crossing the Inner German Border many miles to the west of the city. Slowly, that began to change. The Soviets tightened rules and regulations, especially after the formation of the German Democratic Republic, East Germany, in October 1949. It was called a "socialist workers' and peasants' state." My mother was convinced that Rixdorf and the western sectors would survive, possibly even thrive, while the Soviet sector would languish under the new state.

I remained at my mother's during the blockade, but checked Rickard's apartment after it ended. I talked with Frieda about leaving the American sector, fleeing to West Germany, but my mother wanted to remain in Rixdorf—it was the only home she'd ever known and was also the site of my father's grave. She had lived in Neukölln since she was married and was still friendly with the neighbors.

I had told her about Rickard's apartment and how I viewed it as a window to the past. However, the red-draped room overlooking the park haunted me, connecting me to Laura.

When I could get away from my job at the airport, I spent hours in the room, sometimes just sitting, or watching the snow fall, or gazing out the window as the sky grew dark. I cleaned, dusted, and talked with neighbors who were growing increasingly dissatisfied with their lives on the eastern side. They envied me and my ability to live in the west, but, like me, something stopped them from leaving: money, family, the sense that you belonged where you were born, the feeling in your gut that where you lived was your *home*. I didn't want to stop coming to East Berlin because I knew Laura might have the same feelings.

I spent some nights in the apartment, sleeping in Rickard's former bed. Laura's room, I surmised, was the smaller of the two bedrooms and still held a few items special to her. The apartment had no electricity, so I lit candles—expensive and hard to find. Water ran sporadically, and the only heat filtered up through the residences below. In the winter, I'd smother myself in blankets and not poke my head out until morning.

My time there was painfully beautiful. Often, I'd listen

for footsteps in the hall and imagine that my daughter might knock, or open the door with her own key. The only sounds in the hall were either fancies of my imagination, like phantoms, or neighbors going about their business. Laura never came—but her spirit kept me there. I would have gone to look for her in Leipzig if I had any idea where she lived. Country farms were plentiful.

One day, when I was back at my mother's, I received a letter from Viktor Volkov. I had given him her address during the time that we were conducting "business." The envelope was thin brown paper, certainly nothing of weight, but I dreaded what might be in it. My fingers trembled as I held it. I expected any correspondence from Volkov to be bad news.

I sat on my mother's couch, staring at it for some time. There was no return, only a smeared fingerprint above the address, leading me to believe that the senior sergeant may have handled the letter himself.

I shoved my fingernail under the flap, opened it, and withdrew a letter that was written on something like rice paper. *Dear Marie Rittenhaus*, it read.

*I hope this finds you well in the American sector. We have defeated the National Socialists, but now we have our own war of ideas with our former Allies. The last man that you sent us provided a wealth of information leading to several arrests. The German Democratic Republic thanks you, and I thank you as well. Please remember that I am grateful for your aid in bringing justice to those who deserved to be punished for their crimes.*

*However, the point of this note is not pleasant—and I have no idea how you will take the news—either with sadness or relief. Your former husband, Rickard Länger, is dead. He died in another camp, and his body was buried in a grave provided for prisoners. I can only say*

*that illness took him. By regulation, officers are forbid-*
*den to comment on such matters, or reach out to fami-*
*lies, but I believed you needed to be told. Therefore, I*
*have exceeded my authority at some peril of my own.*

I turned the page over.

*I will express my sympathy for the effect his death*
*may have upon you, but not for his association with*
*National Socialism. Because the remains of Passport*
*Pictures are in the American sector, our former ally*
*should make sure that all of Länger's films are de-*
*stroyed, so they can no longer be a scourge upon the*
*world. The bombings may have already taken care of*
*that, but one never knows.*

*Please feel free to call upon me if you have some*
*need, wish, or desire to be fulfilled in the German*
*Democratic Republic. I must tell you that I still have*
*no word upon the whereabouts of Emil Belmon after*
*Buchenwald. I fear the worst, very few survived. Per-*
*haps the Americans hold records that will shed light.*

*Please destroy this letter, for it will do neither of us*
*any good if it is seen or read by anyone other than our*
*own eyes.*

It was signed, *Respectfully, Your Comrade, Viktor Volkov.*
An address was listed at the bottom for another Soviet special camp, along with a private telephone number.

I stared at the letter for a long time until my mother came
home from shopping. She was not in a good mood, having
been unable to find the ingredients she wanted for the evening meal.

Apparently, my downcast face startled her and took her
away from her own thoughts. "What's wrong?" she asked,
after sitting by me on the couch.

I pointed to the letter. "Rickard is dead."

She touched my shoulder, a display of unexpected sympathy. "I'm sorry."

However, I knew from her tone that she wasn't sad or disappointed. Rickard was another man who had tried to take advantage of power . . . and lost—another man who'd paid with his life. "They will never learn. You sit. I will make dinner from what I could find."

She trundled off to the kitchen and I picked up the letter, rereading the sad contents, wondering if I'd lost Emil as well, another man who had shaped my life. A thought struck me: Laura would need to know about her father . . . but I didn't know where she was.

The front door blew open and I found myself shivering in the cold that rushed through the house. My mother closed the door and looked at me with sad eyes.

I was no closer to finding my daughter than I'd been since the war ended. And now Rickard was dead. Darkness covered me and I shivered, sensing that Emil had not survived. Tears burned my eyes, the pain rising in my chest; but I stifled any outburst, not wanting to disturb my mother.

I had to be strong for my daughter.

I had to believe that she would return to her former home in East Berlin.

# CHAPTER 31

I visited Rickard's apartment four times a year, once in each season. Laura was never there and nothing was ever disturbed, even the note for her that I'd left on the dining table.

I saw Anna Becker's friend again. She told me that she'd received one letter since we'd talked. Rickard had instructed Anna to keep her and Laura's location a secret in order to protect them from reprisals by the Red Army. Even Anna's friend had no idea where they were.

In the letter, the housekeeper indicated that Laura was becoming increasingly irritated with farm life, and she was afraid that the young woman she'd been instructed to look after might run away—return to Berlin and the home she knew. Anna, herself, had no intention of ever returning to the city.

That news didn't please Anna's friend, who believed that Laura might find her way into bad hands. The letter encouraged me, however, and ignited my hope that Laura might find her way back.

A new owner purchased the apartment in East Germany, after the deal had worked its way through the bloated "socialist" court system. The former owner had died near the end of the war and nothing had been done to the building for many years. On one of my visits, I found documents taped to the door saying the apartment would be taken over and its contents liquidated by a certain date if the rent wasn't paid. Nothing in arrears was called for, fortunately, and the new rent was controlled by the government at a decent rate.

I was working now as a secretary in a construction firm in the American sector—a good job that paid well—and doing a little writing under my own name, short stories mostly. I hadn't worked on the novel in months. The stories paid little, but my salary was enough that I was able to pay for food and utilities and have a little left over. Suddenly, I realized that the "little left over" would have to go to Rickard's apartment, unless I wanted to close that chapter of my life.

I talked to my mother about the situation, and, surprisingly, she believed that it would be wise to keep the apartment in the hope that Laura might come back. She offered to put in what she could to preserve the status quo.

Rules for visiting and traveling had become a bit more difficult, but Berliners could still travel between sectors. I signed a lease for the apartment, telling the landlord's agent that I intended to move in soon, a white lie, and in the meantime, I would certainly keep watch on it and spend my free time there. I told him it was "my writing haven." He was glad to get the steady rent, even though I listed an address in the American sector.

"I have my reasons for moving to the GDR," I told him. That seemed to mollify him, and I think he believed that I was a true socialist because of my enthusiasm for the apartment. Other East Berliners were leaving the sector when they could. The Soviets were clamping down on basic freedoms in the GDR, and everyone suspected that conditions might grow worse. The Stasi, the East German secret police, had been created. Its job was to spy on everyone who might be an enemy of the state—anyone who had a different opinion of what constituted freedom and who expressed an objection to a life controlled by the government.

\*   \*   \*

Lotti and Egon married a few years after the war ended and rented a tiny apartment in the Soviet sector. They visited my mother and me when they could, and I had dinner with them when I was staying at Rickard's. Lotti had heard nothing about Rudi, the bartender at the now-closed Leopard Club. Lotti managed to find Rudi's sister, but even she had lost track of her brother after a brutal battle at El Alamein in Egypt. More than ever, we believed he'd been killed in the war and had been omitted from the death rolls.

Another man in my life, Emil, had disappeared as well. I dated a few times, but I was more concerned with finding my daughter than forming a relationship, and no man ignited the spark fired by Emil, or, even Rickard, those many years ago. I was at a loss with men—and it was hard to find someone not formerly connected to National Socialism.

In 1952, the Inner German Border, many miles west of Berlin, was closed to stop emigration to West Germany and beyond. Berliners could still travel somewhat freely in the city, but by 1957 a passport was required of East German residents, another tightening of restrictions, although it had little effect within Berlin other than closing access links of West to East. Of one hundred seventy-eight streets, sixty-three were closed in 1952.

My mother and I kept Rickard's apartment until the spring of 1952, a total of two years—until it became clear that Laura was never returning to Berlin. The rent was beginning to drain us financially as well, and, after much anguish, we agreed that it would be better to let the lease expire.

In the final few months of the lease, I cleaned out the space, taking a few items that I knew were Laura's: some stuffed animals, a picture book that she'd had as a child, the photo of her father and herself that sat in the bookcase. Everything connected to National Socialism I either burned or made sure that it was buried in the trash, including Rickard's commendations for his films. Rickard's clothes and personal objects, I gave to the neighbors, thinking they could use them. My old life had ended and I needed to jump into the new. The door was closing on any happiness that my past had given me.

I finished *Einsamkeit, Loneliness*, working on two typewriters—one I'd purchased cheaply to use at my mother's kitchen table; the other, at Rickard's apartment. Several publishing houses expressed some interest in the novel, but the editors wanted more from me than I could give. They wanted a memoir . . . my life before the Third Reich, through the war, and after it. I wasn't prepared to write such an intimate and subjective portrait. Instead, I waited as one publisher after another rejected *Einsamkeit*. "Too melancholy for our time," one said. "You'd have a much better chance writing under your pseudonym than Marie Rittenhaus," another wrote. I was devastated and prepared to give up . . . when the unthinkable happened.

My life took a sudden turn, the last day I visited Rickard's apartment, at the end of May 1952. I was waiting to turn in the keys to the landlord when a neighbor approached me. She was the same woman who'd been talking to the friend of Anna Becker, the housekeeper. The day was warm, but the billowing clouds threatened spring rain. I sat on the steps, smoking a cigarette, with the last bag of items I'd taken from the apartment. Rickard's typewriter sat by my side. The machine held a sentimental attachment for me because I'd written my first two books on it.

Although we'd said hello a few times, the woman and I had never had a long conversation. "You're Laura's mother, aren't you?" she asked. "I knew her before they left Berlin."

I nodded. "Anna's friend gave me the key to the apartment."

"It's such a shame," the woman said. "Herr Länger was such a nice man—always so kind to his daughter. I heard they arrested him, threw him in a camp for telling the truth."

*Telling the truth.* Here was another ex-Nazi, not to be trusted. "He died," I said somewhat reluctantly, not wanting to shock her, but to let her know that Rickard's words and actions had had deadly consequences.

Her mouth flew open. She planted one hand firmly on the railing as if the news had swamped her, and focused her dark, bird-like eyes upon me. The severity of her face and dress, the gray stockings and the plain black shoes, confirmed that whatever former ideology she'd possessed, she'd made an equal home under Soviet rule.

"Tragic, tragic," she said, her voice filled with remorse.

I remained silent, hoping that the landlord would arrive soon and rescue me. But then she smiled.

"She's here—not far away." Her eyes sparkled like glass hit by sunlight.

"Who?" I asked, my heart racing for a second.

"Your daughter, I believe—Laura."

I rose from the steps, unconcerned about the landlord and the key. "Are you sure?" I looked into her colorless face, trying to discern if she was lying.

"I can't be certain. I saw her a few times from my window, leaving this building, going down these steps. She could be Laura—a woman about the right age—I haven't seen her in years. She's grown up."

"She's twenty—but no one's been in the apartment that I know of. I even left a note."

"Well—it could be her." She stepped away from me as the landlord parked in front of the building.

"Wait . . . you know where she lives?"

The woman turned. "I didn't follow her, but I told someone about Laura. She said the girl lives two blocks to the north and then on the street to the right. Number 68. I don't know which apartment."

"*Guten tag.*" The middle-aged landlord interrupted us.

I remembered little about him other than his worn gray

suit and silver mustache. I handed him the key, grabbed my package and the typewriter, and strode toward number 68, not knowing what I would find there.

I ran the last half block, the typewriter case bumping into my thigh, until I came to a small street north of railroad tracks. The brick building, near the corner, had escaped destruction except for some still evident damage to the upper-level apartments. Two brass buzzers were situated near the oak door. I rang both—the first didn't answer. The second—H. Angermann—seemed as unlikely as the first, and I was about to walk away when the door opened.

She stood there—looking at me as if I was a stranger.

I recognized her instantly. Her face, a bit pale, carried the beauty of the daughter I'd known, but in spite of the laughter and the time we'd shared when she was a child, brittleness, hardness lurked underneath the skin. Her hair was darker, almost brown, cut short and swept back in curls behind her ears. The dress she wore was simple, navy blue with white buttons, falling to the calf, unpretentious and similar to every other housedress in East Berlin.

I lowered the typewriter and the bag to the ground.

"*Ja?*" Her tone was one of irritation rather than inquisitiveness as she looked out on the deserted street. "Who are you?" she asked in German.

I was speechless for a moment, enough time for Laura to sigh and put her hand on the door.

"Wait! You don't remember me . . . I'm your mother . . . Marie Länger."

Her eyes hardened. She stepped back inside and closed the door halfway. "My mother is dead. My father told me."

I walked toward her. "No . . . I orchestrated my death, so I could come back to Germany . . . to find you."

She slammed the door in my face.

I pounded on it. "Please, please," I begged her. "I'll prove it to you. I've just come from your father's apartment. I've been going there for many years. I'd given up on ever seeing you again."

She flung the door open. "Go away! Even if you are my mother, I want nothing to do with you."

I grabbed the bag and opened it. There was nothing much inside except some kitchen utensils and a copy of each of my books that Rickard had kept hidden from Nazi eyes. "Look."

Laura bent over the open bag. "You broke in and stole them. My father hid those books. He never let me read them."

"I found them behind a cabinet. The friend of your house-keeper, Anna Becker, gave me the key because she knew I was looking for you." I withdrew a pen from the bag and opened *The Berlin Woman.* I had signed the copy: *To R. with love and affection. Niki.* I wrote the same inscription below the first and showed it to Laura.

"You're a forger. . . ."

"No, your father and I didn't agree about National Socialism. Do you remember a night with guns long ago?"

Laura looked at me as if I'd dragged her into the past. "I don't want to think about it. I never wanted to think about it. My father told me it was a bad dream. All I remember is the loud noise and the screams."

I put the book back in the bag. "It wasn't a bad dream. An SA officer, Herr Spiegel, his wife, and manservant were killed. It was a night of terror—you weren't even three yet. That was the last time I saw you. . . ."

"I don't know what to think." Her eyes misted with tears. "I don't know what to say."

"May I come in? Can we talk?"

She shook her head and stepped back inside the hall. "No, that's not a good idea. My husband will be home soon from work and I don't think he'd like you being here."

"You're married."

"Yes . . . and going to have a baby." She put her hands on her stomach.

I smiled through the pain in my heart. "Your grandmother is alive in Rixdorf. She'll be so pleased a baby is coming."

"And you? Are you pleased?" The door continued its slow close.

"Yes. I'm happy to see you—glad to know that you're alive. Your father is dead."

"I know." In a scant second, I was staring at the door.

"I love you . . . I've always loved you," I shouted.

I turned away from the apartment for the trip back to my mother's. I hoped that Laura would call out after me, perhaps run to my side and embrace me, but there were no words, no steps toward me.

The street was quiet and deserted. A single tree stood near the sidewalk. It had somehow survived the war as well. I plucked a green leaf from one of its branches and put it in my pocket, vowing to remember where the leaf was picked, where the tree stood in the sun and the rain and the snow, whose apartment it provided shade for, how it endured despite the battles around it.

I vowed to be like the tree. I would keep standing in front of that apartment until I died if I had to—until Laura accepted me as her mother. I wanted her love more than anything in the world, and no battle was too great to be surrendered.

I kept my promise and returned to number 68 when I wasn't working and when the weather would allow. I wasn't foolish, not wanting to be arrested for spying in East Berlin or taken for a madwoman while standing in the sleet and snow. But on days off when it was warm, or on tolerable Sundays, I visited the Angermann apartment only to find it as stark and foreboding as the war-torn buildings of central Berlin. The black curtains remained unmoved; the buzzer ignored.

As time passed, I believed the Angermanns had moved on, but subtle signs remained. Papers and accumulated debris disappeared from the steps; the curtains, though closed, shifted almost imperceptibly from one visit to the next. I left envelopes containing heartfelt messages. They also vanished. So, I believed that Laura might be inside with her baby—but there was nothing I could do to convince her to come out. The decision would be hers.

The economic situation in East Berlin grew dire from the forced collectivization of business and farming. People fled to West Berlin. In June 1953, a strike, resulting in a populist uprising, shook East Berlin and even East Germany. Soviet tanks took positions in Berlin and other cities and towns across the territory. After a few days, the strike disappeared, but the desire by those in power to keep the GDR as a socialist satellite remained.

One day, in the fall of that year, I visited the apartment. I rang the buzzer, again to no answer, and retreated to the curb to study the window—a hand gripped my shoulder like a pincer. The force whirled me around and I found myself facing a young man about Laura's age. He was attired in a uniform similar to those worn by the best dressed Nazi officers at the height of the war. The gray jacket rose to a V below his throat and extended past his waist, cinched by a black belt and silver buckle. The obvious differences between the two uniforms lay in the insignia and the bowl-shaped helmet on the man's head. His polished calf-high boots reflected the afternoon sun.

His skin displayed the freshness of youth, but his eyes and lips showed the same hardness that I'd seen on my daughter. He might have been handsome if not for the severity of his look.

"Come with me," he said in a bitter tone, shuffling me toward the door.

"Wait . . ." I tried to pull away from his grasp, but at forty-two years of age, my strength was no match for his.

He withdrew a key from his trousers, inserted it in the

door, and pulled me into the dark hallway. The air smelled like dry paper and rancid cooking oil, a strange combination that struck my stomach, as well as my nose. My eyes adjusted to the gloomy entrance.

Finally, the door crept open and a shaft of light from a floor lamp extended from the room into the hall. Laura, holding an infant against her breast, stood in shadow behind the door.

"Come in." The clipped words were an order rather than an invitation.

I wasn't frightened, for I believed that Laura would allow nothing to happen to me, but the sense of unease in the room was palpable, as if the Angermanns had dragged an unwelcome stranger inside.

"Let me open the curtains a bit, Herwald," Laura said.

"No, keep them closed." He unstrapped his helmet and threw it on the couch. "Sit."

I unbuttoned my coat, pushed the helmet to one side, and took my place next to it. Laura sat in a rocking chair near the window, cradling the baby in her arms. The young man stood by the stove and lit a cigarette.

The sight of my daughter and her baby reminded me of the times that I'd sat with her and Rickard in his light-filled and luxuriously appointed apartment, of how her father had fashioned a toy over her crib. This room couldn't have been more different, like living in a cave. A room to the right of the door stretched into the darkness. I imagined it contained a small bedroom and bathroom with no room for anything but perhaps a bed and a chest of drawers. No pictures hung on the walls. A set of grimy wooden shelves had been bolted to the wall above the stove.

"What is your name?" I asked the young man.

Puffing on his cigarette, he didn't answer, for he was studying me.

"What is *your* name?" he asked after a time. "And why do you torture Laura with your fantasies?"

"I'm her mother—Marie Länger. My maiden name was Rittenhaus. I wrote books that were banned by the Nazis."

"Anyone could acquire that information," he said.

I smiled, gaining a bit of confidence. Why should I, a woman who'd resisted the Nazis, fear this young man in an East German uniform? "Yes, but I have pictures of Rickard and Laura that I took from the apartment near Helmholtz-platz. I have the books that I wrote and inscribed to Laura's father. I can tell you stories about Berlin and Amsterdam that you could only dream of. Laura remembers the night when Spiegel was killed because it was so terrible. I saw Laura's father before he died. Senior Sergeant Viktor Volkov knows all of this."

At the mention of Volkov's name, the young man straightened from his slouch against the stove, as if he'd been addressed by the officer himself.

"So, you know the man," I said.

He squinted in the dim light, taking a few steps toward me. I'd forced him into a corner. "Yes, I know Volkov. He's now the . . ." He paused, unable to tell what he knew. "He's an important officer. . . ." He walked behind Laura, his gray uniform contrasting with the black curtains.

"Laura and I have talked about you," the young man said. "We can't be friends—not now."

"Why not?" I asked, leaning forward. "Does Laura have anything to say about this?"

The baby squealed, kicked in her arms, and Laura hushed it. "I rely on my husband to make such decisions," she said quietly.

"I am Herwald Angermann and this is our child, Joseph—named after our recently deceased General Secretary. His death was a great blow to us all."

"Stalin." I didn't want to tell them what was in my heart because I knew the "great leader" was as much a butcher as Hitler. My mother would be appalled that her grandson was named after yet another man of dubious political power.

"May I look at my grandson?"

Herwald nodded. I walked to the chair where Laura sat with the baby. He was about a year old, I judged, with fleshy cheeks spotted with red and wisps of black hair that spread like dark spikes over his head. He gurgled when he saw me, his eyes opening and closing in flashes.

"May I hold him?"

Laura looked to her husband, who nodded reluctantly.

I lifted Joseph and felt the warmth of his little body in my arms, the aromatic sweetness of an infant swirling around me. "I wish your great-grandmother could see you," I whispered to the baby. He seemed content in my arms, as I reveled in the touch of his tiny hands tugging at mine.

"What do you do?" I asked Herwald, deducing from the uniform that he was in the East German police or some branch of military service.

"I can't say." His tone was blunt, matter-of-fact.

"My husband can't talk about what he does," Laura said, walking to the stove to get a cigarette of her own. She appeared grateful to have a few minutes apart from the baby. Her hair had grown since I'd seen her last, falling across the back of her neck, nearly to her shoulders. She wore a pair of black slacks and a white blouse. She lit the smoke and leaned against the wall.

My mind raced with possibilities. Was he a spy or a member of the State Security Service, also known as the Stasi? The thought made me shiver, for the Stasi was known for its brutality, its surveillance and espionage capabilities, the detailed files it kept on any citizen deemed an enemy, and the brutal repression of those who dared challenge the state.

If so, Herwald would want me, a West Berliner, as far away from his home as possible, and he would also investigate my politics. Perhaps that was why he'd been so rough with me.

Laura stubbed out her cigarette and returned for the baby. Mother and father looked at me with solemn faces. My time was running out. "Do you enjoy living in East Berlin, under the thumb of the Soviet masters, suffering under the German communists who rule you?"

"Watch your tongue," Herwald said, taking a step toward me. "Are you questioning the sovereign rule of the German Democratic Republic?" His eyes had the hard look of glass, the muscles of his face twitching with anger.

I buttoned my coat, assured that I was no longer welcome in this house. "I live with my mother in Rixdorf in the American sector—I won't always—but the war has changed me as it's changed Berlin. What was once good and whole has been ripped apart. You are always welcome to visit me, for Frieda would love to see her granddaughter and baby. I want to be a mother to my daughter, and know and respect my son-in-law—but that doesn't seem possible. I won't give up, but I won't come begging either."

I touched the baby's head and felt the fine silkiness of his hair, sensing that it might be the last time I'd ever touch the boy.

Herwald opened the door. I stepped across the threshold and then took a last look into the dismal apartment. "I have friends, Egon and Lotti, who live near your father's old apartment on Unter den Linden. If you wish, you can reach me through them." I shouted the address as the door closed.

Strangely, before the dreary hall closed around me, I pictured Laura thrusting out her arms, while holding the baby, as if offering him to me. I held on to this vision, certain I had imagined it.

# CHAPTER 32

Lotti and Egon kept in touch, but to my disappointment, Laura never contacted them. My mother installed a telephone in 1954 as services were restored in Berlin.

My friends now had a small daughter of their own, Kathi. I sat with her when they couldn't be at home. I was still employed by the construction firm, and Egon and Lotti, although living in East Berlin, worked in the West as well. More than fifty thousand residents of East Berlin were employed in the West, and more than ten thousand from the West worked in East Berlin. Lotti had talked about moving to the West, but, like many others, her parents and ancestors had made their homes in the sector occupied by the Soviets after the war. Apartments were scarce and people needed money to move. Therefore, like many, they remained in East Berlin.

A small press published my novel, *Einsamkeit*, but sales were meager. I missed the vivacious talent of Artur Berger, my publisher and editor at Verlangen Press, who'd not only built my career but believed in me as a writer. The Nazis had forced Verlangen and Berger out of business, along with my writing career. No one remembered "the New German Woman" that I'd written about twenty years before. Oddly, "survival" had been the cry of my heroines from the Weimar Republic, but those books were about making a life apart from a man.

After the war ended, a new and desperate kind of survival sprouted in Germany, as well as a new kind of woman—one who avoided the pitfalls of a destroyed city and country.

Only a few critics from small newspapers reviewed my book, most echoing the agents and editors who'd turned it down years before. One wrote that, "I couldn't stand to read anything as morose as this novel after what the country has endured." The sales and reviews prompted me to put down my pen—for a time.

About a year after I'd walked away from Laura and her husband, I got a phone call from Lotti one cold November night while at my mother's.

"Can you be at our apartment next Tuesday afternoon at one?" my friend asked with some urgency.

Of course, I sensed that something was amiss. "I'll have to take off from work. What's wrong?"

"Laura wants to see you. It's the only time that she can escape from her husband without being noticed. We got a note."

The blood rushed to my head—I was elated yet anxious. Had something gone wrong? Were she and my grandson in good health? "Of course, I'll be there—it must be an emergency."

"Good," Lotti said. "I'll leave the key with the woman across the hall who's sitting for Kathi. Egon and I won't be home until late in the afternoon. Lock up when you leave."

I hung up and told my mother about Lotti's call. We both went to bed that night worried about Laura.

The days crept by until Tuesday. I'd arranged for the afternoon off and left work at noon. I was at Egon and Lotti's by 12:45. Unlike my daughter's, this apartment was a jumble of old and new construction with more room and ample windows to let in light. The space made me realize that my daughter's home must have been picked by her husband for its environment: cramped, dark, and secluded, far removed from anything that would reveal its secrets.

I knocked on the neighbor's door and a woman, a ghostly picture, appeared. Her ashen face, silver hair, gray dress, and shoes scuffed to a similar color added to the depressing overcast of the day. Having been told to expect me, she handed me the key. Kathi slept peacefully in a makeshift bed in the corner as a radio played a waltz barely discernible to my ears.

I let myself into Lotti's and opened the curtains covering the large window. The pearly light poured through the glass and illuminated a room that I'd been in many times before. I sat on the couch, which faced the window, and looked at my watch as the time crawled by.

Promptly at one, a knock sounded. I rushed to the door. Laura stood there, tears streaking her eyes, Joseph standing a bit unsteadily by her side, holding on to her hand.

She grabbed her son and lifted him to her chest, fleeing into the room. "Please, close the curtains," she sputtered. "It's too dangerous. He wouldn't want me here." She looked at Joseph, whose face had scrunched into a scowl. "He has to go. Where's the bathroom?"

I pointed. "At the end of the hall."

She led Joseph away, and soon the toilet flushed, water ran, and she returned. "Sit down," I said.

"I must look a mess," she said, taking off her coat.

"No . . . not at all. I'm glad to see you."

She plopped Joseph on the couch and took out a teething toy for him. Tears once again formed in her eyes; she struggled to speak. Finally, the words began. "Mother . . . I've thought about you for a year now. You *are* my mother, aren't you?"

I nodded and held out my hands. She collapsed into them and we hugged as if we'd found each other once again—after years of separation.

"I have so much to tell you," she continued. "I find it hard to start."

I knew we didn't have time to discuss our histories. "Why

did you tell Lotti that we had to meet? Why doesn't Herwald want you here?" We sat on the couch, with Joseph wedged between us.

"I wanted you to know that when I saw you last year, I knew you were my mother. Every day since then I've wanted to tell you what was in my heart. I memorized the address you shouted through the door. I didn't dare call your friends, for our telephone line . . . is compromised. I have their number, but I didn't dare venture out until my husband no longer believed you were a threat."

"A threat? Why are you scared?"

Joseph reached for me as Laura trembled.

"Because my husband works for the Stasi and he believes everyone is an enemy. I think he questions my loyalty to the state. He wants to know when I go out for groceries, what time I do the laundry, if I have a doctor's appointment for Joseph. I never leave the house unless he knows where I'm going. I took a risk today."

I felt myself sliding backward, to the time of Passport Pictures and Herr Spiegel, and the Nazis, and fleeing to Amsterdam. I knew exactly how my daughter felt. I put my arm around her. "Has he threatened you? Hit you?"

She shook her head. "No, but he's so angry all the time, so certain that everyone who doesn't think like he does is evil." She looked at the thin, gold watch on her left wrist. "I hate that I have to sneak around, like a spy, to see you because Herwald thinks you're an enemy of the state."

"I suppose he's right. I am. If my mother taught me one thing, it was that men and their political dreams can destroy the world. Hitler proved it. Stalin proved it as well. I want to live like the Americans, the British, and the French. I want liberty. If I write a book, I don't want it banned. I don't want to hide, or risk death, because I loved a Jew."

Laura frowned. "I know so little about you—I remember so little. Where do we begin?"

Joseph gurgled and drooled. I took a handkerchief from my purse and wiped his mouth. "My grandson. I'm so proud of him, so proud that you survived the war. It was a terrible time . . . but you're telling me that our troubles aren't over?"

She nodded. "I don't know what's happening. Herwald doesn't talk about it much, but sometimes he comes home with blood on his uniform. Often, he goes out at night for meetings. I think the Stasi is arresting anyone they can. He has files that he studies late into the night—and he takes them with him in the morning. I've never been able to see what they contain, except a picture now and then—men and women who are suspects."

I settled against the cushion and ran my fingers through Joseph's fine hair. My heart felt as if it would burst with joy. I never wanted the feeling to end, never wanted my daughter and her son to leave me. "Tell me, Laura, what was your father like . . . after I left?"

She sighed. "I loved him. He was kind to me . . . a good father. Nazis came in and out of our apartment like flies through the window in summer. He would chat with them, serve them dinner and wine and liquor, laugh when he could, but when it was time for me to go to sleep, he would ask them to leave because he needed to put me to bed. When the war came to Berlin, the visits dropped off, and his Nazi "friends" deserted him. When Passport Pictures was destroyed, we were on our own."

Joseph rested his head against her side and his brown eyes fluttered with sleep.

Laura smiled, one of sadness and melancholy rather than laughter. "I don't think Father really liked them. He used them . . . to survive . . . and later, when he saw clearly what was happening, whatever feelings he held for them turned to disgust . . . and guilt. He despised them for all they had done to Germany and Berlin, but it was too late. He admitted to me one night before he sent me away that he had been wrong and that you had been right. At that point, we thought you'd died in Amsterdam. That was what we were told. I wasn't sad because I didn't remember you that well."

"I'm sorry." I took her hand. "I'm happy to know that your father realized what he'd done—that he recanted his connections to National Socialism. I know you're telling the truth, because when I married your father, his attitude was much the same. He always used the Nazis to survive. He threw his hand in with the butchers."

"It cost him his life." Laura gripped my hand and gazed at her son. "Now, I feel the same may happen to my husband."

"Do you love him?" I asked.

She looked away from me toward the black curtains, her eyes focusing on their own dark meaning. "He's the father of my child. I loved him when I married him—at least I thought I did—but life was different in the country. It was an arranged marriage of sorts. Anna Becker, our housekeeper, knew the Angermann family, and Herwald was my age. I was eager, anxious, to be on my own, but at the same time, I needed the stability of the Angermanns. Our marriage seemed like the perfect solution."

"Herwald changed as well?"

"Yes, as the Red Army rolled through Germany, he welcomed them. His family farm was spared because he offered them food, wine, and information, not scorn and derision. He became a devoted follower and when I told him that I wanted to move back to Berlin, he agreed, because he said there were more traitors here than in Leipzig. The Stasi welcomed him. I think he's . . . a killer."

I shook my head in disgust. "You must come to Rixdorf with me. You must leave him for your own safety."

Her eyes reddened. "I can't."

"Why not?"

"You know why. I don't have the strength that you had."

"Not because you love him."

She straightened, pulling away, grabbing Joseph. "I have to go. I want to see you again, but I don't know that I can. I needed to tell you that I know you're my mother."

"Please don't leave," I pleaded. "At least take my mother's address and phone number."

"No," she said firmly. "If Herwald found it . . . I can't leave . . . he'll track me down anywhere I go."

We both stood up. Laura leaned toward me, with Joseph snuggled between us. She hugged me and tears fell upon my neck. I didn't want to let her go.

She broke away. "Help me with my coat. If I need you, I'll contact Lotti. It's safer."

As I was putting on her coat, I asked a question. "Why didn't you respond to my note in the apartment?"

She sighed. "I was never inside. I only went into the building because I wanted to walk the halls—to remember a time when we thought life was good."

"Someone saw you. That's how I found you."

When she was ready to leave, I kissed them both on the cheek. Laura said good-bye and walked out. When the door closed, I felt the gulf widen between East and West and I harbored no hope for reconciliation.

Immersed in my thoughts, I sat for a time on the couch. I wanted my own tears to dry before returning to Rixdorf.

Two days later, I received a late-night call at my mother's. She was already in bed, so I answered the phone.

The voice on the other end was gruff, sounding slightly drunk. "Marie?"

"Yes," I replied, straining to hear. There was no noise in the background, nothing to give away the location of the caller.

"Stay away from her or I'll have you killed."

"Who is this?" I tried to remember the sound of Herwald's voice. It could have been him, or it could have been another man. I wasn't sure.

"Never mind. Stay away or you'll end up dead."

The line clicked and the annoying buzz sounded after a brief silence.

It wasn't the first time in my life I'd been threatened, but it cut more deeply than any other warning I'd received. I didn't know what to do, but I knew nothing could keep me away from my daughter and my grandson. I would make sure of that.

# CHAPTER 33

———◆◆◆———

Laura and her son were never far from my mind.

I thought of them when I was at work, and when I was at home with my mother in Rixdorf. The urge to go to their apartment was even stronger when I visited Egon and Lotti in East Berlin. I worked on another novel, but found myself staring at the blank page rather than writing. When I'd sit at the typewriter, the depressive brick that had been slowly growing in my head blocked the words. No matter how hard I tried, I couldn't crack it.

The Eastern sector deprivations grew, but slowly, almost imperceptibly, like a cancer undiagnosed and untreated. I couldn't convince Egon and Lotti to move to the West. Excuses always crossed their lips—their daughter, Kathi, was growing up; they liked their apartment; life would get better; the government would fail. Like so many, they were rooted to their home.

Days, months, years, slipped away, and any fear I'd carried about the phone call that threatened my death lessened.

But the time came that I could wait no longer to see Laura. My love for her had never lessened, and our separation was tearing me apart. I realized how much I'd become like Rickard, vowing never to lose his daughter.

Again, I found myself haunting number 68, where I presumed that Laura and Herwald still lived. The apartment always looked the same. The drapes were closed, the steps cleared of litter and newspapers, the building unchanged except for the shift of seasons and the play of light and shadow across its façade. The war damage had been repaired gradually.

Sometimes I cried in desperation as I walked past the apartment. Other times, I laughed manically about the futility of ever seeing my daughter and grandson again. On a few visits, my finger lingered above the buzzer, but then I would withdraw in terror. Herwald might be home and unleash the power of the Stasi upon me. I didn't doubt that he, if pushed, would have me thrown in prison somewhere far away from Berlin.

A new decade had begun when I next saw my daughter one Saturday.

The day was warm, the fall sun filling the blue sky with a blinding radiance. Families loved days like these in Berlin, a reminder that summer still held on to its brief life and winter had been pushed into abeyance. I had wandered far from my walk through the Tiergarten, drawn away like a ghost by the melancholy prospect of seeing Laura.

She was not the woman I remembered.

By chance, she opened the door, gazing at the steps as if looking for a delivery of some kind. The wiry bristles of a broom stuck out from its resting place in the hall behind her. She had grown softer, rounder; the sharper angles of her youth had receded as she approached twenty-nine years of age. But the feature that had discernibly changed was her posture. Laura's back was bent, her gaze directed downward, as if taking on the characteristics of a woman hunched over with age. Her hair hung by the side of her face, allowing me only a quick glance at her sad eyes.

I called her name and she started as if someone had jumped at her from a hiding place.

She stared at me, wild-eyed, and I saw the purple bruises on her face and the pale pallor of her skin.

I rushed toward her and she put up her hands impulsively, as if to brush me away.

"What's happened?" I asked with alarm. "Has he done this to you?"

She couldn't speak, only mumble before breaking into sobs.

"Is he here?" I asked.

She shook her head.

"Let's go inside."

Laura stumbled toward the door and I guided her into the shadowy apartment. Not much had changed since I'd last visited. Joseph, however, was gone.

"He's at school," Laura said, drying her eyes with a dish towel. She sat in the chair by the window, where she'd once nursed her son.

I looked over my shoulder expecting to see Herwald gallop into the room, but all was quiet. I closed the door.

"When will he be back?" I asked.

"Not for hours," she said, her voice barely above a whisper. "He's never home . . . and when he is . . ." Laura bent over in the chair, sobbing again.

I lifted her chin with my finger and studied her bruised face. The plum-colored marks covered a quarter of it, spreading from her cheeks, to her eyes, and around her lips.

"He did this to you?"

She nodded, drying her tears on the sleeve of her blouse.

"You must come with me to Rixdorf and bring Joseph."

She exhaled in a fury and slammed her back against the chair. "I can't. He watches Joseph, he watches me . . . he has friends in the Stasi who spy on us. I can't leave. He would swoop down in no time. You and your mother wouldn't be safe. He even knows where Egon and Lotti live with their daughter." She shook her head, her eyes dark and tormented. "There's no way out!"

"I'll find a way," I said, feeling less confident than my words. "Why does he beat you?"

"It started two years ago when I confronted him about the Stasi and the rumors I'd heard about the killings and the torture. He told me to stay out of his work, and I told him that he was no better than the Nazis. He flew into a rage, a fire lighting his eyes, and he struck me so hard he knocked me to the floor. Joseph was five then. His face was filled with fear. He ran to his bed screaming and pulled the blankets over his head. He lay there whimpering until he fell asleep. Herwald told me that he would find me if I ever left him and there would be nothing left of the family. That was his way of telling me that he and the Stasi would kill me . . . and I wondered what he might do to Joseph."

I grasped her hands and looked into her eyes. "I'll get you and Joseph out of here. I promise." At that moment, if I'd had a gun, I would have killed Herwald had he walked in. After what I'd been through, one more death wouldn't have mattered. "So, the beatings haven't stopped?"

"I told him I hated the Stasi and what he did. I told him that I would never have another child with him. Most nights he leaves me alone and goes out to find other women, but sometimes he comes home filled with anger and he beats me for any reason he can find. I want to leave, but I can't endanger Joseph."

"Is there anything I can do? Anyone I can tell?"

She shook her head. "No . . . if you tell anyone it will get back to him. The Stasi has thousands of ears and every one of them is listening. Whatever you do, don't say anything to your Red Army officer friend."

Laura had read my mind, for I had thought of contacting Viktor Volkov. She was right, however. Such a revelation to Viktor could lead to disaster.

"You must leave," she said. "If he catches you here, even if he suspects you've been here . . ."

"How can I reach you?"

Laura thought for a moment. Her eyes brightened briefly. "There's a crack on the foundation on the west side of the house behind the lilac bush. I spotted it when I was looking at the blooms in the spring. I don't think Herwald knows it's there. It must have been from the bombings. You could slip a note inside."

I nodded. "Yes. I won't address it to you, but you'll know it's from me."

"Please leave, Mother," Laura said.

I kissed her on the forehead and was soon out of the house into the sparkling day. I looked for the hiding place she'd mentioned and found it concealed behind the still-green leaves of the lilac.

I walked home, sadness filling me. Despite the beautiful day, I couldn't erase the hate that boiled inside me.

I tried once to reach Viktor Volkov—not to report Herwald and what he was doing to my daughter—Laura and I agreed that would be dangerous—but to find out if he had received any word about Emil. I didn't know where Volkov had ended up, and the GDR kept his assignment a guarded secret. I didn't know if he was still in Germany or had been transferred back to the Soviet Union.

Having no better address, I mailed a letter to the special camp in Hohenschönhausen where Rickard had been held as a prisoner. The Stasi had turned the camp into its own brutal detention center. My letter was never answered. As the years had drifted by, Emil began to seem more like a dream than a person I'd ever loved and touched. My love for him hadn't diminished, but the war had left me and so many others with so little hope of finding, or ever learning, what had happened to those dear to us. Only memories held in our hearts and minds became a solace. Emil, his uncle Levi, and our bartender friend Rudi were among the millions who had disappeared.

I left a few notes of love to Laura in the hiding place, fearing for my own life, sometimes dropping off a note on a dark winter night, being careful to cover any prints I might leave on the frozen ground. I never received an answer, but Lotti told me that she'd seen Laura walking once with a boy on Unter den Linden. My friend had spotted my daughter from afar but didn't approach her on that spring day. The veils of secrecy, retribution, and torture had created a culture of distrust so pervasive that any meeting was dangerous.

In early August of 1961, Lotti called me and we met at my mother's home one day after work.

"Egon has heard things," she told me. My mother listened intently and Lotti had no objection. "If this happens, it will affect us all."

Her words chilled me because I knew that Lotti never exaggerated a situation, if anything she downplayed it.

"We don't know if what we're hearing is true because we can't believe that something like this would slip from the mouth of any official, East German or Stasi. Two months ago, the First Secretary, Walter Ulbricht, told a reporter that 'No one intends to build a wall.'" She took a deep breath and turned her gaze in my direction. "You know Egon—his ears are always open. Ever since his time in the Wehrmacht. . . ."

She stopped, and I knew why she'd paused. Lotti, I was certain, would have no problem exposing Egon's disgust for the National Socialists in front of my mother, but she didn't want to mention how her husband had taken me to Buchenwald or how we had torched a Nazi recruiting center.

Lotti shook her head before continuing. "It's all so unbelievable . . . but Egon believes the GDR is going to build a wall around East Berlin, perhaps around East Germany, cutting us off from the rest of the world. So many people have fled they want to stop us from leaving. We'll become prisoners."

My mother's gasp turned to a laugh. "It's impossible. They could never construct such a wall."

I closed my eyes and thought for a moment. "You should have moved here long ago . . . when I asked you to."

"Our families, our daughter, our home," Lotti responded with sadness in her voice, and I understood.

"Besides, we don't have enough money to uproot our lives," she continued. "I feel like the Jews in Germany who didn't leave and then discovered it was too late. Some even felt that Hitler was a joke not to be taken seriously."

"Emil knew," I said. "He saved me."

The sun's rays slanted into the living room, bathing us in a pink light. It reminded me of the summers I'd spent as a child in this house. Memories flooded me, beginning with the time I'd left home, until I found myself on my mother's couch with the needlepoint pillows listening to Lotti tell me that a wall might be built. I pinched myself under the knee to make sure I wasn't dreaming.

Lotti cleared her throat. "But, Niki, do you understand what this means . . . if it happens?"

I wasn't sure what she was talking about and shook my head.

Her eyes swept over me. "You might never see Laura again . . . for as long as the wall stands. What if the government allows no one to visit? What if they make it impossible to escape?"

I sagged against the couch, fighting the sadness threatening to overtake me. I had been so focused on Lotti and Egon and the wall that I'd forgotten about Laura. I didn't know what to say. I looked at my mother, my head full of questions.

"You must go to East Berlin," my mother said before I could answer Lotti. "You must save Laura and her son."

Her quick response took me by surprise.

"Exactly what I was thinking," Lotti said. "You've slept on my couch before. Pack a few things and come with me."

I wanted to break down, fight against the tears that welled in my eyes. The battle for survival had been so long and hard, I didn't know how much more I could take.

My mother put her hand on my shoulder. "Do it for your daughter. Get her out of East Berlin as soon as you can. You'll always have a home here."

I swiped at the tears on my cheeks and got up. I walked to my bedroom at the front of the house and stared at the bed that I'd slept in for many years at various times in my life. I ran my hands over the bedclothes and fluffed the pillow, knowing that what lay in front of me was as dangerous a task as any I'd faced. Rescuing my daughter and grandson from the Stasi's hands would not be easy.

I packed my bag, kissed my mother good-bye, and got into a taxi with Lotti. Soon, we were at her apartment in the Eastern sector. Egon was reading a paper. Kathi was already in bed.

As soon as I walked into my new surroundings, I felt the world close around me.

# CHAPTER 34

I tried for several days, but failed, to slip a note to Laura in the hiding place. One afternoon, I spotted Herwald walking several streets away. At first, I didn't recognize him because he was dressed in a dark suit. But as he approached, I quickly turned and rushed down a side street. He hadn't seen me because he was studying a document encased in the black folder in his hands—the Stasi's business was never finished. He walked, hardly looking up, as if he'd memorized the route in front of him.

Because I didn't know when I'd return to the American sector, I resigned at work. I knew my employer would have no trouble filling my job. He was a bit perplexed, but when I told him that I was moving to East Berlin, he understood my concern and said good-bye. I had mentioned my daughter and grandson many times over the course of years. He could read the political climate in Berlin as well as anyone.

When we woke up on the morning of August 13, 1961, Berlin, Germany, and the world took notice of an earth-shattering change. In the course of two nights, the GDR had divided Berlin with a one hundred and fifty-three-kilometer-long wall.

Egon was the first to return home as Lotti was preparing for work. I was to look after Kathi that day.

"It's happened," he said, his cheeks red from sprinting to tell us the news. "We can't leave. And we're out of work!" Lotti and Egon were two of the thousands of East Berliners who were employed in the West. "It's not a wall—just fencing and barbed wire—but streets are closed and patrolled, and checkpoints have been set up at the few that are open. It's chaos. I couldn't get through. People are milling about wondering what's next. I'm sure this isn't the end of it."

Because I no longer had to stay with Kathi, I left the breakfast dishes in the sink and hurried to the Brandenburg Gate. Through its classical columns, the barbed wire flashed in vicious circles on the other side of the perimeter fencing. To hold the sectional barriers in place, metal posts had been sunk into concrete cubes resembling a pyramid chopped in half above the base. At the main gate entrance, beneath the quadriga, armored personnel carriers resembling tanks stood guard, keeping anyone from venturing into the West.

In the crowd, I spotted a young man carrying a briefcase who appeared to be shaken up by the sudden appearance of the fencing. Dressed in his polished black shoes, stovepipe pants, and jacket, he looked as if he'd been stopped on his way to work. I stood by his side and asked him if he knew if there were any open streets.

"Fourteen," he said, "but with checkpoints. The guards aren't letting just anyone through. You have to have a special permit. Work in the western sectors isn't good enough."

"Do you know what happened?" I asked this young man because I was surprised that Egon, with his nose for rumors, hadn't alerted Lotti and me to any news regarding the wall.

"I didn't see it," he said, "but a neighbor told me the lights went out at the Gate the last two nights at one in the morning. The border police and the combat units worked quickly, putting up fencing and laying down the barbed wire. I heard the government is calling it an 'Anti-fascist Protection Rampart.'"

When Lotti had told my mother and me that such a plan

might be put into place, I was as skeptical as Frieda. It's impossible, I'd thought, echoing her words.

"My wife and I moved into a new apartment two days ago," he continued. His gaze lowered and he adjusted his black-rimmed glasses on his nose.

"Do you mean . . . ?"

"Yes, she's in the West. Tonight was to be our first night together in our new home. I have relatives here, but I didn't intend to live with them for the rest of my life. I hope the border brigade and police find it in their hearts to let me through. . . ."

I wasn't confident that his request would be granted.

We parted and I walked back to the apartment. Lotti had finished the dishes and Egon was sitting on the couch next to Kathi. She, at almost eight years of age, was reading a book. He lifted a cigarette that I'd left on a table and spun it in his fingers like a magician doing sleight of hand tricks. Egon didn't smoke, so I knew something else was occupying his mind. He scowled as I sat across from him, his expression sad and perplexed. His body had filled out and his blond hair had begun to thin. Although he was still fit, he no longer looked like a man who could scale fences after setting a Nazi recruiting office on fire.

"You didn't know?" I asked, hoping that he wouldn't take my question as a criticism.

"No, all I heard were the rumors, but that's not what's worrying me." He looked at his daughter to make sure she was reading, and then cocked his head backward toward Lotti, who stood in their small kitchen. "They need to leave while there's still time. The fence is weak in points . . . people told me so this morning. I need to find those points. Lotti and Kathi have to go . . . to your mother's."

"What are you talking about, Father?" Kathi asked. Lotti didn't seem to hear our conversation and continued to put away the breakfast dishes.

"Go back to your reading," Egon said, and patted his daughter's hand. "It's nothing for you to worry about."

"It's difficult now," I said, not wanting to use the word "dangerous."

He nodded. "But conditions will get worse as time goes on. I know that. Your son-in law knows that as well, but he's determined to . . . find people like us." He looked at his daughter. "Lotti, please come here for a moment."

She wiped her hands on a dish towel and came into the room. The sunlight, bright that day, belying the misery in East Berlin, lit the world beyond the window. Looking out, everything seemed normal: the trees full and verdant, the cars parked as they always were by the curb, the bushes green with leaves, the morning dew still sparkling on the summer grass.

Egon scooted away from his daughter, allowing Lotti to sit between them. She looked at him expectantly, as he flicked my cigarette back to the table.

He put his hands on his palms and leaned forward. "How would you and Kathi like to visit Niki's mother in Rixdorf?"

Lotti's lips parted and she took a deep breath. It was hard to tell whether her face bore an expression of shock or disgust. "Kathi, take your book and go to your room," she told her daughter.

"Must I?" Kathi asked. "I want to be with you. How long will we be there? I'm old enough to listen. I won't say a word."

Lotti pointed to the hall. "No. Your father, Niki, and I have an important issue to discuss."

Kathi snorted, closed her book, and headed to her room. The door slammed a few seconds later.

"She doesn't need to know what's going on," Lotti said. "I'll tell her this afternoon when we have a chance to talk."

"The fence is imperfect," Egon said. "There's no wall yet. We can cut through the barbed wire if we find the right location. Maybe it's already been done. They don't have enough units to keep everyone from slipping through."

Lotti pushed her back against the couch. "I'm surprised at you, Egon, and you, Niki, for even thinking that I would agree to such a plan."

"I didn't agree," I protested. "I said it's dangerous . . . but if there was ever a time to escape . . ."

"I'm not going anywhere," Lotti said firmly. "I don't care if I have to swear allegiance to the GDR and the Stasi, I'm not putting my daughter in danger, and I'm not leaving my husband and my best friend behind. We'll get by until all of us can escape or this horrible time has passed."

"What if I . . ."

Lotti put a finger to Egon's lips. "I don't care how much you beg. I am not leaving you." And with that, Lotti burst into tears.

Egon took her in his arms and kissed her and I watched as they consoled each other with hugs and loving looks. I thought of Emil and wished that he was by my side.

Lotti had made up her mind and in a matter of minutes the discussion was over. Kathi returned to the couch, Lotti paced in the kitchen deciding what she would prepare for lunch, and Egon sat brooding next to his daughter. I could tell from the subtle shifts in his eyes that he was thinking—attempting to find a solution to a problem that wasn't going away soon.

I still had to contact my daughter and hope that she would follow me back to West Berlin.


Every person on the street was a potential threat.

After the wall was put in place, the Stasi recruited its spies and operatives, even seeking out West Berliners sympathetic to its mission—to deter all enemies and traitors, and to end desertion from the GDR. Reprisals were swift and brutal, including arrest, imprisonment, and torture. As in Germany under Hitler's rule, people disappeared. It seemed as if the goal of the government was to imprison all of its citizens or to brand them as criminals.

Egon found a job as a shipping manager with a rail company—employment was relatively easy to find because so many people had fled East Berlin. Lotti found work as an assistant to a wealthy businessman who had connections to the Soviet Union. Both of them were happy to find jobs that made them seem like supporters of the government. My duties, in exchange for the couch at night and food, were readying Kathi for school, taking her to class in the morning, and picking her up in the afternoon. In addition, I helped with the cooking, shopping, and cleaning. For most of the day my time was my own.

My solitary hours were a blessing and a curse. Many times I found myself awash in tears and desperate thoughts while curled up on the couch. Would our struggles ever end? Laura never called and, with each day, as the summer fled and fall brought its cold winds to Berlin, I despaired of ever seeing her. I thought the same of Emil. My personal mission to find them, rescue them from horror, had failed.

On other days, my emotions bordered on the manic. I was convinced that I could take on the Stasi single-handedly, that all I needed to do was to walk into Laura's apartment and rescue her and Joseph. But where would we go? Everything seemed hopeless as the GDR crushed its people with its iron fist.

In the fall, before snow covered the city, I knew I had to get word to Laura.

One night, I decided to take a chance and deliver a coded message to the hiding place. I couldn't spell out my name, or those of Lotti and Egon, but I hoped Laura could decipher my message. If I had written it out, it would have read: *I'm staying in East Berlin with Egon and Lotti and am working on a way to get you and Joseph back to the West. As soon as I know the plan, I will be in touch. You know where to reach me.*

Instead, my short note read: *Here with friends. Planning a party. See you soon.*

I chose the October evening because of the elements. Rain fell—sometimes in a mist, sometimes in spurts like bullets. The wind ripped through the streets. Sane people would be inside on such a miserable night.

When I arrived at Laura's apartment, the eerie sense that nothing and everything had changed filled me. I pictured a beaten and defeated Laura sitting in her chair, perhaps trying to read a book of no interest to her; Joseph would be studying under the meager light of a bulb hanging above the small kitchen table. Herwald was out—prowling the neighborhood, or most likely, searching the wall's perimeters for deserters and traitors, pistol drawn in case he had to shoot.

The setting of the vampire movie Rickard had hired me for so many years ago seemed tame compared to the night I had stepped into. As I bent behind the lilac bush, which offered little cover, my overcoat flapped in the wind. I quickly inserted the note into the crack and slipped away, pressing the folds of my garment against my body. I looked over my shoulder often as I made my way back to Unter den Linden.

Egon, dressed only in his underwear, a pile of dirty clothes at his feet, stared at me as I entered the apartment. I was soaked to the skin and looked like a bedraggled cat that had been caught in a downpour. I was surprised by his appearance as well. Lotti and Kathi were in the kitchen.

"I worked late tonight," he said, pointing to the mud-stained garments. "I got dirty."

"You don't get dirty in your job. You manage people who sort and load packages."

He smiled. "Soon, in a matter of months, in less than a year, we will be in West Berlin."

I took off my wet coat and hung it on a rack near the door. "How?"

"You'll find out." He scraped sand off his arms onto the clothes. "Maybe you can help."

A burst of excitement surged through me. "Please, tell me."

"A tunnel . . . connecting East and West. All we have to do is make sure the Stasi doesn't discover it."

"A tunnel. Of course." The GDR had begun to reinforce the wall and add additional layers and a no-man's-land as a deterrent, but there were still sections less than one hundred meters wide separating East from West.

"They can blow up all the border buildings they want, they can brick up all the windows, they can close the apartment entrances bordering the wall and move people out of their homes on the first and second floors—so you have to risk death to escape . . . but they won't stop us."

"So you're working late at this job?"

"Yes, and I'll be sleeping there if it's safe."

I looked toward the kitchen. Lotti held up her hands knowing there was nothing she could do. "We should have left long ago as you suggested."

"You have a job, too," Egon said, looking at me. "You need to tell Laura about our plan, and hope she reveals nothing to her husband. The Stasi's spies are everywhere."

I made my bed on the couch that night and, after turning out the lights, opened the curtains so I could look out on the street. The wind howled through the trees and the rain had gotten worse. All I wanted to do was fall asleep and dream of freedom for me, my daughter, and my grandson.

# CHAPTER 35

We heard the blasts.

Sometimes the apartment shook and the dishes rattled as the GDR leveled vacant apartment buildings bordering the wall. By November 1961, the "death strip," a no-man's-land, had been widened in many areas, and anti-tank barriers and camouflage nets had been added as defensive measures.

After dropping Kathi off at school, I sometimes walked the streets, noting the strategic positions of the border patrol and the continuing reinforcement of the wall with concrete blocks and barbed wire. The Stasi was determined to succeed in its mission.

At first, people were able to talk over chest-high barriers, always in sight of border guards, or they waved to family members across the divide. Food and clothing were hoisted from sidewalks situated in West Berlin to neighbors who lived in apartments along the border in East Berlin. Not an organization to wallow in sentimentality, the Stasi took note. Gradually, the provisional walls were replaced with higher, more solid structures. Families were moved away from the border, the ground-floor windows of the remaining structures were laced with barbed wire, and front entrances were closed. People had to enter through the back of the building.

I saw how quickly the GDR was working to achieve its

goal of complete repression and restricted movement, but we couldn't rush our process. It had to be done methodically and with painstaking care.

One evening, under the blanket of darkness, Egon took me to the dig site to show me how meticulous the job had become.

"There will be two men working there, in addition to those working on the other side, from the West," he told me as we left the apartment. "At some point, we will meet and then we can escape. People live on the top floors, but they know about our work and want to come with us when it's done."

"You trust them?"

He nodded. "Yes, they are young and don't want to live out their lives in East Berlin."

We kept quiet the remainder of our journey, walking south about a kilometer from Unter den Linden until we reached a forlorn brick apartment building in sight of the concrete wall. The barrier was topped by a string of barbed wire held in place by Y-shaped metal brackets. We passed police along the way and as we got closer to the wall, we ducked out of sight of a few border patrol guards. The evening was cold and windy, and the few men that we saw were huddled together smoking cigarettes, backs braced against the cold.

We cut through a vacant lot filled with twisted metal and refuse. Egon opened a flimsy wooden door and put a finger to his lips. He had told me that once we got to the site, no talking was allowed. The Stasi had positioned microphones and motion detectors at suspected escape tunnels. A set of wooden stairs led to a basement. We took off our shoes, holding them in our hands, and tiptoed down the boards attempting not to make a sound.

At the bottom, we encountered another door—this one more solid and reinforced with metal edging. Egon tapped on the wood—so faintly, I barely heard the knock.

Slowly, the door opened toward us. We put on our shoes

and stepped into a world unlike any I'd ever experienced. The first thing I noticed was that the ground was elevated; we stepped onto a growing basement floor. Wooden racks lining three of the walls were filled with items that you would find in any city basement: rusty gardening tools that hadn't been used in twenty years, cleaning supplies, buckets, pails, rat poison, battered luggage, and old window frames. The shelves, nearly hidden behind the contents of the dig, contained all the collected detritus of seventy years.

The air was cold and damp and smelled of smoke and burning wax. That was how the space was lighted. A candle burned near each of the racks, and, at the back, more flickered in the dark. Another set of shelves, fashioned more like a bookcase with a solid backing, had been pulled out from the south wall. A black tarp covered a narrow hole just wide enough for a man to crawl into. Buckets of dirt and sand lay on the tops of larger mounds of excavated material.

The young man in his twenties, who'd opened the door, sat on the floor taking a rest. He was covered in dirt but didn't seem to care as he ate a piece of bread and jam, probably covered in just as much grit. Another man, older, clambered out of the hole.

Egon was to take his place in the shift. He silently mouthed the words so close to my face I could feel his warm breath on my cheeks. "Take a look. I don't expect you to work. We're making progress."

I skirted the candles and lifted the tarp. A spot of yellow light shone from a point deep within the tunnel. The crew wasn't digging under water; only earth and the wall stood above their heads. Less than seventy-five meters away, I estimated, the two crews would meet and the tunnel would open to its full length.

I bent down and crawled into the hole, the earth forming a shallow arch over me. One could worry about the tunnel caving in and burying you alive, but all I could think about as I pushed onward was bringing my family to freedom. At equi-distant locations heavy posts had been laid into the walls, giving some sense of solidity to the work.

The earth was a combination of clay, pebbles, and sand; damp in spots, dry in others. The light, an oil lamp, sat twenty meters ahead of me. It was surrounded by metal pails and buckets resting against an imposing barrier of semidark earth. I wondered if I was under the wall or West Berlin. I wished that I was a mole and could dig my way up and out.

I scrunched my body into a ball and turned in the tunnel, working my way carefully back to the tarp. When I emerged, Egon nodded and pointed to the seat of a broken chair he'd positioned in front of one of the walls. I took my place there as Egon crawled into the tunnel first, followed by the young man, leaving the older man near the entrance. The work was silent, but an assembly line had been formed. Egon filled the pails at the end of the tunnel, and then by stop-and-go carried his weighty loads to the younger man, who then relayed them to the older man at the entrance. The last man emptied the buckets onto the ever-growing piles that rose like an earthen barrier, nearly topping the shelving on each of the walls, almost concealing their contents.

When the work was finished for the evening, all three men, grimy and dirty, left the tunnel and secured the tarp across the entrance. The bookcase was then pulled in front of it, and opaque netting stretched across the dirt on either side, shortening the length of the basement. Egon smiled, happy with the work done for the night.

The younger man left first and then the older fifteen minutes later. We waited as well. Egon blew out all the candles and withdrew a small electric torch from his coat pocket. We made our way to the door, which he closed slowly. Again, we took off our shoes and climbed the stairs until we were in back of the Zimmerstrasse house once again. Rain had fallen during our time in the basement, and a fog had settled over the city.

When we arrived home, Lotti was sitting on the couch. Kathi had been put to bed. I noticed a white envelope in my friend's hand. I was excited to talk to Egon about the tunnel and its progress, but Lotti thrust the paper toward me. "This came for you when I was with Kathi in her bedroom. I didn't hear a knock or see anyone. I wouldn't have noticed, but the edge of it had been jammed underneath the door."

Lotti had opened it because there was no name on the outside. My heart quickened, hoping it was a note from Laura. I opened the envelope and pulled out a folded piece of paper. It read:

*Herwald works various hours now that the Stasi is determined to bring traitors to justice. He is part of a unit to infiltrate and spy upon his own border guards. I received your notes. It's become dangerous to pass these because everyone has turned into a spy. But he is working tonight, so I took the risk.*

*I am ready to leave. I can take no more. I hope that my son will follow, but I won't force him. He is old enough to understand, and he also knows what his father has done to me. Despite Herwald's efforts to mold him into something like a brutal animal, I sense a resistance—a goodness that can't be snuffed out despite his father's savage thinking. Escape is the only way to keep Herwald from turning him into a killer. I've seen too much death—witnessed too much retribution. Just as you resisted your husband, I'm doing the same.*

*I am free to leave the house when Herwald is working and Joseph is in school, but I still fear eyes follow me. We must change our communications to the park*

*at Helmholtzplatz. There is a flat-stone walkway lead-*
*ing into it. The stones can be lifted from the ground.*
*The tenth one from the entrance curves away from the*
*grass. Leave your messages under that stone on the fif-*
*teenth of each month. It's safe to deliver them at night.*
  *This is all I can write. I hope that we can live and*
*talk one day in freedom.*
    *Your daughter*

I sat on the couch next to Lotti, unsure what I was feeling.
I knew the park, for it was near the apartment where Rickard and Laura had lived. Every action against the GDR was
a risk in East Berlin, but if all worked according to plan, my
daughter and her son would be free at last.

"Are you all right?" Lotti asked.

I nodded. Yes . . . but I'm scared to death."

"We're far from done," Egon said, walking to the bathroom to take off his dirty clothes.

"How long will it take?" I called out after him.

"Late spring, early summer, I think. We know how fast
we're working, but reports from the other side are sketchy."

"I'll write to Laura telling her I got the note," I said to
Lotti. "I'll let her know we are planning an escape."

Lotti said good night and left me alone. Once again, I
pulled open the curtains in darkness to look out upon the
damp night. The only streetlamp on the block cast misty light
against the trees, forcing their black shadows into the room
like knives.

I made my bed on the couch and closed my eyes. In a half
state of dreams, I pictured myself and the others crawling
through the tunnel as men as vague as the fog outside raced after us. I blinked and sat up, convinced that I'd had a nightmare.

Through the winter and the spring, Egon and the other men
continued work at the site, sometimes staying overnight. We

prayed that they would be safe and that the Stasi would never discover the tunnel. Our luck held despite the border guards on Zimmerstrasse who questioned Egon and the others from time to time. Familiarity with the guards soon took over and the threat lessened. Egon and the men had come up with alibis and even befriended a few, offering them pats on the back, and cigarettes and chocolate purchased from his paycheck.

Laura and I wrote coded notes to each other once a month on the fifteenth. She reported that Herwald had been promoted within the Stasi and was now overseeing a large group of guards.

One night in early June of 1962, Egon came home with a scowl on his face.

"Sit," he instructed Lotti and me, as he sat in the chair opposite the couch. From his expression and tone of voice, I expected bad news. Perhaps, the tunnel had collapsed, or everyone had given up, or the Stasi had discovered it.

His scowl shifted to a smile. "We heard them—on the other side. We're probably three or four meters from completion. We wanted to scream, but we couldn't. We heard a few scrapes and that was all."

I clutched Lotti's hand—the news was so exciting. "So, we can leave after the fifteenth?"

"Probably. We won't know until it's open, but we need to be ready to leave on a moment's notice. We can't walk through the streets with luggage, so we must carry only what we can conceal in our clothing. We'll have to start over in West Berlin."

Lotti sighed and managed a half smile. "When the war ended we had nothing. We can do it again. It wasn't so bad. We're alive and have our Kathi."

"Yes," Egon said. "Our children deserve to live in freedom."

That evening, I composed a note to Laura telling her to "plan for a party," with the time and date to be announced. I left the apartment and walked to the park, making sure that no one was following me. When I arrived, I circled it before stepping onto the pathway. The lights were on in the neighboring apartment buildings, but no one was looking out the windows. Satisfied that everything was safe, I slid the note under the rock and left. The earth was damp from spring rains, and I hoped that the ink I'd used wouldn't smear.

As I walked home, a man's footsteps sounded behind me. I didn't dare look over my shoulder for fear that he would think I was scared and had something to hide. I picked up my pace a bit, and only when I'd reached the apartment door did I look back. The steps had faded and the street, as far as I could see, was empty.

I stepped inside and collapsed against the door, my heart pounding. Everyone was asleep and the rooms were dark.

I hoped that fleeing from brutal regimes and years of desperation were about to end. I sat on the couch and vowed to bring my daughter and her son to West Berlin.

# CHAPTER 36

In the late afternoon of June 27, 1962, the tunnel that Egon had been working on opened between East and West.

He and the two other men who had toiled so hard shook hands with the three men from the West who had finished their hard and painstaking job. After a brief exchange of silent good wishes, everyone retreated to their respective sides.

His face glowed as he told us the news. "We leave at noon tomorrow and we must be ready, even if we have to stay up all night." He hugged Lotti and then me.

Kathi walked into the room. "Papa, are we leaving?"

"Yes, tomorrow. You won't see your friends again for a long time, but you will make new ones."

She thought for a moment and then said, "I don't want to go. This is our home."

Egon kneeled before her and took her small hands in his. "This is difficult, but you can't imagine what it will be like on the other side. You'll be able to travel, read any book you want. You won't have to worry about food, or getting a piece of candy. We will have freedom."

Kathi nodded reluctantly.

Egon took her in his arms. "But when we leave, you must be quiet and do everything your mother and I tell you to do. We'll be going with other people. Do you understand?"

Kathi nodded, this time with more conviction.

"Mother will help you with the things you can take."

Lotti took her daughter back to her bedroom, as a lump formed in my throat. "What should I do, Egon? Laura might not see the note."

He lowered his gaze, stroked the stubble on his chin, and then shook his head. "Six people from the building, plus the men who helped me and their families, are going through to-night. I told them that we will come later because you needed to contact your daughter and grandson. If any of them are caught, or they talk, we'll be stuck in East Berlin, perhaps forever." He paused. "I would go to her—take the chance that Herwald isn't home. But she and Joseph must come to the apartment by eleven tomorrow because once we're through the tunnel, the western end might be sealed."

"What if Herwald is off duty tomorrow?"

Egon shrugged. "Then Laura must find a way to come."

"I'll go tonight at nine as the sun is setting," I said. "Maybe he won't be there."

"Lotti and I will be praying for you. You are a brave woman. This is the final test."

I wrote a note, just in case. All it said was, *You must come to the apartment tomorrow morning at eleven. It's finished.*

The message was as direct and clear as I could make it. It was also dangerously detailed for the wrong eyes. I would have to take that chance.

When the time drew near, I left the apartment. The evening was warm, the damp air settling on my face and arms. In the west, where I hoped we soon would be going, the setting sun streaked the clouds straddling the horizon with azure.

Skirting the park, I took my time walking to Laura's apart-ment. As I neared her home, I took the note out of my purse and wadded it in my hand. The building looked the same as it had for years: the blinds drawn at the Angermanns, the steps swept clean. Two pots of red geraniums had been set on each side of the bottom step. I walked up, trying to calm myself with each lift of my foot.

I rang the buzzer and waited.

A few moments later, Herwald Angermann answered the door.

I trembled a bit, but retained my composure. "I must see my daughter," I said as forcefully as I could.

"You can make no demands here," he responded, his voice full of contempt.

"I'm not leaving until I see her," I said.

"I will have you arrested. Don't press me."

It had been many years since I'd seen him. He looked dead to me, his skin drawn and tough. Time had hardened him, and I felt no hint of compassion or joy in his soul.

Laura appeared at the apartment door behind him.

"Go back inside," he ordered.

Laura's eyes were dull, her expression flat. "No, I want to see my mother . . . I will see my mother."

Herwald's lip curled in disdain, but he let Laura approach. I knew that she would pay dearly for defying him. She stepped around him.

I hugged her and spoke so that Herwald could hear. Joseph peeked around the door, his eyes taking in another confrontation between his parents.

"I wanted you to know that I'm safe and living in East Berlin," I said.

"I know where you live," Herwald said, hissing out the words. "You think the Stasi doesn't know where you live—everything about you—and those two misfits you call friends? You are on our list."

Was he exaggerating to scare me? Surely, he didn't know about the tunnel or he would have arrested Egon and the others.

Laura pivoted toward him. "Leave my mother alone. She's done nothing wrong. All she's done is care for me."

Herwald spit on the hall floor.

I grasped Laura's hands in mine, pressing the note against her palm, and then squeezed her fingers into a fist, concealing it from her husband. That was all I could do. I couldn't stay longer—Herwald would become suspicious. I hoped Laura would carry the note safely back into the apartment, read it, and destroy it.

I said good-bye, turned and strode away, hoping that my daughter and her son would be at Lotti's door at eleven tomorrow morning.

When the knock came, my heart jumped into my throat. It sounded soft, like a woman's, not the bruising knock of the Stasi or the long-disbanded Gestapo.

We sat waiting, Egon looking at his watch every two minutes. Lotti had concealed money and a few pieces of jewelry in a light overcoat she would carry for the journey to Zimmerstrasse, much as I had years before when I'd taken the emerald bracelet to Amsterdam. Egon fashioned a thin bag that hung over his neck, which was hidden under an oversize shirt. It held important papers and watches and rings. A shoulder holster carried the one pistol he owned. Kathi took the one doll she wouldn't give up. Who would question a girl with a doll? I took only the clothes that I was wearing, leaving the rest behind in my old suitcase, knowing that a few things remained at my mother's in Rixdorf.

I sprang from the couch and opened the door.

Laura and Joseph stood there, both looking anxious and confused. I wanted to ask them how they'd escaped, but there was no time.

Egon waved them in. "Hurry! Inside."

I closed the door and hugged them. Laura and Joseph responded to my touch, but not in the way I'd expected. Both cringed a little, as if a loving touch was foreign to them. Laura turned into the light, for we had closed the curtains, and removed the scarf from her head. I saw what Herwald had done to her last night. Her left eye was swollen and bruised; a red streak ran from the hairline to her chin on the right side of her face. He had taken out my visit on her.

"We must leave, now," Egon said. "No time for tears. We can cry when we reach the West." He then took charge, telling us that he, Lotti, and Kathi would go first toward Zimmerstrasse. Laura and Joseph were to follow across the street, and I would lag behind. When we got to the tunnel, Lotti would go first, followed by Kathi; then Joseph and Laura. Egon and I would be the last to leave. "When we approach the wall, turn right on Zimmerstrasse," he said, giving the address as a final instruction. "I will stand at the door until we are all safe in the basement. If you're stopped, don't show fear. You are out for a walk on a summer day. Walk quietly down the basement steps and say nothing once we're inside."

Egon and Lotti took a final look at what they were leaving behind: the furniture, the cookware, and the few items they had collected. All would be donated gratefully to the Stasi or the next tenant. He locked the door and we stepped into the sun.

We did as he instructed. I held my breath along the way as we strolled south. I carried a shopping bag with a few vegetables in it, so I could pretend that I'd been to the market, if the border guards stopped me.

Other East Berliners were on the streets. Those people made me feel better, knowing that the police and border guards would have more to look at than just us. If we looked normal—not suspicious in any way—our chances of making it to the tunnel were good.

As we approached Zimmerstrasse, Egon broke away from Lotti and Kathi and approached a border guard. I knew it had to be one he'd met before, for the man smiled at him. He shook the guard's hand and offered him a piece of chocolate, and then, amazingly, introduced him to Lotti and Kathi.

Kathi shook hands with the guard, and he bent down to admire the doll.

I looked at Laura, who returned my gaze. I wanted her and Joseph to slow down for a moment. She stopped and wrapped the scarf around her head to hide the bruises on her face.

Soon, Egon was on his way toward the apartment building that held the tunnel. I kept to his side of the street. Laura and Joseph veered away from the guard, who gave them only a glance as he munched on the chocolate. Soon, we were all at the back door.

I squeezed Egon's hand as we descended the stairs to the basement. He had planned it perfectly, including his interaction with the border guard.

He acknowledged my appreciation with a nod and then directed everyone to the back wall. The ceiling seemed lower, the shelves hidden by dirt.

Keeping one for herself, Lotti pulled out two small electric torches from her coat pocket and handed the other to Egon. We pulled away what was left of the bookcase that covered the tarp. Egon lifted the covering and motioned for his wife and daughter to crawl into the tunnel.

Lotti kissed Egon and shined the light into the narrow opening. She lifted Kathi and her doll inside and then followed. Joseph and Laura were next, following the beam of light directed down the shaft.

The basement air was damp and cool. I could hear the scrape of dirt and sand against their bodies as they made their way through the tunnel.

Egon waved me in with his torch light. I left the shopping bag against the earthen wall and took one last look at my dismal surroundings—a dark mess of useless objects and refuse in East Berlin—and put my hands on the earth that would lead me to light and freedom.

Egon crawled in after me, the pinpoint beam of his torch

bouncing around me and over my head. Ahead, I spotted the dark outlines of those who had gone before.

We were about eight meters into the tunnel when a shout sounded behind us.

"*Du! Halt!*" The order came several times, fast and frantic. I couldn't be certain, but the voice sounded like Herwald's.

Egon switched off his torch and shouted for the others to go ahead. I lurched a few meters forward and then looked back, unwilling to leave him behind.

The tarp had been torn from the wall. Near the tunnel entrance, in the shadowy outlines of the basement, lights flashed and men crowded near the entrance.

Egon squirmed back toward the entrance and reached into his shirt to withdraw his pistol. The man who had just crawled in behind us also had a gun in his hand.

Egon fired first and the report blasted through the tunnel like a shock wave. Bits of earth fell from the ceiling. Egon paddled his feet, sending up a spray of dirt and sand, propelling him backward.

When the haze cleared, the man who had followed tried to rise up on his knees. A blast of gunfire came from the tunnel entrance and the man fell, blocking the way of those who came behind us.

"Ahead! Go!" Egon screamed in the dark.

I scrambled through the seemingly unending darkness, until a shaft of light fell on the earth in front of me. A ladder had been positioned against the tunnel wall. When I reached it, I looked up into the faces of Laura, Joseph, Kathi, and Lotti.

I waited at the ladder's base as Egon hobbled toward me. The left side of his shirt was covered in blood.

"My shoulder," he said. "They won't follow us. Go."

I shook my head. "No, you first."

I moved aside as he reached out with his right hand and climbed slowly up the rungs, wincing with each step.

No one followed us. The tunnel was quiet.

Six other Berliners waited for us in the large metal shed that concealed the tunnel's exit. They greeted us with kisses, flowers, and champagne.

Lotti ripped Egon's shirt open and tended to his wound. He'd been struck in the left shoulder, directly above his armpit. Soon, American soldiers and West Berlin police scrambled in, greeting us and asking how we had done it. I was too shaken to talk.

Two of the soldiers ushered Egon, Lotti, and Kathi into a military car outside. I told them to come to my mother's house when they could. We would welcome each other there.

Laura cried as she fell into my arms. Joseph clutched her hand, and I shed tears over both of them.

As we stepped into the sun, the light and air warmed me. We were standing on American sector soil and I was free once again. To the right of the shed the view opened. Across the wall, in East Berlin, border guards carried a body out of the back of the house on Zimmerstrasse. They lowered it carefully to the walk in front of the vacant lot filled with trash.

Laura started to look, but I told her to turn away.

I would tell her later that her husband, Joseph's father, was dead.

# CHAPTER 37

We were interviewed by West German police and American officers for a few hours. They inspected the tunnel and left the ladder in place. They knew the East Germans would block the other entrance, most likely caving it in so no one could get through.

Finally, in the late afternoon, we were allowed to leave. I had a little money on me, so I paid for a taxi to my mother's house for the three of us. Joseph had said nothing since he'd arrived at Egon's apartment, but he began to speak up on the ride. I didn't know what to expect from a nine-year-old boy whose world had changed so drastically. He had seen much violence in his life—a good deal of it at home—and heard tales of Stasi atrocities from his father, I was certain.

Joseph looked ahead through the windscreen as we wound our way to Rixdorf. "He knew," the boy said.

"Knew what?" I asked.

"Father knew that we were going to escape."

Laura looked at him, her eyes growing large at this admission.

"How?" she asked. "How did he know?"

"He told me so last night. They heard things through microphones that had been placed a few houses away."

Laura gasped. "He knew . . . suspected . . . but didn't stop us?"

Joseph clasped his hands and placed them in his lap. "He wanted me to stay after everyone else was arrested so we could be together. He said Mother was a traitor, but he wanted more enemies—like he was hunting, collecting trophies for the Stasi. He wanted to arrest everyone who tried to escape and then put them in prison until they died. I don't think he loves anyone—not even me."

Laura leaned against him, trying to reassure her son. "I'm sure he loves you." Her voice was weak, not convincing.

Joseph turned to her, his brown eyes sparkling. "Does he? Or does he only love the Stasi?"

Laura didn't answer. She put her arm around his shoulder. "It doesn't matter now. You came with me and your grandmother. We're safe and free."

"He told me someone might die," Joseph said. "Someone I loved might die . . . maybe even he because what he was doing was so dangerous. I heard his voice in the tunnel . . . and then the shots."

I looked at Laura. Shock and remorse danced across her face.

"Do you want to go back?" I asked Joseph. "Are you sad you left?"

He shook his head. "No. He beat Mother. He never beat me because I listened to him. He *made* me listen. Now, I don't have to listen anymore."

Laura turned her head toward the window to avoid breaking down.

When we arrived at my mother's, I paid the driver. Joseph walked ahead of us on the path. I held on to Laura's arm, holding her back for a moment. "Herwald is dead. I'm sure of it." I didn't tell her that Egon had shot first. But other shots were fired by the East Germans. Perhaps those bullets had killed him.

She stumbled a bit and sucked in a breath. "Joseph, wait before you knock." She clutched my arm. "I'll tell Joseph. Oh, God, what's happened? Why is there all this sadness?"

"Your great-grandmother will tell you the reason. She's been telling me for years." I pointed to the door. "Knock, Joseph. Frieda will be happy to meet you."

He did.

My mother, wearing one of her usual housedresses, opened the door a few moments later. When she saw the three of us, her expression shifted from amazement to a broad smile.

Three days later, Egon, Lotti, and Kathi joined us in the small house. Seven of us were crammed into it, but we made it work, and I hadn't been so happy in years despite our close and familiar circumstances. We were resigned to make the best of it because we knew it wouldn't last.

Egon had been shot in the left shoulder. The bullet had plowed through flesh, passing between an artery and bone. The doctors had sewed up the entrance and exit wounds and bound his shoulder, placing his arm in a sling. They expected a healing time of two months.

Once again, I found myself sleeping on the couch until new living spaces and jobs could be arranged. Frieda gave Lotti, Egon, and Kathi her room because it had the biggest bed. Laura and Joseph made their home in my old bedroom. A neighbor kindly took in my mother at night so she could sleep in a spare room. During the day, we cooked and laughed and enjoyed our freedom. However, what had happened in Germany in the past forty years was never far from our minds.

Laura told Joseph that his father was dead. There had been few tears from her son and even fewer words and that worried Laura. She was concerned that the abuse Joseph had witnessed had affected him and would continue to haunt him. That was something we needed to plan for.

One evening, as we were gathered in the living room after

supper, Egon told us what had happened in the tunnel and what might have to be done.

"Herwald is dead," he said, directing his words to Laura and Joseph, "but I want you to know that I didn't shoot him. I fired a shot into the tunnel ceiling, hoping that part of it might crumble and at least stop him. He rose from the tunnel floor to see through the grit, but the guards, or the Stasi, returned the fire. The Americans think that those men killed Herwald as he tried to kill me, but we'll never know. The Stasi is going to make a martyr of him. The name of Herwald Angermann will live in history as the GDR tries to extradite me for murder."

Laura put a hand over her mouth. Joseph lowered his head.

"I didn't kill your father," Egon said to Joseph. "I hope you believe me."

Joseph looked up. "I believe you. The Stasi will do anything to protect its name."

Egon stretched his free hand toward Joseph and patted his knee. "Thank you. I'm sorry this happened."

"Are you in trouble?" I asked.

"We may be moved from West Berlin to West Germany for our own safety—we'll begin another new life. The Americans aren't going to give me up." He looked at Lotti and Kathi, who sat on the floor in front of her mother. "We're used to starting over."

The evening ended with all of us grateful to be alive. Perhaps Kathi and Joseph weren't as grateful for what they had gained because of their losses of home, friends, and a father. Those would fade with time, but, for now, they stung.

I was stung by a loss as well, by a man who still haunted me. I wanted more than ever to find out what happened to Emil Belmon and, also, to his uncle Levi.

Zehlendorf, a locale of forest and lakes, stood about seventeen kilometers to the southwest of my mother's home, not far from Wannsee, where the Nazis crafted the "Final Solution" to their "Jewish question" in 1942.

The neighborhoods, the cobblestone streets, the surviving trees and buildings retained the feeling of "old Berlin" when I visited. Most of the area looked as it did in the Weimar Republic, but it was 1962, nearly twenty years after the war ended.

Zehlendorf was also home to the U.S. Army Berlin headquarters, sometimes called the Berlin Command. It was housed in a large group of buildings that had an ominous feel. My appointment with a "Community Commander" had taken weeks to get, after much phone calling and wrangling with minor officials. For years, I had tried before to arrange a meeting with someone in the American army who might know what happened at the liberated concentration camps, but in the chaos of the post-war years, my requests were either turned down or ignored. The excuses ranged from "we don't have that information" to "those files aren't available to the public."

Finally, my appointment arrived in late summer, when the weather was clear and the air smelled of pine. The gate was guarded and it was a long walk to the main building. My visit was confirmed by a guard and I had no trouble getting inside the compound. As I approached my destination, I realized why I'd felt so strange. These were former Nazi military buildings, constructed in the monumental style so favored by Hitler, throwing me back to the days of the Third Reich. The rows of American flags lining the drive did little to soothe my discomfort.

Inside, I was met by desk officers who, again, affirmed my meeting. After sitting for twenty minutes in a hallway, I was escorted to an office at the rear of the building. It was much like Viktor Volkov's after the Red Army had taken Berlin: a simple oak desk, a narrow, vertical window behind the desk letting in natural light, maps of Berlin and Germany taped to one wall, and an American flag attached to the other.

The man sitting behind the desk bore no resemblance to Volkov, however. He was young, good looking, with a bright smile and easy manner. He stood when I entered and invited me to sit in a leather office chair in front of him. His blue eyes accented the robust color of his skin, but presented a striking contrast to his pomaded black hair.

"Mrs. Länger," he said. "A pleasure to meet you. I hear you've had some trouble getting an answer to a question." He spoke perfect German.

I was taken aback by the way he addressed me. No one had called me by my married name in years, even though I was still Rickard's wife. He'd introduced himself as Captain Fields, but seemed relaxed about how I should address him.

I looked past him for a moment, into the trees that shivered behind the window. "I'd like to find out about someone who went missing during the war—arrested by the Nazis in Amsterdam and transferred to Buchenwald." I stopped, the words catching in my throat. "I heard that those Jewish prisoners were taken to Mauthausen. That camp was liberated by the United States Army. Is that correct?"

He nodded, opened a file on his desk, and studied a page before speaking. "This is what I do know. Only two of the Jewish prisoners taken to Mauthausen from Amsterdam survived. You are inquiring about Emil Belmon. There is no such name on the list, either dead or alive." He looked at me, a kindness suffusing his eyes. "I did further research, however, and I found something amazing. I looked at the camp records recovered from the Nazis, for they kept meticulous files, and searched for all men with the first name Emil."

I nodded, waiting for him to continue.

"This will be difficult to hear," he said. "It's equally difficult for me to tell you. Are you Jewish?"

"No."

He ran a finger over another page. "I found an Emil Länger—the same last name as yours. He told the Nazis that he was married to a woman named Marie, who had died during the Netherlands invasion."

"That has to be Emil," I said, trying to make sense of what the captain was telling me. "My name is Marie Rittenhaus . . . it has to be my Emil."

"He also told them that he had relatives in Amsterdam, but would not give any names. He probably used Länger to direct the Nazis away from any person they might connect to him. The record indicates that when he arrived at the camp he was stronger than most and a good worker . . . so they didn't execute him." He paused. "Unfortunately, Emil Länger died of typhus in 1944. So the record indicates."

I lowered my head, knowing that what I had suspected for years had been confirmed.

"I'm sorry for his death," the captain said. "There were so many. I'm sure he was a brave man."

"Yes, he was." Sorrow rose from my chest to my eyes.

"I wish I had better news for you and more information to share, but I don't. If there's anything else I can do, please call on me."

"Thank you." We both rose from our chairs, and I shook his hand. "You've been a great help."

My legs felt weak and numb as I walked past the offices, out the door, and into the sunlight, the warm air, the scents of the nearby lakes and woods rushing toward me. Emil was dead, just as I had suspected. Another sad chapter of my life had been written and completed. Now I had to go on. I had to survive.

Emil was dead, but Laura and Joseph were alive. Egon, Lotti, and their daughter were the dearest of friends. My mother had become a rock in my steadfast foundation. Life would continue.

After I left the compound, I hailed a cab. Riding back to my mother's house, I pondered whether I would ever write another novel again.

# EPILOGUE

After my mother's death during the winter of 1965, I made a life for myself in a village not far from Berlin. The name isn't important.

My mother had been right—she had been carried out of her house in a coffin. We buried her in a gentle snow that had fallen for two days in Rixdorf. Laura had remarried—a kind and loving man—and Joseph, now going on thirteen, seemed to be adjusting well to his stepfather, new school friends, and life in Berlin. I was happy for them, and there was nothing more for me to do other than to wish them well. We visited each other often and I stayed at their home in Berlin on holidays and special occasions.

I wrote letters to Toos in Amsterdam, but they were returned unopened. I had no idea where Karin and Derk lived; the same with Ruud. The Wednesday Night Club's veil of secrecy made it difficult for me to find out what happened to its members—if any remained at all. Although I doubted that I would succeed, I also sent a few letters to Uncle Levi, hoping to get a response. Those also remained unanswered. I suspected that Levi might have met the same fate as Emil in one of the many death camps built by the Nazis.

Egon, Lotti, and Kathi were relocated to West Germany, and though we kept in touch, our contact diminished over the years. Our bartender friend, Rudi, disappeared in Africa and was never heard from again. Lotti tried to find out what happened, but every inquiry to his whereabouts led to an unanswered question.

I sold Mother's house in Rixdorf and moved to the village west of Berlin, where I could live out my life in peace. I adopted homeless cats and dogs, who kept me company at my small house. I helped run a garden for our community.

Sometimes I would get a letter from a publisher asking for the rights to reprint my novels, *The Berlin Woman* and *Confessions of a Vampire's Wife*. After much thought, I declined. Another wanted me to write my autobiography. I declined. I didn't want the attention. I was comfortable with what money I had and I dreaded getting into the business again. I never finished *The Last Man*, but, for my own pleasure, I revised the ending of *Einsamkeit, Loneliness*, which had been published years before.

Instead of my heroine asking how she could find the happiness she threw away, railing against the "life of the lonely," I wrote about survival, and the various shades of love—from pink to red, from white to black—the sustaining characteristics that had guided me through life.

*I look into the deep black and marvel at the stars—mostly white, but some yellow and red, heaven's colors stretching into infinity.*

*I think of the dead who have gone before me, but also of the living, who, at times, I've denied, like Peter denied Christ.*

*But I search the sky, looking to galaxies that stretch beyond our human concept of time, and wonder why I've survived and others have died. No answer comes to mind, save that of the self and the good fortune that I survived and might do good.*

*I am happy within my small world—the feel of a*

*cat's soft fur upon my fingers; a dog's warm, friendly lick on my leg; the heady perfume of the rose in summer; the earthy aroma of fall's decaying leaves; the chill, arctic air lashing my face in winter.*

*These small things of life live with me now, along with small gifts of love.*

*Do I need others to make my life complete as I once did?*

*I am happy now alone, but I cherish the love and understanding of others.*

*That is enough.*

# AUTHOR'S NOTE

As the back cover copy of this book states, *The Novelist from Berlin* is loosely based on the life of Irmgard Keun, a writer who was forced into exile because her novels defied the accepted norms of the National Socialists as they rose to power. I, of course, have created my heroine and embellished her life for the benefit of fiction; however, several of Keun's major life experiences were used as settings in the novel.

Arvind Dilawar, writing for the *Smithsonian*, in early 2021 stated, "The greatest trick that Irmgard Keun ever played was convincing the world she didn't exist. . . . She took her own life . . . but the story was false. Keun had used it as a cover to return to Germany to see her parents."

I chose to explore Keun's life for several reasons of interest to me, and, hopefully, the reader will find them interesting as well.

First, much of her biography remains a mystery, the time line and events of her life vary according to differing accounts. Her story is fairly straightforward during her time as a novelist as the Nazis rose to power, and there is some biographic evidence regarding her expatriate life once she'd fled Germany in the mid-1930s. The books that made her rich and famous had been blacklisted by the Nazis. Suddenly, she found herself in political danger and with no income. She sued the Gestapo for her losses, but failed in a court ruled by the government.

For a time she was in the Netherlands, where she joined other writers in exile, including Thomas Mann and Joseph Roth, with whom she had an affair. After her faked suicide and return to Germany, she wanted nothing to do with politics, much like my heroine's mother, Frieda. She was invited to write her memoirs, but declined. Her last novel, published in 1950, describes a man, Ferdinand, who wants nothing more than to be left alone, who wants to live a "normal" life. Despite Keun's efforts to blend in, to live out her life in anonymity, her books were reissued in German in the 1970s and have since been rediscovered internationally for their unique viewpoint on German women and society between the world wars.

Second on my list of reasons was Keun's courage. She took the Nazis to court, knowing that she was putting herself in danger, while facing the end of her writing career. The critics of the time trashed her books, labeling them as assaults against German women, and also for their "incompatibility" with Nazi ideals. It took guts to stand up against the fascists and she did it. I imbued my heroine, Niki, with some of the characteristics gleaned from my research on Keun.

Third, and perhaps most important from an artistic viewpoint, Keun portrayed German women in a light never before explored. As Dilawar points out, a contemporary *New York Times* review called one of her most famous novels "a delightful contrast to books written by men." Keun has been described as a leading author of the late Weimar period and a proponent of *die Neue Sachlichkeit, The New Objectivity*, a rejection of German Expressionism and the romantic ideal. When reading her books, I found a realism that even some of today's readers might find disturbing, and perhaps incompatible with their own ideas of what a heroine should be. The New German Woman of Keun's novels smoked, drank, went from man to man, boyfriend to boyfriend, in order to survive. Her women looked for love, and sometimes found it and other times rejected it. Survival is a key theme in her books. Malaise, ennui, the sense of just getting by fills her writing. Happy endings are almost nonexistent and, in the context of her novels, wouldn't make sense if she had written them. Scholars are rediscovering her work. More details about her life and writings will be published in the coming years.

Keun, a striking woman with sensuous lips and doe-like eyes set in an oval face, wasn't prolific in the sense that some modern novelists are, but one must consider the time and place of her publication. I read most of Keun's major works as research for *The Novelist from Berlin*. The list and dates of the novels are as follows:

*Gilgi, One of Us* (1931)
*The Artificial Silk Girl* (1932)
*After Midnight* (1937)
*Child of All Nations* (1938)
*Ferdinand, the Man with the Kind Heart* (1950)

Other books that I found helpful in the writing of the novel were *The Hiding Place*, Corrie ten Boom; *Berlin Alexanderplatz*, Alfred Döblin; and *The Passenger*, Ulrich Alexander Boschwitz.

Unfortunately, Keun was never able to achieve her previous success as a novelist and, perhaps, found such a goal unnecessary. She remained in hiding until the end of the war and in the 1960s suffered from homelessness and was treated for alcoholism. For six years, she remained in the psychiatric ward of a German hospital. She died of lung cancer in 1982.

Much of Keun's life remains locked in shadow. Her daughter, in a later interview, said that her mother felt that the Nazis "took her best years." It's my hope that this novel does justice to such a theme—the rise of a fascist government that took away years from so many and ended the lives of millions.

For the creation of this book, I must give my heartfelt thanks, once again, to Bob Pinsky, the beta reader for all my novels, who also took on editorial duties during a tight deadline. He is a wonder.

As always, thanks go to John Scognamiglio, my editor at Kensington, and Evan S. Marshall, my steadfast agent. My sincere thanks go to the readers who have supported me through seven books. You have allowed V. S. Alexander to thrive.

# THE NOVELIST FROM BERLIN

## ABOUT THIS GUIDE

The suggested questions are included
to enhance your group's reading of
V. S. Alexander's *The Novelist from Berlin*!

# DISCUSSION QUESTIONS

1. From your reading of the book, what defining characteristic drove Niki?

2. Did you find this story to be propelled by love, by revenge, or by a quest?

3. Rickard bows to the National Socialist Party in order to save his business and provide for Niki and their daughter. What would you have done if you had been in that situation?

4. "The New German Woman" that Niki wrote about relied on her wits and talents to get by in the Weimar Republic. Irmgard Keun wrote about this woman in her books. Had you heard of the author or read similar works by other writers?

5. Many historical events are explored in *The Novelist from Berlin*. Were you familiar with them, for example, the Night of the Long Knives or the Nazi book burnings?

6. Could you have done what Niki did in Amsterdam with the Wednesday Night Club to the German officer?

7. Niki takes a piece of jewelry she found at a Nazi gathering. Would you have done the same?

8. A British soldier parachuted into Berlin after his plane was hit. A Soviet officer had information about Rickard. How would you have handled both situations?

9. *The Hiding Place* by Corrie ten Boom and *The Diary of a Young Girl* by Anne Frank take place in the Netherlands. Both are stories of the Nazi occupation. Have you read either of them?

10. How far would you go, what steps would you take, to find your child?